D1246181

CONSCRIPTED CITY

Norfolk In World War II

CONSCRIPTED CITY

Norfolk In World War II

Marvin W. Schlegel

The Virginian-Pilot and The Ledger-Star

PUBLISHER'S NOTE

Editors and reporters at The Virginian-Pilot and The Ledger-Star rediscovered *Conscripted City: Norfolk in World War II* as we were preparing our own special report, "Hampton Roads Goes to War," published each day of December, 1991, in commemoration of the 50th anniversary of the bombing of Pearl Harbor and the ensuing entry of the United States into World War II.

In his book, published in 1951 to commemorate the 10th anniversary of the attack, Dr. Marvin W. Schlegel committed to history much of our newspapers' coverage of the war years. We were impressed with Dr. Schlegel's insights and storytelling and thought it fitting that we give his work new life by republishing it as a service for the readers and communities we serve.

For this new edition, we have added eight pages of contemporary photographs from the Borjes Collection. These, along with the foreword by former Congressman Bill Whitehurst, are the only additions we have made to the 1951 edition. The text is reprinted uncut and unaltered.

FOREWORD
TO THE 1991 EDITION

Two generations after "The Day of Infamy," Americans are revisiting World War II with a mixture of nostalgia and curiosity. It is unlikely that 25 or 50 years hence, the events of 1941-45 will spark as much interest in the Second World War as we know feel when we look back on it. By then, those with direct memories of it will be gone, and it will be just another remote occurrence in American history, an event to be treated like other conflicts in the nation's past.

Fifty years after Pearl Harbor, however, there is a compulsion to look back with a fresh eye one last time, a moment for veterans to remember their experiences, a time for every American whose memory stretches back to those days to recall their own wartime encounters and share them with each other and their children and grandchildren, if they can persuade them to listen without being bored!

Cataclysmic events so etch themselves in our memories that all of us can recall where we were and what we were doing at the moment they occurred. Such was the case of Dec. 7, 1941. Whether you lived in Norfolk, Nebraska, or Norfolk, Virginia, the odds are that if you were at least 10 years old at the time, you will recall the moment clearly. Moreover, there was a sense that the nation was not only about to embark on a great adventure but that a corner had been turned in history. A decade of depression was over, and gone with it were the isolation and self-absorption that had been the hallmarks of the 1930s. For the second time in this century, Americans would embark on a crusade.

Yet somehow, even in the earliest days of the war, there was a feeling that, when it was over, we would never turn back and withdraw from the world as we had in 1920. Americans seemed to realize that a new era, an American-dominated one, was dawning, and the war was fought, at home and abroad, with a conviction that there was more at stake than the military defeat of our enemies. We saw on the horizon not the long Cold War that was to follow but an age of peace and prosperity driven by American inspiration and ingenuity. The "Can Do" spirit that typified wartime America fueled that postwar dream.

It was in this spirit that America went to war 50 years ago. Norfolk, Virginia, a Navy time with a mixed reputation, was a microcosm of the nation itself in those years. Awakened abruptly from a peaceful slumber, the city went on an immediate war footing like that of the Navy in its midst. Norfolkians of my generation will remember it well, but for those born too late, it is hard to envision a community of less than 150,000, whose urban density did not spill far beyond Ward's Corner, connected to Virginia Beach by a two-lane highway and to Portsmouth, the Peninsula and the Eastern Shore by ferry. Pour nearly 60,000 more people into an unprepared city, and one can only imagine the problems that arose. The title of this book is not an overstatement. Norfolk natives truly felt that their city had been conscripted, and their story is told with understanding, compassion, and not a little humor in the following pages.

Marvin Schlegel first published *Conscripted City* in 1951, just 10 years after the onset of the Second World War. Like a good wine, his story can be savored better now than then. The reader who lived through those years will smile with recollection, while those younger will have a first-hand view of the past. It is the story of a city whose citizens endeavored to do their part in support of their own sons and daughters who had gone off to war and also to accommodate and make welcome the visitors among them — the sons and daughters of others. For all the memories are bittersweet, like those of the war itself.

G. William Whitehurst
U.S. Representative,
2nd Congressional District, 1969-87
Lecturer in Public Affairs,
Old Dominion University

CONSCRIPTED CITY

Norfolk In World War II

FOREWORD

The guns and bombs of World War II had not ceased their ominous rumble when the Virginia legislature in its session of 1944 paused in the middle of routine duties to seek the answer to some questions that seemed pertinent.

How had the war affected the Commonwealth and its communities? How should the records of this war be preserved as a guide in future crises of a similar nature? How could sign-posts be set up for the historian of tomorrow?

These, and collateral questions, seemed best answered by the creation of a World War II History Commission, appointed for the purpose of "collecting, editing, assembling, and publishing information and materials with respect to the contributions to World War II made by Virginia and Virginians, its primary purpose being the development of several historical volumes of State-wide interest." Under the same act, all localities chartered by the State were authorized to appropriate what sums they thought necessary to carry out a similar program.

Norfolk was one of the first communities to underwrite its share in responsibility for the plan. City Manager Charles B. Borland appointed a Norfolk War History Commission, composed of Mr. Frank Pace, Chairman, Miss Mary D. Pretlow, Mr. E. S. Brinkley, Dr. W. H. T. Squires, and Mr. Frank Turin. The city also generously implemented the work of the Commission with funds for the maintenance of an office and a full time secretary.

Mr. Pace and Mr. Turin resigned from the Commission in 1947, and were replaced by Mr. John A. Norton and Mr. S. H. Ferebee; Dr. Squires and Mr. Brinkley died in office, and their places were assumed by Mrs. Frances B. Sawyer and Mr. H. M. Williams.

Whether we like it or not, war periods are important historically. War always marks a turning point. It inevitably brings a quickened tempo, a new set of technological procedures, different values in manners and morals, new social problems. Wartime bring out an intensity of life and effort we never find in peace-time. We deplore war, with its waste and its horrors, but it is undeniably true that war brings a richness and vitality that are missing from ordinary days.

The documentation of such a period in Norfolk's history was a tedious business. Much material continues to be elusive.

In September, 1948, the Commission, feeling it should no longer be a drain on the public purse, made a final report to the city manager, took receipt for its archives from the city librarian, and asked that it be discharged.

Norfolk's Council, however, impressed by the work of the Commission as shown in its report, and by a commendation of the Virginia World War II History Commission, declined to make the discharge asked. Instead, without solicitation, they requested the Commission to remain in being, and to prepare a budget that would cover the cost of engaging a historian to write a story of the period based on the Commission's records, and the cost of printing and distributing such a history.

By the Spring of 1949 the budget was approved and the Commission entered into a contract with Dr. Marvin W. Schlegel, Associate Professor of History at Longwood College, to write the book. Dr. Schlegel seemed well qualified for the task; he had been in charge of Pennsylvania's war history program for five years and after coming to Virginia had spent two summers with the Virginia World War II History Commission. In these capacities he had written several books and articles on the effects of the war on these two states. Moreover, he had become acquainted with Norfolk's particular problems while teaching at the St. Helena Extension of the College of William & Mary.

This foreword cannot possibly acknowledge all the sources of help that have been given the Commission in assembling its records; that would be a book in itself. A few acknowledgements must be made.

The Norfolk City Council and the city manager gave the Commission an absolutely free hand to produce an unbiased history that was free from any censorship; by their tolerance, this book, which pictures Norfolk's ugly aspects alongside its noble ones, was made possible.

The Commission thanks the Alderman Library at the University of Virginia for its aid while the work was in progress. For two summers it offered its research facilities and working quarters for Dr. Schlegel, and is now the careful custodian of the Commission's records until such time as Norfolk has a library equipped to care for these valuable archives.

Thanks, too, must go to the Virginia World War II History Commission, which was both a goad and an inspiration to our work.

Perhaps the chief criticism that will be made of this book is that it speaks but little of the men and women who served, and often gave their lives on all our World War II battlefronts. The omission was deliberate. It was felt that Norfolk was but one common denominator of all American cities, towns, villages and counties which gave their sons and daughters to our country. What the citizens of Norfolk did during the war was but background music to their superb sacrifices.

The important thing is that Norfolk, suffering all the personal anguish and anxiety for its loved ones, responded magnificently to the country's need for a city that was not afraid. The war brought problems to Norfolk, problems that would have seemed insoluble a few years before, and they were solved. Norfolk demanded the last measure of war effort from its citizens—and got it.

Here is the story.

S. H. FEREBEE.

Norfolk, Virginia
March 10, 1951

PREFACE

This is the story of how one American city accepted the burden which was thrust upon its reluctant shoulders by militaristic aggression abroad. Norfolk was drafted for war as truly as was the average American soldier and carried out its unpleasant assignment just as he did—in the democratic way, grumbling and criticizing, debating and squabbling, but somehow surpassing the vaunted efficiency of dictated unanimity.

The ultimate result of Norfolk's war service was the victories of the United States Navy. That story will be told and retold in naval annals for generations to come. But back of that is the Norfolk story, the story of how the city and the Navy learned to work in double harness. Norfolk has asked for no glorified, flattering historical portrait; it has insisted on a realistic picture, showing the sordid as well as the splendid.

To achieve such a picture is the goal the author has set for himself. Within the limits of his materials and his own abilities he has tried to tell the story just as it happened, striving to recapture some of the excitement of those hectic days of the early 1940's, already fast fading in memory. Realizing the hazards of venturing into a field where the dust of controversy has not yet settled, he has attempted to give fair treatment to both sides of every dispute. He has tried to treat the persons mentioned in these pages with as much detachment as if this had all happened in another century and hopes that they will be able to accept this treatment in the same impersonal spirit. Those who are mentioned in what might appear an unfavorable light have generally been reduced to anonymity unless their names were essential to the story.

While the author has full responsibility for everything that is said in these pages, his work would have been impossible without the help of many hands. The Norfolk War History Commission collected most of the records; the Virginia World War II History

Commission (now the History Division of the Virginia State Library), made available all its vast collection. The Public Relations Office of the Norfolk Naval Base also opened many of its records. Dozens of persons, including many former Navy men who had been stationed in Norfolk during the war, gave him valuable background information in informal interviews.

He is especially grateful to his good friends W. Edwin Hemphill and William M. E. Rachal and their fellow workers in the Virginia War History Commission, who were always unstinting in their loyal support; to Harry Clemons and Jack Dalton and the staff of the Alderman Library of the University of Virginia, whose unfailing courtesy has made Charlottesville his favorite summer resort; and to the members of the Norfolk War History Commission, who read and criticized his manuscript. Special tribute is due the Commission's chairman, who was among the first to volunteer to serve in the city's war effort and is now fittingly bringing to a close the last item on the World War II program. His sacrifices of time, money, and energy to see that this volume came into existence have had no reward save his own satisfaction in completing an assignment imposed upon him by his fellow citizens.

MARVIN W. SCHLEGEL

Farmville, Virginia
April 14, 1951

TABLE OF CONTENTS

I

THE FACE OF A CITY

THE final edition had been put to bed, but the lights were still on in the *Virginian-Pilot* newsroom. The lounging staff eyed the teletype expectantly. Suddenly a bell jangled, and the machine began to clatter out the awaited message: "Berlin, Sept. 1 . . . ." At once the office sprang into action. Snatching the story with its hastily-written heads, copy boys hustled it off to the linotypes. The presses rolled into action, and soon newsboys were on the streets with bundles of freshly-printed papers, shouting, "Extra, extra, read all about it! Germany invades Poland! War breaks out in Europe."

The people of Norfolk grabbed eagerly at the papers, looking for more details of the news they had already heard over their radios at breakfast. Here at last was the answer to the question with which they had been wearying each other's ears for days: "What's the latest on the European situation?"[1] Almost with a sigh of relief they learned that the war of nerves had finally become a shooting war. Eventual American involvement they accepted as a certainty, although they gave little thought to what such involvement might mean to Norfolk.[2]

For the moment the war seemed to be making no change in the city's routine. Out at the Naval Operating Base the salty commandant of the Fifth Naval District, Rear Admiral Joseph K. Taussig, told a reporter that the war had had no effect on the operation of the Navy, and foreign freighters sailed in and out of Hampton Roads as if nothing had happened.[3] With this reassur-

---

[1] Norfolk *Virginian-Pilot*, September 3, 1939, Part II, p. 1. The *Virginian-Pilot* is hereafter cited as *V-P*.

[2] Congressman Colgate W. Darden, Jr., of Norfolk, reported that 75 per cent of his callers thought that the United States would inevitably be drawn into the war. *V-P*, September 20, 1939.

[3] *V-P*, September 2, 1939, p. 16.

ance the people of Norfolk relaxed and returned to their own affairs. They scanned three columns of "Real Estate for Rent" ads in the morning paper and noticed that a last year's Plymouth could be bought for $545. They saw that the week-end specials included butter at 28 cents a pound and ham at 21 cents. They went to Loew's to see Robert Taylor and Hedy LaMarr in a "Flaming Love Drama,"entitled *Lady of the Tropics*, or to the Norva for Bing Crosby's latest picture. Baseball fans took the ferry to Portsmouth to see the Cubs knock the local Tars down into the second division. As usual, Norfolkians prepared to head for the beaches for the Labor Day week end.

Basking on the sand at Ocean View or Virginia Beach, they could look back with satisfaction on the most prosperous summer the city had known in many years. In 1939 at last Norfolk was beginning to recover from the blows of fate. The troubles, it was ominous to recall, had begun the last time the Germans had broken loose in Europe. Before 1917 Norfolk had been a little Southern city, making slow but steady progress. It was a commercial center for southeastern Virginia and northeastern North Carolina with many small industries. Located on Hampton Roads, one of the finest natural harbors in the world, it was striving to make better use of the port. The development of two coal railroads, the Norfolk and Western and the Virginian, had given it an important export to supplement its shipments of cotton to New England, although it still lacked counter-balancing imports.

Then, when war was declared on Germany in 1917, both the Army and the Navy suddenly discovered these unused port facilities. The Army set up a vast supply base in the open countryside at Sewells Point, north of the Lafayette River. The Navy went farther north to the abandoned site of the Jamestown Exposition of 1907 on Pine Beach and converted it into an operating base. A large naval training station was built there to replace the small school located on the St. Helena Reservation in Berkley. As the demand for sailors grew, a second and even larger training station was constructed beside the first. Across the river in Portsmouth employment at the Navy Yard tripled.

Middle-aged Norfolkians in 1939 could still recall the crowded discomfort these abrupt changes had thrust upon their city, as more than 100,000 newcomers had pushed their way into a community with a population of only 67,452 in 1910.[4] Trolley cars had been jammed, houses packed so tight that beds had to be rented in shifts. A government housing program, started with belated haste, only brought in more construction workers and increased the crowding. The chief compensation for the shoving had been the promise that these new government projects would bring Norfolk peacetime prosperity. Postwar employment at the Navy Yard, it was predicted, would be 8,000, more than twice the prewar figure, while the new Army Supply Base would furnish permanent employment for 1100 more.[5]

Those rosy estimates faded quickly, however, as the gloom of disarmament blanketed Hampton Roads in the 1920's. The Washington Naval Conference of 1921 scrapped the half-built battleship *North Carolina* where it stood on the ways in the Navy Yard, and employment at the Yard dropped back to the 1899 level. The Navy tore down East Camp, the second naval training station it had just completed, and sold the land back to private owners. The old St. Helena Reservation grew up in a wilderness of weeds, and the Army closed down its supply base entirely.

Civic leaders made a mighty effort to create new jobs for the stranded workers. A grain elevator was built and piers expanded to improve shipping facilities. New industries were brought in, notably the Ford assembly plant, the largest private business on the south side of Hampton Roads. In a moment of optimism the city reached out six miles across the open countryside to annex the beach resort of Ocean View at the other end of the Granby Street trolley line, and the Norfolk Advertising Board was created to proclaim the city's merits as a tourist center.

All these measures helped, but they did not succeed in creating a sound basis for a prosperous economy. The cotton trade vanished as the textile mills migrated from New England to the South, leaving the port dependent on its coal shipments. Its shipyards could find little work, and its construction workers were

---

[4] U. S. Department of Labor, Bureau of Labor Statistics, Employment and Occupation Outlook Branch, *The Impact of War on the Hampton Roads Area*, Part II, "Impact of World War I on the Hampton Roads Area," (Historical Study No. 69, January, 1944), p. 55. This work is hereafter cited as *Impact of War on the Hampton Roads Area*.

[5] Survey by the U. S. Housing Corporation, January, 1918, cited in *ibid.*, pp. 13, 22.

idle in a city that had more houses than it could use. When the depression hit in 1929, all the efforts at recovery collapsed. Then, two years later came the crowning blow. The United States Fleet left its base at Norfolk and moved to new quarters in the Pacific where it could keep a watchful eye on Japan, which had just embarked on its career of aggression in Manchuria. In 1939 merchants still talked mournfully of the day the fleet had left.

The very forces which had drawn the fleet into the Pacific, however, were now contributing to Norfolk's revival. With the dark cloud of economic discontent hanging low over the world and militarism reigning in Germany and Japan, the United States was quietly rebuilding the defenses torn down in the 1920's. While most Americans still had their heads buried in the isolationist sands, the President of the United States was unobtrusively getting the Navy back into fighting shape. Employment at the Navy Yard had already shot up from 3,500 in the summer of 1938 to 7,600.[6] The keel for a new battleship was about to be laid on the ways where the ill-fated *North Carolina* had been junked nearly twenty years before. At the Naval Base a $4,000,000 construction program was under way, and Congress had already authorized the repurchase of the East Camp tract for expansion of the Naval Air Station.[7]

Signs of this new-found prosperity were to be seen in the city's main business section on Granby Street. The stores were losing their air of shabby gentility and were being dressed in bright new clothes. The corner shop in the Monticello Hotel was being completely remodeled for its new tenant, The Hub. Rice's was moving across Freemason Street into a building with a shiny new face to make way for a modern Woolworth's. Showiest of all was the new home of the Ames and Brownley department store, six stories tall, air-conditioned and windowless, which had just been completed on March 1.[8]

Sears Roebuck was putting up a new store on Freemason Street at Monticello Avenue. Only the year before Pender's grocery chain, not yet turned Colonial, had opened up Norfolk's first super-market, and already there were four of these giant food

---

[6] Statement of Rear Admiral Manley H. Simons, *V-P*, July 30, p. 2.
[7] *V-P*, December 31, 1939, Part I, p. 4.
[8] *Know Norfolk*, 1943, p. 56; *V-P*, December 31, 1939, Part I, p. 2.

stores in the city. On Hampton Boulevard the city was getting
the first railroad underpass to permit traffic to the Naval Base
to flow without interruption from Norfolk and Western freight
trains. A new bridge across an arm of the Lafayette River at
26th Street provided easier access to the eastern part of the city.
A soon-to-be-completed toll-free highway would permit travelers,
for the first time in the city's history, to enter Norfolk from the
west without paying toll.[9]

Federal aid was making possible many other civic improvements. The new Municipal Airport, out near the city's reservoir,
had put Norfolk back on the airline map. Pennsylvania-Central
Airlines had begun a daily flight to Washington a year earlier
and on September 1 inaugurated twice-a-day service, duly welcomed at the airport by Mayor John A. Gurkin and other local
officials.[10] Near the landing field a WPA project was at work
creating an azalea garden which was intended to rival Charleston's when completed. At Ocean View jetties had at last been
erected to preserve the beach from wave erosion. A Community
Hospital for Negroes was being built to provide better medical
care for colored persons.[11] The rough stone-block paving on Church
Street was finally being covered with a smooth surface.[12]

Signs of a growing population were two new schools about to
be opened, an elementary school in bright modernistic concrete
at Ocean View and a colonial brick high school on Granby Street,
north of the Lafayette River, ready at last to take some of the
pressure off Maury High, bursting in its cramped downtown quarters. The location of the new schools itself was evidence that the
city had again resumed its relentless march to the north. Fine
homes were appearing in the suburban area along upper Granby
Street and were spreading out along the northern shore of the
Lafayette River, where exclusive Algonquin Park rubbed elbows
with shabby Titustown, a remnant of World War I emergency
building. The residential frontier was steadily making its way up

[9] *Know Norfolk*, First Quarter, 1940, p. 12; *ibid.* 1943, p. 58; *V-P*, September
10, 1939, Part I, pp. 1, 9.

[10] *V-P*, September 2, 1939.

[11] The hospital opened December 17, providing 64 beds instead of the 25 in
the old frame building previously occupied. *V-P*, December 18, 1939, p. 14.

[12] *V-P*, September 19, 1939, p. 18.

Granby Street toward Sewells Point Road, where there was a country crossroads known as Ward's Corner. The 172 homes in Larchmont Village, north of Foreman Field, built in 1938, were already fully occupied.

All this new prosperity was one aspect of Norfolk's enforced marriage with the Navy. Another less pleasant side of the relationship was seldom publicly discussed. The presence of the Navy meant sailors on the streets, sometimes many of them, and the people of Norfolk did not have a very high opinion of sailors. To make matters even, the sailors did not have a very high opinion of Norfolk. This did not mean that there was anything the matter with either Norfolk or the sailors, except that they were both human. As long as human beings have existed, there has been friction between the insiders and outsiders in any community. This friction is increased when there is some obvious mark of distinction on the outsider, such as the shape of his nose, the color of his skin, or the cut of his clothes. This identifying badge causes the permanent resident to notice any offense committed by an outsider and to attribute it to the group rather than to the individual. These offenses are more frequent when the outsiders are men without families, living in bedrooms or in barracks, who are forced to seek recreation in public spots, such as taverns. This quest for diversion is especially strong in men who have been shut up in confined quarters, as on board ships at sea. Ill-feeling is also increased when outsiders are forced to be in the community without any choice of their own in the matter.

It would not have been remarkable then if some ill-feeling had existed between sailor and citizen in Norfolk; in fact, it was remarkable that the two groups got along as well as they did. The people of Norfolk, conscious of the city's dependence on the Navy, controlled their instinctive dislike of the sailors, even though the seamen had no reason to restrain their grumbling. Over the years the two groups had worked out a way of living with a minimum of friction.

By tacit agreement the sailors had been allotted East Main Street from the ferry landings to the Union Station. It was a street fitted out with everything a sailor could possibly ask for—except peace and relaxation. It was lined with glaring neon lights and blaring juke boxes. It held the dingy Gaiety, where sailors could get a close-up revelation of feminine charms. There were penny arcades with peep shows and shooting galleries and stands where an accurate baseball thrower could knock a girl out of bed. There were tattoo parlors and flophouses. Everywhere there were barrooms. There was plenty of wine, women, and song to be had for the right price.

This was the sailors' territory, and they had jurisdiction there. The city police kept out, and the only law-enforcing agency was the shore patrol, made up of friendly shipmates, not anxious to create any trouble. As long as the sailors brawled with each other, no one noticed. It was only occasionally when a fight with civilians broke out that the city police had to be called in. The police had accepted the same arrangement about the girls who worked on East Main Street. It seemed simpler to keep vice regulated in a confined area than to attempt to suppress it. The laws against prostitution were thus quietly suspended, and the only interest the police took in the girls was to see that they stayed inside their district and that they were examined regularly by a physician to keep them from spreading disease.

East Main Street fitted perfectly the civilian conception of Navy tastes. It was true that men joined the Navy without a taste for beer and burlesque, but East Main Street usually converted them. The other alternative was the Navy Y. M. C. A. on Brooke Avenue, where religion and recreation mingled. For the enlisted men, segregation was almost as complete as for the Negro. No "nice" girl was allowed to go out with a sailor. Most civilians accepted the popular conception of the peacetime Navy that a man who enlisted was probably a failure as a civilian and had no decent moral standards. While they would tolerate him on the street, they would not have him in their homes. Only the officers with their Annapolis education and their family backgrounds could hope to escape the caste system, and they usually did. This was not an ideal solution to the problem of social friction, but it was accepted with a minimum of complaint by all concerned.

The only other problem created by the business recovery was the remote possibility that it might turn into a boom. The memory of the crash after the World War was engraved deeply in the minds of the businessmen who ruled the city, and they were determined to prevent another over-optimistic expansion, with its aftermath of heavy debts and high taxes. This time, they were resolved, the city's growth should be held down to a slower, steadier rate. If the Navy insisted on moving more rapidly than that, it should do so with a minimum of interference with Norfolk's normal way of life. This conservative attitude was well expressed by the city manager, Colonel Charles B. Borland, reporting with pride on his first year in office:

While Norfolk is not booming, and I hope it will not, the city is in a mighty healthy condition. On Granby Street, for instance, as late as Friday night there weren't two vacant store buildings from Brambleton Avenue to Main Street.

There is no question of tremendous expansion due to Federal activities. If the Navy takes the East Camp property for enlarging the air station, we will have less than 2,000 undeveloped acres left in Norfolk, and that's not too much for a city this size. . . .

I believe we have hit our stride, gentlemen, but the war has thrown everything offside. Inflations and booms have to be watched carefully. I am going to stand fast by an attempt to keep the tax rate no higher than it is and to provide improvements with what is left over.[13]

[13] *V-P*, September 19, 1939, p. 18.

2

BILLIONS FOR DEFENSE

SEPTEMBER faded into October, and the guns grew silent in Poland. As the war settled down into a dull "sitzkrieg," the people of Norfolk gradually abandoned their gloomy expectation of United States involvement. All through the winter there was little sign of the European hostilities in the city's streets. Trade was not affected by the war, and local business was continuing to improve. The neutrality patrol of American waters was requiring added strength for the Atlantic squadron and was thus increasing activity at the Naval Base, but the steadily quickening beat of the Navy's pulse was scarcely perceptible to civilian ears. Businessmen, in fact, saw more promise of prosperity in the prediction that would-be travelers to Europe might spend their dollars in Norfolk instead during the coming summer.[1]

The spring, however, sent this air-castle of security suddenly tumbling. As Hitler's *panzers* gobbled up Norway and then swallowed the Low Countries, Americans discovered that the Atlantic Ocean was uncomfortably small. Norfolk joined the rest of the nation in cheering President Franklin D. Roosevelt's ringing request for a rapid rearmament. The *Virginian-Pilot* spoke for its readers:

> Let us make no mistake about this: The President is asking for protection, but he is calling also for sacrifices. This program means toil and sweat. It means high taxes. It calls for high intelligence and skill in application. It should be utterly divorced from partisanship. It is the American will and, in broad outline, it deserves approval.[2]

A few days later headlines in the morning paper brought this toil and sweat a little closer home to Norfolk:

[1] *V-P*, December 18, 1939.
[2] *V-P*, May 17, 1940, Part I, p. 6.

9

Germans 12 Miles From English Channel
Britain Confident Home Fleet Can Turn Back Any Invasion
Civilians Flee Paris as Nazi Hordes Near Capital
Million Allied Soldiers Trapped by 'Pincher' as Death Threats to
    Britain Grow Acute Hourly
15,000 Naval Workers To Get New Jobs Under Speed-Up Defense
    Plan
Speed-Up Orders to Mean Large Increase in Force of Workers In
    Navy Yard
Air Base to Get $13,246,000 Fund[3]

These were only shadows of forthcoming events, however, in
that frustrating summer of 1940. The people of Norfolk, as pro-
Allied in sentiment as any American city, for the moment could
work off their wrathful indignation at the collapse of France only
by volunteer efforts to aid Britain or repair American defenses.
The city council, glancing nervously about for potential spies and
saboteurs, voted unanimously to petition Congress for a law requiring all aliens to be registered, fingerprinted, and photographed.[4] The people were annoyed that Hampton Roads had to
offer shelter to ten Italian freighters, driven off the high seas by
British cruisers immediately after Italy's entry into the war, and
silently cheered when a new regulation thought up by the Immi-
gration Bureau temporarily confined the Italians to their ships.[5]
Some Norfolkians with more enthusiasm than discretion set
out on their own to hunt down spies. Excited patriots ran to the
Federal Bureau of Investigation with tales about their neighbors,
and war hysteria magnified suspicion into rumor. The city was
flooded with stories that the FBI had discovered secret short-wave
radio sets and concealed ammunition, that confidential naval data
had been stolen, that several prominent persons had been arrested as Nazis. The *Ledger-Dispatch* printed repeated denials of
the rumors, and finally appeals from Governor James H. Price

  [3] *V-P*, May 22, 1940.
  [4] *V-P*, May 22, 1940, p. 18.
  [5] The regulation required fingerprints on the passports of all seamen on
foreign ships. Norfolk *Ledger-Dispatch*, June 14, 1940. p. 4. The *Ledger-Dispatch*
is hereafter cited as *L-D*.

and the FBI head, J. Edgar Hoover, put an end to this witch-hunting.[6]

More purposeful enthusiasm was shown by the Norfolk chapter of the American Red Cross, which plunged into work to aid the war victims of Europe and turned out nearly 30,000 surgical dressings in four weeks.[7] The Norfolk branch of the American Association of University Women prepared to provide homes for children who were to be evacuated from the bomb-threatened cities of England. Struck by an appeal from national headquarters, the new president of the local branch, Miss Lynette Hamlet, mathematics teacher at Maury High School, decided to act at once. She filled the newspapers with publicity, called a meeting of representative citizens to form plans, organized the Refugee Children's Aid of Norfolk, Inc., started a campaign to collect $10,000 in pledges, obtained a rent-free office, staffed it with volunteers, and gathered the names of 200 families who were ready to receive the British evacuees.[7] Unfortunately, all this well-meant activity went to waste when the English decided to keep their children at home after all.

It was well that Norfolk could think about Europe in this summer of 1940, for this was the last summer it was going to have free to think about anyone else's troubles for the next five years. Already the war had been dumped on the city's doorstep, and before long the infant which had been taken in and cared for would be growing to such sprawling size that it would be driving the family out of the house. On either side of the city the Navy was expanding more rapidly every day. On the left bank of the Elizabeth River the Navy Yard with 11,000 employees in June, was adding a thousand new workers a month, and the commandant, Rear Admiral Manley H. Simons, was constantly demanding new homes in Portsmouth for his civilian employees; in fact, he had

[6] *L-D*, June 8, 1940, p. 2; June 13, 1940, pp. 13, 22; June 28, 1940, p. 18. Neither Price's nor Hoover's appeal was made directly to Norfolk, of course, as this spy hysteria was prevalent all over the United States.

[7] *L-D*, June 29, 1940, pp. 1, 12; July 1, 1940, p. 3; July 3, 1940, p. 2. See also Miss Hamlet's files on the subject in Norfolk Refugee Children's Aid file, Norfolk War History Commission records (hereafter cited as NWHC records).

even turned real-estate man himself and laid out the development of Simonsdale, when businessmen failed to act.[8]

At the north end of Norfolk's Hampton Boulevard the Naval Operating Base, already bustling with 8,000 employees in and out of uniform, not counting the sailors on ships based there, was planning to double that number.[9] In July, just as the defense boom was getting under way, it was estimated that the Navy in the Norfolk area was handing out monthly pay envelopes filled with $3,500,000, dollars which were dropping into Norfolk cash registers.[10] Unemployment began to dwindle. The number of job-seekers registered at the Norfolk office of the Virginia Employment Service dropped from 4,967 on June 15 to 4,636 on July 13 and 4,484 three days later. Newspaper stories were already attracting outsiders in search of jobs. The Employment Service reported that about ten newcomers a day, mostly from North Carolina, were showing up at its office.[11]

This last trace of the depressed thirties, however, was vanishing rapidly. The city stared in open-mouthed astonishment at the Navy's sudden burst of speed. After dawdling for a year over the proposed expansion of the Naval Air Station at the base, the Navy now moved with bewildering rapidity. On July 11 it took by condemnation 1,034 acres of land stretching east from the Naval Base towards Granby Street. The owners of the property involved were given notice to deliver the land by August 15. Next day the contract for the new construction was awarded, and workmen began moving in.[12] Ten days after carpenters started nailing together a headquarters building for the contractor's office, the first

[8] The admiral, of course, did it on a non-profit basis. He earned $25 on the venture in addition to winning a $25 bet with the Portsmouth City Manager that it could be done. Admiral Simons' testimony, March 24, 1943, *Investigation of Congested Areas. Hearings before a Subcommittee of the Committee on Naval Affairs, House of Representatives . . . Part I, Hampton Roads, Virginia, Area.* (Hereafter cited as *Hampton Roads Investigation*).

[9] *V-P*, July 13, 1940, p. 16.

[10] *V-P*, July 26, 1940, Part II, p. 12. Employment figures at this time were: Navy Yard, 11,893; Naval Base, 9,430; all Navy installations in the area, 26,623.

[11] These unemployed were of course unskilled labor. *V-P*, July 17, 1940, p. 20.

[12] *V-P*, July 12, 1940, Part II, p. 16; July 13, 1940, p. 16.

members of the staff were working in it. Flood lights hung on poles kept workmen going on a double shift to finish the barracks and mess hall by September 15. Mammoth dredges dug up the bottom of Willoughby Bay and pumped it across the fields into Boush Creek, which gradually disappeared.[13]

The importance of Hampton Roads as a defense center was dramatized on July 29 by the visit of the President of the United States. Franklin D. Roosevelt, just renominated for a precedent-breaking third term, chose the Norfolk area for the first of his "non-political" inspection tours. As his yacht *Potomac* tied up at the Navy Yard at 9:45 A.M., Rear Admiral Joseph K. Taussig, commandant of the Fifth Naval District, and Rear Admiral Manley H. Simons, commander of the Navy Yard, greeted him, followed by Norfolk's Congressman, Colgate W. Darden, Jr. Norfolk's Mayor John A. Gurkin was also on hand to welcome him. After a tour of the buzzing Navy Yard, the President was driven through cheering crowds to the new toll-free highway to give him a glimpse of what Federal aid had already done for the area. The route over which he traveled had been paved with New Deal dollars: the toll-free bridge across the Elizabeth River; two railroad overpasses; the free Campostella bridge; the underpass and the Lafayette River bridge on Hampton Boulevard. Thousands of men, women, and children stood at every intersection to cheer as he went past, and, in spite of the blazing sun which was beating down upon him, the President returned every greeting with a smile and a wave of his big right hand.[14]

At the end of Hampton Boulevard he reached the Naval Base, which had been born in 1917 while he was Assistant Secretary of the Navy. As he drove past the officers' homes, survivals of the Jamestown Exposition of 1907, he could recognize familiar buildings, seen on his visits then. Elsewhere, however, the Base had become unrecognizable through changes made during his administration. New brick barracks and mess hall had replaced the old frame buildings. Already workers were clearing the land just acquired in the East Camp tract, which had nearly doubled the size of the Base. Encouraged by the signs of progress, President

[13] *V-P*, August 2, 1940, Part II, p. 16.
[14] *V-P*, July 30, 1940, pp. 1, 2.

Roosevelt summed up his visit in a sentence: "A year from now we are going to be a lot safer."[15]

Even with the defense boom just getting under way, housing was already becoming a problem. Only four years earlier 5,000 of the city's 34,000 homes had stood vacant,[16] or a vacancy rate of 15 per cent. The census takers in April 1940, had counted 38,753 dwelling units with only 1,156 of these for sale or rent. This was a vancancy rate of 3 per cent, less than the 5 per cent which is considered necessary to give tenants freedom of choice. The situation was actually considerably worse than this since 20 per cent of Norfolk's dwelling units needed major repairs to make them inhabitable. Including the homes lacking a private bath, 42 per cent were substandard, and 69 per cent were more than twenty years old.[17]

These shabby homes pockmarked the face of the city, breaking out into open sores in several sections. Concerned with the danger of infection from these squalid slums, Norfolk had appointed a Citizens' Committee on Crime, which in 1937 had presented some startling statistics, showing that the crime rate in the slum areas was four and one-half times greater than that of the rest of the city, and that the taxpayers of the rest of the city were paying a subsidy of three-quarters of a million dollars a year to keep up the slums.[18]

A year later Virginia had authorized its cities and counties to cooperate with the newly created United States Housing Authority, which offered Federal aid to local communities for slum clearance projects, but Norfolk spent two more years in deliberation. At last, on April 30, 1940, the city council decided to bring the subject up again and reappointed the earlier Citizens' Com-

[15] *Ibid.*

[16] Sue R. Slaughter, "Migration of Defense Workers and Housing Problems," *The Family*, XXI, 339–340 (February 1941). The terms "homes" is used here instead of the more technically correct "dwelling units", which includes houses, tenements, or apartments.

[17] U. S. Department of Commerce, Bureau of the Census, *Sixteenth Census of the United States: 1940. Housing*, Volume I, Part II, p. 663; *Impact of War on Hampton Roads*, Part I, p. 121. The exact figures for substandard housing were 14,323 dwelling units out of 34,453 for which the information was reported, including 6,835 considered uninhabitable.

[18] Housing Authority of the City of Norfolk, *This Is It* (Norfolk, 1946), p. 3.

mittee to study the question. The committee at once went into action without even waiting for formal notification of its appointment. The very next day it met and prepared the requested report; the members explained that they had gathered enough facts three years before to demonstrate the need for slum clearance.[19]

A public meeting called by the committee to discuss the slum-clearance project revealed both misunderstanding and opposition. The theory of the USHA was relatively simple: People live in slums because they cannot afford to pay for decent housing. The USHA proposed to provide adequate homes for these families at rents they could afford to pay, making up the losses by a subsidy from the Federal treasury. The intricacies of New Dealing economics, however, baffled many of the audience. James E. Etheridge, Norfolk realtor, could not understand why the project was not designed to help the very poor, who could not afford to pay the proposed rent of ten dollars a month. Another man thought it unfair to grant the project an exemption from local taxes, as proposed. One conservative attorney maintained that slum occupants were largely responsible for their own living conditions because they failed to take care of the property, and indignantly denied that there were houses in Norfolk not connected with the sewer, until City Manager Borland assured him that the statement was true.[20]

In spite of the lack of understanding, it seemed clear that the majority of the people of Norfolk were in favor of the program. There was therefore considerable surprise when the city council rejected the project by a 3–2 vote on June 25, allegedly because it failed to provide housing for the very poor. The council embarked on a slum-clearance program of its own by instructing the city manager to enforce the building code.[21]

Fortunately for Colonel Borland, he did not have to carry out these impossible instructions. A roar of protest arose from the city at the council's blundering action. Meetings were held, committees formed, and petitions were circulated. Even such a bul-

[19] *V-P*, May 2, 1940, p. 18. Members of the original committee were Charles L. Kaufman, David Pender, George H. Lewis, C. Wiley Grandy, and L. H. Windholz.
[20] *V-P*, May 7, 1940, pp. 18, 9.
[21] *V-P*, June 26, 1940, p. 24.

wark of business as the board of directors of the Association of Commerce asked the council to reconsider. Council members hasily began to back water, explaining that they would be glad to vote for establishing a housing authority if that was the only way to get rid of slums.[22]

While the debate was running on, however, Washington had been switching from New Deal to National Defense. The USHA had shifted from slum clearance to defense housing, and its funds were now set aside for homes for war workers. An appeal from Admiral Taussig to create the housing authority to provide quarters for his sailors' families saved the council's face. Protesting that they would not think of standing in the way of National Defense, the members on July 23 unanimously voted to establish the Norfolk Housing Authority.[23] The original members of the investigating committee were named to the authority and at once set about their unexpected task of being landlords to the Navy.

In spite of the transformation of purpose the job was fundamentally the same. The problem of the enlisted man with his salary of $60 to $157 a month was to find a suitable home for his family at a rent he could afford to pay. It had never been easy, but now with 38,000 sailors based on Norfolk, it was impossible.[24] As early as February, 1939, Admiral Taussig had attempted to get Federal funds to provide low-cost housing for his married sailors. Referred to local authorities, he had met with a special joint committee of Norfolk businessmen and on May 31, 1939, received from them a report full of conservative optimism, declaring that there seemed to be no shortage of housing for rent at $35 a month and over and that local capital would probably provide whatever additional construction that was needed. Looking back on this report a year later, the plainspoken admiral called it "very disappointing," since he had been primarily interested in obtaining more homes at less than $35 a

[22] *V-P*, July 2, 1940, p. 22; July 3, 1940, p. 20; July 10, 1940, p. 16.

[23] *V-P*, July 23, 1940, p. 18. Because of a technical flaw in the resolution the council had to vote it over again a week later; hence the authority celebrates its birthday on July 30.

[24] Housing Authority of the City of Norfolk, *This Is It*, p. 6.

month. Local capital, he pointed out, had failed to furnish such houses for his enlisted men, and the recent increase in personnel had made the situation worse than when he first brought up the subject.[25]

The good admiral was no longer to be put off by committees. On July 31, the day after the Housing Authority took on legal life, he conferred with its members. When he told them that he needed a thousand low-cost units for his married enlisted men, the authority promptly dispatched a letter to Washington, asking for four million dollars to build the thousand homes. In just four weeks the application crossed the necessary number of desks and came back with half the requested amount approved.[26] A site was found in Ocean View on an 87-acre peninsula in Mason's Creek, just at the back door of the Naval Base.

In the meantime Admiral Taussig was experimenting with direct action. On August 7 he obtained approval by telephone from Rear Admiral Ben Moreell, head of the Navy Department's Bureau of Yards and Docks, for a test project. Admiral Moreell authorized the construction of fifty homes for enlisted men inside the Base as a trial run for future housing to be provided by the Navy. Admiral Taussig demonstrated how fast the Navy could solve its own problems by letting the contract two weeks later and seeing that the houses were ready for occupancy just 48 days after that.[27]

Having made these gains for his enlisted men, Admiral Taussig now turned to the defense of his officers. As it came time to renew the leases which expired September 30, some of the officers noticed that the new contracts called for higher rents. When their complaints came to the ear of the commandant, the admiral fired another broadside into the ranks of the local realtors. He announced that he was making an application to Washington for funds to build officers' quarters. Pointing out that he had called the Norfolk Real Estate Board's attention to rising rents

[25] *V-P*, June 29, 1940, p. 18.

[26] *V-P*, August 2, 1940, Part II, p. 16; Housing Authority of the City of Norfolk, *This Is It*, p. 6.

[27] *V-P*, August 8, 1940, p. 20; U. S. Navy Department, *Building the Navy's Bases in World War II* (Washington, 1947), I, p. 372.

in June, he asserted that the increases were still going on, and implied that the Navy would have to protect its officers from grasping landlords.[28]

The real estate men had good grounds to argue that an increase in rent was justified. From September, 1921, to March, 1935, rents in Norfolk had dropped 47 per cent while the cost of living had fallen only 24 per cent. From March, 1935, to March, 1940, rents had risen only 3 per cent. Landlords therefore could maintain with some show of justice that they were entitled to a 10 or 20 per cent increase to bring rents into balance with other living costs. On the other hand, Norfolk's rents were not far out of line with those in similar cities. Its median rental in March 1940, was $19.72. This was slightly less than the median for the urban areas of Virginia, $21.58, but slightly higher than the median for eight cities of the southeastern United States of comparable size, $18.36.[29]

With tempers still somewhat ruffled, a citizens' committee met in a prompt conference with the admiral, just three days after his blast. Admiral Taussig renewed his charges, reading letters of complaint from his officers. He mentioned a house on La Salle Avenue where the rent had jumped from $50 to $70 a month. In addition, he told them that Norfolk had no really modern apartments and that rents for comparable accommodations were lower in California.

Otto Hollowell, secretary of the Norfolk Real Estate Board, offered as his opinion that the Navy should go ahead and provide quarters for its officers. Navy families were not desirable tenants, anyhow, he added, since their frequent transfers, sometimes in the middle of the rental year, often left property owners with vacant houses on their hands for several months. Of course, if the officers lived on the Base, the Navy should pay the city for the municipal services furnished them, such as schools.[30]

The implied tone of "good riddance" in this speech brought John Twohy II, president of the Norfolk Advertising Board, quickly to his feet. He said that Hollowell was not expressing

---

[28] *V-P*, August 14, 1940, p. 20.

[29] Figures taken or computed from tables in *Impact of War on Hampton Roads*, Part I, pp. 50, 51, 122.

[30] *V-P*, August 17, 1940, p. 16.

the sentiments of the people of Norfolk. "They realize the value of the Navy to local business and that the city is absolutely dependent on the Navy," he declared. "We had our greatest depression when the Navy was transferred to the West Coast, and now real prosperity has returned with the resumption of large-scale Navy activities here." With the troubled waters thus calmed, the committee decided to make a survey of rent increases to find out how general they were.[31]

At a second conference on August 28, the Real Estate Board reported that a survey of 21 rental agencies, covering 5,648 white rental units, showed increases on only 540 units. Of 278 naval officer tenants, three had had their rents raised, three reduced. Of 85 enlisted men, 23 had had their rents increased. In many cases the increases were accompanied by improvements, and in one instance, the board gleefully reported, the rent-raising landlord had been a naval officer himself.[32]

On the issue of housing for enlisted men the decision was clear-cut. Admiral Taussig explained that the Navy was reluctant to authorize more housing for fear of competition with private builders. He estimated that there were now 7,500 married enlisted men in the Norfolk-Portsmouth area, with 22,000 dependents, and many more who would like to bring their families. The real estate men replied quite definitely that the Navy would have to provide homes for them.

The Real Estate Board, however, saw little difficulty in taking care of the officers. Their survey seemed to indicate that the officers living in Norfolk were being well-treated. As for new arrivals in the area, the board declared that new units were being constructed at the rate of 150 per month and that "it is doubtful whether or not Norfolk is growing at a rate that can permanently absorb more than 150 families per month."[33]

[31] *V-P*, August 17, 1940, p. 16.
[32] *V-P*, August 29, 1940.
[33] *V-P*, August 29, 1940.

3

COORDINATED CHAOS

LABOR Day in 1940 brought an end to the first hot summer of National Defense in Norfolk. The tourists at Virginia Beach and Ocean View went home, cottages were boarded up, and amusement parks shut down, as in previous years, but Norfolk grew even busier. While the Navy was preparing more expansion plans, the Army moved in on the area. The Army leased the Virginia Military Reservation at the south end of Virginia Beach,[1] renaming it Camp Pendleton, and expanded Fort Story at the other end by leasing 700 acres of the Seashore State Park.[2] On September 24, the 246th Coast Artillery Regiment of Virginia's National Guard arrived at Fort Story to begin a year of military training, while New York's 244th Coast Artillery moved into Camp Pendleton, to be followed a day later by Pennsylvania's 213th Coast Artillery.[3] With the Virginia Beach amusements in hibernation the National Guardsmen frequently ended a day's drill by a bus trip to Norfolk. In turn, the Navy moved out towards the beach by acquiring a large tract of land near Oceana for an auxiliary air field.[4]

The expansion brought protests from disturbed civilians. Scientists and nature-lovers objected when the Army violated the virgin wilderness of the Seashore State Park,[5] and the site of the Fort Story hospital had to be moved inland so as not to disturb the shore scenery.[6] The Navy took great pains to try to select a site for its practice bombing target which would not disturb

[1] *V-P*, September 5, 1940, p. 22.
[2] *V-P*, September 19, 1940, p. 20.
[3] *V-P*, September 24, 1940, p. 20.
[4] *V-P*, December 19, 1940.
[5] *V-P*, September 29, 1940, Part II, p. 1.
[6] *V-P*, October 5, 1940.

the duck hunters. The acting commandant of the Naval Air Station, Commander Gordon Rowe, finally selected Troublesome Point on the advice of one local duck hunter, only to be overwhelmed by complaints from others. The exasperated commandant relived his feelings with a public protest:

From the opposition that always appears when efforts are made to install bombing and ground gunnery targets along the seacoast, the Commanding Officer is forced to the conclusion that the property owners, duck hunters, guides and keepers expect the Navy to meet their every wish but at the same time they have either no conception or no interest in the question of national defense. These individuals must be made to realize that if our aerial gunners and bombers are not thoroughly trained there is no sense in continuing the aviation part of the national defense program now under way. These parties must make some sacrifice. . . .[7]

It was not only the Navy that was losing patience. Civilian tempers snapped even more quickly. The night of the football game between William and Mary and North Carolina State 17,000 fans overflowed Foreman Field, among them many sailors. A special section had been set aside for the Navy men, who were admitted at the reduced price of fifty cents. Someone in a moment of enthusiasm, however, had sold twice as many tickets as there were seats in the section. The sailors therefore overflowed into the $1.65 reserved seats, and belated arrivals found their seats already taken. In spite of appeals over the loudspeaker system the sailors refused to budge. When indignant reserved-seat holders demanded that the usurpers be removed by force, Police Chief John F. Woods objected that such action might cause a riot, and the latecomers had to be satisfied with a refund of their money.[8]

One of the disappointed football fans insisted on airing his grievance at the next meeting of the Junior Chamber of Commerce. A former president of the organization, citing the police failure to obtain his seat for him, declared that every courtesy

[7] *V-P*, December 7, 1940, p. 16. The commandant, himself a duck hunter, went on to explain that bombing practice would actually have little effect on the sport.

[8] *V-P*, September 21, 1940, p. 10; September 26, 1940, p. 26.

should be extended to sailors and that they should be made to feel at home, but "there is no reason why they should come in here and tell our police where to get off." The Chamber's secretary, William Kilgore, replied that two Navy men had helped him to get a couple of William and Mary students out of his seats and that he did not think anything should be done to antagonize any group. The ex-president insisted, however: "We've got to live in Norfolk as civilians for a long time, and if mob rule by sailors is to be countenanced, then something should be done."[9]

Flaring tempers were only one sign of the quickening tempo of the defense boom. Every index told the same story of more people and more money in Norfolk. Sales in the city's liquor stores during the summer were up 40 per cent over the previous year.[10] Retail sales in November were up 28 per cent over the same month in 1939, and unemployment was down 31 per cent.[11] The State's Norfolk office sold 4,320 more auto license tags in eight months than it had in the entire preceding year.[12] Construction figures for the city in 1940 were nearly nine times the 1939 totals.[13] The city post office had the first million-dollar year in its history.[14]

These defense dollars were bringing problems as well as prosperity, and the dizzy spiral of expansion was threatening to sweep the people of Norfolk off their feet. Caught up as they were by this mad whirl, they scarcely had time to notice any problems but their own. While other sections had debated the issue of a peacetime draft during the summer, Norfolk from its post in the front line of defense had accepted it as a vital

[9] *V-P*, September 26, 1940, p. 26.

[10] The increase was 39.82 per cent for the first quarter of the fiscal year beginning July 1, 1940. There were actually fewer bottles sold, as the increase was due to rising taxes. *V-P*, November 28, 1940, p. 32.

[11] *V-P*, December 11, 1940, December 15, 1940, Part II, p. 1.

[12] *L-D*, December 13, 1940, p. 1. Sales of city licenses, however, were up only 2,000 over 1939.

[13] The figures, compiled by the Builders and Contractors Exchange, were Norfolk City, private builders, $7,007,473 in 1940, $3,310,410 in 1939; government construction, $23,060,908 in 1940, $170,283 in 1939. For the entire Norfolk area, including Portsmouth, and Norfolk and Princess Anne Counties, the totals for 1940 were $49,917,144; for 1939, $6,720,038. *L-D*, February 1, 1941, p. 4.

[14] *V-P*, December 4, 1940, p. 13.

necessity. Where other cities found in the first registration day for Selective Service on October 16 a sign that national rearmament was beginning, Norfolk tried to carry out its registration without interrupting its defense tasks.

Organization went off without a hitch. The city was divided into five draft board areas according to election precincts. Fourteen registration places were set up and staffed by volunteers. At 7:00 A.M. some young men were already in line at the registration offices, and when closing time arrived at 9:00 P.M. some were still waiting to sign up. By the time all these had been taken care of, 19,996 men between the ages of 21 and 35 had enrolled their names. Six of these were the sons of James Edward Shipley of Berkley, who proudly told reporters that he had two more who were not yet old enough to register.[15]

Thus draft registration passed without incident and without fanfare. Equally quiet was the departure of the first contingent of draftees six weeks later. On the morning of November 28, seven young men, four white, three Negro, reported to draft board headquarters. All were volunteers. After a brief talk by one of the draft board members they departed for the station to take the train to Richmond for induction. There were no bands, no cheering crowds of friends to see them off.[16]

Other evidences of the approach of conflict were accepted with no more excitement. The public schools announced a federally-aided program of vocational education for national defense to meet the shortage of skilled workers. More ominously, the National Youth Administration set up courses in practical nursing for unemployed young women because of an expected shortage of nurses.[17] The Navy surprised civilians by suddenly blacking out the Navy Yard and the Naval Base one Sunday night at 10:15, while planes roared overhead to simulate dive-bombing attacks.[18]

In the meantime Norfolk for a moment threatened to disrupt the state's plans for civil protection. At the request of the National Advisory Commission on Defense, the first of a series of

---

[15] *V-P*, October 17, 1940, pp. 1, 24.
[16] *V-P*, November 28, 1940, p. 32.
[17] *L-D*, July 3, 1940, p. 5; *V-P*, November 23, 1940, p. 16.
[18] *V-P*, November 4, 1940, p. 14; November 5, 1940, p. 18.

Washington agencies to be in charge of the defense program, Governor James H. Price prepared a Civil Protective Mobilization Plan, which was designed to form the local police of the state into a mobile reserve, which could be moved into any area in an emergency. The Governor was to be authorized to call out these local policemen for temporary service in other cities. The purpose, of course, was to provide an extra force of trained police for a community which might meet a sudden disaster, such as an unannounced air raid by an undeclared enemy. The possibility of any such force ever being called out was so exceedingly remote that other cities in the state accepted the plan without hesitation.

City Manager Borland, however, proved intransigent. In spite of the fact that the plan seemed intended primarily for Norfolk's protection, he objected to the city's participation in it on the grounds that the local police force was at such a low level that no men could be spared even for emergencies. To save his plan Governor Price revised it so that local authorities could retain their policemen if necessary and sent Weldon T. Ellis, of the State budget office, as his personal representative to explain the plan to the city council. The *Virginian-Pilot* chimed in with its advice:

> . . . the city of Norfolk cannot decently hang up a "do not disturb" sign when it is called upon to make a pro rata local contribution to an emergency mobile police force that the other counties, cities, and towns, with negligible exceptions, have approved. The city which, in an economic sense, is peculiarly benefitting from the national emergency, cannot decently become a hold-out from a State policing plan which grows directly out of that emergency.[19]

Persuaded by this sound lecture and by the Governor's concessions, the city council voted to support the plan, even though the city manager refused to withdraw his objections.[20]

Although the Civil Protective Mobilization Plan was never called upon to function, another action of the Governor's was to have a more important effect on the Hampton Roads area. On May 29 he had appointed a Virginia Defense Council to coordi-

[19] *V-P*, November 30, 1940, p. 4.
[20] *V-P*, December 4, 1940, p. 22.

nate the State's defense efforts. After spending the summer trying
to define its hazy responsibilities by discussing such subjects
as putting armor on the State Highway trucks and stepping up
mule production,[21] the council in September discovered the problems of Hampton Roads.

At a special meeting on September 17, the defense group heard
two representatives of the National Advisory Commission on
Defense discuss the housing situation in Hampton Roads. A
member of the council, Homer L. Ferguson, president of the
Newport News Shipbuilding and Dry Dock Company, described
conditions on the north side in detail. The situation there was
worse than in Norfolk, since even furnished rooms were scarce,
while on the south side it was only apartments that were hard
to find. A representative of the Defense Housing Coordinators'
office, Carl M. Monseese, presented a detailed picture of the
anticipated housing needs of the Hampton Roads area. He estimated the requirements of the Norfolk area as 4,000 housing
units, of which 1500 should be temporary, with 1800 more permanent units needed on the Portsmouth side. The Federal plan for
satisfying this demand demonstrated the dire need for coordination of defense housing. The Navy was to build 101 permanent
and 1100 temporary units; the Federal Housing Administration
would construct 500 units, the Defense Housing Coordinator,
500, the United States Housing Authority, 500, and the Reconstruction Finance Corporation, 550, leaving 750 to be furnished
by private builders. Monseese asked the Defense Council to cooperate in an experiment to explain the Federal program to the
localities and to furnish information to the Defense Housing
Coordinator. As a result of the discussion, the council recommended the appointment of a committee to work with the Federal
agencies and private interests in meeting the housing needs of
Hampton Roads.[22]

Acting promptly, Governor Price two days later appointed a
Temporary Committee for the Hampton Roads Area. Chair-

[21] See editorial, "Where Do We Go From Mules?" *V-P*, June 7, 1940, Part
I, p. 6.
[22] *V-P*, September 18, 1940; Minutes, Virginia Defense Council, 1940, pp. 13-
16, records of the Virginia Office of Civilian Defense, Archives Division, Virginia State Library. These records are hereafter cited as VOCD records.

man of the eight-member committee was Dwight Morgan of
Norfolk, president of the Virginia Manufacturers Association,
with Winder Harris, managing editor of the *Virginian-Pilot*, as
the other Norfolk representative. At its first meeting on September 26 the committee heard an elaborate report recommending
the establishment of a regional defense council. This had been
prepared by Hugh R. Pomeroy, director of the State Planning
Board, who had been named executive secretary of the committee
by Governor Price. At a second meeting on October 1 the committee approved the Pomeroy report and sent it to the Governor.[23]

Governor Price on October 16 appointed a fifteen-man Regional Defense Council, representing all the cities and counties
of the Hampton Roads area, which met in Norfolk to organize
on October 25.[24] At the moment a coordinating agency seemed
essential. The Navy was concentrating on getting housing, the
city was intent on keeping expenses down, the State was trying
to lend a hand, and various Washington agencies were stumbling
over each other in their efforts to help. Moreover, there had
been no agency to coordinate the activities of the various units
of local government around Hampton Roads.

Unfortunately, however, the Regional Defense Council concealed several fatal weaknesses. The whole framework had been
handed down from the state and did not represent a voluntary
effort of the local communities to cooperate. The original membership did not include an official of any of the three major cities
in the area, nor a representative of the major employers, the
Newport News shipyards and the Navy. Cloaked with no authority, the council was without effective powers of coordination.

In spite of the fact that it had not been consulted in advance,
the Norfolk city council voted $2,000 to pay its share of the
Regional Council's expenses. Portsmouth and Newport News each
appropriated $1,000, with the state furnishing the rest of the
$12,000 budget through the Port Authority.[25] The council ac-

[23] *V-P*, September 27, 1940, Part II, p. 14; October 2, 1940, p. 18. Minutes of
the Temporary Committee, September 26, 1940, October 1, 1940, in Hampton
Roads Regional Defense Council file, VOCD records.
[24] *L-D*, October 16, 1940, p. 3; *V-P*, October 26, 1940, p. 18.
[25] Marvin W. Schlegel, *Virginia on Guard* (Richmond, 1949) p. 13.

quired an office next door to the Port Authority's, and used that agency's secretary on a part-time basis. After a long search the council obtained an executive director, André Melville Faure, town planner of Montclair, New Jersey.[26]

One of the problems which was being handed the new Defense Council was that of providing recreation for defense workers and servicemen, but here there was nothing to coordinate. A few of Norfolk's citizens were beginning to realize that the Navy Y and East Main Street could not provide adequate entertainment for the rapidly growing Navy, either in quality or quantity, but for most persons the readjustment of traditional mental attitudes was slow and difficult.

The problem first became apparent when the beaches and their amusement parks shut down after Labor Day. With no other place to go, sailors swarmed over downtown Norfolk until there was a Navy man in almost every ten-foot square. On Saturdays 3,000 recruits in training at the Base piled into the battered old trolleys at the gate and headed downtown. The 400 who had week-end passes bulged the walls of the old Y every Saturday night. The Y had 284 beds in its 225 rooms and set up 200 extra cots, but even with that it had turned away 7,000 bedseeking sailors in the first eight months of 1940. In the same period it had welcomed 213,000 more sailors than in 1939. "How to entertain them is a situation that is calling for serious thought these days" a reporter commented.[27]

Thought the problem may have been getting, but there was little evidence of action. The city council did appoint a special committee, headed by Louis Lee Guy, to investigate the need for recreation. Chairman Guy reported the obvious, that the rapid influx of military and civilian personnel made it necessary that greater recreational facilities be provided. The problem, however, seemed too great for local solution. As it was reported that President Roosevelt had a $25,000,000 fund for recreation, the council declared an "urgent need" for recreational facilities and empowered City Manager Borland to apply for funds.[28]

Not until the end of November was there anything like con-

[26] V-P, October 26, 1940, p. 18; December 12, 1940, p. 32.
[27] V-P, September 8, 1940, Part II, pp. 1, 2.
[28] V-P, October 2, 1940, p. 18.

crete action. Then the executive board of the Navy Y authorized the expenditure of $15,000 for remodeling of the old *Virginian-Pilot* building on Brooke Avenue. This amount would convert the first floor into a social room to provide many varieties of entertainment and space for another 150 cots at night. In another year, it was hoped, money would be available to convert the second floor into a standard-size gymnasium with room for 150 more cots.[29]

What was needed most, however, was a touch of friendliness. In the peacetime pattern of segregation, friendship with the Navy's enlisted men had been not so much frowned on as unthought of. Now Norfolk was beginning to think about it, inspired perhaps by the presence of the National Guard at Virginia Beach. It was natural to accept these soldiers as civilians temporarily in uniform for the defense of their country. From this it was only a short leap to the realization that the men in blue were also part of the nation's defenses.

Whatever the reasoning involved, Norfolk took its first step towards fraternization with the Navy. The men's committee of St. Paul's Church took the initiative in interesting a number of civic organizations to arrange for a dance every Saturday night in the old city auditorium, which would be solely for the entertainment of Army and Navy personnel and civilian workers on national defense projects.[30]

Pending the formation of this organization, a group of public-spirited citizens contributed funds to get a program started. On December 7 they began a series of Saturday night dances in the city auditorium with a hired orchestra. Screening the guest list was a ticklish problem, since letting in either the wrong type of sailor or the wrong type of girl would ruin the dances. Navy tickets were distributed at the Base and at the Navy Y. Some girls were invited, and all who wished could obtain tickets from the Y. W. C. A. or the City Recreation Bureau. To assure doubting parents of the safety of their daughters, forty matrons chap-

[29] *V-P*, November 30, 1940, p. 18.
[30] William McC. Paxton, member of the Regional Defense Council, made this announcement at the council's meeting on November 22. *V-P*, November 23, 1940, pp. 16, 9.

eroned the dance and introduced the boys and girls to each other.[31]

The sailors were enthusiastic about the dances. It was not merely that they wanted a place to go on Saturday night. More important was the opportunity to meet decent girls in respectable surroundings, as well as the friendly welcome the dance indicated. Sailors and girls were unanimous in approving the social events. "We want the dances to be informal but on a high plane," said Mrs. Norwood Pinder, chairman of the hostesses. "We are trying to build the dances on a sound basis. We are proceeding carefully so as to keep the confidence of the community."[32]

It was well that sailors were getting an opportunity to meet decent girls because it would soon be harder for them to meet the other kind. In October Dr. J. A. Goldberg of the American Social Hygiene Association suddenly arrived in Norfolk and headed for East Main Street. He had brought with him a list of places where Navy men had contracted venereal disease. Into each one he went, inspecting each house carefully, even the beds. He seemed to be surprised at what he found. Of a roadhouse on Cottage Toll Road, he declared: "I don't see how a place like that can exist around here."[33]

Rumor had it that the Navy had been alarmed about an increase in the venereal disease rate and that the orders were out to close up the red-light district. For a week there was a glum silence around police headquarters, and then City Manager Borland finally admitted the truth in an ambiguous statement:

It is the policy of the city government to prosecute vigorously vice in all its phases. Prostitution has been practiced in every age. Those in authority have tried to the utmost to curb and correct this evil.

The administration of the City of Norfolk has been experimenting along various lines over a period of years in connection with the curbing of prostitution. It appears that so far very little definite improvement has been made.

No one in authority looks with favor upon commercialized vice in

[31] *V-P*, December 14, 1940, pp. 18, 9.
[32] *V-P*, December 15, 1940, Part I, p. 8.
[33] *V-P*, November 1, 1940, Part II, p. 14; Minutes, Hampton Roads Regional Defense Council, November 22, 1940, VOCD records.

any form. The City of Norfolk is undergoing a vast change. The population is increasing at a rapid rate. Naturally this brings with it many complications in government activities. We are trying to meet these as best we can.

As segregation has met with much opposition, we shall have to abolish it and change our methods. But the people of Norfolk can rest assured that every effort will be made to make Norfolk a clean and respectable city in which to live.[34]

In other words, if the Navy wanted the girls of East Main Street to be put out of business, the city would close up the district, regardless of any misgivings the police might have as to the wisdom of such a step. The word went quietly out that the law would be enforced after the Christmas holidays, and on January 1, 1941, the red lights went out.

[34] *V-P*, November 8, 1940, Part II, p. 16.

4

BURSTING AT THE SEAMS

MEANWHILE the housing situation was rapidly going from difficult to impossible. Newcomers were arriving faster than homes were being built for them. In August, 1940, the Real Estate Board had declared that houses were being put up at the rate of 150 a month. In the first half of September new families moved into Norfolk at the rate of four a day, in the last half, six a day, and in the first half of October, ten a day, according to estimates of the Norfolk Advertising Board.[1] Ten a day meant 300 a month, or twice as many as the available new homes. Even in September a survey made by the letter carriers at the request of the Norfolk Housing Authority found only 352 vacant dwellings out of 34,236, and more than half of these empty homes were considered uninhabitable.[2] There was no relief to be found in crossing the ferry to Portsmouth or taking the long trip across Hampton Roads to Newport News, for civilian shipyard workers had crowded those cities even more than Norfolk. The only vacancies were the heatless summer cottages at Virginia Beach.

Houses were a-building, however, all over the open countryside that had once separated downtown Norfolk from Ocean View. Government money was supplying homes for Admiral Taussig's enlisted men. On October 16 the contract was let for Merrimack Park, the Norfolk Housing Authority's 500-unit project on Mason's Creek, adjoining the new extension of the Naval Air Station. The next day the Navy let the contract for 1,042 units more, which it was to rent to its enlisted men.[3] These units

[1] *V-P*, October 17, 1940, p. 24.
[2] Housing Authority of the City of Norfolk, *This Is It*, p. 7; *V-P*, September 24, 1940, pp. 20, 15.
[3] *V-P*, October 18, 1940, Part II, p. 16.

were the result of the success of the trial project of fifty units constructed on the Base in August and September. The new group of homes, to be named Benmoreell, after the admiral who, as head of the Bureau of Yards and Docks, had obtained approval of the project, were located on part of the old Army Base, just east of Hampton Boulevard.

Private builders were putting up more individual homes and small apartment units than ever, and out-of-town builders were moving in to take on larger projects. Biggest of these was Suburban Park near Ward's Corner, where Sewells Point Road crossed Granby Street. Started in September, 1940, by a Baltimore firm as a 101-apartment unit, it was shortly doubled in size. A Richmond organization laid plans for an even larger project in Commodore Park, hoping to put up 240 homes there. Other contractors started developments in Glenwood Park, just north of Benmoreell, and in Fairmount Manor, on the old fairgrounds on the east side of the city.[4] Still the Navy did not have enough. Admiral Taussig told the Norfolk Housing Authority that 500 furnished homes for officers were still needed. Conceding that there was a great amount of building going on, he pointed out that the new construction was intended largely for sale rather than for rent.[5]

All this hectic activity, supported largely by FHA loans, aroused unpleasant memories in conservative financial circles in Norfolk. Real estate men remembered all too vividly how lending institutions had collapsed when property values crashed not so many years before. The current temporary need, they felt, should be met entirely by temporary construction. These hundreds of permanent homes being thrown up by out-of-town builders with the aid of Federal funds threatened to cause another crash as soon as the emergency had passed.

In order to protect their capital invested in Norfolk real estate, the local building and loan associations therefore decided to cooperate to keep the housing situation under control. They named a committee, headed by John R. Sears of the Berkley Permanent Building and Loan Association, which was joined by Otto Hollowell, executive secretary of the Norfolk Real Estate Board. On a

    [4] V-P, September 14, 1940, p. 16; September 24, 1940, p. 13; October 9, 1940, p. 18; December 4, 1940, p. 18; December 29, 1940, Part II, p. 1.
    [5] V-P, November 5, 1940, p. 18.

trip to Washington in September, the group tried to present its case to Federal officials, warning that 10 per cent overbuilding might reduce property values 30 to 40 per cent. The only assurance they were able to obtain was the suggestion that they work with the Temporary Committee on Housing just named by Governor Price to determine what the permanent needs were. Then they should use their efforts to see that temporary needs were met by temporary construction.[6]

As soon as the Temporary Committee on Housing had given way to the Hampton Roads Regional Defense Council, the joint committee of the building and loan associations and the Real Estate Board tried to carry out the advice they had received in Washington. They appeared at the council's second meeting to repeat their warning about overbuilding. Answering some unfriendly criticism that had developed, W. C. Pender of the Federal Mutual Savings and Loan Association explained that the fact that they had turned down several groups which had applied for loans did not mean that they were opposed to further building. They objected only to loans on housing intended for the defense workers to be brought into the area on a temporary basis. Although they could not risk their depositors' funds in such projects, they were willing to go the limit on loans for permanent housing.[7]

In spite of the fact that the Regional Defense Council had been created primarily to meet the housing problem, it took little interest in the joint committee's ideas. Nevertheless, the group went ahead on its own to make a survey of the building under way. Chairman John R. Sears announced that Norfolk would have 6,500 additional family housing units by the spring of 1941. On closer analysis, however, this figure did not seem quite so overwhelming, since it included only 3,469 units actually started since January 1, while the rest of the total was obtained by including the 1,300 vacancies found by the census takers in April and some 1,700 more homes that builders would probably start in the next few months.[8]

The figures were meaningless, in any case, unless the demand

[6] V-P, September 24, 1940, p. 13; September 25, 1940, p. 10.
[7] V-P, November 7, 1940, p. 17; Hampton Roads Regional Defense Council Minutes, November 6, 1940, VOCD records.
[8] V-P, November 10, 1940, Part II, p. 1.

could be measured alongside the supply. The joint committee therefore called upon the Regional Council to make a survey of permanent housing needs, but the council was still without a staff. Chairman Sears reminded the public that the current shortage was merely temporary, as it was caused largely by the construction workers on the new housing projects and the big expansion at the Naval Air Station. As soon as these jobs were finished, the newcomers could be expected to leave the area.[9]

While local capital was holding back so reluctantly from the building boom, other investors were cheerfully investing their money in expansion, regardless of the future. The Virginia Electric and Power Company spent $4,300,000 expanding its Reeves Avenue plant capacity by 50 per cent and constructed a connection with Virginia Public Service on the north side of Hampton Roads for an exchange of power.[10] The Chesapeake and Potomac Telephone Company, completing in May a million-dollar expansion intended to take care of ten years' growth, had to enlarge its long-distance switchboard by Christmas.[11]

The city had to expand its water system, but the Federal Government paid most of this bill. The Navy insisted that the city pay 25 per cent of the $515,000 cost of laying new mains to supply water to the Naval Base, in spite of Colonel Borland's argument that the improvements were needed only for the Navy, not for the city. As the city manager told the council:

Norfolk's water supply is more than adequate for its own needs, the deficiency being in the manner and means of distributing the water from the two pumping stations. In other words, our reservoirs are adequate, our pumping stations are more than adequate, but the old pipes within the city limits are rather seriously impaired and deliveries cannot be made in the outlying districts. . . .[12]

With the Army the colonel proved a more effective negotiator. When the Army asked for water for Fort Story and Camp Pendleton, the city laid eleven miles of main to reach these camps

[9] *V-P*, November 24, 1940, Part II, p. 6.
[10] *V-P*, August 6, 1940, p. 18.
[11] *L-D*, December 27, 1940, p. 2.
[12] *V-P*, August 6, 1940, p. 18; *Civic Affairs, Annual Report of the City Manager, Norfolk, Virginia, 1940*, pp. 40–41.

and installed a pumping station on the line. The entire cost of $138,500 was supplied by the Federal Government, since the extension was of no benefit to the city.[13]

The sewers were the only utility that could handle their added load. In spite of all the construction going on, the city spent less on new sewers in 1940 than it had in 1939. Increasing sewage, however, was intensifying a problem of long standing. Untreated sewage was already being dumped into local waters faster than the waters could purify it. The oyster beds of the lower James and Hampton Roads had long been contaminated, and the water of the area was too filthy for swimming. It seemed but a question of time until sewage would be seeping out into the Chesapeake and defiling the beaches of Ocean View.

The cities of Hampton Roads had evaded responsibility for this problem, partly because of reluctance to assume the additional debt burden of constructing sewage treatment plants and partly because of the lack of any coordinating agency to bring the cities into cooperation in meeting the situation. In 1940 the General Assembly had offered a solution to the problem by authorizing the creation of a Hampton Roads Sanitation District, subject to the approval of the voters in the area. This super-government agency could sell its own bonds without affecting the debt of the cities and counties concerned and pay for its operations by collecting fees from the users of the sewage-treatment plants.

The referendum on the creation of the districts brought out a group of embattled citizens who seemed intent on defending Norfolk's sacred right to dump its sewage where it pleased. A self-appointed "Fact-Finding Committee" took a full-page advertisement to lambast the proposed Sanitation Commission. Demanding that the State and Federal Government pay two-thirds of the cost, it called for the defeat of this "half-baked measure," and scoffed at the idea of the polluted waters causing epidemics.[14]

Ideas like these prevailed on the west side of the Elizabeth River, where Portsmouth city officials were in loud opposition to the sanitation measure, but when Norfolk went to the polls that November day to choose Franklin D. Roosevelt over Wendell

[13] *Civic Affairs,... 1940*, p. 41.
[14] *V-P*, November 4, 1940, p. 8.

Willkie, it endorsed the sewage-treatment proposal. Although Portsmouth, South Norfolk, and Norfolk County were opposed, the voters of the area as a whole approved the creation of the district, and the first step was taken in cleaning up Hampton Roads.[15]

More noticeable than any other of the problems of expansion was the traffic situation. Norfolk's narrow, crooked downtown streets had long been clogged with trolley cars and buses. Now that the newcomers had added more thousands of automobiles to the city's traffic, lines of vehicles threatened to tangle in hopeless snarls. In September the city council requested City Manager Borland to make a survey to see what might be done about the situation. He conferred with local transit officials about taking the streetcars off Monticello Avenue to give motorists a free route north, but found that Monticello merchants objected.[16] There was a possibility of removing the trolleys which jammed Granby Street, but Granby Street merchants objected to that.

While motorists objected to the trolleys on any street, carless commuters wanted more of them. Naval Base streetcars were jammed to the doors every morning, and squeezed straphangers clamored for better service. Colonel Borland once more conferred with Virginia Electric and Power Company officials. R. J. Throckmorton, Norfolk vice-president of the company, and Raymond G. Carroll, transportation manager, assured him that the company had ordered both streetcars and buses, but that with all the defense work going on there was no telling when they could expect delivery. Nevertheless, they would make every effort to get the needed equipment.[17]

The Navy fortunately came to the rescue with an offer to help in expediting the traffic it had created. Admiral Taussig stared at the stalled lines of cars leading into the Naval Base in the morning and out in the afternoon, as 12,000 tried to pass through the gate, and declared emphatically:

It takes an hour to get our traffic out, and sometimes it is held up by the railroad trains. Communications are not reasonable now—not even

[15] V-P, November 6, 1940, pp. 1, 2; Reid W. Digges, "Abatement of Pollution in Hampton Roads," Lynchburg Foundry Company's The Iron Worker, Summer, 1949, pp. 11–15, 30–32 (Vol. XII, No. 3).
[16] V-P, October 5, 1940, p. 18.
[17] V-P, November 23, 1940, p. 16.

satisfactory. And in view of the fact that we will have twice or maybe three times as many ships here in the future, due to the two-ocean Navy, as we have now, we had better get some funds for roads right away.[18]

At a meeting in the city council chamber the commandant promised that he would ask the Navy for funds to improve streets and highways in the Norfolk area. His recommendations called first for the improvement of the streets leading to Granby Street and Ocean View Avenue from the new gate at the Naval Air Station extension on the east side of Mason Creek. Second on his list was the construction of overpasses at the two railroad crossings on Hampton Boulevard and the one on Granby Street. Next he wanted Sewells Point Road improved and a new road constructed to connect it with the Virginia Beach Boulevard and provide easy access to the new auxiliary landing fields near the ocean. In addition he would ask for funds to widen Hampton Boulevard as far south as the Lafayette River.[19]

A few days later the Regional Defense Council held a highway traffic conference to discuss the problem for all of Hampton Roads. A crowd of civic leaders, state and local officials, and Army and Navy officers appeared for the meeting, among them two Washington officials, Frank Bane, of the National Advisory Commission on Defense, and a representative of the Public Roads Administration. Admiral Taussig once more promised his aid in obtaining Federal funds. He said that it would take some education of Congress to make the legislators see that Hampton Roads was different from the Navy bases in New York, Philadelphia, and Boston. Defense workers made up about 20 per cent of the population in this area, he declared, while they constituted only about 1 per cent of New York City's population.

The cities chimed in to offer their mites. Portsmouth was "poor but patriotic," said its City Manager Charles E. Harper, as he offered $4,600. Colonel Borland declared that Norfolk received only $90,000 a year from the state for road-building. Suffolk could offer nothing but a right-of-way. Their poverty did not limit their requests, however, By the time the localities were through offering suggestions they had turned in $6,000,000 worth of recommendations. Portsmouth suggested a new highway to

[18] *V-P*, November 29, 1940, Part II, pp. 18, 7. Total shore-based personnel, naval and civilian, was 14,000 at this time.
[19] *V-P*, November 13, 1940, p. 20.

8 CONSCRIPTED CITY

link the Navy Yard with the Naval Base, starting from the toll-free highway and circling east of Norfolk to connect with the Sewells Point Road. Norfolk had no new projects, but City Manager Borland urged: "If it's an emergency, we ought to put it right in Washington's lap."[20]

Local authorities were not merely twiddling their thumbs, waiting for dollars from Washington. The State in September let contracts for widening the rest of the Beach Boulevard into Virginia Beach and for doubling the width of the toll-free highway before it was a year old.[21] The city chopped off part of the sidewalks on Bank Street to provide more room for autos. The city also resurfaced a half-mile of Hampton Boulevard at Foreman Field, paving in the streetcar tracks to provide a wider street. Kersloe Road, running from Hampton Boulevard to Granby Street along the edge of the new Naval Air Station expansion, was improved by the Navy in compensation for closing off the Mason Creek Road, and renamed Admiral Taussig Boulevard by the grateful city.[22]

The city was meanwhile girding up its financial loins. A New York expert, Norman S. Taber, was called in to submit a plan to lighten the burden of debt, which was taking 41 per cent of the city's revenue. The Taber plan promised the city a saving of $400,000 in 1941, an important item in the city's $7,000,000 budget. This was accomplished by the expedient of partially postponing debt retirement for the next few years until the emergency was over. In addition, taxes on the new buildings being constructed were expected to make city revenue in 1941 a half-million dollars higher than in 1939. This new income, together with the savings on debt retirement, would cover increasing expenses. As the city manager's report proudly declared:

The tax rate for 1941 was retained at $2.50 per $100.00 assessed valuation despite the fact that the additional population of the City and defense requirements placed heavier demands for municipal services.[23]

[20] *V-P*, November 29, 1940, Part II, pp. 18, 7, 5.
[21] *V-P*, September 27, 1940, Part II, p. 14.
[22] *Civic Affairs, . . . 1940*, p. 20.
[23] *Civic Affairs, . . . 1940*, pp. 9, 167–170. The Commissioner of the Revenue commented: "Yet, revenue provided by the 1940 tax levy, the principal source of municipal funds, was well over a million dollars less than that for some of the other previous years." *Ibid.*, p. 158.

5

HALF-WAY TO WAR

THE Navy's rapid expansion could not be interrupted even by disaster. Nerve-center of the Fifth Naval District was the administration building at the Base. A survival of the Jamestown Exposition of 1907, it was an imposing brick-faced structure topped by a dome, but within it had a heart of tinder-dry wood. When the cry of "Fire!"rang through its empty corridors on a quiet Sunday morning in January, 1941, it was obvious in a few moments that the building was doomed, and the Navy's firemen had to content themselves with saving the two adjoining wings.[1]

In the roaring flames the Base lost not only its auditorium and post office but also its vital communication center. A few minutes after the two telephone operators on duty had given the alarm, every phone on the base was dead. Repairmen of the Chesapeake and Potomac Telephone Company rushed to the scene to restore the Navy's nerves. An hour and a half after the fire broke out they had a line to the city working again, and by Friday every telephone on the Base was back in operation.[2] Admiral Taussig immediately asked the Navy Department's approval for the construction of a new building, and plans for the proposed structure were already in Washington on Thursday.[3] Meanwhile, in emergency quarters, the Navy's work went on without pause.

Already crowded, even with its 1,034-acre addition of the previous summer, the Naval Air Station kept nibbling at other properties in its vicinity until it finally gobbled up the last 227 acres which separated it from Granby Street, including, appro-

[1] *V-P*, January 27, 1941, p. 1.
[2] *L-D*, January 31, 1941, p. 22.
[3] *L-D*, January 27, 1941, pp. 1, 3; January 30, 1941, p. 2.

priately enough, the old Norfolk Airport. This completed an
extension of more than 1,500 acres in the Station's area since
July 1, 1940.[4] Not content with this, the Air Station also took
over more Princess Anne County farms to make two additional
auxiliary fields along the coast.[5]

Another acquisition of the Navy was 38 acres of land at Little
Creek. This, it was announced, was to be converted into a "section base," for small naval vessels, principally patrol boats.[6]
The Navy also found some use for its St. Helena Reservation in
Berkley, idle since the Naval Training Station had moved out
to the Base in 1917. It was first projected as a storage base for
the landing craft the Navy was planning to build in case it
should ever be called upon to land troops on foreign shores.[7] An
even larger function was revealed on the occasion of Secretary
of the Navy Frank Knox's visit to Norfolk on July 9, when plans
were announced for building an auxiliary navy yard on the reservation for the repair of small vessels.[8] The project was to cost
four million dollars and to employ a thousand men on each
shift.[9]

Even a four-million-dollar construction program was no longer
big news in dollar-dizzy Norfolk. Millions were crowding millions
in the headlines, and contracts had grown so large that even the
Navy's paper clips and erasers cost $17,000.[10] The Naval Air
Station program was doubled with twelve more million heaped
on top of the original twelve.[11] The Naval Supply Depot was
granted $4,400,000 for construction,[12] and the Naval Training
Station was awarded $1,700,000 to expand its facilities.[13] An ap-
propriation of a million and a quarter was authorized for replacing the administration building,[14] with another half million

[4] *V-P*, July 22, 1941, p. 18.
[5] *V-P*, February 6, 1941, p. 22; March 21, 1941, Part II, p. 14.
[6] *V-P*, February 19, 1941, p. 20.
[7] *V-P*, February 26, 1941, p. 1.
[8] *V-P*, July 10, 1941, p. 1.
[9] *V-P*, July 13, 1941, Part II, p. 1.
[10] *L-D*, March 4, 1941, p. 13.
[11] *L-D*, March 4, 1941, p. 13.
[12] *L-D*, February 15, 1941, p. 2.
[13] *L-D*, May 28, 1941, p. 18.
[14] *L-D*, February 13, 1941, p. 1.

for permanent Marine barracks.[15] Even these sums paled into insignificance beside the millions allocated to the Navy Yard for construction of warships, ranging from minesweepers to battleships.

These activities expanded so rapidly that no one could keep up with them. Norfolkians, each busily preoccupied with his own section of the defense effort, seldom saw the picture as a whole. The Hampton Roads Defense Council, to get a better picture of its problems, hired a bus and made an inspection tour of the area from Camp Pendleton to Portsmouth. Even local people were impressed and surprised at what was happening. Colonel Borland's executive secretary, Aubrey G. Graham, exclaimed: "I never dreamed this much was going on or that it had progressed so far."[16]

Feverish haste was imposed by America's progress toward war. At the moment Congress was still debating President Roosevelt's proposal to lend or lease war supplies to Britain. In Norfolk there was no debate, however. When the Kiwanians planned a pro-and-con discussion of all-out aid to England, not a single member could be found who was opposed to the idea.[17] In fact, Norfolk so completely forgot the sensitivity of tender-skinned isolationists elsewhere that it almost precipitated an international incident.

The *Virginian-Pilot* one March morning prominently displayed some Navy Yard gossip about two new minesweepers which had just been completed there. Workers noticed that they were being covered with the same dark-gray paint which had been used on the ten destroyers the Yard had prepared for transfer to England the summer before. Since they were being painted the English color instead of the lighter United States shade, it was natural for the workmen to assume that the minesweepers would shortly be transferred to Britain under the lend-lease agreement, and the *Pilot* printed the report.[18]

An unidentified Navy Yard official saw the story and hastened to set the matter straight. The minesweepers were not going to be

[15] *L-D*, May 28, 1941, p. 18.
[16] *V-P*, March 19, 1941, pp. 18, 13.
[17] *V-P*, March 7, 1941, Part II, p. 12.
[18] *V-P*, March 18, 1941, p. 18.

transferred to England, he explained. The new dark gray was being adopted as a standard color by the Navy, and all ships would be painted that color. He added that this was going to give Hitler's U-boats a tough time since they would not be able to tell whether ships they sighted were American or British. The next day the newspaper played up this clever bit of strategy as another blow at the Nazis.[19] In Washington, however, the story did not meet with universal applause. An isolationist Congressman rose on the floor of the House, brandishing a copy of the *Pilot*, and demanded to know why the Navy was deliberately painting its ships to make them targets for German torpedoes. The embarrassed Secretary of the Navy was forced to deny the whole story, explaining that the change of color was merely routine procedure and that any resemblance to the British Navy was purely coincidental.[20]

Escaping without a public scolding from this fracas, the Norfolk newspapers kept a tighter lip thereafter. A few weeks later the *Pilot* righteously upbraided the New York *Herald-Tribune* for reporting the arrival of the British warship *Malaya* when it sailed up the Hudson in plain view of millions.[21] A month later the Norfolk papers had a chance to practice their own preaching when the crippled British carrier *Illustrious* passed through Hampton Roads on May 12 and headed for a Navy Yard dry dock. All summer repairs to the *Illustrious* went on, while the British sailors with their ship's name on their caps swarmed over Norfolk. Everyone seemed to know of the *Illustrious's* presence, but not a word about her appeared in the papers. The *Pilot* even scolded the British for talking about her:

What has possessed the British Ministry of Information to announce that Captain Lord Louis Mountbatten, recently arrived in the United States, will command the British carrier *Illustrious*, and that the *Illustrious* is "in an American shipyard undergoing repairs," is beyond our guessing. Except for the arrival of the British battleship *Malaya* in New York months ago, the first of the British naval vessels to seek repair or overhaul in the United States, there has been no public mention of such arrivals.[22]

[19] *V-P*, March 19, 1941, p. 18.
[20] *V-P*, March 20, 1941, p. 22.
[21] *V-P*, April 10, 1941, p. 6.
[22] *V-P*, August 24, 1941, Part I, p. 10.

The *Ledger-Dispatch* put its tongue in its cheek and soberly reported that the dispatch from London had not revealed which American shipyard was sheltering the carrier.[23] Even when the Duke of Kent visited Norfolk in the full glare of publicity, the papers reported only that he went on board "a British vessel" in the Navy Yard.[24] At length, when Lord Mountbatten arrived in Norfolk to take command of the carrier, the papers were at last allowed to reveal the well-kept "secret."[25]

Censorship, even voluntarily accepted, was one more sign that the United States was already at war. Norfolk, in fact, could feel Mars's hot breath on the back of its neck. In March Coast Guardsmen boarded the Italian and Danish ships anchored in Hampton Roads and discovered that several of the Italian ships had been sabotaged. To prevent any further damage to the vessels, their crews were removed to exile in St. Helena.[26] Navy wives found that letters from husbands at sea no longer mentioned what their ships were doing, and some got only printed postcards with the message indicated by checkmarks.[27]

The Coast Guard gave reserve commissions to owners of forty- to fifty-foot cruisers, and called them into active service to patrol the harbor. Owners of smaller boats were organized into an auxiliary to be ready for emergency duty.[28] Guards suddenly appeared on the waterfront and halted every visitor to important piers.[29] War games held in Hampton Roads were a grim reminder that an actual hostile force might be expected, and an "enemy" plane with ominous success dropped an imaginary bomb on the Navy Yard, causing fictional casualties in Norfolk.[30]

On June 9 the city learned that the first American ship had been sunk by a Nazi torpedo. Aboard the *Robin Moor* as assistant engineer was a Portsmouth man, Frank Ward, Jr., and a Norfolk boy named Virgil Sanderlin was a member of her crew.[31] The

[23] *L-D*, August 22, 1941, p. 10.
[24] *V-P*, August 26, 1941, p. 1.
[25] *V-P*, August 29, 1941, Part II, p. 12.
[26] *V-P*, March 31, 1941, p. 1. The Coast Guard incidentally found itself stuck with the care of a pig and two canaries, which were left aboard the ships.
[27] *V-P*, May 12, 1941, p. 14.
[28] *V-P*, May 16, 1941, Part II, p. 16.
[29] *V-P*, May 31, 1941, p. 18.
[30] *V-P*, May 20, 1941, p. 18.
[31] *V-P*, June 10, 1941, p. 1; June 12, 1941, p. 1.

shooting war had begun. As if in reply, the guns of Fort Story boomed out next day for the first time since 1928 in regular service practice. With utter disregard for the fact that the shells cost $2,000 apiece, the sixteen-inch howitzers blazed away again and again at the target.[32]

Almost equally unmindful of the cost of warfare were the people of Norfolk. While other cities were teetering painfully between their fear of Hitler and their fear of conflict, Norfolk left no doubt where it stood. The new congressman from Virginia's Second District, Winder R. Harris, who succeeded Colgate Darden on April 15, at once took a firm stand in favor of all-out aid to Britain without receiving a single letter opposing his position. Some of his correspondents, in fact, urged him on even further, demanding a break in relations with the Axis powers.[33]

Although not all Norfolkians were willing to endorse such a policy, they accepted the fact that the United States was already virtually in the war. Hoping, like every American, that some miracle would overthrow Hitler and make it unnecessary for American soldiers and sailors to fight, they were prepared to shoot before they would surrender. The miracle did not come when Hitler turned on Russia in June. As the *Wehrmacht* rolled over the Russian plains, it became obvious to the realist that American guns could not destroy Nazism unless they were fired by American soldiers. The *Virginian-Pilot* took a stand "On a Hitherto Taboo Subject" and declared boldly:

. . . if our safety and security require full-scale war, we shall fight it with whatever resources in manpower and weapons we can command and wherever military strategy calls for it to be fought. Any other course, and in particular any half-way course, would be very near the topmost peak of folly.[34]

Norfolk meanwhile had been helping to build up these resources in manpower. Each month a slightly larger contingent of unmarried young men answered the call of their draft board and set out to Richmond for induction. The largest single departure came on February 3, 1941, when the 500 members of the Norfolk units of the National Guard were formally inducted into Federal

[32] *V-P*, June 11, 1941, p. 20.
[33] *V-P*, May 25, 1941, Part II, pp. 1, 7.
[34] *V-P*, July 21, 1941, p. 6.

service for a year of military training. The Guardsmen were given a farewell party at the Town Club on February 6, but, with a bit of anti-climax, remained camped out at the armories for another week. At length, Fort Meade was in condition to receive them, and on Monday, February, 17 the first units started pulling out.[35]

The departure of the National Guard left the city without any organized military force, but it was prepared for this emergency. In accordance with plans drafted the preceding summer, Governor James H. Price had summoned Brigadier General E. E. Goodwyn of Emporia out of retirement to organize a Virginia Protective Force to function as a home guard while the National Guard units were away. On January 7 General Goodwyn was in Norfolk to discuss plans for organizing this force with City Manager Borland and Brigadier General William H. Sands of the National Guard. A few days later the result of this conference appeared in the appointment of Robert P. Beaman as lieutenant colonel of the First Battalion of the Virginia Protective Force, to consist of four companies in Norfolk and one in Portsmouth.

The naming of Colonel Beaman, president of the National Bank of Commerce and Norfolk's "First Citizen" of 1940, was warmly applauded. The *Virginian-Pilot* commented:

> The appointment of Mr. Beaman is to be welcomed. He has had active military experience. He has executive ability. He is schooled in the importance of sound organization and he has the judgment to institute it. This is a good start for a reliable and effective Protective Force in the Norfolk-Portsmouth area.[36]

The praise proved justified. Colonel Beaman was soon able to announce the captains of his five companies, all of them leading citizens who had served overseas in World War I. All were first choices, he proudly announced; no one had turned him down.[37]

[35] *L-D*, February 3, 1941, p. 1; February 7, 1941, p. 3. The last company left on Thursday, February 20. *V-P*, February 18, 1941, p. 18.

[36] *V-P*, January 10, 1941, Part I, p. 6.

[37] The captains named were: First Company, R. W. Webb, president of the Tazewell Garage Corporation; Second, James W. Roberts, vice-president of Henry B. Gilpin Company; Third, John Cahill, Jr., vice-president of Thomas A. Bain and Company; Fourth, Julien R. Hume, deputy city sergeant. Captain of the Fifth (Portsmouth) Company was Judge Robert R. Beaton. *V-P*, January 19, 1941, Part II, p. 1.

The duty of each captain was to recruit his men and to organize and drill his company. On February 5 the captains started looking about for likely volunteers and three days later had their companies up to half-strength. By the time the four companies were scheduled to be mustered in, 210 officers and men had been enlisted, only 42 less than authorized strength. On February 19, even before the last National Guardsmen had left the city, the companies were sworn into service in the Twelfth Street Armory. General Goodwyn himself was on hand for the ceremony and handed the officers the first commissions to be issued in the state. The next Monday the volunteers, middle-aged veterans of World War I and young men not yet drafted, began their weekly training in the armories.[38]

The United States provided the rifles—Springfields of 1917 vintage; the National Guard furnished the armories; the volunteers supplied the energy; but who was to supply the uniforms? That question had been passed over lightly in January when the Ledger-Dispatch had mentioned that "the units themselves, or their communities, will furnish the uniforms." When Colonel Beaman, however, approached City Manager Borland with the reminder that the State was making no provision for uniforms and that the city was expected to provide $10,000 to outfit the four Norfolk companies, Colonel Borland swung into instant action. He promptly called the city council and all six local members of the General Assembly into a special conference on the subject and sent off a telegram to the Governor, asking the State to pay for the uniforms.[39]

Colonel Borland sent copies of his telegram to all other cities responsible for units of the V. P. F. in order to gain additional support for his plea and was rewarded when Farmville chimed in with a similar request to the Governor. No pleas could move that adamant executive, however. When Colonel Beaman renewed his request for uniforms, City Manager Borland approved an appropriation of $3,200 for summer uniforms. "Just because the Governor of Virginia has fallen down on the job is no reason why the City of Norfolk should do so," agreed Councilman L.

[38] V-P, February 6, 1941, p. 22; February 9, 1941, Part I, p. 12; February 20, 1941, p. 18; February 24, 1941, p. 14.
[39] V-P, March 29, 1941, p. 16.

P. Roberts, and the council "reluctantly" voted the appropriation.[40]

Fortunately, the only casualty in this buck-passing battle was the Norfolk city treasury. The First Battalion had been drilling throughout the debate with unlowered morale. The men were already well trained, Colonel Beaman declared, and would be prepared for duty as soon as they had received their new uniforms.[41] The uniforms arrived, and all through the hot summer the volunteers continued at their weekly drills. By September the entire battalion was ready to put on a parade performance under the floodlights of Foreman Field. When they had finished, there was a round of editorial applause from the *Ledger-Dispatch*:

> If there were any among the spectators who had gone there in the expectation of witnessing a faltering, halting demonstration by an aggregation of civilians who have been called upon to act as soldiers on a part-time basis, they were completely disappointed. They saw, instead, a smart, alert, spick-and-span organization, well-drilled and well turned out, and obviously intensely in earnest about the role they have assumed. Despite the fact that these companies are composed in some part of men who are no longer eligible for regular military duty, there was decidedly no evidence of creaking at the knees or of incapacity of these men for whatever service they may be called upon to perform in the emergency.[42]

Norfolk was full of many other opportunities for volunteers to give up time or money to the defense effort. The American Legion appointed a committee to handle the registration of all veterans for possible future defense service. The Business and Professional Women's Club made a survey of defense jobs for women.[43] Bundles for Britain functioned regularly, while a special drive in honor of a visiting British woman made Norfolk the first city in the United States to provide funds to maintain a communal kitchen in England.[44] A "Young America Wants to

---

[40] *V-P*, April 4, 1941, Part I, p. 16; April 16, 1941, pp. 22, 15.

[41] *V-P*, April 18, 1941, Part II, p. 16.

[42] *L-D*, September 10, 1941.

[43] *V-P*, February 19, 1941, p. 8; *L-D*, January 25, 1941, p. 8.

[44] *L-D*, March 17, 1941. The money was originally raised to buy an ambulance but was diverted to the community kitchen at the request of the mayor of Lambeth, England.

Help" drive among the city's school children raised over a thousand dollars to aid the British.[45]

These activities, however, could no longer command the popular attention they had had in the summer of 1940. Other cities, bursting with patriotic fervor, were to seize upon such campaigns as outlets for their righteous zeal. Norfolk, however, had no reason to look so far afield for ways of helping the defense effort. The people of Norfolk could do their bit simply by keeping their noses to the grindstone.

The urgent nature of the emergency was emphasized by the call for volunteers to organize an Aircraft Warning Service. This plan to create a network of observation posts along the East Coast got under way in a familiar snarl of confused responsibilities. The American Legion was given the task of recruiting the volunteers to man the posts, but the first public announcement ignored the Legion entirely. In April the Hampton Roads Defense Council received a mimeographed release from Frank Bane of the Division of State and Local Cooperation in Washington, reporting that the council would soon be selecting volunteer plane spotters and registering them for service. The customary sesquipedalian officialese of the release so thoroughly concealed the duties and qualifications of the plane spotters that neither Executive Director Faure nor the reporter who wrote up the story could make any sense out of it. Faure, in fact, pleaded with the public not to try to volunteer through his office until he found out more about the plan.[46]

A month later the organizational responsibility was made clear when Governor Price proclaimed Norfolk the center of the Virginia Aircraft Warning Service and ordered the service to be mobilized and ready for action by June 15. The Legion's State Adjutant, W. Glenn Elliott, was placed in charge of the program. He was to name 111 organizers for the state, each of whom was in turn to find a chief oberver for the ten posts in his district. Then each chief observer was to locate fifteen observers to help man his post. Within ten days the fifteen posts in the Norfolk and Princess Anne area were fully staffed, a greater speed than any other section in the state could boast.[47]

[45] *L-D*, March 17, 1941, p. 12.
[46] *V-P*, April 30, 1941, p. 20.
[47] *V-P*, May 25, 1941, Part II, p. 1; June 3, 1941, p. 20.

Norfolk's task was only begun, however, for the city had been designated as the state's filter center. To recruit the 400 to 750 women who were needed to keep the proposed filter center going, John Twohy II, chief organizer of the Aircraft Warning Service for Norfolk, wisely called in the women. He asked representatives of the feminine organizations of the city to meet at his home on May 28 to draw up plans for the recruiting campaign. Miss Dora Schofield, head of the Business and Professional Women's Club, was named chairman of the general committee to obtain the volunteers, while Miss Lynette Hamlet, still president of the American Association of University Women, was placed in charge of obtaining the interviewers to handle the registration.[48]

Miss Hamlet's interviewers opened up three registration centers on June 3, but instead of the expected 400 volunteers only forty showed up. The next day would have been even worse if it had not been for a pep talk given the Colonial Stores clerical workers by Organizer Twohy, which brought a flood of fifty girls to swamp the downtown registration office. Disturbed by the lack of public response, Twohy discussed the problem with the Hampton Roads Defense Council, saying that there was a whispering campaign against the recruiting program which he believed was inspired by a fifth column. "There is a definite inclination to consider this as playing war and as a perfectly superfluous and futile gesture," he said. "They say it is a publicity stunt to stimulate a feeling of impending disaster in order to get us into war." A subtler form of sabotage, he reported, was being carried on by husbands who laughed at their wives when they proposed to enlist.[49]

This complaint had an unexpected result. Nearly a hundred women next day decided to defy ridicule and demonstrate their patriotism by volunteering. The day after, however, only 25 showed up, and a big rally at the Monticello Hotel on Friday, June 13, scheduled to celebrate the completion of the drive two days before the Governor's deadline, found the recruiters still 25 short of the minimum goal of 400. At this point Miss Hamlet took unofficial charge to put the drive over the top. She sent a letter to every white pastor in town, asking him to read the announcement at his Sunday service and to publish it in his

[48] *V-P*, May 29, 1941.
[49] *V-P*, June 4, 5, 1941; *L-D*, June 5, 1941.

bulletin. She sent an appeal to the head of every woman's organization in the city and asked every classroom teacher to urge their students to invite their mothers to volunteer. She talked stores into paying for posters and put them up all over the city. Opening up new registration offices uptown and downtown, she had some two hundred new volunteers by the following Wednesday.[50]

Still the recruits had only the faintest idea of their duties, but they were told that they would be given a two-week training course in July in preparation for maneuvers in August. They patriotically revised their vacation plans and waited patiently for the call to action. July turned into August without any news about the promised training course. Vacationless volunteers began to jangle telephones to learn what was the matter. Members of the A. A. U. W. called Miss Hamlet to ask when the training would begin, but she knew no more than they did. Organizer Twohy was in the hospital and could not be reached. Finally, his assistant, Major Francis E. Turin, wrote to State Organizer Elliott: "What in the world has happened to the Virginia Aircraft Warning Service?" The answer came back in time to save some of the vacations: The delay had been caused by failure to get the service organized in some parts of the state, but the Army would arrive in September.[51]

[50] Hamlet scrapbook in Hamlet, Lynette: Aircraft Warning Volunteers file, NWHC records.
[51] Turin to W. Glenn Elliott, August 29, 1941, Elliott to Turin, August 22, 1941, Major Gordon P. Saville to Elliott, August 20, 1941, in Turin, Frank E.: Virginia Aircraft Warning Service file, NWHC records.

6

TO BUILD OR NOT TO BUILD

T HE well-meant efforts of the joint housing committee seemed to be having no effect on checking the housing boom as 1941 began. In addition to private housing, which was going up at a rate faster than the city had seen in twenty years, the Federal Government was erecting homes by the thousands. The Norfolk Housing Authority was at work on its 500 homes in Merrimack Park, and the Navy would soon have its 1,042 units in Benmoreell to add to the fifty already built inside the Base. Across the river, the Portsmouth Housing Authority had partly finished 300 Dale Homes and was starting the 210-unit Swanson Homes project. The Navy was building 250 homes at New Gosport for enlisted men stationed at the Yard. A Reconstruction Finance Corporation subsidiary, National Defense Homes, was scheduled to build 250 homes in Simonsdale for officers and defense workers, but had not yet started; with true bankers' caution the RFC was spending the winter having the title searched.[1]

To many Norfolkians these 2500 homes being built by various agencies of the Federal Government seemed more than enough to take care of the demand, but suddenly a new agency appeared with plans for 665 more. Late on January 17 a dispatch came over the Associated Press wires from Washington announcing that President Roosevelt had just approved a recommendation by the Defense Housing Coordinator that the Federal Works Agency be authorized to build 665 homes for workers in the Navy Yard. Surprised editors in the *Virginian-Pilot* newsroom called up Admiral Manley H. Simons, Navy Yard commandant, to ask him for more details and were even more suprised to find that he knew nothing about the proposal. A check with

---

[1] *V-P*, March 2, 1941, Part II, p. 3.

the AP confirmed that this was indeed a brand-new housing project.[2]

Once more the joint housing committee jumped in alarm. Chairman John R. Sears declared that it looked as if these Federal agencies were duplicating each other's work. Furthermore, the committee saw no reason why tax-free homes should be built for well-paid defense workers and Navy officers; houses for them should be left up to private enterprise. In any case, Sears felt, the demand for housing had been much exaggerated. He had heard that only fifty of the 300 Dale Homes in Portsmouth had been rented since the project was completed.[3]

The statement of Chairman Sears indicated that his committee was misinformed as well as uninformed. The *Ledger-Dispatch* the night before had told its readers that there were already 62 families living in Dale Homes and that there were more than enough applications to fill the other units as soon as they were finished.[4] The joint housing committee in its fright was showing a tendency to talk the housing shortage out of existence. Even if its facts were not straight, however, they were the only facts available to the public. No one had yet told the people of Norfolk that the Federal Government as far back as September, 1940, had planned to build 5,800 homes in Norfolk and Portsmouth or explained that all this construction was only the beginning of a plan to meet the minimum needs for the proposed expansion of the Navy Yard. Although the Regional Defense Council had been created for the express purpose of explaining this program to the public, its new director was still floundering in the uncharted seas of his job. The Office of Defense Housing, which had been so eager to have the council established, now seemed to be neglecting it entirely.

Even though the future remained foggy, as far as the people of Norfolk were concerned, there was no doubt about the present. Everywhere workers were clamoring for homes that were not yet finished. A single advertisement offering a $35-a-month bungalow for rent brought out fifty applicants.[5] E. S. Smith, chairman

[2] *V-P*, January 18, 1941, pp. 16, 5.
[3] *V-P*, January 19, 1941, Part II, p. 1.
[4] *L-D*, January 17, 1941, clipping in Turin, Frank E.: Defense Housing file, NWHC records.
[5] *V-P*, March 7, 1941, p. 1.

of the housing committee at the Navy Yard, declared that many of the workers at the Yard were quitting because they could not find a place to live and called for at least a thousand more homes.[6]

On the Norfolk side of the river Admiral Taussig grew similarly concerned over the morale of his officers. The situation had grown steadily worse since the commandant had issued his blast against rent increases the previous August. Landlords still continued to discriminate against Navy officers because of the uncertainty of their stay, making it difficult for newcomers to find homes. Real estate men relieved the plight of those who had places to live by permitting them to terminate their leases with only thirty days' notice instead of the customary sixty, but one firm in the city charged officers $10 a month extra for the first six months of their lease, reducing their rent by the same amount during the last six months. Officers who were transferred before the year was out thus had to pay an increased rent.

Some officers, unable to find a home for rent, bought houses under the liberal FHA terms and abandoned the homes and the down payments when they were transferred. Those who located apartments were disappointed by their shabbiness and irked by easygoing Southern ways when they demanded repairs. One Navy wife, whose husband was in the Caribbean, reported her troubles to Admiral Taussig. She had to pay $85 a month, she complained, for an apartment in extremely bad repair, with dirty, torn wallpaper, cracked walls and floors, old plumbing, and shabby furniture. When she reported to her landlady that the refrigerator was not working, the landlady told her just to put her food outside on the window sill, and the wife had to put up with this primitive form of refrigeration for a week before the icebox was repaired. Several times, she declared, the heat had not come on promptly in the mornings, and her children had had to wear overcoats at the breakfast table.[7]

Worried over such complaints, Admiral Taussig once more plunged into the housing situation. In a public statement he asked for more rental homes for his officers so that they could vacate their uncomfortable, expensive quarters. President Robert F. Baldwin, Jr., replied for the Norfolk Real Estate Board, explaining that private builders did not feel that they could safely

[6] *V-P*, February 21, 1941, Part II, p. 14.
[7] *V-P*, February 22, 1941, pp. 16, 7.

invest in apartments for Navy officers, who were likely to be transferred out of the city at any time. The Real Estate Board, however, appreciated their needs and was willing to cooperate with the admiral to help them. The board would render whatever service it could to aid the commandant in his efforts to have homes built on the Base. To demonstrate its willingness it worked with Admiral Taussig to obtain FHA financing for a 164-unit apartment project in Larchmont. Baldwin said he was very much gratified over this project and hoped that it would relieve considerably the acute shortage that the commandant said existed in housing for Navy officers.[8]

Hope of better housing in the future at least lightened the dingy quarters of the moment, and by the spring of 1941 some hopes were being realized, as Benmoreell and Merrimack Park threw open their first units at the end of March. The first couple into Benmoreell told a revealing story. Chief Water Tender J. B. Landers had been living in Norfolk when he was called back into the Navy the previous summer. The next day his rent had been raised. He and his wife had been paying $35 a month for three rooms and a chance at the bath whenever one of six other people was not using it. Mrs. Landers, a Norfolk girl herself, had been hoping for a transfer to California, but with a Benmoreell apartment at $17 a month she now wanted to stay in Norfolk. Another typical couple had spent the last three months in a furnished room. All of them agreed: "We like Norfolk better now!"[9]

The most ominous thing about these comments was what they implied about the less fortunate Navy families. Admiral Taussig estimated that there were six or seven thousand enlisted men trying to live with their families in the area. Benmoreell and Merrimack Park would provide for only a quarter of these, leaving the rest to grumble about the local landlords. It was no matter that the Government was at fault for shoving them into an unprepared community—that their pay was too low to buy decent housing anywhere—that they themselves were sometimes responsible for the run-down condition of their quarters. Inevitably they blamed their discomfort on the city and its people.

    [8] V-P, February 22, 1941, pp. 16, 7; February 23, 1941, Part II, p. 1; February 26, 1941, pp. 18, 10.
    [9] V-P, March 26, 1941, pp. 18, 9.

In spite of the fact that these complaints threatened to echo through the Navy and blacken Norfolk's reputation everywhere, the city remained apathetic. Hardened to the Navy's criticisms, it saw no reason for getting excited about the situation. Most people expected the housing shortage to disappear as soon as the new projects were finished and the construction workers went home. In any case, putting money into more houses was too risky an investment for men who remembered the crash after the last boom.

There was some effort to convince the city that the current expansion would be permanent. Charles P. Taft of the Federal Security Agency, in Norfolk for a study of its problems in March, told local officials that they could dismiss any fears that they might have that the present boom was only temporary. Admiral Taussig said that it appeared that the United States was going to maintain a two-ocean Navy, regardless of the outcome of the war, indicating that Norfolk would continue to be an important naval base. The morning paper gave the story a four-column headline:

Defense Boom Not a Passing Bubble
Charles P. Taft and Taussig Agree;
Norfolk Is Urged to Expand Solidly[10]

Nothing, however, could quite convince the joint housing committee that the boom had come to stay, or even that it had come. Otto Hollowell suggested that the current shortage was being exaggerated by the same persons registering their wants with many different agencies.[11] What was needed was a central housing bureau where everyone looking for a home might register. In this way the need could be measured more exactly. Such a plan had been recommended to the Hampton Roads Defense Council in February by Thomas S. Green of the National Defense Housing Coordination Office. Green declared that an inventory of all housing facilities should be made, explaining that it was the hope of the authorities in Washington that every available housing unit would be used before new projects were authorized. In this way Government spending could be held to a minimum and

[10] *V-P*, March 28, 1941, Part II, p. 14.
[11] *V-P*, March 15, 1941, p. 18.

the joint housing committee's fears of a ghost city could be averted.[12]

The chief difficulty over the proposal was financing it. Council Director Faure enthusiastically approved the idea, but Chairman Bottom reminded him that the council's limited budget could not provide for it. The joint housing committee endorsed the project and promised its support, but it too had no funds. Faure and Green set to work to enlist local support through a committee headed by the city's Public Welfare Director, H. G. Parker. Parker obtained clerical help from the WPA, assigning one of his own staff to part-time duty directing the office. With this local cooperation Robert B. Wilson, a new emissary from the Defense Housing Office in Washington, was able to announce that a Norfolk Homes Registration Office would be opened on Friday, June 13.[13]

The Defense Housing Coordination Office made another effort to coordinate local housing activities. The Regional Defense Housing Coordinator, C. W. Farrier, told the Hampton Roads Council that there should be some sort of committee, representing all types of agencies concerned with housing in the area, to work together to prevent any disastrous aftereffects of the boom. City Manager Borland heartily agreed: "The lack of coordination in defense housing activities here has reached such proportions that it is terrifying to me. In fact, I think we have become so muddled that we have got to make plans for coordinated effort." Everyone approved of the idea, and "initial steps" were taken.[14] Unfortunately, nothing more came of the proposal as the Hampton Roads Council was about to fall apart. With a clumsy organization, an inadequate budget, and an ineffectual director, it was sinking from paralysis into suspended animation while a resurrection in a new form was being discussed.

Meanwhile the Regional Council had summoned up enough energy to meet another aspect of the housing situation. Two representatives of the rent section of the Office of Price Administration and Civilian Supply, Tom Tippett and Frank Ralls, arrived in Norfolk in June to confer with Council Chairman Bot-

[12] *V-P*, February 15, 1941, pp. 16, 7.
[13] *V-P*, February 15, 1941, pp. 16, 7; March 15, 1941, p. 18; June 13, 1941, Part II, p. 1.
[14] *V-P*, June 27, 1941.

tom and other officials. Bottom endorsed their idea that fair rent committees should be appointed to investigate complaints about unfair rent increases.[15] The committees, of course, would be without legal authority, but the pressure of public opinion might be enough to curb rapacious landlords.

Norfolk accepted the idea without question. Colonel Borland promptly agreed to appoint a committee and within two days named Robert F. Baldwin, Jr., president of the Norfolk Real Estate Board, as chairman, along with two other businessmen, a naval officer in charge of housing, and E. M. Moore, president of the Central Labor Union.[16] While outsiders might have scoffed at the idea of obtaining any effective rent control from a committee headed by a representative of the landlords, the appointments were in the Norfolk tradition of civic responsibility, based on the assumption that businessmen had a gentleman's sense of honor. The new committee was expected to talk over any increases brought up before it, explain to both sides what was fair, and reach a gentleman's agreement satisfactory to all concerned.

The Real Estate Board, in fact, did not feel that responsible landlords had made any unfair rent increases. Otto Hollowell declared that there were only isolated instances of tenants protesting against higher rents, as most tenants realized that increases were justified. There had been an unreasonable increase in room rents, he said, "on the part of a very few mercenary rooming-house operators, many of whom are newcomers to Norfolk, and are intent upon exacting every last penny the traffic will bear."[17] The Fair Rent Committee, however, was surprised to learn that rent boosts had been much greater than was originally supposed. Even before the committee had an office, it was overwhelmed with protests from angry tenants. Many landlords, it discovered, had raised rents as much as 15 per cent, whereas the committee had thought 5 to 10 per cent was fair. Loudest complaints came from the Negroes, whose increases were not large in dollars but were enormous percentagewise. One boost of 60 per cent was reported on a home that had rented for $10 a month.[18]

15 *V-P*, June 19, 1941, p. 22.
16 *V-P*, June 20, 1941, Part II, p. 14; June 22, 1941, Part II, p. 1.
17 *V-P*, June 22, 1941, Part I, p. 12.
18 *V-P*, June 29, 1941, Part II, p. 2.

By the middle of July the committee had found an office and furniture to put in it. The group made matters as easy as possible for the landlords by ruling that a "moderate" increase since January 1 would be considered fair. Even with these relatively lenient rules, it discovered nineteen landlords who had been immoderate and asked them to appear before the committee and explain their action. Eleven of the nineteen offenders entirely ignored the request. Six explained by letter or telephone that their tenants had voluntarily offered to pay higher rents when they had been ordered to move. Three of those invited appeared for a hearing, and one of the three agreed that perhaps his increase had been a little too much and ought to be reduced; on the other hand, he had been thinking of doing a little repairing so that he had better talk it over with the committee again sometime in the future.[19]

The committee continued to treat the offenders as gentlemen, relying entirely on its powers of persuasion. It kept the names of the accused landlords out of the papers to protect them from unpleasant publicity. The fair-rent formula was revised to permit increases up to 20 per cent, with a maximum of $5.00. Even with fairness stretched this far, however, some property-owners still demanded more and stubbornly ignored the committee. Chairman Baldwin himself began to concede that some reasonable legislation controlling rents would be beneficial.[20]

The reason why rents were spiraling upwards was not hard to find. The 2,500 housing units, which the joint committee had thought might solve the problem by summer, had been swallowed up without making any more impression on the shortage than a pebble on a pond. Admiral Taussig, retired from the Navy but still concerned about his enlisted men, declared that there were some five or six thousand of their families living in disgraceful conditions, three or four persons in a single room, sharing the bath with several families, and paying more for their room than the cost of a five-room apartment in Benmoreell. The Norfolk Homes Registration Bureau corroborated the admiral by reporting an investigation it had made. It had found 26 apartments, averaging four rooms each, in which 58 families lived.

[19] *V-P*, July 20, 1941, Part II, p. 1; August 2, 1941, p. 16.
[20] *V-P*, August 17, 1941, Part II, p. 1.

In 208 residences of four or five rooms each, it had discovered 306 families, practically all of them with children. At least three families had had to spend several nights sleeping in their car, with the children under the steering wheel and the parents in the back seat.[21]

Although the joint housing committee continued to insist that the shortage was only temporary, a study by the State Planning Board in cooperation with the Hampton Roads Defense Council reported that thousands of homes were still needed. The survey, conducted by Lorin A. Thompson, estimated that population on the south side, including Norfolk and Princess Anne counties and the three cities, had risen from 258,927 on April 1, 1940, to 318,695 in May, 1941, or 23 per cent. Dwelling units in the area during the same period had risen from 69,425, to 76,421, or an increase of only 10 per cent. This seemed to indicate that the area was already 8,000 homes short. Moreover, Doctor Thompson estimated that expansion planned for the next five years would require a total of 107,500 dwelling units, or over 30,000 more than were available in May.[22]

Only slight progress was being made to handle this additional demand. Another public housing project was undertaken by the FWA on Campostella Road to provide 300 homes for Negro defense workers. This development was the only provision being made anywhere in the area for Negroes, whose living conditions even in pre-boom times had been indescribably bad. One other Negro project was lost on a Washington desk. Early in the spring funds had been granted for 230 homes in Roberts Park as a slum clearance program, but the development was being held up because Washington officials refused to approve the proposed central heating system, while the Norfolk Housing Authority insisted that it was essential.[23]

[21] *V-P*, June 21, 1941, pp. 16, 7; July 30, 1941, p. 18.

[22] *V-P*, June 20, 1941, Part II, p. 14. In May, 1944, there were approximately 101,000 units in the area. The additional 6,500 units would have been necessary if the Navy Yard had been able to carry through its original plans for expansion.

[23] *V-P*, June 6, 1941, Part I, p. 16; Norfolk *Journal and Guide*, February 28, 1942, p. 10; Housing Authority of the City of Norfolk, *This Is It*, p. 24. There were also twenty homes for colored enlisted men in Titustown.

The FHA encouraged private contractors by insuring their mortgages up to 90 per cent of the value of the buildings and authorizing the builder to sell without any down payment or to rent the property. This chance to invest money at almost no risk attracted more builders. Rose Gardens and Suburban Park Homes started 175 homes at Ward's Corner. Other promoters turned to the area east of Lafayette River in their search for more sites. Lafayette Shores was opened up with lots for 350 homes. A local firm started fifty FHA-financed homes in Willard Park, but an out-of-town builder took over the other 119 lots they had laid out. The contractor, James Rosati of New York, incorporated under the appropriately Italian name of Monticello Homes, had just finished 114 homes in Newport News and had moved across Hampton Roads in search of new worlds to conquer. He planned to put up 119 homes on the lots in Willard Park and to add 400 more as soon as he could find the ground to build them on. "Tremendously impressed" with local possibilities, Rosati declared: "Things are just starting in Norfolk, and we feel fortunate in being able to enter the real estate field here."[24]

Local real estate men were not quite so impressed by the out-of-town builders. The president of the Real Estate Board issued a public warning to home-buyers to beware of builders they did not know, declaring that "undesirable persons flock to centers of activity, especially in times of emergency."[25] The joint housing committee also raised an admonishing finger. Pointing out that more than four times as many new homes had been started in the area so far in 1941 as compared with the same period in 1940, and more than seven times as many as in 1939, Chairman Sears declared: "... it would appear that intelligent builders will be very careful of future projects until data on the permanency of our population is available."[26]

[24] *V-P*, July 18, 1941, Part II, p. 12.

[25] *V-P*, June 8, 1941, Part II, p. 5. On the opposite page was a story assuring prospective buyers that FHA appraisals guaranteed them full value when they bought FHA-financed houses, which included practically all the homes being built in Norfolk.

[26] *V-P*, June 15, 1941, Part II, p. 5.

7

HELP WANTED

EVERY day in 1941 the meaning of a boom was becoming clearer to Norfolk. The housing shortage did not itself affect the older residents. Some had their rents raised or were ordered to move, but their number was relatively few. Most pre-boom Norfolkians went on living in the same houses at the same rent as before and knew of the home-hunters' troubles only what they read in the papers. Once they left the shelter of their own roofs, however, they could not escape the boomers. The buses they took to work were jammed with passengers and delayed by traffic. The restaurants where they tried to eat were crowded, and they had to stand in line at the movies. It was sometimes hard to obtain fresh milk, and there was talk of a water shortage. There were not enough seats for the children in the schoolrooms or enough beds in the hospitals.

Norfolkians sighed for the peaceful days of yesteryear and wished the newcomers would go back to North Carolina.[1] This was excellent emotional catharsis, but more concrete steps were needed. In general, private commercial capital met its responsibilities well. In the first year of the boom, three new movie theaters were added to Norfolk's fourteen, an increase in keeping

[1] The feeling of many Norfolkians was unintentionally expressed by a slip of ex-Congressman Colgate W. Darden, Jr., when he was telling a House committee about Norfolk's needs. "The building of the air base there will be completed in July and under our present plan there are several thousand workmen that will leave there," he said, "so that we don't have to make provision for the numbers that are now there that appear to be on our shoulders because I very much hope—" then hastily correcting himself, "I know that they will go back to the States from which they came." U. S. House of Representatives, Public Buildings and Grounds Committee, *Hearings . . . on H. R. 3213 . . . and H. R. 3570, A Bill Authorizing an Appropriation for Providing Additional Community Facilities Made Necessary by National-Defense Activities, and For Other Purposes, March, 4, 5, 6, 7, 12, and 13, 1941* (Washington, 1941), p. 211.

with the growing population.[2] The number of restaurants also increased rapidly. Where the profit motive did not offer an incentive, however, the response was much less rapid. Municipal services did not expand in proportion to the population; in fact, they scarcely expanded at all. While the number of the people to protect was increasing, the police force remained at its rock-bottom minimum. Although new houses were going up by the thousands, the city bought no new fire equipment.

This cautious frugality was even more evident when it came to capital expenditures. Colonel Borland's attitude was quite clear in this matter. As he told the Norfolk and Portsmouth Traffic Club:

> The Government should carry most of the burden in putting our roads in first-class condition. The Titustown road must be rebuilt and the sewage disposal question must be taken care of. The Government must come in on that cost too.
>
> We want the Navy here, but the Government must realize Norfolk's strategic location and assist in providing the things we need. The city is growing by leaps and bounds. We don't know just how much we should expand. Certainly we don't want to overexpand.[3]

Colonel Borland had several sound arguments in his case for Federal aid. All of the added expenditures were forced on the city by the Navy's expansion, in which Norfolk was a rather reluctant partner. It was therefore unfair to expect the city to foot the bill. Moreover, the Navy was already the beneficiary of many municipal services, for which it paid no taxes, and was now demanding more, such as tax-free education of the children of Benmoreell. Overshadowing all these arguments, of course, was the city manager's loyalty to his tax rate, which he was determined to preserve through peace and war.

One difficulty with this policy of having the United States share the expense of local improvements was to persuade the United States to pay. Chairman Bottom discovered the problem when he tried to learn what was being done about the $7,000,000 road program, which had been elaborated with such fanfare the preceding Thanksgiving. Bottom had worked out the details with

[2] *V-P*, May 30, 1941, p. 6.
[3] *V-P*, January 17, 1941, Part II, p. 12.

Admiral Taussig and sent the plan to Richmond for clearance with the Virginia Defense Council. On a trip to Washington Bottom traced the plan from desk to desk until he discovered that the Acting Commissioner of Public Roads had passed it on to Transportation Coordinator Ralph Budd a month before. On Budd's desk it still was, because Budd had no place to send it; there was no agency with any money to build roads. Chairman Bottom told his troubles to the Regional Defense Council, and the group performed its function. It passed a resolution calling on the State Defense Council and the National Defense Council to act.[4] By some dispensation of fate, this plea did not get lost in the usual channels, and the mills of Washington started to grind out aid to Hampton Roads in their slow, methodical way.

Meanwhile, there was time to consider the needs. The hospitals were discussed by the Regional Defense Council at its January 22 meeting. City Manager Borland lost no time in introducing his favorite topic. State and Federal aid were necessary, he pointed out. "Health is important," he said, "but that is only one of the functions of government. We have our roads, police, fire, schools, etc., to consider also, and an increased tax rate would be the only way to provide more of these services."[5]

The doctors, however, seemed to refute earlier reports that hospitals were overcrowded. Newspapers had reported that Leigh Memorial and Norfolk General hospitals had been full for varying periods and had been compelled to turn away all but emergency patients. St. Vincent's, Norfolk's oldest, dating back to the yellow fever epidemic of 1855, had also been filled at times.[6] A government survey several years earlier had reported that the city was 25 per cent short of its hospital needs, but part of that deficiency was being made up. Leigh Memorial was adding fifty beds to more than double its capacity and the Norfolk General was building another thirty-bed extension. The opening of the Norfolk Community Hospital in 1939 had also added 39 more Negro beds.

The doctors felt that this expansion was enough to meet the city's needs. Dr. Walter B. Martin, president of the State Medi-

[4] *V-P*, January 23, 1941, p. 22.
[5] *V-P*, January 23, 1941, pp. 22, 15.
[6] *V-P*, January 8, 1941, p. 18.

cal Society, calculated that the city had 1,123 beds, including those of the Marine Hospital. Leaving the Marine facilities out of consideration, there were 479 adult white beds and 147 adult Negro beds, with 175 more that could be added in emergencies. This he thought sufficient for the present population.[7] On the other hand, the Rev. B. W. Harris, president of the Norfolk Community Hospital, pointed out the need for at least eighty more Negro beds. There was no need for concern about doctors, said Dr. James W. Anderson, president of the County Medical Society. Even though seven or eight had left for military service in recent months, sixteen new ones had arrived. "We are, in fact, rather overloaded," he added.

While the hospitals were apparently taken care of, this was not true of the schools in the northern part of the city. Ocean View and Granby High in the second year of their existence were already overcrowded. To relieve the pressure on these schools Norfolk applied through the Regional Defense Council for a Federal grant of $600,000. This was to provide three new grammar schools in the section. One was to be in Bay View, another on Granby Street, and a third for Benmoreell.[8] High school needs could be taken care of by transferring the grammar grades out of Granby High. This plan met with protests from Talbot Park residents, who objected to having their children taken out of the building. Insisting that they had been promised elementary seats in Granby High when the building was constructed, they declared that permanent residents ought to be taken care of first, and that the defense workers should undergo whatever hardships had to be undergone as a result of the sudden population increase.[9]

Children of the defense workers were already undergoing hardships. The sailors' sons in Benmoreell were being distributed all over the city, slipping into whatever vacant seats were available. The city insisted, on very solid grounds, that, since the Navy was paying no school taxes on their homes, the United States should pay for their education.[10] For the Bay View school, the city ac-

[7] Minutes of Hampton Roads Regional Defense Council, January 22, 1941, VOCD records; *V-P*, January 23, 1941, pp. 22, 15.
[8] *V-P*, February 21, 1941, Part II, p. 14.
[9] *V-P*, June 27, 1941, Part I, p. 13.
[10] *V-P*, May 14, 1941, p. 22.

quired a 22-acre site, long before there was any hint of Federal approval of funds for the building. "With the completion of the homes in Merrimack, Commodore, and Suburban parks, the problem will become acute," said City Manager Borland.[11]

The city followed the same general policy in increasing the water supply. It appealed to the Federal government for aid and in the meantime applied emergency measures of its own. In spite of Colonel Borland's optimism about the adequacy of the city's pumping stations the previous summer, they were already being pushed to their limits. The pumps at Moore's Bridges east of the city and at Lake Prince eighteen miles west were working their hearts out to produce 21 million gallons a day instead of the 13 million they had furnished a year before.[12] Help, however, would soon be coming from the unused pumping station on North Landing River, which was being re-equipped and put back into service as part of the expansion agreed upon the summer before.[13] This would pump water from the North Landing Reservoir to the Moore's Bridges station.

City Manager Borland also decided to seek an additional source of water. He had applied for a Federal grant to build a second line from Lake Prince, but that would take a year to complete after the money had been allotted. From the city council he obtained authorization to apply for a WPA project to construct an eight-mile pipe line from West Neck Creek to the North Landing pumping station. "In order to safeguard against a possible drought during the remainder of the year," said Borland, "I feel it is absolutely necessary that the city make provisions to obtain more water at our Moore's Bridges pumping station."[14]

The city's water supply did prove adequate for the summer, however, in spite of a drought which stretched all through May. When an anxious reporter began to worry about the effects of the long dry spell, Colonel Borland reassured him. Care in using water would be appreciated, the city manager said, such as filling the bathtub only half-full, but there was no cause for alarm. The North Landing system was now bringing in enough water. If the

[11] *V-P*, May 14, 1941, pp. 6, 22.
[12] *V-P*, April 30, 1941, p. 12.
[13] *Civic Affairs, . . . 1940*, p. 41.
[14] *V-P*, April 30, 1941, p. 12.

faucets did not flow very rapidly, that was because the pumps were weak, not because the water was low.[15]

As for the traffic situation, virtually the only action taken locally was another resolution by the Regional Defense Council in April, urging action on the defense roads program.[16] The State did start work in June on the overpass at the city limits carrying the Beach Boulevard over the Virginian Railroad,[17] but it ignored the Fort Story problem. Although it had long been known that the commander of Fort Story would eventually have to close the portion of the Shore Drive inside the camp gates, the State Highway Department's only provision for this emergency was to plan a detour. When the Army announced that the road through the post would be closed to traffic on April 15, the State was ready with a roundabout detour over the Great Neck road between Lynnhaven and Broad Bay. The building of a new road would depend on Federal appropriations.[18]

Although this detour was actually a shorter route to downtown Virginia Beach than the closed highway it aroused a storm of protest. One of the most alarmed of all at the slamming of Fort Story's gates was Mrs. Frantz Naylor, president of the Tidewater Virginia Women and Order of Cape Henry 1607. If the road were closed, it would be impossible for her to lead her annual pilgrimage to the cape on April 26 to commemorate the landing of the first settlers. With undaunted courage she assaulted the fort and quickly compelled its surrender. The gallant commander promised that not only would he open up his gates to her forces, but he would also bring up a thousand chairs from the Cavalier Hotel for her guests and line up his troops on parade to receive the visitors.[19]

Mrs. Naylor could not keep the gates open, however, and State Highway officials, nature lovers, and Virginia Beach residents locked horns over a new route which would satisfy the people of the upper end of Virginia Beach without injuring the Seashore State Park. A final compromise was worked out to build the new

[15] *V-P*, May 24, 1941, p. 18.
[16] Minutes of Hampton Roads Regional Defense Council, April, 1941, VOCD records.
[17] *V-P*, May 23, 1941, Part II, p. 14.
[18] *V-P*, March 5, 1941, pp. 20, 13.
[19] *V-P*, March 9, 1941, Part II, p. 3.

road along the edge of Fort Story, thus doing little more harm to the Park than that already done by the Army. Approval of this route was obtained from the War Department just a month after the road closed, and the State Highway Department was authorized to start to work.[20] Meanwhile, the effects were already being felt, even in April. The first Sunday after the fort gates were shut happened to be a fine day, and that afternoon cars were lined up in bumper-to-bumper travel on the three lanes of the Beach Boulevard.[21]

All through the spring of 1941 the city too waited patiently for the Federal aid which was to improve its streets, but at length Colonel Borland went to the WPA and obtained grants for the proposed improving and widening of the streets in the vicinity of the Naval Base.[22] In the meantime, the city's major accomplishment was the installation of the new timed traffic lights on Boush Street, which were designed to keep traffic moving rapidly, and instead created the worst traffic jam that had been seen since Christmas.[23] Later adjustments gradually got the snarls untangled, and Boush Street moved along as rapidly as before.

The sailors at the Base benefited largely from two other traffic changes. After months of discussion as to whether the city needed more taxicabs, the city council at last tried to settle the question by reducing the fares. Rates for travel beyond the first mile were reduced from ten cents a half mile to five cents. Sailors who kept an eye on the meter thus saved half a dollar on a trip from downtown out to the Base.[24] Late travelers no longer had to take a cab, even at the reduced rates, as VEPCO added three "owl cars" on the run out to the Base, providing all-night service.[25]

This improvement in service seemed to be unique. The promised new trolleys were a long time in coming, and when they did arrive the company had trouble in finding men to operate them, for who would bear the whips and scorns of outraged com-

[20] *V-P*, May 16, 1941, Part II, p. 16.

[21] *V-P*, April 21, 1941, p. 14.

[22] *V-P*, June 20, 1941, Part II, p. 14.

[23] *V-P*, March 9, 1941, Part II, p. 1.

[24] *V-P*, June 18, 1941, pp. 6, 10.

[25] *V-P*, August 24, 1941, Part II, p. 1. Some stranded sailors "borrowed" parked cars late at night to get back to the Base, abandoning the autos near the gates.

muters when he himself might his departure make to some high-paid defense job? A veteran straphanger on the long ride from Ocean View downtown, who somehow managed to keep his sense of humor, described the tribulations of his fellow-travelers:

Being one of the many unfortunates forced to rely on the V. E. P. Co. for conveyance to and from work, the writer is well acquainted with the seemingly, unsolvable problem. He has read with interest the reports on the many obstacles to be overcome and the difficulty in obtaining operators for the several new cars, and, as a good commuter should, he has waited patiently—but now with patience exhausted he is taking advantage of his good ole' American privilege of "airing" his views on the subject.

Why not distribute the available cars as to demand? Why not treat the tired working people as passengers instead of cattle to be herded into a stall?

Personally, this disgusted reader is an expert in the art of exhaling an unnecessary breath from his lungs, folding his body into a compact bundle and plunging into the swaying, stumbling mass of humanity hanging from straps, bars, or just balancing themselves as best they can.

He has suffered the indignities of waiting for the "next car" in hopes there will be just a little more breathing space, and then after "oozing" aboard, has been forced to inhale everything from stale beer to South Church Street on Saturday night.

Doesn't it seem that any self-respecting commuter (or are we of Ocean View considered such) is entitled to just a little more consideration while riding a street car?

We're not asking for seats to and from Norfolk—Heavens no! No such luxury as that, because what would be the use of those "oh so comfortable straps"?

Just a little more standingroom, please! If this isn't possible, then let's call it "The Toonerville Trolley"—half fare on top.[26]

The interurban buses, however, moved to give better service. The lines coming into the city had outgrown their quarters in the city market and the previous fall had begun construction of a union bus terminal on the site of the old *Ledger-Dispatch* building, on Plume near Main. Before the building was finished, the Greyhound Lines decided to| construct their own terminal on a vacant lot at Granby Street and Brambleton Avenue. So rapidly was the demand for buses growing that the president of the

[26] Letter of Sam T. Barfield, *V-P*, July 31, 1941, p. 6.

half-completed union terminal said: "It is probably to the best interests of all concerned that this thing happened, because we will need all the facilities in our new terminal for the lines remaining."[27]

In entertaining the servicemen within their midst, the people of Norfolk assumed the same attitude taken toward the other problems of congestion: that the Federal government had created the problem and therefore should rightly bear the financial burden imposed. Nevertheless, the city met this situation with more energy than it had shown in attacking any other question. The police cooperated with the Navy in the negative side of controlling the sailors' recreation. Police Chief John F. Woods may have grumbled, as he did to the Cosmopolitan Club, about the pressure which had compelled him to close up East Main Street, but he was determined to enfore the law.[28] Policemen went up and down the street, checking the familiar addresses. Most of the places were dark, with padlocks on the door, although some claimed to be rooming houses. Occasionally the patrolmen found a madam who had not taken the warning seriously, and hauled her and her staff off to jail.[29]

Police Chief Woods kept his eye out for the old business popping up under new disguises. He shook a club at the licensed liquor dealers of the area:

I am inclined to believe it is not in the best interests to have women selling beer and wine in establishments. . . . We may make a rule to eliminate women. . . . If they are there to solicit the sale of wine and beer, then I am opposed to it . . . and the establishment is not fit for a license.[30]

The city also accepted the challenge the volunteer committee had flung it by starting the Saturday night dance program in December. City Manager Borland was as much concerned about the problem of entertaining the servicemen as he was about any of the others the city had faced. He told one civic group:

With very few exceptions most of the cities in America are just cities. They are not attractive places in which to make your homes.

[27] *V-P*, April 30, 1941, p. 20.
[28] *V-P*, January 17, 1941, Part II, p. 12.
[29] *V-P*, January 14, 1941, pp. 18, 8.
[30] *V-P*, March 15, 1941, p. 18.

A father said to me a short time ago that he did not want his son to go into camp with the militia at Virginia Beach. The man lives at Virginia Beach.

I asked him why and he said because Norfolk had nothing—just a few movies and East Main Street. (We haven't got East Main Street now.)

I said to him that Norfolk is a great place in which to live, and it will become even greater if we all help to make it so.[31]

One step taken was to reorganize the City Advisory Committee on Recreation, which had been inactive for months because its chairman had been too busy on other matters. A new chairman was named and an executive committee was appointed to co-ordinate the activities of ten lesser committees, devoted to information and hospitality, women's and girls' recreation, servicemen's centers and clubs, entertainment and dances, church cooperation, and similar purposes.[32]

Colonel Borland pledged that the city would do the utmost in its power to meet the recreational needs of the armed forces in the area, cooperating with every agency represented by the reorganized committee. He stressed the fact that the work of providing recreation was an integral part of the defense program, and that men, not machines, were the nation's defense. Their morale, he declared, was the community's most important concern.[33]

The recreational program got an additional paper push from the Hampton Roads Regional Defense Council. When Chairman Bottom on February 14 suggested that all localities in the area be called upon to provide recreational facilities for servicemen without waiting for Federal aid, the council approved.[34] Federal aid of a sort arrived in the person of Arthur H. Jones, regional defense representative attached to the office of Paul V. McNutt, coordinator of health, welfare, and related activities. His coming was celebrated by the usual conference with officials to discuss problems and by the regular publicity announcement. "I believe my appointment to the Hampton Roads area is one of the first

[31] V-P, January 17, 1941, Part II, p. 12.
[32] V-P, January 9, 1941, p. 22, 12.
[33] V-P, January 9, 1941, pp. 22, 12.
[34] V-P, February 14, 1941, p. 7.

half dozen or so in the nation," Jones said. "I know that the Federal Security Agency regards Hampton Roads as one of the hot spots of the nation in so far as the intensity of defense activity here and the potentially overtaxed recreational and welfare facilities are concerned." His duties, he explained, would be to coordinate the program already going on, in cooperation with the city's recreation committee, and to stimulate other activities, when necessary.[35]

More stimulation was provided by the visit of another FSA representative, Charles P. Taft, son of the late president and chief justice, and brother of the senator. Taft's remarks to a group of local officials attracted widespread publicity and did more to focus the community's attention on the problem than any other recent event. He itemized the problems which had not yet been faced: setting up enough ordinary comfort stations for the downtown sailors; providing places where servicemen could dine reasonably, where they could gather and meet other people; providing showers, lockers, an information service, a room registry center, furnishing facilities to make wives of servicemen feel at home.[36]

The Federal government, he said, was not planning "to run the show," but only "to pull things together," and provide financial assistance when necessary. The building of the proper "community attitude toward the man in uniform is a slow educational job," he told the officials. "We must learn to interpret the servicemen to the civilians, showing that they are just as fine and decent as those known to the community." Part of the job, he pointed out, was to take the servicemen into the city's homes and churches.[37]

Speaking on the same day, Admiral Taussig flung the challenge directly at the people of Norfolk:

The fascinating problem is how to bring to individual soldier and sailor boys and defense workers and their families, crowded into a place much too small for them at the start, the decent, pleasant, and interesting life of the home town, inspired now by the fire of a burning love of country.

No Federal Government can do that. It isn't the Federal Govern-

[35] *V-P*, March 13, 1941, pp. 20, 13.
[36] *V-P*, March 28, 1941, Part II, p. 14.
[37] *V-P*, March 28, 1941, Part II, p. 14.

ment you love with your heart and soul, or even the flag of our country. You love the people, the men and the women and the children, the queer ones and the fine ones and the dirty ones, all the ones that feel American. You love the soil and the streets and the mountains.

The Federal government cannot organize your community for you. You are the only ones in the end that can do the job. We can give you information and show you some methods and ideas that other places have found useful. We can do some mighty important financing for you. But the job is yours.[38]

The most effective response to this challenge had been offered by the band of volunteers who had assumed responsibility for the Saturday night dances. What they could do was only a drop in the bucket, but at least they were able to make a few splashes on the bottom of the pail. The free dances for servicemen they had begun on December 7, 1940, were among the first to be held in the United States. A representative of the National Recreation Association attended one of the dances in January and was quite impressed.[39]

In spite of every conceivable handicap the committee kept up its Saturday night dances without interruption and even expanded the program. They financed their operating expenses by persuading local business firms to take turns sponsoring the dances,[40] until eventually they obtained a $2,500 grant from the City Council for that purpose.[41] Dates were harder to get than dollars, however. In most American cities the novel sight of a uniform was making every young girl come running, but in Norfolk Navy blues still had their traditional reaction and sent girls running in the opposite direction. Norfolk looked on rather enviously in March when the Associated Press told the world about Richmond's plans for finding girls to dance with the soldiers who would shortly be coming to Camp Lee. Norfolk had tried the same scheme months earlier with much less publicity and with much less success.

Mrs. Fred Stewart, wife of the city recreation director, had named women in various sections of the city to recruit dancing partners. In four months of trying the women had found only

[38] *V-P*, March 28, 1941, Part II, p. 14.
[39] *V-P*, January 9, 1941, pp. 22, 12.
[40] *V-P*, March 14, 1941, Part I, p. 9.
[41] *V-P*, July 9, 1941, p. 18.

900 girls in the city who were willing to take a chance on dancing with a sailor. The committee issued a public appeal to every organization in the city for help in its search for volunteers,[42] and even pleaded with girls to give up their Saturday night dates with civilians in order to come to the dances.[43] They provided door prizes for the girls and printed the pictures of several of them in the papers every week as sponsors, but even these devices failed to draw a large enough attendance. One March night 1400 sailors and marines showed up, undiscouraged by a flurry of snow and sleet, but less than 400 girls braved the weather.[44]

The girls' tickets had to be checked carefully, of course, to make sure that no refugees from East Main Street tried to crash the gate. The chaperones in all innocence were quite pleased at the number of sailors who brought their wives. There were sometimes as many as 150 married couples in attendance.[45] A little skeptical investigation, however, revealed that some of the girls were "wives" for the night only, and the rules had to be revised.[46]

In spite of these handicaps, the committee arranged dances for the soldiers at the beach camps. A thousand soldiers packed into Army trucks and came into the city auditorium for the inaugural dance of the series. It was a gala occasion with the entire city council, the city manager, ex-Congressman Darden, and Congressman-to-be Harris all present.[47] Not having been indoctrinated against khaki uniforms, the girls were a little less shy of the Army dances. In fact, when the first dance was held at Camp Pendleton, 140 girls showed up for 160 soldiers.[48]

A noteworthy accomplishment was the starting of a series of Saturday night dances for the Negro sailor, hitherto a totally neglected man. C. Wiley Grandy, chairman of the committee on recreation for the Negro enlisted men, reported there were 1,500 to 2,000 of them in the area, and that facilities for them were "woefully inadequate."[49] They were barred from the Navy

[42] V-P, March 23, 1941, Part II, p. 1.
[43] V-P, April 11, 1941, Part I, p. 16.
[44] V-P, March 14, 1941, Part II, p. 9; March 30, 1941, Part I, p. 10.
[45] V-P, March 14, 1941, Part I, p. 9.
[46] S. H. Ferebee to the author, July 17, 1949.
[47] V-P, March 26, 1941, p. 11.
[48] V-P, May 4, 1941, Part II, p. 1.
[49] V-P, March 28, 1941, Part II, p. 14.

Y and even from the dives of East Main Street. All that was open to them was the scanty resources of the civilian Negroes of Norfolk. The Saturday night dances held for them in the Booker T. Washington High School gave them at least one decent place to go.[50]

Meanwhile, other organizations were accepting some of the obligations of hospitality. The Navy Y, crowded as it was with a million visitors, in 1939, a million and a half in 1940, and no one could say how many there would be in 1941, still managed to squeeze in a few hours for gym, chorus, and other activities for Navy wives.[51] Now the P. T. A. held out a friendly hand. At a meeting of the city Federation of Parent-Teachers Associations Mrs. I. T. Van Patten reminded the group of the presence of 8,000 wives of enlisted men and asked the associations to help organize the Navy wives into clubs. Mrs. A. O. Calcott, member of the city recreation committee, urged each of the P. T. A.'s to search for the Navy wives in their community and to invite them with typical Norfolk friendliness to come to P. T. A. meetings and to church and Sunday School.[52] The churches too organized their hospitality. Many of them began holding parties on Friday nights, inviting from thirty to sixty servicemen. The church people arranged games and various forms of entertainment with the aid of the City Recreation Bureau.[53]

Well as Norfolk was beginning to handle the problem of recreation it was still making no impression; the Navy was growing even faster. There were 10,000 "boots" alone in the Naval Training Station, compared to the 3,000 that had made the streets look blue the previous fall. In the middle of June there were 15,559 officers and enlisted men on the Base and 14,426 more on ships based there, not to mention 12,706 civilians, many of whom were newcomers to the city.[54] In addition, the thousands of shipyard workers and sailors at the Navy Yard and the thousands

[50] V-P, March 21, 1941, Part I, p. 8.
[51] See, for example, V-P, March 30, 1941, Part I, p. 12.
[52] V-P, March 22, 1941, p. 18.
[53] V-P, June 12, 1941, p. 26.
[54] Admiral Taussig's figures for June 16, the last day of his command. V-P, June 21, 1941, pp. 16, 7. Other figures were: Navy Yard: civilians, 20,893; Navy personnel, 3,716. Total Navy employees in the area: 71,669. Wives and children of employees: 37,916.

of soldiers at the beach also regarded Norfolk as their recreation center. Coordinator Taft, in fact, thought the Hampton Roads area "probably the greatest concentration of Army, Navy, and industrial defense activities in the country."[55]

The city therefore welcomed the proffered help of the USO. So preoccupied had it been with its own problems that it only vaguely realized what Thomas E. Dewey represented when he arrived in Norfolk in May as national chairman of the newly organized United Service Organizations. Probably few Norfolkians ever did understand that USO was merely a coordinating agency to collect and distribute funds among the six organizations primarily responsible for servicemen's welfare,[56] but they did know that the letters stood for aid to the soldier and sailor.

The New York district attorney was much impressed with what he saw. "Efforts of the local people are extraordinary," he exclaimed enthusiastically. "Norfolk has been dealing with the problem of entertaining enlisted men for many years and is at a decided advantage. All you need here is help. You don't need people to take over the work entirely as they do in other places. A little financial aid and everything will be fine."[57]

A visit with the New York National Guardsmen at Camp Pendleton gave the USO chairman a slightly different picture. The soldiers there, he learned, had found the beach rather dead in the off-season. A round-trip to Norfolk on the bus cost 75 cents, and then they had trouble finding a place to sleep. There was no place to go but the Y, and that was always overcrowded. The five things the soldiers and sailors wanted most were: beds; transportation; a 10-cent glass of beer; "a decent place to take a nice girl to dance under good auspices"; and a place to meet each other after the movies to play games and swim.[58]

Complaints like this could have been heard in almost any Army or Navy post in May of 1941, and they were probably just

[55] U. S. House of Representatives, Public Buildings and Grounds Committee, *Hearings . . . March 4, 5, 6, 7, 12, and 13, 1941* (Washington, 1941), p. 291.

[56] The Y. M. C. A., the Y. W. C. A., National Catholic Community Service, National Jewish Welfare Board, the Salvation Army, and the Travelers Aid Society. Only in unusual circumstances did the USO operate a center directly and not through one of its member organizations.

[57] *V-P*, May 9, 1941, Part II, p. 16.

[58] *V-P*, May 10, 1941, pp. 16, 7.

as loud in San Antonio or San Diego. Norfolk, however, was attracting more attention, was, in fact, getting as much publicity as the Norfolk Advertising Board could wish. In Washington Commander John L. Reynolds, head of the recreation section of the Bureau of Navigation, trying to help the Federal aid bill along, told a Senate committee, "Our worst spot in the United States is Norfolk", adding that Taussig had "repeatedly referred to conditions there as intolerable." Before an indignation meeting could be called, the admiral explained that he had not said "intolerable," but merely "inadequate."[59] Other publicity was received from "the writer-sleuths assigned by pix-and-slick weeklies to tell the story of the national defense program," who wrote "hard things about the inadequacy of Norfolk's recreational facilities," as the *Virginian-Pilot* commented.[60]

The chairmen of the drive for USO funds in Norfolk determined to prove that the city did not have the hard heart its critics charged. They decided to open the campaign for $22,500 five days ahead of schedule so that Norfolk could vindicate its reputation by becoming the first city in the United States to go over the top. Another unusual feature of the drive was that there was to be no canvassing. The chairmen would merely open up headquarters and wait for the money to pour in from enthusiastic donors.[61] It was supposed that firms benefiting from the defense boom would be glad to share their profits.

Unfortunately the chairmen had overestimated Norfolk's enthusiasm. Unsolicited contributions came in, but not in the expected volume. On the day the drive was supposed to end only $7,685.50 had been received, and a week later the city was still $5,000 short of its goal.[62] At the end of the third week a check for $3,200, contributed by Navy Yard employees, finally raised the total to $23,225.50, and Norfolk's reputation was saved.[63]

While the USO funds were being raised all over the nation to help provide recreation, Federal aid was coming nearer reality. In February, the Regional Defense Council learned that its request of January had been channeled into Washington and prog-

[59] *V-P*, May 20, 1941, p. 18.
[60] *V-P*, May 30, 1941, p. 6.
[61] *V-P*, May 31, 1941, p. 1; June 6, 1941, Part II, p. 12.
[62] *V-P*, May 31, 1941, p. 1; June 6, 1941, Part II, p. 12.
[63] *V-P*, June 13, 1941, Part I, p. 14.

ress was reported.[64] By March the House Public Buildings and Grounds Committee, headed by Fritz G. Lanham, was holding hearings on a bill to appropriate $150,000,000 for community facilities in defense areas.[65] As part of its investigation the committee spent a Saturday touring the Norfolk area.[66] After another month of careful consideration the House committee approved the Lanham Act,[67] and the House sent it on to the Senate. At length the act passed all the Senate hurdles, and on June 30 the accompanying appropriation of $150,000,000 was approved. Norfolk immediately went to work on its requests, which already totaled $7,000,000.[68]

[64] *V-P*, February 15, 1941, p. 16.
[65] *V-P*, March 8, 1941, p. 16.
[66] *V-P*, March 30, 1941, Part II, p. 1.
[67] *V-P*, April 30, 1941, p. 20.
[68] *V-P*, July 2, 1941, p. 13.

8

TEN THOUSAND HOMES?

W HILE the joint housing committee was vainly breaking
its lances on the Federal housing projects, a new champion entered the lists. W. Bruce Shafer, Jr., a produce
dealer by profession and an inveterate booster by inclination, had
always had a loud faith in Norfolk's future. He had been a warm
supporter of Admiral Simons' efforts to get more housing in Portsmouth for Navy Yard workers and had even dabbled in a small
real-estate project there himself.[1] When Admiral Simons moved
across the river in June, 1941, to succeed Admiral Taussig as
commandant at the Naval Base, Shafer's interests moved with
him.

Striking up an acquaintance with the out-of-town builders who
were arriving in Norfolk, he was delighted to find that their
visions were even grander than his own. He tried to dispel some
of the pessimism that was shrouding the city by publicizing these
rosy predictions in a letter to the editor:

Most of the national developers that have followed the big booms like
the Detroit and Los Angeles booms, predict that Norfolk will have over
a half-million people when this boom stops. Most of them say that all
booms usually stop in seven years, but they contend the Norfolk boom
is very much like the Detroit boom which ran for 21 years.

One of the main things that is attracting the big investor to put his
money in Norfolk is the fact that Government employees around here
need 10,000 new homes and will buy them like rent. They also are informed by the Senators from their States that the Government is going
to bring in 20,000 new defense workers in the next few months in the
Norfolk area, if the big national builders can build the homes to house
them.[2]

[1] *V-P*, June 19, 1941, p. 6.
[2] Letter, August 1, in *V-P*, August 7, 1941, p. 6.

A few days later he learned how much effect his arguments had had in convincing the skeptical. Picking up his Sunday paper, he noted with satisfaction the display given to his proposed business center and dance casino on Beach Boulevard. Then his eye shifted to the next page and fell on the usual statement by the joint housing committee. Chairman Sears gloomily reported that housing was going up four times as fast as a year earlier and announced that his committee had forwarded a request to Washington that no more large-scale government projects be assigned to the area.[3]

Indignant at this attempt to slap brakes on the boom, Shafer promptly dashed off a telegram to Defense Housing Coordinator Palmer:

Press states Norfolk Realty Board and Building Loans Committee requesting Government to stop large housing projects here. Take their request with a grain of salt, for it is largely due to their song of fear that this section is now 10,000 houses short. . . . The Norfolk committee should be pitied more than censured as they represent home and apartment owners who seek high rents. Acute housing shortage plays into their hands to gouge the defense worker for high rents. Most Norfolk people thank you for helping us build a greater Norfolk. Forgive them for they know not what harm they are doing to national defense by opposing more homes.[4]

The controversy swirled away in a haze of figures. The joint housing committee had counted 8,330 new homes in the area since January, 1940, and had decided that was too many; Shafer exuberantly declared that 25,000 were needed. Another more conservative optimist put the demand at 21,430.[5] The real debate, however, was not over the size of the demand; even the joint committee was ready to admit that there were not enough homes to satisfy everyone. The committee, nevertheless, believed the shortage was caused by the construction workers out at the Naval Base, who could be expected to head back to North Carolina in a few months as soon as their job was done. For their temporary accommodation, the committee felt, it would be better

[3] *V-P*, August 10, 1941, Part I, p. 13.
[4] *V-P*, August 11, 1941, p. 14.
[5] *V-P*, August 10, 1941, Part I, p. 13; August 11, 1941, p. 14; August 16, 1941, p. 6.

to rent out rooms in existing homes than to build houses which could not be finished before the transient workers had left.

Although this viewpoint was generally held in Norfolk, anyone reading the papers carefully could have realized that there was no prospect of the construction projects being completed within a few months. The original contract at the Naval Air Station had been expected to last until December, 1941, and that original contract was already buried under millions of dollars more. On top of all the other building at the Base, the Navy announced plans for an Atlantic Fleet School on a twenty-acre site on the Army Base, and Congressman Harris revealed that a 750-bed hospital would be built on the old golf course there.[6] A new $5,000,000 shipyard in Berkley was assigned to the Norfolk Shipbuilding and Dry Dock Company for operation, and the St. Helena shipyard grew from its original four million to six or seven.[7]

Government construction alone could thus be expected to last for at least another year, and after that there would have to be workers to operate all these new facilities. Civilian and Navy personnel at the Base in June, 1941, had already been up over 19,000 from a year earlier, and the Navy Yard had added 11,000 workers in the same period. Moreover, the Navy Yard was planning to hire another 13,000 employees to hit a 35,000 ceiling.[8] This meant new houses by the tens of thousands, no matter how the figures were discounted, and affirmed Doctor Thompson's prediction of June that 38,000 new housing units were needed on the south side of Hampton Roads.

Fortunately, the protests of the joint housing committee had little effect in Washington. The Defense Housing Office from the first had been as concerned as the joint committee about the dangers of overbuilding and was making every effort to keep construction to a minimum. It had taken the lead in urging the establishment of a central housing registration office to measure the demand and had assigned a full-time staff member to study the Norfolk situation. Although it had failed to publicize its information, the Defense Housing Office had quite accurate figures

[6] *V-P*, September 10, 1941, p. 18; September 16, 1941, p. 18.
[7] *V-P*, September 12, 1941, Part II, p. 14; September 17, 1941, p. 20.
[8] *V-P*, September 17, 1941, p. 20; October 5, 1941, Part IV, p. 8.

as to the need in Hampton Roads and was preparing to satisfy it. A special National Committee on Emergency Housing, headed by Mrs. Samuel Rosenman of New York City, was cooperating with the State Planning Board in selecting sites for the large-scale projects still to come.

Unaware of all this planning, Norfolk continued to fight its housing battle. Booster Shafer renewed the contest by starting a one-man campaign to solicit more out-of-town builders to help out the local contractors, who were unprepared for the mass production needed for these large developments. Naming himself chairman of an "Emergency Housing Committee," he started to write letters—to the New York *Times*, to engineering journals, wherever his message might strike a contractor's eye:

Norfolk is getting a lot of unfavorable publicity because of the acute housing shortage here.

Local builders have built 2,900 houses in the last year trying to help house the influx of defense workers, but it is out of the question for local developers to build fast enough to keep up, as Norfolk's population has increased from 119,000 to 222,000 in two years.

A few wealthy public-spirited citizens have purchased 5,000 lots to give to any out-of-town builders that will build in groups of fifty or more homes and help Norfolk get the 10,000 new homes we have promised the Navy Department we would build during the next six months.

When the Navy started recently to build two new shipyards we promised the 10,000 new homes with the aid of the FHA, and we want the public to know that Norfolk is doing everything possible to keep our word.[9]

This notice attracted the attention of several prospects, and one of them wrote to the Norfolk Association of Commerce for more details. Since Shafer's 5,000 free lots had not been mentioned in the local papers, the Association's Manager W. S. Harney found the proposition "not altogether clear" and asked for more information himself.[10] After he had received a copy of the Shafer

[9] Clipping from New York *Times*, October 7, 1941, in Turin, Francis E.: Defense Housing file, NWHC records. The population figures are highly inaccurate. The city's population in April, 1940, was 144,332, and the peak never exceeded 200,000. The estimates of the Norfolk Advertising Board were based on figures which included the county east of the Elizabeth River.

[10] W. S. Harney to Jerome Jolin, Newark, October 23, 1941, copy in Turin, Francis E.: Defense Housing file, NWHC records.

letter, he was still mystified by the mysterious "Emergency Housing Committee," the anonymous "wealthy public-spirited citizens," and the unlocated lots.

Since this national airing of Norfolk's housing quarrel seemed to deserve some local consideration, Manager Harney invited several prominent citizens to discuss the problem with him. The group came to the sensible conclusion that the way to settle the dispute would be through an impartial survey and asked the Hampton Roads Defense Council to make an investigation.[11] "There has been a diversity of opinion," Harney explained to the public, "on how much of a shortage exists, and we believe the most logical way of getting something accurate and useful to the Defense Council and to business and others interested is through an actual survey."[12] The council's new executive director, Dr. W. T. Hodges, was happy to reply that such a survey had been under way for the past two months. He disclosed that Robert Wilson had been assigned to the study by the Defense Housing Coordinator and was working full time in the Defense Council's office, making a complete check of both supply of and demand for housing.[13]

In the meantime the joint housing committee returned to the fray with another letter to Washington requesting that no more large-scale public-housing projects be assigned to the area. Chairman Sears declared that housing questionnaires should be taken with "a grain of salt." It would be ridiculous, he felt, to ask tenants whether they wanted new and larger quarters at less rent and expect anything but a loud, long clamor for more and more housing. The committee could see no reason why "the highly paid workers, who are temporarily making Norfolk their home, should expect us to have ready for their selection a wide choice of rentable properties. We are inclined to the belief that since all Americans are putting up with varying degrees of inconvenience these highly paid transient workers should also be willing to put up with their portion of inconvenience."[14]

[11] Harney to A. B. Schwarzkopf et al., October 27, 1941, Turin memorandum, October 28, 1941, Turin, Francis E.: Defense Housing file, NWHC records.
[12] V-P, October 29, 1941.
[13] V-P, October 30, 1941, p. 7.
[14] V-P, October 30, 1941, p. 7.

Once again Booster Shafer fired a telegram to Washington in reply, urging the need of 10,000 new homes. Rumbling up in his support came the big guns of the Navy. Admiral Simons, battling the bureaucracy of Washington in his effort to get more housing for his men, lost his patience at this sniping in his rear. After ten days of preparation he brought all his sixteen-inchers into line and unloosed a barrage which reduced the batteries of the joint housing committee to sputtering silence. The commandant thundered:

> Not only is housing falling short of the needs of service and industrial personnel, but the difficult problems of planning and building, for the best interests of both city and national defense, are being complicated by active opposition to needed construction here.

> Organizations, as well as individuals, in Norfolk will no doubt quickly dissociate themselves from attitudes harmful to the effective solution of the housing situation, particularly if they realize that, under present conditions, the net effect of such attitudes is almost a direct sabotage of the defense effort in this area.

> Loose talking today is extremely dangerous. We must not lose our footing now, not even if it requires taking an "emergency view" of every single problem we face, large or small. Housing is in the vanguard of the formidable list of problems before us and it is important that anyone interested in such matters inform himself fully on all implications of the situation before bringing to the public a picture which may not only be false but dangerous, as well, to the citizens of Norfolk in terms of the future of the city. . . .

> It was four years ago that the U. S. Navy began to take a serious look at housing matters here, and about then that the first general "behind-the-scenes" quickening occurred in Navy circles, long before most citizens thought of an emergency. The methods used in studying and acting upon the conditions were the methodical, precise ones characteristic of Navy planning, a fact to be borne in mind in the face of recent utterances that such study and survey should be "taken with a grain of salt." That "grain of salt" might well be reserved for those suspiciously loud and general statements which indicate, rather than careful study and communal interest, an alarming component of group and personal prejudice. . . .[15]

Admiral Simons was the topic of conversation in every real estate office in town that Friday morning. A reporter making the

[15] *V-P*, November 7, 1941, Part II, p. 16.

rounds found "considerable furor" but no one willing to make a public statement. He also discovered "much support among the citizenry" for the admiral's position.[16] Not until Saturday did the joint committee recover its voice. "Under the impression that Rear Admiral Simons," as the *Ledger-Dispatch* amusedly commented, "might be aiming his big guns in their direction," the "saboteurs" met in the Mutual Federal Savings and Loan Office to prepare a reply. They indignantly asked the admiral to point out anything they had done which looked like sabotage. Recalling their unsuccessful attempt a year earlier to get the Hampton Roads Regional Defense Council to make a survey, they declared that they had been able to obtain only "vague, incomplete information" from the Navy. Once more they affirmed their resolution to protect the city:

> The committee is vitally interested in the permanent welfare of this community. The funds its members have for investment purposes are the life's savings of many families. Being fully aware of the economic disaster that befell the community following World War I, the committee believes it to be its duty to prevent a recurrence of such a disaster.[17]

To soothe the ruffled feelings of the joint housing committee, resentful at having its patriotism impugned, the public relations office at the Naval Base prepared a tactful reply for the admiral. The statement reported that Navy officials were "pleased" at the assurances given by "some of the citizens of Norfolk concerning their determination to prevent overbuilding while at the same time expressing themselves ready to help in whatever manner possible to satisfy defense and long-range housing needs." The release repeated the Navy's figures on anticipated demand and the promise that Norfolk's growth would be permanent. On the "sabotage" charge, however, the Navy refused to yield, insisting that interference with the housing program would hinder the defense effort, no matter how high-minded the motive.[18]

One Norfolk realtor, who preferred to keep his name out of the controversy, next day gave a reporter a sane summary of the dispute. If you wanted to start an argument any time, any

---

[16] *V-P*, November 8, 1941, p. 16.
[17] *L-D*, November 8, 1941, p. 2; *V-P*, November 9, 1941, Part II, p. 1.
[18] *L-D*, November 14, 1941, pp. 1, 12.

place, he said, all you had to do was to say something about Norfolk housing. Hitler, the war in Europe, and the chances of war with Japan, he declared, were sure-fire debates, but Norfolk housing was even hotter stuff, since local interests and sensitive pocketbooks made the debators more intense in their partisanship. The real estate man defended the right of high-ranking Navy officials to express their views, even if they had no financial interests at stake. Local realtors, he said, were not discouraging out-of-town builders. The ones most concerned were the building and loan associations with mortgages not covered by FHA insurance, as they were in danger of losing their investments if property values fell.[19]

More fuel to feed the fires of controversy was provided a day later by the appearance of the Hampton Roads Council's housing report. It estimated the population of the city at 194,000 on November 1, nearly 29,000 less than the estimate made by the Norfolk Advertising Board on September 15. The increase for the entire Norfolk area since April, 1940, it placed at 80,724. For these newcomers the report calculated that 10,764 homes were needed. The Defense Council counted only 8,293 new units so far completed or under construction, pointing out that several errors in the joint housing committee's figures had made its total nearly 1,000 too high. There was thus an immediate shortage of 2,471 homes with an anticipated need of 416 more by January 1. By February and March, 1942, construction workers might start leaving the area, the report conceded; on the other hand, if anticipated government contracts should be awarded, "this region has witnessed only the beginning of the population increase and the housing construction program."[20]

Although the report stated that the council had attempted "an absolutely factual, cautious and analytical approach" in order "to establish as nearly as possible the unbiased truth about the controversial subject of housing and population," it was met with

[19] L-D, November 15, 1941, p. 4. The so-called "joint" housing committee had seldon had at its meetings any representative of the Norfolk Real Estate Board other than Otto Hollowell, the board's executive secretary.
[20] V-P, November 16, 1941, Part II, pp. 1, 2; "Housing and Population Report . . . November 1, 1941," in Hampton Roads Regional Defense Council file, VOCD records.

criticism from both sides in the dispute. Manager Francis E. Turin of the Norfolk Advertising Board launched an attack on the Defense Council's population figures and tried to convince Doctor Hodges that the report's total for Norfolk was 30,000 too low.[21] While the Advertising Board was in effect arguing for the need of 4,000 more houses, Otto Hollowell, sole survivor of the joint housing committee, stubbornly refused to admit that there was any shortage. From his citadel in the Norfolk Real Estate Board's office he fired his final shot before striking his colors.

Hollowell released figures showing a total of 2,456 homes under construction in the area. This number virtually equalled the shortage calculated by the Defense Council and seemed to imply that the demand would soon be satisfied, although the Defense Council's estimates had called for 2,471 homes in addition to all those being built. The Real Estate Board secretary said he did not see how there could be a severe housing shortage in view of the houses and rooms which he saw advertised in the papers every day. He declared:

I cannot imagine a greater catastrophe than to have the out-of-town builders construct the thousands of houses they say they are going to build under Title Six of the FHA. Some of these promoters are honest enough to admit they are going to build all the housing they can, under this title, which requires no down payment. They will take their profit and run, leaving our citizens to struggle with a greatly overbuilt community with its disastrous economic effects.[22]

It remained for the ebullient "real estate developer" to fire the final shot in the battle of the builders. Shafer sent off to the *Virginian-Pilot* his own version of the housing question:

Naturally there are two sides to every question. Everyone agrees that we have an acute housing shortage here, but whether we should build 5,000, 10,000, or 50,000 homes is the question to be answered. If the Association of Commerce estimate is correct that Norfolk's population has grown from 119,000 to 222,000 it is reasonable to suppose that the surrounding counties, cities and towns have increased their populations by another 100,000, making a 200,000 increase in all. If you figure

[21] *L-D*, November 19, 1941, p. 2.
[22] *L-D*, November 18, 1941, pp. 1, 2.

four people to live in every small defense home that would show a need of 50,000 new homes.

Personally, I don't think this section should jump in and build 40,000 or 50,000 homes, but I do feel we could build and sell a minimum of 10,000 homes within the next six months and benefit the defense worker and the Norfolk section and everyone in it.[23]

The end of the housing hostilities was celebrated by a feast given by the victor. Shafer and his associates, N. C. Wright and Oscar Smith, gave an oyster roast to some fifty distinguished guests on November 18 at the Arrowhead Inn on Campostella Road, near their 343-acre development that was being graded into sites for 1,200 homes. Among the oyster-swallowers were the mayor of South Norfolk, two members of Norfolk's city council, representatives of Admiral Simons and of the new commandant at the Navy Yard, Admiral Felix X. Gygax, and several New York builders, unmindful of the 5,000 free lots which seemed to have vanished. Even Chairman Sears of the late joint housing committee came to the party, although there was no sign of Otto Hollowell. All was harmony. A Long Island investor named John Halperin announced that he had opened a Norfolk office and was ready to finance any of the several thousand needed homes that the FHA would insure. The city councilmen said the city would cooperate, and the Navy men said the Navy would fill up the houses.[24]

The end of the housing war seemed to open the gates for the outside contractors. Barred by priorities from non-defense areas, builders were converging on Norfolk. M. Kraft and Harry Karpel of Washington, having put up 49 homes in Monticello Village on Sewells Point Road, were ready to start on 150 more. Dan M. Dalis of New York acquired sites for 175 houses on Sewells Point Road and Cottage Toll Road. Sam Walter of New York purchased the Hyslop farm on Indian River and planned to put up 650 homes there. Altogether, 1,450 more new homes were scheduled to be erected by next June, the *Virginian-Pilot* reported in its issue of Sunday, December 7.[25]

[23] *V-P*, November 20, 1941, p. 6.
[24] *V-P*, November 19, 1941, p. 15; *L-D*, November 19, 1941, p. 20.
[25] *V-P*, December 7, 1941, Part IV, p. 4.

9

HALF A LOAF

THE moment the Lanham Act's $150,000,000 became available, every defense area in the country added up the bill it was going to submit to the Federal Government. The very next day Norfolk was ready with requests for over $6,000,000. High on the list was a million-dollar item to provide some of the badly-needed recreation spots for the sailors. City Manager Borland recommended that $600,000 of this be used to provide the adequate auditorium which the city had so long desired, now even more essential as a theater to entertain large crowds of servicemen. The rest of the million was asked to renovate the old city auditorium and to provide smaller recreation centers in Berkley and Ocean View, in addition to one for Negroes. The other millions were needed to meet the new demands caused by the defense boom: expansion of the water supply, including a second pipe line from Lake Prince to the city, a new hospital, four new schools and street improvements.[1]

Since defense area requests added up to far more than the $150,000,000 granted, the Federal Works Agency appointed regional priorities boards to determine which needs should be satisfied. When the regional priorities board arrived in Norfolk on July 18, it heard requests for $20,000,000 from the Hampton Roads communities. Half of this sum was asked by the Hampton Roads Sanitation District Commission to build its entire sewage-disposal system. Retired Admiral Taussig, working hard at his brand-new job as chairman of the commission, asked the United States to assume this burden as a defense measure. The cities and counties were no more modest in their requests, asking for Federal funds to take care of all their new needs, including a second-hand

[1] *V-P*, July 2, 1941, p. 13; *L-D*, July 12, 1941, p. 2.

ferryboat to improve the service between Norfolk and Portsmouth. When members of the priorities board remarked that they understood money would be available for operating schools as well as building them, Colonel Borland promptly ordered an application prepared for another $175,000 for that purpose.[2]

The regional priorities board rushed through its approval of the projects in what one of the members later called "the most fantastic bit of futility" he had ever witnessed.[3] There was no time to spend in consideration; since Congressional action had taken six months, the FWA was determined to rush the projects through. Exactly a month later the first Washington decision came through. Newspapers announced that presidential approval had been obtained for a $2,240,000 project to expand Norfolk's water system.[4] Next day, however, spirits fell when it turned out that the FWA grant was for only 30 per cent of the total cost, and that the city was expected to pay the rest.[5]

At once Colonel Borland called upon Congressman Harris to come to the aid of his district. Harris went to work on the FWA to get it to raise its grant to 50 per cent. Borland also went to Washington to try his powers of persuasion. Defense Council Chairman Bottom declared indignantly that it was "distressing to see a vital aspect of the defense effort suffering under suspicious, questioning, pinch-penny administration."[6] Representative Harris tried to soothe the Regional Council by explaining that the FWA was doing its best but that it had to make the $150,000,000 go around. That was the reason it could grant only about 30 per cent of the amount asked. He suggested that the council appeal to the President for the appropriation of another $300,000,000 and without further urging the council adopted such a resolution.[7]

Major Bottom phrased the council's plea in urgent terms in a letter to Governor Price calling for the State's cooperation. As-

[2] V-P, July 19, 1941, p. 16.
[3] Hugh R. Pomeroy, speaking to the Engineers Club of Hampton Roads, V-P, September 27, 1941, p. 16.
[4] V-P, August 19, 1941, p. 18.
[5] V-P, August 20, 1941, p. 18.
[6] V-P, August 23, 1941, p. 16.
[7] V-P, August 28, 1941, p. 24.

serting that $20,000,000 was required to meet the "minimum needed expansion" of community facilities in Hampton Roads, he declared the localities could not be expected to furnish 70 per cent of this cost. "The simplest examination of the resources of the communities involved," he maintained, "will evidence the practical impossibility of their shouldering the burden of a $14,000,000 debt for capital investments in expansion of community facilities, together with the added burden of the substantially increased overhead costs involved in operation of these facilities."[8]

The Norfolk city council directed Colonel Borland to use the same argument on the FWA. The city was within about $5,000,000 of the limit of its bonded indebtedness, the council asserted, and it would be required to issue $2,500,000 or $3,000,000 in bonds if the FWA did not increase its grants. Moreover, all the projects had been made necessary only by the national defense program in the area.[9]

The arguments of poverty and need made some impression in Washington. The FWA yielded here and there, as Colonel Borland marshalled Congressman Harris by his side and fought for one project after another. The first victory came over the waterworks grant. After Borland and Harris had told the FWA that the city's water supply had been planned to take care of all expansion until 1965 and that only the defense program had upset the schedule, the Federal officials agreed to boost the grant to 50 per cent of the total, which was as much as the city had expected.[10]

The new line from Lake Prince to the city made possible by the grant would increase the water supply by more than 50 per cent and take care of any foreseeable contingency, but it could not be completed for at least a year. Meanwhile, the dry summer was being succeeded by a fall drought, and the water supply was no longer a question of additional pumps. The council on August 12 approved a $355,000 bond issue for the construction of the temporary pipe line which had been planned in April as a

---

[8] *V-P*, September 4, 1941, p. 8.
[9] *V-P*, September 4, 1941, pp. 18, 8.
[10] *V-P*, September 24, 1941, p. 20. The FWA grant was $1,080,620 of the $2,240,500 total.

WPA project. This was to run from the North Landing Reservoir to the Dismal Swamp Canal, where it could tap the juniper-flavored water flowing from Lake Drummond, deep in the heart of the swamp.[11]

Work on the new line was under way by September and scheduled to be finished by December 1, but already the city lakes to the east were drying up, and the game wardens were preparing to remove the fish which could no longer live in the muddy bottoms. The supply from the Lake Prince line could have been increased another 2,000,000 gallons a day, but defense work was delaying the arrival of the booster pump ordered seven months before.[12] By the middle of October City Manager Borland was issuing public appeals to save water. He urged the public to wash cars as little as possible and to sprinkle lawns only when necessary to save valuable shrubs. All the city lakes were dry except Little Creek, which was down more than four feet from its normal six-foot level. That water the city was hoping to save in order to dilute the juniper water from Lake Drummond when it arrived in December.[13]

Residents of the northern part of the city, including the bustling Naval Base, on Tuesday morning, October 28, got a foretaste of what might happen. Late Monday night a runaway Army barrage balloon dragged a steel cable over the power line running to the Lake Prince pumping station and stopped the pump temporarily. The resulting air-lock blew a huge hole in the line and cut off all pressure in part of the city. Early risers, turning on the faucet for a morning bath, got a trickle of water, but stay-a-beds got none. Not until nightfall was the pressure back to normal again.[14]

While bathtubs were dry that morning, Nature played its little joke by filling up the streets with water. The heavy two-inch rainfall, followed by other showers, gradually filled up the city lakes, and the danger seemed past.[15] Troubles were not over, however. As the line to the Dismal Swamp Canal neared completion on its scheduled date, it was discovered that the city

---

[11] *V-P*, August 13, 1941, p. 18.
[12] *V-P*, September 28, 1941, Part IV, p. 4.
[13] *V-P*, October 17, 1941, Part II, p. 16.
[14] *V-P*, October 29, 1941, p. 20.
[15] *V-P*, November 8, 1941, p. 16.

would not have Lake Drummond water after all. The level there had fallen so low that water would not flow into the canal. The canal itself was low, as it had been cut to let out water to fight the fires that were sweeping over the dry forests of the swamp. A pump, therefore, would have to be installed on the Pasquotank River to pump water into the canal.[16] This did not mean, however, that Norfolk would be denied the juniper water traditionally conducive to longevity, as the Pasquotank was as junipery as Lake Drummond. Moreover, water from North Carolina should give a taste of home to many people in Norfolk.

By a lucky coincidence, Army engineers at this moment found the canal too low for navigation and ordered it closed, making it possible for the city to pump water out at one end before it was ready to pump water in at the other.[17] On December 1 the new line with its 8,000,000 gallons a day capacity went into action, but after the pumps had been going for several days there was still no water coming out the other end. Investigation disclosed that the water had all been going into the Elizabeth River. A barge which had run aground had knocked the pipe apart. Repair crews went to work, and by Saturday, December 6, the line was at last in full operation.[18]

Meanwhile, the city was negotiating for other Federal grants. The need for new schools was emphasized when the new term began in September. First day enrollment showed 21,914 pupils, 510 more than a year earlier, although later figures cut this increase to 217, with a total enrollment of 23,307.[19] This increase of slightly less than 1 per cent might have been handled readily if it had been evenly distributed, but it was concentrated in the schools in the northern part of the city. Madison School was up 173, Meadowbrook, 93. Granby High, with two elementary grades added, was 148 over its 1500 capacity. Worst of all was the new Ocean View School, which had been near its 800 capacity a year earlier, and was now squeezing in 1,005 children every day.[20]

[16] V-P, November 28, 1941, Part II, p. 16.

[17] V-P, November 30, 1941, Part II, p. 1.

[18] V-P, December 4, 1941, p. 24. The city continued to have trouble at this spot and finally had to bury the pipe in the river bottom. V-P, December 27, 1941, p. 16.

[19] V-P, September 11, 1941, p. 22; September 20, 1941, p. 20.

[20] V-P, September 20, 1941, p. 20. Enrollment in other city schools had declined substantially. High school pupils were down 238; Negro pupils, down 113.

The city had originally requested Lanham Act funds for four new schools, but was told to select the two most needed. It chose the school on the Granby Street site already purchased and the Negro elementary school in Campostella to take care of the prospective residents of Oak Leaf Park. The FWA thereupon authorized a grant of $446,850 toward the total cost of these two schools, which it put at $783,947. This latter figure mystified Colonel Borland and the school board officials, as their last estimate had been $346,924 for the Granby Street school, and $168,075.40 for Campostella.[21]

The result of this confusion was another job for Congressman Harris. Two months of patient negotiations finally worked out an odd compromise. The FWA agreed to construct the Granby Street school for the estimated price, with the city turning the site over to the FWA, and leasing the school back for $1.00 the first year, and whatever the city could afford to pay thereafter. The FWA also agreed to allot $100,000 to the construction of the Campostella school, the city to furnish the site and pay the rest of the cost. As a bonus the city was also awarded $75,000 towards the cost of operating its schools through 1942.[22] Although the city council grumbled about the indefinite terms of the lease, it decided not to look a gift school in the mouth and accepted the agreement.

The negotiations over the hospitals were less easily settled and in fact precipitated a local debate very similar to the housing dispute, although on a much more dignified level. A special committee named by City Manager Borland, with Dr. Walter B. Martin, president of the State Medical Society, at its head, had long ago reversed the stand taken by Doctor Martin in January, when he had thought no additional hospital beds were necessary, and an application for a new hospital had been among the city's first requests. The expansion of the Norfolk Community Hospital for Negroes was settled with a minimum of haggling. The city asked for a $333,364 grant for a 67-bed expansion. The FWA granted half, provided the city would furnish the other half.[23]

[21] *V-P*, September 19, 1941, Part II, p. 18.

[22] *V-P*, November 19, 1941, p. 22. The city, of course, had a much easier time than the rapidly expanding counties. Princess Anne's new Bayside school was 125 pupils over capacity the day it opened. *V-P*, November 19, 1941, p. 18.

[23] *V-P*, September 4, 1941, pp. 18, 8.

Then Colonel Borland went to Washington, cut a few corners on the construction plans, pared costs by $93,364, and persuaded the FWA to let the city have the benefit of all the saving.[24]

With the white hospital, however, he had less luck. Even though he cut the cost from the original $1,840,000 down to $1,500,000 for a 270-bed hospital, he could not persuade the FWA to go any higher than $750,000 for a new hospital. With negotiations stymied the local hospitals decided to try their luck. Each of them prepared an application to the FWA. Norfolk General Hospital asked for $550,000 to add a new, 100-bed wing to its 278 beds; St. Vincent's for $502,000 to increase its 225-bed capacity by 106; and Leigh Memorial needed $330,000 to expand from 90 beds to 161.[25]

This threat of having Norfolk's prospects for a brand-new hospital frittered away excited Doctor Martin's committee. Martin at once issued a statement urging that a new hospital be constructed instead of expanding the old ones. He argued:

We feel that this community has an unusual opportunity to secure a hospital unit constructed along modern lines, situated in the direction of population growth, with adequate surrounding space, and readily accessible to the general public.

We believe that such a hospital properly constructed can be operated more economically, with less per unit personnel, and can render more effective public service. . . . In this opinion we are supported by the official action of the Norfolk County Medical Society and by the Hampton Roads Regional Defense Council.[26]

To corroborate Doctor Martin all six members of his committee met and again endorsed his views. Dr. M. S. Pritchett, president of the Norfolk County Medical Society, said that his society had approved the new hospital on October 3, and Executive Director Hodges announced that the Regional Defense Council had given its approval on August 27.[27]

Into this solid wall of unanimity one of Norfolk's most public-spirited citizens dared to plunge his head. David Pender, president

[24] V-P, September 25, 1941, p. 20; November 19, 1941, p. 22.
[25] V-P, October 25, 1941, p. 16; November 19, 1941, p. 22.
[26] V-P, October 27, 1941, p. 14.
[27] V-P, October 28, 1941, p. 18.

of the Norfolk General Hospital, expressed the views of men who are charged with the trusteeship of community property. In courteous tones he explained:

> In reference to the new hospital in Norfolk, our board is thoroughly sympathetic and we all recognize the splendid work done by Dr. Martin and his committee. We appreciate that they are interested only in what is best for the community. Our board of management, consisting of 35 of Norfolk's most prominent citizens, after a very long discussion, were unanimous in endorsing the enlargement of our institution, provided the money could be made available. . . .
>
> If a new hospital is built here, responsibility for operating same would fall upon the taxpayers of the city—certainly the government is not going to furnish the funds unless somebody is responsible for its operation. . . . If we had a city-owned hospital, all the clinic patients would necessarily be sent there, and if we should lose these patients, it would very much interfere with our securing internes and training nurses, to which the clinic service is absolutely necessary. . . .
>
> After mature consideration, if the citizens think it is best to have a new hospital here, we will gladly extend our full co-operation.[28]

A month later the controversy flared anew when Doctor Martin explained the plans his committee was making for an emergency. The committee was preparing to take over schools, churches, and clubs for emergency hospital space in case of an epidemic, and was making a survey of all women in the city with nursing training who might be pressed into temporary service. He explained incidentally that Norfolk's hospital shortage at the moment was 223 beds on the basis of the estimated population, while Portsmouth with only 157 beds needed 160 more.[29]

It was hard for any businessman to see how there could be such a great shortage when there were empty beds in every hospital in the city. Since President Pender had already given Doctor Martin this information the day before the public statement was issued, Pender now decided to give the facts to the public. If there had been 300 additional beds available in Norfolk for the last nine months, he said, every hospital in the city would

---

[28] *V-P*, October 28, 1941, p. 18.
[29] *V-P*, November 27, 1941, p. 22. A "very conservative" estimate of the anticipated shortage made earlier was 332, or, deducting the 67 beds allocated to the Negro hospital, 265. *V-P*, October 27, 1941, p. 14.

have been bankrupt by now. On the average only 395 of the 593 beds in the three hospitals had been occupied over that time. He admitted that at times it had been hard to make the service match the demand, but the hospitals had already added seventy beds during the year, and all could increase their capacity 50 per cent in case of an emergency. He urged financial caution:

All three hospitals have a large indebtedness, which their respective boards feel honor bound to protect. Certainly, to greatly increase all beds available would jeopardize same. My personal opinion is that 100 additional at this time would meet the demand. In addition to this, to properly staff the fourth hospital would be almost impossible from personnel standpoint, as all the hospitals throughout the United States are undermanned at this time.

I have the strongest desire to cooperate in the fullest in everything for the best interest of Norfolk. . . .[30]

This time Pender received a glare from the Hampton Roads Regional Defense Council for his obstinacy in again butting this stone wall. The council's anonymous statement said in annoyed patience:

The Defense Council has hoped that it would not be necessary to reopen the hospital controversy in Norfolk. But in view of statements which have appeared in the press to the effect that there is no hospital shortage here, the council feels it cannot let the matter pass. If it let such a statement go unchallenged, there is danger that the public might be lulled into feeling that the community is adequately protected in case of a winter epidemic or the usual winter increment in disease incidence, whereas this is not the case. . . .

The fact that this has been a mild season so far, with a low incidence of illness, should not blind us to the realization that with the advent of the winter season there will be a rising curve of illness, and that our present hospital accommodations are totally inadequate to meet the expected load.

There is no reason to anticipate that we have entered on an area of permanent decreases in illness sufficient to upset figures based on past experience. It was a matter of common experience among physicians that during the past winter our hospitals were intolerably crowded. With the present population increase, patients can be accommodated during the coming winter by placing additional beds in every available

[30] *V-P*, November 28, 1941, Part II, p. 10.

space in our hospitals. While this is justified as an emergency measure, it is no answer to our problem.[31]

The statement seemed to demolish all but one of the arguments against the new hospital. In the excitement of the debate the contestants seemed to have overlooked the fact that there was still no answer to the $750,000 question: Who was going to pay for the new hospital?

While the city had been declining to pay its allotted share of the cost of the new hospital, it had been putting up a battle to share in the cost of the new auditorium. This ironical development had resulted from the FWA's policy on recreation facilities. The city had leaped at the chance of getting its long-wanted auditorium as a defense measure. The city recreation committee, in fact, as early as June had prepared plans for a combination recreation center, auditorium, and arena on the city-owned site at Ninth and Granby, and sent them on to the Federal Security Administration for approval.[32]

The need for recreation centers had been stressed before the regional priorities board by former City Manager Thomas P. Thompson, a member of the city recreation committee, who said:

I hope you gentlemen will realize, much better than others in high places appear to know, that we have a bigger recreation problem here than probably any other place in America.

We have both the Army and Navy with us and there are times when we have 10,000 to 15,000 soldiers and sailors on our streets.... This has resulted in a most acute situation. We are dealing here in human values, and if this job is not done and done well, then the fathers and mothers who have sent their boys into the service here will have a just complaint against us.

We need means for furnishing mass entertainment, and we have made our plans to meet this need.[33]

Even though the erection of a large auditorium was somewhat out of line with the usual policy of building small, club-room-type recreation centers, the FWA looked kindly on the city's

[31] V-P, November 30, 1941, Part I, p. 9.
[32] V-P, June 12, 1941, p. 26.
[33] V-P, July 19, 1941, p. 16.

request. As early as August 8 Colonel Borland was able to announce that a tentative allocation of $420,000 had been made to Norfolk, including $278,000 for the new auditorium.[34] It was September 30, however, before the exact size of the grants became known in Norfolk. There was to be a $60,000 recreational center for Benmoreell, a $73,000 Negro recreation center, and a $280,000 temporary white recreation center.[35]

The idea of temporary buildings was a great disappointment, but the *Virginian-Pilot* proposed an idea:

 In its present form, the PWA allocation contemplates the construction of temporary buildings, the entire cost of structure and equipment to be borne by the government. If Secretary Knox is correct in his estimate of Norfolk's future as a permanently enlarged naval center, temporary structures for local defense recreation facilities would hardly seem to qualify as a sound solution of the problem. Certainly, if by moderately increasing the $353,000 allocation now approved, the PWA could, with some municipal aid make possible the building of permanent, instead of perishable frame recreation structures, such a change is worth exploring. It could be explored and acted upon without undue delay.[36]

The city recreation committee needed no urging to carry out this idea. They at once set out for Washington with Colonel Borland to arrange the compromise. Unfortunately for their purpose, they ran smack into the Army. The FWA, they learned, was handing the building of all recreation centers over to the construction section of the Army Quartermaster Corps. The committee called on the man in charge, Brigadier General Brehon P. Somervell, and found that he was in no mood to negotiate. The general, in fact, was determined to start to work right away. Calling in Congressman Harris as reinforcement, the committee launched a week-long battle with the Army.[37]

Winder Harris was equal to his assignment. He blocked Army action for the moment and, even though he was forced into the hospital, from his sick-bed arranged a conference with General Somervell. When the general surrendered, the city council met for three consecutive days to thresh out the details of the arrange-

[34] *V-P*, August 9, 1941, p. 16.
[35] *V-P*, October 1, 1941, p. 18.
[36] *V-P*, October 1, 1941, p. 6.
[37] *V-P*, October 3, 1941, Part II, p. 16.

ment, incidentally settling the Negro recreation center problem by transferring the site to the Federal government.[38]

As finally worked out, the Army agreed to let the city have the $280,000 allocated to the temporary project. The city was to contribute $245,000 so that the building could be made permanent. To save costs the original game-room feature was eliminated, but there still remained a theater with 2,000 seats, and an arena which could hold 5,000 persons. The city would own the project but would lease it to the Federal government for a dollar a year for the duration.[39] While another eight weeks passed, arguments over the plans went on. The Army engineer who had to approve looked at the local architect's drawings for a cinder-block structure faced with stone and ruled it too weak. Colonel Borland snorted that the Army wanted to make the building safe from earthquakes and hurricanes, but a compromise between economy and security was finally reached on December 3.[40]

Even though all these entertainment projects were still on the drafting board with 1941 nearly run out, there had been some progress in entertaining the sailors. The coming of summer had brought back into action the area's natural recreational resource, the beaches. As the *Virginian-Pilot* pointed out:

Save only for a few clubs operating on a private-membership basis, this whole vast bay-and-shore recreation facility is open to the service personnel as freely as to civilians. Civilians come here every summer from far distant places, by the tens of thousands, to enjoy these facilities. The army and navy men concentrated here are either domiciled next door to them, or can reach them with a 10-cent bus fare.[41]

Soldiers and sailors sprawled on the sands that summer beside civilians from New York, North Carolina, and Norfolk, all reduced to the common denominator of human beings by the anonymity of bathing suits. Some of the coldness toward the serviceman thawed out under the warm beach sun, as accidental acquaintances turned into friends. Girls even agreed to go out with sailors, provided they did not wear their uniforms to the

[38] *V-P*, October 9, 1941, p. 22.
[39] *V-P*, October 10, 1941, Part I, p. 6, Part II, p. 14.
[40] *V-P*, December 4, 1941, p. 24.
[41] *V-P*, May 30, 1941, p. 6.

house. The serviceman's chief handicap at the beach was lack of money, for defense dollars were sweeping over the resorts in waves so that one reporter noted "a Gold Coast confusion of spending that has never been equaled at Virginia Beach or Ocean View, the two major resort centers." In fact, the amusement spots had to prolong the season after Labor Day in order to take care of belated spenders.[42]

The sailors swimming at Ocean View had the advantage of a Navy Y Beach Club nearly twice as big as before.[43] Since there were three times as many sailors, however, this failed to help much. When the servicemen were driven back into town by the closing of the beaches, they found the town more crowded than ever, but at least there were some alternatives to fighting one's way into the Navy Y or spending a month's pay in an East Main Street dive. Up to now the only other place a sailor without money had been welcome was at some of the churches on Friday nights and at the city auditorium dances on Saturdays. By September there were several full-time centers in operation. The Methodist women of the city had prepared a hostess house at 236 Court Street, which they kept open every afternoon and evening. They had opened it on July 2 with some misgivings about whether the sailors would come, but even on that midsummer night the first bluejackets who discovered the place gobbled up gallons of ice-cream and dozens of Methodist-made cookies.[44] In August the Catholic ladies started dances at Ocean View, which had furnished at least one sailor a wife by October.[45]

Other centers were the result of outside enterprise. The Salvation Army in June received approval from national headquarters for a $75,000 renovation of their Granby and Plume Street building to turn it into a servicemen's recreation center.[46] About the same time the Reverend Frederick A. Smith, representing the National Lutheran Council, arrived in Norfolk to see whether a Lutheran service center was needed.[47] In July Miss E. Jacque

[42] V-P, September 2, 1941, p. 16. One reason for extending the season was that Labor Day came on September 1 that year.

[43] V-P, June 15, 1941, Part I, p. 7.

[44] V-P, July 3, 1941, Part II, p. 12.

[45] V-P, September 22, 1941, p. 14.

[46] V-P, June 14, 1941, p. 16.

[47] V-P, June 16, 1941, p. 14.

Poole arrived on assignment from the National Y. W. C. A. as a USO worker.[48] Devoted primarily to Navy wives and children, she so endeared herself to service families that one Merrimack Park child toddled to the telephone to call "Jacky" to settle a fight with his brother.

By August both Lutherans and Catholics were at work furnishing new recreation centers. The Lutheran survey had shown Norfolk to have a greater need than any other spot in the country except little Alexandria, Louisiana, surrounded by three Army camps. The National Lutheran Council spent $75,000 at 114 City Hall Avenue to develop an attractive room. The lounge was dazzling in red, black, and blue leather and chromium, and the washroom was provided with outlets for electric razors. There was a radio strong enough to bring in home-town stations and ping-pong tables for diversion. Appropriately, the first thing to strike the visitor's eye was the chapel, where at night a spotlight fell upon the cross.[49] One enlisted man was so taken by the friendly atmosphere that he remarked: "All you need is Pop and Mom there in the corner, and it's home."[50]

The Catholic center was even better. It set up quarters on the second and third floors of the old Woolworth building at 259 Granby Street. The second floor was designed as a lounge and recreation room with a snack-bar in the rear. When the third floor was finished as a 100-bed dormitory, the center would be open around the clock. In the meantime servicemen could come in from ten to ten for any of the entertainment offered. Most popular was a recording device, permitting sailors to mail their voices home. "A major function of the club," said Philip Dean, president of the Norfolk branch of the National Catholic Community Service, "is to provide a home away from home for the boys in uniform."[51] The center was open, it was stressed, to men of all denominations and to men of no denomination. Admiral Simons, after taking a look around, said succinctly: "You've got something."[52]

[48] *V-P*, July 19, 1941, p. 16.
[49] *V-P*, August 18, 1941, p. 14.
[50] *V-P*, September 13, 1941, p. 9.
[51] *V-P*, September 21, 1941, Part I, p. 14.
[52] *V-P*, September 22, 1941, p. 14.

At the same time effort was being made to suppress the illegal forms of recreation. The police periodically raided the East Main Street houses which had refused to close and carried the girls off to jail for a fine and a physical examination. Other places opened up in more respectable parts of the city. "All over Ghent and in other sections of Norfolk, little nests of vice have sprung up," one reporter declared.[53] Police Chief Woods explained:

> We know we haven't cleaned up the town, but we're doing our best. There are houses scattered around town, but we harass them as much as possible. Two nights last week we had approximately 100 arrests involving some form of prostitution. All we can do is our best and we'll do it. This is something that can never be eradicated, and anyone who believes it can is fooling himself.[54]

The chief effect of Norfolk's vigorous enforcement was to drive the oldest profession out into the counties where the police were less strict. There it joined hands with the liquor law evaders. Since it was impossible to buy a drink of whiskey in Virginia legally without buying a bottle, "social clubs" went through the motions of buying bottles for their "members" and pouring drinks for them.

The effort of the Alcoholic Beverage Control agents to close up these clubs was blocked in the Tidewater by the tacit opposition of the public and even of the courts. Arrests made in Princess Anne in July, for example, were still before the courts in October. Raids were tipped off in advance, and, even when an operator was fined, he put it down as part of the cost of doing business. Business was booming, especially when tourist cabins were attached. At one place at least one couple every minute for an hour appeared and asked for a cabin, and that was only on Friday night. One A. B. C. officer declared that the situation was the most vicious he had yet observed in the state of Virginia.[55]

Although this problem was beyond the city's jurisdiction, it had one at home for which the people were responsible. Most conspicuous and most regrettable failure was the inability of the average person to adjust his prejudices to the new Navy. There

[53] *V-P*, October 19, 1941, Part II, p. 1.
[54] *V-P*, October 22, 1941, p. 15.
[55] *V-P*, October 18, 1941, p. 16; October 19, 1941, Part II, p. 1.

was little active hostility; virtually no brawling between sailor and civilian, as one might have expected. All that the ordinary Norfolkian was doing was to continue the way of living which had preserved the local peace for many years. As before, he went about his business, completely ignoring the men in the bell-bottom trousers.

The Navy veteran was used to this attitude and had accepted it, but homesick youngsters inevitably were rebuffed and found the city cold and arrogant. The only place, it seemed, that they could expect an outstretched hand was on East Main Street, and there the hands were extended palms upward. Thousands of "boots" at the Naval Training Station were being sent out to man the nation's ships with a hatred of Norfolk in their hearts.

It would have been too much to have expected anything different, of course. Human habits cannot be remolded in a year, even in such a year as 1941 was for Norfolk. Especially in such a year, for the hectic haste, the annoying inconveniences, the pushing and the shoving, all so foreign to the city's old ways, did not make it easier to love one's fellowman. Then, too, the sailors did their part to increase the irritation. They got drunk, they destroyed property, they played practical jokes with more cruelty than humor, they were rude and contemptuous—in short, they behaved like any group of young men away from home and the restraint of family influence.

Sailors on the rear platform of a Naval Base trolley one night, for example, discovered that by turning out a light in the back they could put out the car's headlight. When the light went off, the motorman resignedly stopped the car, trotted around to the back, and screwed the bulb back in again. When the light went off again a block later, he stopped the car and remained in his seat. At last he raised his head above the curtain behind him and called back, "When you fellows get through playing and screw that bulb back in, we'll go on to the Base. Otherwise, I can sit here all night." The light went back on.[56]

Another sailor stopped to watch Porky-Pie at Ocean View Park. Porky-Pie was a little pig in a cage. A well-tossed baseball would knock open his cage door and send Porky-Pie sliding down a chute. The sailor paid for his three throws and decided to

[56] *V-P*, September 20, 1941, p. 20.

improve upon the game. With his first toss he sent Porky-Pie tumbling down the slide and with his second he hit Porky-Pie squarely between the eyes, sending the little pig to a premature sausagehood. The indignant owner of the concession had the sailor hauled off to court where he was fined $25.[57] Three other sailors paid $50 each for the pleasure of carrying off a downtown parking meter and taking seven nickels out of it.[58]

It was regrettable, but inevitable, that Norfolk's relations with the Navy had not yet approached cordiality. Perhaps more significant, however, were the signs that the leaven of friendship was gradually working its way down from the top. The churches were reaching a few of the thousands of sailors every week and extending a welcoming hand. The presence of the USO "homes away from home" was helping, and the USO announced in November that a permanent staff would soon be assigned to the old city auditorium to keep that going full-time. Oldest veteran of the warm handclasp, however, was the city dance committee. Through winter and summer, through sleet and heat, with money and without money, it had carried on, missing only two Saturday nights,[59] until it rounded out a full year of service on Saturday, December 6, 1941.

[57] *V-P*, July 18, 1941, Part II, p. 12.
[58] *V-P*, October 10, 1941, Part II, p. 14.
[59] Newspapers called the dance on November 29, the 50th, which would have meant two missing Saturdays. *V-P*, November 30, 1941, Part I, p. 9.

10

PLANNING FOR DISASTER

B Y the summer of 1941 Norfolk was beginning to learn some of the new discomforts of defense. It was reminded of impending shortages in July when the nation was called upon to search its attics and its cellars for old aluminum to put wings on the 50,000 planes that Franklin D. Roosevelt had asked for. Norfolk started off its drive with both enthusiasm and organization. One eager donor brought his contribution into the city's fire headquarters more than a week before the campaign began.[1] A young Ghent girl named Kay Larson held an aluminum scavenger hunt in honor of a Rehoboth Beach visitor. Guests scurried around looking for aluminum saucepans, coffeepots, pie-plates, and hair curlers, and carried their miscellaneous collection off to the firehouse in triumph, where the girls were rewarded by being allowed to try on the firemen's boots.[2]

Plans for the formal collection were thoroughly prepared. A vacant lot across the street from the City Hall was fenced in to receive the huge piles of scrap to be gathered, and sections of the city were divided among the Scouts, the American Legion, and the Red Cross. The newspapers gave the campaign full publicity, and Mayor Wood went on the air on Friday night to urge co-operation. "This is a job for all the people," he declared, "for no one man, and no one group of men and women in any locality, can make the campaign a success. Everyone must help. This is an opportunity for every man, woman, and child in America to make a valuable contribution to the national defense effort without cost to anyone."[3]

On Monday, July 21, the volunteers started out. American Legionnaires donned their overseas caps, and the feminine mem-

[1] *V-P*, July 13, 1941, Part II, p. 1.
[2] *V-P*, July 17, 1941, p. 20.
[3] *V-P*, July 20, 1941, Part II, p. 1.

bers of the auxiliary put on their identification badges before they got into the collection cars. The Sons of the Legion dressed in white pants and shirts, members of the Junior Red Cross put on their armbands, and the Scouts appeared in neat uniforms. From house to house they went, ringing doorbells and asking for aluminum. When the housewife answered the bell, she usually tried to find something to give the youngsters. Unfortunately, in busy Norfolk, the housewife was frequently out working on a defense job and too rushed at home even to think about setting aluminum out on the curb.[4]

The trucks seemed to be equally busy. A general appeal for the contribution of fifteen trucks from the city's merchants to gather up the scrap from the local firehouses and haul it to the central collection point persuaded only one truck to volunteer the first day and a day later there were still only two. The truck shortage was not as serious as it might have been, however, because it turned out there was not much aluminum to haul. Although the Estabrook Girl Scouts and all the Negro Boy and Girl Scouts had done an excellent job, the pile of scrap collected by the other organizations was disappointingly small.[5]

Norfolk had planned to make swift work of the campaign, getting in all the local collections in three days and hauling them in to the central point on Thursday. By Thursday night, however, the heap across from the City Hall was only one-fifth of its expected size. The drive was extended to July 29, national closing date, and Mayor Wood asked for renewed effort. "There are 30,000 families in Norfolk," he said, "and it seems to me we ought to be able to collect an average of one pound of aluminum per family."[6] In spite of every appeal the city could not reach even this minimum quota. When the collection was hauled out to the Army Base, where all the Hampton Roads contributions were gathered, it weighed only 12,250 pounds.[7]

Although the lack of aluminum seemed to have made little impression in Norfolk, there were other shortages of which the city did not need to be reminded. On July 1 Colonel Borland informed the council that contractors would no longer bid for

[4] *V-P*, July 22, 1941, p. 18.
[5] *V-P*, July 23, 1941, p. 18; July 25, 1941, Part II, p. 12.
[6] *V-P*, July 25, 1941, Part II, p. 12.
[7] *V-P*, August 9, 1941, p. 16.

improvements of the city streets because they could not get the materials.[8] By September hardware shelves were looking like Mother Hubbard's cupboard. Finding nails was a game which only the patient could play. One dealer said there were not more than 300 pounds of galvanized roofing nails in the city. All galvanized materials were scarce, even water buckets, as well as aluminum and chrome. As for electric wiring, a dealer said the situation was "just as bad as it could possibly be."[9]

Manager Turin of the Advertising Board foresightedly warned appliance dealers to seek priorities for the area from the manufacturers. Already customers had some difficulty in finding the right kind of electric refrigerator or stove. If manufacturers were to put local dealers on a quota based on previous sales, he pointed out, Norfolk would receive far less than its rightful share. "If Norfolk is negative in the national manufacturer's viewpoint," he said, "then the entire community will be negative, and it might result in adverse comment about our city. Secondly, the national defense workers should be given every comfort and convenience to keep their morale up. We want to keep the business volume up too."[10]

There even seemed to be a shortage of daylight. In the spring of 1941 Admiral Taussig had urged Norfolk to adopt daylight saving time, unheard of in the state since World War I. Mayor Wood's response was: "I have always opposed daylight saving law and always will. It does no good. Ships sail by the sun, by God Almighty's time, and I'm not in favor of changing it."[11] When the subject was again brought up in city council, the 75-year-old mayor commented: "There's nothing in the law to keep people from getting up at six, five, or four o'clock, or not going to bed at all if they don't want to. A lot of them don't, anyway."[12]

A more general reason for opposing the daylight saving inovation was the confusion which would result from action by individual communities. The Hampton Roads Regional Defense Council attempted to avoid this by urging President Roosevelt

[8] *V-P*, July 2, 1941, p. 22.
[9] *V-P*, September 23, 1941, p. 18.
[10] *V-P*, September 21, 1941, Part I, p. 11.
[11] *V-P*, April 2, 1941, p. 20.
[12] *V-P*, May 14, 1941, p. 9.

to proclaim daylight saving over the nation.[13] Governor Price was also requested to order the time shift for the state, but he procrastinated on the grounds that he had no legal authority for the proclamation.[14]

At length the Governor yielded so far as to ask, rather than order, the state to go on daylight saving time. Norfolk's city council promptly cooperated by voting the city clocks ahead, with even Mayor Wood's approval.[15] Confusion was not entirely eliminated, however, as Norfolk decided to change its clocks at two o'clock Sunday morning, August 10, while Portsmouth and the rest of the state did not reset their timepieces until Sunday midnight. Ferry travelers that Sunday reached Portsmouth fifty minutes before they left Norfolk, and even on Monday the time was still uncertain. Many a businessman missed his breakfast because his maid had forgotten about the new time. Mayor Wood was twenty minutes late for his appointment with the new Navy Yard commandant, Admiral Felix X. Gygax, but he denied that his failure to reset his watch had been intentional.[16]

Admiral Simons made an effort to persuade the city to keep its clocks fast after September, asserting that daylight saving increased efficiency 25 to 50 per cent. "Naturally," he complained, "if the community adopts the old time as of midnight on September 28, we shall have to follow suit, but I feel that it is scarcely a step forward when we are bending every effort to increase our productive capacity for defense."[17] Nevertheless, the Navy was forced to take this step in the wrong direction. On Sunday, September 28, Norfolk returned to standard time—22 hours ahead of Portsmouth.[18]

The shortage that caused the most talk and the least inconvenience was the oft-proclaimed lack of gasoline. As early as June it was predicted by the *Ledger-Dispatch:*

Recently the possibility of a gasoline rationing plan for the mid-Atlantic seaboard was discussed in these columns. Such a development

[13] *V-P*, June 5, 1941, p. 22.
[14] Schlegel, *Virginia on Guard*, p. 28. The Governor may also have been influenced by the opposition of all rural Virginia to the measure.
[15] *V-P*, August 7, 1941, p. 20.
[16] *V-P*, August 12, 1941, p. 18.
[17] *V-P*, September 21, 1941, Part II, p. 1.
[18] *V-P*, September 27, 1941, p. 16.

has now become a distinct probability. The requisitioning by the government of a number of tankers operated by the oil companies threatens to cut down the supply of oil to this section of the United States. The transfer of the tankers to the government for use in aiding the British is likely to continue. And unless pipe lines from the oil fields can be laid quickly to the section of the East which has been largely supplied with fuel oil and gasoline by tankers, a gasoline rationing plan is regarded by the authorities as inevitable. The motor car owner, who has always looked upon the supply of gasoline as virtually inexhaustible, may find himself face to face pretty soon with a government restriction on the use of his car for pleasure purposes. It is well to be prepared to face this issue.[19]

By July it seemed as if the issue was to be faced squarely. One hundred American tankers were to be transferred to Britain, and Secretary of the Interior Harold Ickes in his extra-curricular capacity as Defense Petroleum Coordinator was clamoring for a reduction in the use of gasoline, first by 20 per cent, next by 25 per cent, then by 33⅓ per cent. Governor Price issued an appeal to save gasoline and ordered the State police to stop all speeding motorists. Norfolk's Retail Merchants Association co-operated by asking the stores to request their customers to carry small packages and save the gasoline that would have been used by the delivery trucks.[20]

To curtail sales, Coordinator Ickes ordered all gas stations on the East Coast to close for twelve hours each day. Although the order could not be legally enforced, most service station owners welcomed the compulsory holiday. In Norfolk when the Ickes-imposed curfew went into effect at seven on Sunday night, August 3, only one filling station remained open, to the indignation of all his competitors.[21] Restriction of hours was followed by informal rationing of sales. At Ickes' request the Office of Price Administration and Civilian Supply ordered deliveries to all stations reduced by 10 per cent. The dealers were then expected to reduce their sales to non-essential users by a corresponding amount.[22]

A few dealers tried to carry out the reduction in sales by setting

[19] L-D, June 5, 1941, p. 10.
[20] Schlegel, Virginia on Guard, pp. 27–28; V-P, July 22, 1941, pp. 6, 18.
[21] V-P, August 4, 1941, p. 14.
[22] V-P, August 16, 1941, p. 1.

up a daily quota and closing when that was sold. Still, storage tanks in Norfolk were full, deliveries continued to come in regularly, and distributors did not take their instructions from Washington too literally.[23] Even though business was not actually falling off, however, the much-publicized shortage offered a not-to-be-neglected excuse for raising prices.

Just ten days after the restriction on sales was announced, most Norfolk stations raised their prices a cent a gallon. Since they were going to sell fewer gallons, they explained, they would have to make a larger profit on each gallon, although the operators of some filling stations pointed out that all the stations were getting enough gas. About sixty of the gasoline dealers held a meeting and decided to stick by their price boost, keeping gas at 21.3 cents a gallon, and also voted to stop giving the customary discount to trucks and other commercial vehicles.[24]

This firm front was subject to assault from all directions. The chief of the Office of Price Administration and Civilian Supply, Leon Henderson, wired Mayor Wood that the maximum fair retail price in Norfolk should be only 19.75 cents. Colonel Borland released the telegram and declared that he did not want Norfolk citizens to allow anyone to take advantage of them. Gasoline distributors called the price-boost "unnecessary and unjustified," and incidentally revealed that the local stations had raised their profit margin a half-cent not long before.[25]

Nothing could shake the gas dealers from their determination to get their share of the defense dollars. OPACS tried again in October, pointing out in a letter to Mayor Wood that Norfolk's average price was a cent and a half above the maximum price, the highest in forty cities. Moreover, with a promised increase of deliveries in October, there was now even less excuse for the price boost. There was nothing the city could do, however, said the mayor helplessly, except hope for cooperation.[26] One distributor explained that the stations would not actually be getting more gas in October, even though the October quotas were higher than

[23] V-P, August 22, 1941, Part II, p. 12; August 28, 1941, p. 24.
[24] V-P, August 26, 1941, p. 18; August 29, 1941, Part I, p. 16.
[25] V-P, September 6, 1941, pp. 16, 9. Retailers bought gasoline for 15.75 cents, including tax. The normal four-cent margin had made the price 19.75 cents. The retailers had increased this profit to four and a half cents in the fall of 1940, and were now making it five and a half cents.
[26] V-P, October 10, 1941, Part I, p. 14.

those in September. The new order on gasoline distribution had
teeth in it, he said, and the October quotas were only 56.5 per
cent of actual sales in September. One dealer asserted that the
stations would be sold out for the month by October 20.[27]
Filling stations fortunately did not have to pay the penalty for
their refusal to observe quotas. On October 22, the shortage scare
vanished as suddenly as a Halloween spook. Ickes lifted all restrictions, and customers waited for the price of gas to drop
back to normal.[28] The service station men, however, decided not
to give up the benefits that went with the late shortage. They
formed an association which agreed to retain the 12-hour day
and to set "prices which will return a reasonable profit and not
gouge the consumer."[29]

Gasoline was not the only commodity rising in price, although
other increases were not such obvious local profiteering. Milk
producers and distributors, having already upped milk from fifteen
to sixteen cents a quart, applied to the State Milk Commission
for another increase. Local dairymen had boosted their normal
production by 45 per cent, to meet the expanded demand, and
this increase had been accompanied by rising production costs.
They complained of the "trifling nature" of the workers they were
able to get, even with a 28 per cent wage increase recently granted.
A sympathetic State Milk Commission listened to the complaints
of the milkmen and granted half of their requested increase,
raising the price to eighteen cents a quart.[30]

The inflation-evader could not shift to beer, for 10-cent beer
was already up to twelve or fifteen cents, depending upon where
you bought it, while 15-cent beer cost either seventeen or twenty
cents, even though one distributor insisted that twelve and fifteen
cents was enough for these respective qualities.[30a] Food had been
edging its way upward for several months, and breakfasts at the
drug-store counter jumped a nickel in August, making two eggs,
toast, and coffee cost twenty cents.

Chairman Bottom asked the Hampton Roads Regional De-

[27] *V-P*, October 11, 1941, p. 16.
[28] *V-P*, October 23, 1941, p. 1.
[29] *V-P*, November 26, 1941, p. 8.
[30] *V-P*, October 9, 1941, p. 22; October 30, 1941, p. 22; November 8, 1941, p.
16. Already two to four thousand gallons of milk were being brought into the
area daily from as far away as Pennsylvania.
[30a] *V-P*, August 22, 1941, Part II, p. 12.

fense Council to look into the rising cost of living and in September received a report which showed that in food, rent, and other items Norfolk was far higher than Richmond. For the last four years Norfolk's living costs had been below average, now they were above. In the past year bread had risen from 8.6 to 9.2 cents a pound loaf; bacon from 26.2 to 35.2 cents; butter from 35.9 to 44.7 cents; and sugar from five to six cents.[31] In the barber shops shaves were raised to 35 cents with the formula explanation: "Increased costs of supplies and the taxes imposed on materials necessitated the increase."[31a] A survey made by *Business Week* revealed that the local cost of living was up 11.5 per cent since September 1, 1939, sharpest increase of any of 33 cities surveyed. Richmond's increase in the same time had been 7.5 per cent, exactly the national average. This did not mean, of course, that Norfolk's cost of living was the highest in the country, since the city had started from a lower level.[32]

Hidden aspects of inflation were immeasurable changes in quality and service. Only the strong-stomached defense worker could survive daily meals in some of the restaurants. One girl after trying out most of the Tidewater eating-spots wrote of her troubles:

Invariably, the peas are canned, the stewed tomatoes are canned, the spinach is canned, the butter beans are cooked to a watery, mashy death; the snap beans to a dull, leathery, greenish brown. The corn is canned, seldom on the cob. The peaches—and this right in the middle of the summer—were canned; the pineapple canned. The fruit for sundaes and sodas at the soda fountains is canned. Where in Norfolk is there a fresh peach sundae? . . .

Convenient to many vegetable and fruit-growing centers, prices should not be as high for vegetables and fruits as they are here. We are afraid we are inclined to believe that, as is probably the case elsewhere in the country, those who can are making hay while the sun shines. A restaurant, no matter how bad its food, how ill kept its tables, how dilettante or hectic its service, how shoddy its walls and floors and front, can do a land-office business here at the moment, and will for the duration, simply because there is always a line of defense workers, soldiers, sailors waiting for a table.

[31] *V-P*, September 23, 1941, p. 18.
[31a] *V-P*, November 1, 1941, p. 18.
[32] *V-P* November 23, 1941, Part II, p. 1.

Young, overworked waiters and waitresses, indifferent or else poorly trained originally in neatness and cleanliness, seem to be the localities' standard or lack of it. With their often bad-smelling, damp cleansing cloths pushing crumbs and refuse from the tables to the already slippery floors, there is about many of the restaurants the atmosphere of a backwoods village eatery—of "hick" places that have grown up overnight—and of places where the regular chefs, waiters, bus boys have all gone away to the wars, leaving behind the younger brothers and sisters of the town to cope with the terrifying inrush of hungry and impatient strangers.

It is either eat in these places or starve.[33]

This was all part of the cost of war, for the Tidewater had already given up the weasel word, "defense." Norfolk had supported lend-lease in the spring with the full knowledge that "all aid short of war" meant "all aid whether or not it means war." When the need for convoying goods to Britain became urgent, the *Ledger-Dispatch* stated without hesitation:

We must move these supplies to Britain—supplies of planes and guns and ammunition with which the British can carry the fight to Germany now, and supplies of weapons and of foodstuffs and other war materials which could be laid up against the time of dire need when the climactic struggle for England comes. We must move these supplies even if it becomes necessary to employ the American Navy to guarantee them a safe passage—and even if the employment of this force results in carrying us into the "shooting" phase of a war in which we have for all practical purposes been involved almost from its beginning. The time for convoy is here.[34]

When the first shots in the undeclared war were fired in the far-off North Atlantic, the *Virginian-Pilot* calmly dismissed all quibbling as to whether the attack on the *U. S. S. Greer* was the result of German or American aggression. It said plainly:

It would be a mistake of the first order to believe that the *Greer* incident is an isolated affair to be settled by settling the question of original aggression and exchanging suitable explanations or apologies. It is an incident of a German-American tension which is bound to grow

[33] Louise White, "A Vegetarian Starves in Tidewater Virginia," *V-P*, September 14, 1941, Part IV, p. 4.
[34] *L-D*, June 25, 1941, p. 6.

worse before it grows better, because it is a tension growing out of an American aid-to-Britain program which is steadily becoming a greater menace to Germany's war effort, and which, soon or late, Germany must strike at openly and without any logic-chopping over the minor question of which started shooting first in any particular episode of a continuing and relentless movement.

It is not the *Greer* incident that has moved us closer to a shooting war with Germany, but the gathering momentum of the British-aid program which is its background.[35]

Six weeks later Norfolk suffered its first casualty in the unadmitted war at sea. A telegraph boy knocked on the door of 370 Hamilton Avenue and delivered to Elsie Mae Frontakowski the first fateful telegram:

The Navy Department regrets having to inform you that your husband, Leonard Frontakowsky, boatswain's mate, first class, U. S. Navy, is in a critical condition as the result of the torpedoing of the *U. S. S. Kearny.* . . .

C. W. Nimitz
Chief of the Bureau of Navigation[36]

The *Virginian-Pilot* again commented with sane realism:

If we are honest we will accept the torpedoing of the *Kearny* for what it is—an act of war in an undeclared sea war which Germany precipitated with the attack on the *Greer* and which the President's "shoot on sight" order of September 11 accepted as reality. It is hardly ground for a war declaration. But it is emphatic reason for redoubling our efforts to wipe the Nazi raiders, both surface and undersea, from those waters which, as the President has said, are vital to our defense.[37]

The first damage to an American warship was followed inevitably by the first sinking. The loss of the *Reuben James* on October 30 was a real blow to Norfolk, for both the destroyer and its commander, Lieutenant Commander H. L. Edwards, had been well known in Norfolk, and boys from Berkley and Ocean View were in its crew. Nevertheless, compassion did not flame into futile anger. Both Norfolk papers accepted the fact with their

[35] *V-P*, September 7, 1941, Part I, p. 10.
[36] *V-P*, October 20, 1941, p. 1.
[37] *V-P*, October 18, 1941, p. 4.

wonted calm. The *Ledger-Dispatch* declared: ". . . there is nothing . new about the sinking of the *Reuben James*. The act is merely cumulative; it drives us a bit closer to open war."[38] The *Virginian-Pilot* was even franker, speaking of an "open and undisguised war conducted by Germany against the United States, itself resulting from an American policy of delivering war materials to Germany's enemy and ordering the United States Navy to protect this transportation with fire if necessary."[39]

With its eyes focused on the North Atlantic, it was natural for Norfolk to prepare itself against reprisals which might be expected without warning at any time. By the summer of 1941 the emphasis of the Regional Defense Council had begun to shift slowly towards preparation for defense against enemy attack, especially since Hampton Roads appeared to be the most inviting target for any long-range planes Hitler might have.

The first step necessary was a strengthening and reorganization of the council itself. In July it rid itself of the paper organization provided for it by the Governor's advisory committee. The large, unwieldy council, representing all the outlying districts, was unofficially discarded. Full powers were lodged in the hands of a compact executive committee, composed of the officials of the Hampton Roads cities, representatives of the Army, the Navy and the Newport News Shipbuilding Company, and several other citizens.[40]

The first act of the new committee was to recommend a greatly expanded budget. Weldon T. Ellis, Jr., chief of the administrative planning section, State Bureau of the Budget, temporarily assigned to the council by the Governor, was appointed to draw up a statement of needs, along with J. C. Biggins, Newport News city manager. Two weeks later the executive committee endorsed an expanded program with a $51,420 budget, two-thirds to be contributed by the State, the rest by the localities.[41] Governor Price accepted the new budget in August and called upon the counties and cities assigned to the Hampton Roads Council to

[38] *V-P*, November 1, 1941, p. 1; November 5, 1941, p. 1; *L-D*, November 1, 1941, p. 6.
[39] *V-P*, November 1, 1941, p. 6.
[40] *L-D*, July 12, 1941, p. 2.
[41] *L-D*, July 12, 1941, p. 2; *V-P*, July 26, 1941, p. 16.

contribute $17,140, apportioned on a per capita basis. Norfolk's share of the expense was $4,615.88.[42]

With this financial transfusion in its veins, the Defense Council took on new life. The hapless executive officer, who had found the hectic problems of Hampton Roads far more complicated than laying out the quiet streets of Montclair, was shunted off as chief of the planning section.[43] As the new executive director, the council selected Dr. William T. Hodges, ex-dean of the Norfolk Division of the College of William and Mary.

The reinvigorated Defense Council began moving swiftly even before its popular new director took over on October 1. It endorsed a proposed survey for a Major Thoroughfare Plan to keep roads open for civilian as well as military traffic; it called for a housing survey; it approved the expansion of home nursing classes. Significantly, it recommended the establishment of a permanent registration office for civilian defense volunteers and called for coordination of planning for disaster.[44]

Preparations for defending the city against a possible sneak air raid were just beginning to get under way. To the Aircraft Warning Service, still waiting for some word from the Army, was to be added the Air Raid Warden Service, which was to be responsible for receiving warnings from the information center and passing the signals on to the public. Each community in addition was to have a director of disaster planning who would take charge of preparing his area for defense against actual attack. Although the general organization was clear enough as drawn up by the U. S. Office of Civilian Defense after a study of British experience, details were still unsettled and responsibilities still unapportioned. Moreover, what original clarity there was in the plan was muddied by its trip through the official channels of national headquarters to regional headquarters to state headquarters to local headquarters.

The resulting confusion soon entangled Norfolk's defense. On Friday, September 12, Chairman Bottom of the Hampton Roads

[42] *V-P*, August 22, 1941, Part I, p. 16. The new budget was to be effective as of July 1, 1941.

[43] Faure slipped quietly out of town for another position at the end of the year. *V-P*, November 27, 1941, p. 22.

[44] *V-P*, September 23, 1941, p. 18.

Council asked Richard M. Marshall, civic-minded insurance executive, whether he would become director of disaster planning for Norfolk. On the same day Marshall was appointed chief air raid warden for the Hampton Roads area by the state's chief air raid warden, Mayor Frank H. Wheeler of Clifton Forge.[45] The insurance man plunged into his new jobs with enthusiasm, even though he had yet only the vaguest idea what he was supposed to do.

Since an advance contingent of the Army company which was to set up the Norfolk information center had arrived in town that very day, he arranged a conference the next morning with the lieutenants in charge and City Manager Borland. He also called up Clifton Forge to get more exact information about his job, but discovered that Mayor Wheeler could tell him little more than that he was supposed to work in close cooperation with the Aircraft Warning Service in communicating air raid signals. Marshall therefore decided to help out the Signal Corps lieutenants, who had arrived with almost no information about the volunteer organization they were supposed to take over. Marshall remembered the women recruited in June, located the registration cards, set the lieutenants up in his office with a telephone, and let them go to work. He himself took part in the interviewing as the volunteers appeared, and prepared plans for their training.[46]

In the meantime, however, the Hampton Roads Defense Council asked Major Francis E. Turin to head a committee charged with recruiting additional volunteers for the Aircraft Warning Service.[47] This well-meant action succeeded only in beclouding the situation further. Jack Twohy had been placed in charge of getting information center recruits by State AWS Chief Elliott; Chief Air Raid Warden Marshall had taken over the responsibility under the mistaken assumption that this was part of his duties under his appointment from Mayor Wheeler; and now the Hampton Roads Council was handing the job over to a brand-new committee. Warden Marshall, interpreting the action as a re-

[45] Memorandum by Marshall, Civilian Defense: Histories file, NWHC records; *V-P*, September 13, 1941.

[46] Memoranda by Marshall in Civilian Defense: Civil Air Raid Warning and in Civilian Defense: Histories files, NWHC records.

[47] Weldon T. Ellis, Jr., to Turin, September 15, 1941, Turin, F. E.: Virginia Aircraft Warning Service file, NWHC records.

pudiation of his efforts, handed in his resignation to the Defense
Council and went off to Asheville on vacation.[48]

A wire from the Defense Council, however, served to bring
the sulking Achilles out of his North Carolina tent. The telegram
renewed the appointment as director of disaster plans for Norfolk,
which had never been formally accepted, and urged him to continue as chief air raid warden. Marshall promptly agreed and
returned on Monday, September 29, to go to work on plans for
the maneuvers scheduled to begin on October 9.

Meanwhile the Army had been moving rapidly to make up for
the lost summer. Training of the June volunteers got under way
by September 20 in the city council chamber in the old city hall,
while other Signal Corps men worked busily at installing the
equipment for the information center in the basement of the
Federal Building. Major Turin borrowed a battery of anti-aircraft searchlights from Fort Story and set them up in Plume Street
as an advertisement for his recruiting campaign. For two nights
their beams prowled about the sky while Signal Corps men stood
by to sign up the girls. Although not many new volunteers were
gained, there were enough left over from June to take care of the
impending maneuvers.[49]

Norfolk's new director of disaster planning discovered that his
job had been defined for him during his absence. The Hampton
Roads Council had worked out an organizational chart explaining
how the defenses should be prepared. Mayor Wheeler was attend-
ing conferences and reading directives to explain the job of the
chief air raid warden, who seemed to be stationed simultaneously
inside the information center and outside patrolling the streets.
Fortunately, the new Hampton Roads organization solved this
split personality problem by assigning the original duties of the
chief air raid warden to a group of "Liason (*sic*) Officers from
Office of Director of Disaster Plans," who were shortly to become
"Civil Air Raid Warning Officers." The chief air raid warden's
title was now transferred to a subordinate of the Director of
Disaster Plans, who was in charge of groups of zone and section
wardens.[50]

[48] Memoranda by Marshall in Civilian Defense: Civil Air Raid Warning and
in Civilian Defense: Histories files, NWHC records.

[49] *V-P*, September 21, 1941, Part II, p. 1, September 27, 1941, p. 6.

[50] Civilian Defense: October Maneuvers file, NWHC records.

Director Marshall set up an office in the Pender Building, talked with his friend, S. Harrell Ferebee, who had been carrying on preliminary work in his absence, and started to study the new chart. Within the week the chart had been filled out with the names of volunteers. He had six men lined up to serve as civil air raid warning officers and had appointed a central committee for preparing plans. Ferebee took over the position of chief air raid warden with its new duties, named zone wardens for each of the six zones into which the city had been divided, and told them to start recruiting section wardens. A specialist from the U. S. Office of Civilian Defense, who had studied England's air raid precautions, came to Norfolk to offer his advice.[51]

Disaster Director Marshall tested out the city's facilities for giving an authentic air raid alarm by sounding all the available sirens at once. At 11:30 A.M. on Thursday, October 2, sirens on fire trucks and police cars scattered around the city burst into simultaneous shrieks. Three times they unleashed a thirty-second blast, but no one paid any attention. Even Director Marshall, straining his ears in front of the Federal Building, found the sirens drowned in the rumbles of Granby Street. In disgust he said that five or six large sirens would be placed on top of downtown buildings, and by Monday one of the sirens was up on the roof of the Courthouse.[52] As a further reminder to the public, he arranged to have a demonstration air raid shelter erected on the Courthouse lawn.[53]

Further realism was lent the maneuvers when a squadron of new fast pursuit planes, Curtiss P-40's, arrived from the West Coast and set up a base at the Municipal Airport. The 74th Coast Artillery Regiment moved in from Camp Pendleton to take up field positions around Norfolk. Disaster Director Marshall called his planning committee together in its first meeting on Monday afternoon to test the city's newly-thrown-together defenses. He reminded the group that these "play" exercises should be taken seriously because only in this way could Norfolk prepare itself for actual attack.[54]

[51] Civilian Defense: October Maneuvers file, NWHC records; *V-P*, October 3, 1941.
[52] *V-P*, October 3, 1941, Part II, p. 1; October 7, 1941.
[53] Civilian Defense: October Maneuvers file, NWHC records.
[54] *V-P*, October 5, 1941, Part II, p. 1; October 9, 1941, p. 22.

On Thursday, October 9, the Army put its new system into operation. Observers climbed into their lookout posts at 6:00 A.M. to watch for groups of planes. In the post office basement the feminine volunteers put on their telephone headsets and prepared to shove their markers about the big board there. The civil air raid warning officer took charge of the communications panel where telephone operators prepared to flash lights in the warning centers set up throughout Tidewater Virginia. As the Army sent its planes up into the air, spotters passed the word along to the information center, and the warning that "enemy" aircraft were approaching went out over the CARW equipment.

In Director Marshall's temporary office in the Pender Building a warning yellow light flashed on. The telephone operator pushed a button, answering, "Norfolk, yellow," and then proceeded to call the two local radio stations and the State Police. A few minutes later a blue light came on, warning that "enemy" planes were only twelve minutes away. The radio stations interrupted their programs to make the announcement to the public, and the city sirens sounded, as loudly as they could, a warbling blast, indicating an impending raid. The blue was followed by a red, meaning that an attack could be expected momentarily, and then a flashing white gave the all clear, which was sounded by a sustained note on the sirens.

No response was expected from the public to any of these alarms, since they were merely intended to test the communications system; in fact, the radio stations broadcast only four of the seven alerts it received during the day. The volunteers who were on duty soon got adjusted to their new tasks, and the signals went through without a hitch. Director Marshall, keeping an interested eye on the information center, pointed out that that installation had not been given a fair test, since the "enemy" planes had all been sent up locally and had not flown over a definite course long enough to allow the spotters' reports to indicate their approach.[55] That had not been a serious handicap, however, since the information center knew in advance where and when the "enemy" planes were going.

The public was provided more of a show that night as search-

[55] *L-D*, October 10, 1941; Civilian Defense: October Maneuvers file, NWHC records.

light batteries stabbed the sky and trapped a pair of Flying Fortresses in their beams. A rescue squad trained by the Red Cross also put on a demonstration at Twelfth Street and Monticello Avenue where an incendiary bomb was imagined to have just missed the huge gas tanks nearby. The most realistic demonstration of air-raid conditions, however, came on the following night, according to Director Marshall's carefully laid plans. At 7:40 P.M. the flashing yellow in the CARW equipment in Marshall's office announced the start of the drill, and the alert was passed on to the radio stations and to the participating agencies. Five blocks of Dunmore Street in the vicinity of the Pender warehouse were blacked out, and at eight o'clock city firemen started a blaze on the warehouse rooftop to simulate an incendiary bomb. Communications received a test as the orders to fight this fire went out. A city fire truck raced to the scene, and the police arrived to rope off the area to hold back a crowd of curious onlookers who had followed the fire sirens. Trucks from the telephone and the power companies rushed in to repair any damages to utility lines. A group of Boy Scouts came out to act as messengers, and the Red Cross arrived with a first-aid squad and a canteen squad to serve coffee and doughnuts, which were not imaginary. The only hitch in the proceedings came over a mix-up in the orders to the V. P. F., who, instead of reporting at the Pender warehouse, patrolled the entire downtown area with their rifles. Their presence resulted in the false report of the dropping of a number of other imaginary bombs, which was printed in the morning paper before the error was discovered.[56]

Although the Army continued its exercises until the following Thursday, October 16, there were no further staged incidents. Civilian participation was confined to the Aircraft Warning Service and the operation of the civil air raid warning equipment. The girls at the information center felt as if they were practically in the Army. When Major General Herbert A. Dargue, commander of the First Air Force, walked into the center on an inspection trip, the Signal Corps lieutenants snapped to attention at the sight of his two bright stars. The volunteers, uncertain what to do, did their best to snap too, until the general told them to be at ease.

[56] *V-P*, October 11, 1941; *L-D*, October 11, 1941; Civilian Defense: October Maneuvers file, NWHC records.

If war were to come, it was said, they would, in fact, be taken into the Army with regular rank and pay; the nation's leading dress designers were already at work designing them a uniform.[57]

Meanwhile the Army's fighter planes flew away and the anti-aircraft guns disappeared. The CARW equipment in Marshall's office and in the other Tidewater communities was removed because it was too expensive to pay for the leased wires. About ninety of the information center volunteers were to be called back for further training in another six weeks or so. Director Marshall asked the members of his planning committee to remain on the job and stand by for further instructions.

Time passed, however, and civilian defense seemed to have been forgotten. Finally Virginia's Chief Air Raid Warden Wheeler showed up in town on Monday, November 24, to discuss the organizational plans used during the October maneuvers. He conferred with Disaster Planning Director Marshall and Chief Air Raid Warden Ferebee and their Portsmouth counterparts, J. Lawrence Smith and R. E. B. Stewart. The group promised to draw up an organizational plan based on their experience and submit it to the State Defense Council by December 1.[58]

Before anything could be done about this, a brand-new set of plans arrived from the U. S. Office of Civilian Defense. On Wednesday Colonel Clifton Lisle, regional director for the U. S. OCD, came to Norfolk to explain the program to the Hampton Roads Defense Council. There were to be two groups of services, one devoted to protection, the other to participation. Each community was to have a director of the protective services and a chief for volunteer participation, with an over-all coordinator. Volunteers were to be recruited immediately for all these services with priority for the moment going to the protective group. Most urgently needed were air raid wardens, auxiliary firemen, and auxiliary policemen.

The Defense Council at one promised to set up the registration office for volunteers which it had authorized in September. That night a conference was held with representatives of all the organizations which had taken part in the October maneuvers to per-

[57] *V-P*, October 12, 1941, Part II, p. 1.
[58] Hampton Roads Regional Defense Council file, VOCD records.

suade them to join in enlisting recruits for this new program.[59] By Friday the council's genial director, Doctor Hodges, was writing to the State Defense Council that he hoped to get the ground laid for the new plan during the coming week. A week later he wrote again that he was planning an important conference on the subject with Council Chairman Bottom on Monday afternoon, December 8. By then, he said, he expected to "be really ready to proceed."[60]

[59] *V-P*, November 27, 1941, p. 22. The air raid wardens already had their basic organization functioning, although many more volunteers were still needed.

[60] Hodges to J. H. Wyse, November 29, December 5, 1941, Hampton Roads Regional Defense Council file, VOCD records.

II

DECEMBER SUNDAY

IT had turned cold over night, and the chill air was a reminder that this was the first Sunday in December. Norfolkians sleepily stepped out into the bright wintry sunshine to bring in the paper on their doorsteps. "Roosevelt Sends Personal Plea To Mikado," the headlines said. "Direct Action Seen Last Move To Avert Open Break; Tokyo Is Now Mobilizing Vast Army." According to the story, the two Japanese envoys in Washington had failed. War, it seemed, might be only a matter of weeks. A disquieting article on "Japan's Tricks: Duplicity and Broken Pledges Mark All of Island Empire's Dealings" warned against possible treachery, while an editorial pointed out the danger of "Under-Estimating Japan."

On the other hand, a Democratic senator named Truman was going to demand a defense production czar to solve industrial troubles, and Secretary Knox said we already had the greatest Navy in the world. In any case, it was too pleasant a day to worry about trouble on the other side of the world, when there was already enough trouble on this side. Some Norfolkians got into their cars for a drive in the country to take advantage of the fine weather. Others went downtown to Granby Street where sailors were piling off the Naval Base trolleys to head for the new show at the Gaiety or to see the "Billy Rose Girls" in the Granby stage show, which sometimes threatened to outstrip the East Main Street attraction.

As usual, many persons simply stayed at home and after the comfort of a good dinner relaxed to the two o'clock dance music over WTAR. Then, as the program neared its end, the music was abruptly cut off. An excited voice began: "Stand by for a special news flash." Half-drowsing listeners, inured to war bulletins, wondered idly whether this was a Russian or a German claim of

victory. The voice went on: "The White House says that the
Japanese are attacking Pearl Harbor."

For moments radio listeners sat in stunned consternation, then
rushed to the telephone to call the newspaper offices to make
sure they had heard aright. The lone copy boy on duty in the
Virginian-Pilot newsroom gave confirmation of the news until
the telephones jammed in helpless confusion. Without waiting
for orders reporters headed at once for the office. Newsmen, but-
tonholing servicemen to get their opinions on the outbreak of
war, discovered that many of them had not yet heard the news.
One reporter called Colonel Borland to ask what action the city
planned to take in the emergency. The colonel, relaxing at home
with his radio turned off, was startled to learn what had happened.
In a few minutes he called back to announce that he had ordered
the immediate arrest of all alien Japanese in the city. Fifteen
minutes later he heard over his own radio a news flash from New
York, reporting that Norfolk was arresting its Japanese aliens.[1]

The Japanese round-up proceeded swiftly. At the suggestion
of Naval Intelligence, Police Captain Ted Miller had long before
been assigned to checking all Japanese in the Hampton Roads
area, and Police Headquarters had ready a file on the forty aliens
discovered in the district. Forty minutes after the police radio
had broadcast the names and addresses of the fourteen living in
Norfolk, patrol cars had them all at headquarters. Other Hampton Roads communities followed Norfolk's lead in gathering in
their Japanese that afternoon.[2]

The Army immediately ordered all soldiers back to their posts.
The Navy went under wartime security; the Marine sentries at
the entrances to the Naval Base suddenly became strict, and an
officer's wife who had driven up without her pass was firmly
turned back at the gate in spite of all her arguments. Flotilla No.
10 of the Coast Guard Reserve was called to active duty as a
24-hour-a-day harbor patrol. The V. P. F. was put on the alert,
and the city police posted guards at all the utility centers. Dean
Hodges promised that the Regional Defense Council would speed
up its plans for registering civilian defense volunteers.[3]

[1] *V-P*, December 6, 1942, **Part II, pp. 1, 16.**
[2] *V-P*, December 8, 1941.
[3] *V-P*, December 8, 1941.

As the December dusk closed in over Norfolk late on Sunday afternoon, private citizens still twisted radio dials, listening to streams of rumor and opinion, mingled with an occasional fact. Avid for details, they overwhelmed the newsboys who started selling the *Virginian-Pilot* extra at six o'clock. Eager customers snatched up the copies as fast as the boys could carry them out. Drivers passing the newspaper building slammed their cars to a stop and called out for copies. Motorists behind them honked their horns impatiently, then bought copies and read too.[4]

Out of the flood of news there slowly emerged some comprehension of the disaster at Pearl Harbor, and the first stunned shock gave way to other feelings. There was worry for the safety of friends and relatives in Honolulu. There was shame that the Navy had been caught so flat-footed. There was anger that the attack had come with such treacherous suddenness. There was unity, pledged by the spokesman of the small group of America Firsters in the city. Above all, there was determination that this fight would be fought to the end, regardless of what it might cost the people of Norfolk.

On Monday morning the civilian defense organization prepared to go into action. Disaster Planner Marshall received a telegram from Chief Air Raid Warden Wheeler, notifying him that the instruments in the civil air raid warning center set up in the Federal Building had been reconnected and requesting him to recruit volunteers to man the center on a 24-hour schedule.[5] At the meeting of the Regional Defense Council that day Marshall was named coordinator of Civilian Defense for Norfolk, as part of the reorganization recommended several weeks earlier. The American Legion and the Association of Commerce pledged their cooperation for defense, and Colonel Borland promised the city's official aid in all plans for defense work. The Defense Council set December 30 as the registration day for all volunteers in order to have time to print cards and plan procedures. The registration was to be held in the polling places with the aid of the teachers who had cooperated in registering for the draft. Meanwhile, Fire Chief E. J. Cannon appealed for the immediate enlistment of auxiliary

[4] *V-P*, December 8, 1941.
[5] Memo in Civilian Defense: Hampton Roads Regional Defense Council file, NWHC records.

firemen, asking for all the volunteers he could get and promising them speedy training. Chief Air Raid Warden Ferebee called a meeting of all air raid wardens for Wednesday night at the John Marshall School to enlist more wardens and to organize a training school.[6]

The *Ledger-Dispatch* stressed the city's changed outlook:

Until last Sunday the general public did not consider with full seriousness the necessity for an all-out civilian defense organization in this area. Now the public is beginning to know the danger which confronts us. There is no longer anything perfunctory about the formation of civilian defense units. It is serious business and it becomes the duty of every person to co-operate to the limit of his ability.

The air-raid warning service, the organization of which has dragged along month by month, now becomes a matter of grave importance. The mock air raids which were held in this vicinity some weeks ago gave a sketchy outline of the work that must be done. The time for action has arrived.

A call has been issued for volunteer firefighters to augment the regular force of the Fire Department. This volunteer service contributed tremendously to saving London and other British cities from far graver disaster than that which befell them when the German air squadrons roared above them to send down death and destruction. There is the most urgent need for full public co-operation with the civilian defense authorities in working out a plan to safeguard this area, as far as it is possible to do so, from the effects of attacks which it is no longer inconceivable can be launched against it. . . .

This civilian service, which must be organized as closely and as completely as possible, recognizes no social, racial, or other lines. It is a service which demands all the sacrifice and hard work and self denial on the part of all the public that is necessary to make it wholly effective. The time has come to consider this matter with deadly seriousness and grim purpose.[7]

On Tuesday the Army threw a protective wall of antiaircraft batteries around the city. The Aircraft Warning Service was ordered back into operation, and the skeleton staff of the spotters recruited in June attempted to keep their observation posts open all day and all night. A hasty effort was made to summon the women volunteers for the information center, but the only ones

[6] *V-P*, December 9, 1941, pp. 22, 7.
[7] *L-D*, December 10, 1941, p. 6.

who had been kept available were those taking the special training course started after the maneuvers. The campaign to enlist new recruits was once more placed in the hands of John Twohy II who had started the program off in June. Meanwhile, the few who were on hand attempted to keep the center going 24 hours a day.[8] In its crowded quarters in the basement of the post office building the Army moved over to make room for Coordinator Marshall, who hired a secretary and set up a full-time office with borrowed furniture and supplies.[9]

The same day the new city coordinator went on the air to tell the curious public that

this city may be attacked by German airplanes any night now. We naturally don't know when that attack will take place, or whether it will take place at all. We are simply making full preparations to defend your homes and your lives as far as possible from the effects of airplane bombing.[10]

He gave grim instructions: "If there are several members of the family, you should have them lie on the floor in different rooms so that if one room is hit by a fire bomb, the other members of the family will be able to do rescue work. . . . Don't throw water on the bomb, for, if you do, it will explode and probably kill you."

Wednesday brought 75 new women volunteers at the information center, and the American Legion Auxiliary agreed to take over the duty of staffing the Norfolk warning center which relayed air raid signals to other Tidewater communities and the military installations in the area. Colored organizations formed the Norfolk Negro Council for Defense. Five hundred persons turned out for the air raid wardens meeting at John Marshall School, and 200 of them signed up for training.[11]

On Thursday Coordinator Marshall announced the appointment of another aide, J. Branham Cooke, as chief civilian air raid warning officer. His duty was to supervise the regional warning center, which passed the news of impending air raids received from

[8] V-P, December 10, 1941.
[9] Memo in Civilian Defense: Hampton Roads Regional Defense Council file, NWHC records.
[10] V-P, December 10, 1941, p. 22.
[11] V-P, December 11, 1941, pp. 24, 13.

the information center along to the district warning centers in other Virginia cities. Cooke was at once able to announce the staff which would keep the center open on a 24-hour schedule. Telephone calls overwhelmed the Regional Defense Council offices with inquiries about whether there would be a blackout and what should be done if there was one. Army convoys moved in and out of the city, the Navy announced that the Chesapeake Capes had been mined, and the sale of automobile tires was banned on an order from Washington.[12]

On Friday newspapers printed a full page of instructions of what to do in case of an air raid, the first time the public had seen these details. Orders from the Governor in Richmond called the First Battalion of the V. P. F. out to guard the toll-free bridge across the Elizabeth River, although the presence of the sentries there was an official secret. Fortunately, the uniform mackinaws had just arrived, as the only official uniform up to now had been shirt and trousers. John Twohy II appealed to all the women who had taken part in the October maneuvers to come out and work at the information center, "no matter what sacrifice they have to make in order to keep this center operating efficiently now." That night sirens shrieked at the Navy Yard and the Naval Base when ships sighted an unidentified dirigible off the coast. Lights went out on the Navy reservations, and civilians started rumors that enemy planes had been sighted.[13]

That very evening city and defense officials agreed that the emergency demanded an immediate test of the protective organiaztion. A blackout was called for the following night, in spite of the confusion it would cause among Saturday night Christmas shoppers. At 1:15 Saturday afternoon radio stations broadcast the news of the lights-out order. Irate merchants called up Coordinator Marshall and demanded to know why he had chosen Saturday night out of all the possible nights of the week, but he replied, "The Germans and the Japanese won't let us know when they are coming."

Surprised citizens tried to find out what they were supposed to do during a blackout or else guessed at what would be adequate protection. Crowds surrounded every flashlight counter in the

[12] *V-P*, December 12, 1941, Part I, pp. 1, 17; Part II, p. 18.
[13] *V-P*, December 13, 1941, p. 18.

city in the search for emergency lighting, and, while they were waiting for service, debated the relative merits of the vest-pocket flash over the large searchlight type. Radio Station WTAR enthusiastically bought both black enamel and black oilcloth, and the entire staff went to work covering every one of its twenty windows for the duration. The *Virginian-Pilot* newsroom was satisfied merely to tack up black paper. One restaurant had the clever idea of buying black water-color paint which could be used to cover up the windows at night and, it was hoped, could be easily washed off the next day.

As dusk fell around five o'clock Saturday night, the city assumed a satisfactory gloom. Street lights remained off. Most stores shut up entirely, while others blacked out successfully. Granby Street's "white way" was obscured in Stygian darkness relieved only by the dimmed headlights of passing automobiles, which proved to be entirely too bright. Only a few merchants refused the voluntary cooperation asked of them, and in at least one case the violation was unintentional. A Freemason Street shopkeeper turned off all his lights and went home, forgetful of the time clock which promptly lit up his show windows. Passersby immediately noticing this glaring violation, took it upon themselves to summon the merchant to come down and turn off his lights.

Defense officials were highly pleased with the results of the test. A general darkness reigned east of the Elizabeth River, bringing Portsmouth's bright lights into brilliant contrast from the air, and Norfolk for once admitted that it had been outshone by its sister city. The only accident occurred when a Negro fell overboard at the Southgate Terminals, but the policemen who fished him out said his unsteady footing was not entirely caused by the lack of light.

Colonel Borland, Coordinator Marshall, Assistant Coordinator J. H. Wood, and Chief Air Raid Warden Ferebee, comprising the general staff of Norfolk's Civilian Defense, agreed that there had been a few flaws. One of the worst was the eagerness with which people had called police headquarters for information, blocking the lines and preventing the transmission of emergency calls. Once again citizens were reminded that they must use the telephone only for emergencies during blackouts. Many persons had unwittingly let their lights shine out by relying on such inadequate protection as ordinary household shades. Only special blackout curtains would serve, they were reminded. It was also revealed, to no one's surprise, that the Civilian Defense organization was not yet functioning effectively.[14]

On Monday morning, December 15, a conference was held in Admiral Simons' office at the Naval Base to discuss defense problems. It was decided to educate the public further by a series of daily radio talks. Although local blackouts already scheduled in Hampton Roads communities would be held, all future drills were to be called through the Regional Defense Council. Actual air raids would be announced by the Army Interceptor Command, operating through the chain already set up, running from aircraft spotter to information center to J. Branham Cooke's civilian air raid warning center to district warning centers to local control centers. Colonel Borland handed over to the city attorney for study a model blackout ordinance prepared by the League of Virginia Municipalities.[15]

On Tuesday the new agreement on blackouts was tossed out the window by the arrival of an officer from the staff of Brigadier General John C. McDonnell, head of the First Interceptor Command at Mitchel Field, New York. Local communities, it was announced, could hold blackouts if their requests went through proper channels. The procedure was from the defense coordinator to the Hampton Roads Council to the regional commander at the information center to General McDonnell, who would do the approving. Army and Navy posts, however, could blackout at their own pleasure.

The city council devoted its Tuesday meeting to defense measures. It appropriated funds to buy and install eight large sirens. It gave retroactive approval to Colonel Borland's action in turning over city property for the use of the Army anti-aircraft regiments guarding the city and gave blanket authorization for such measures in the future. It also adopted the model blackout ordinance, empowering the city manager to make and enforce any necessary rules and regulations.

The keen interest that had developed in Civilian Defense was

[14] *V-P*, December 14, 1941, Part II, pp. 1, 7.
[15] *V-P*, December 16, 1941, p. 22.

illustrated by the unexpected attendance at the meeting called by the Hampton Roads Regional Defense Council. Members who had hitherto accepted their duties as purely honorary began arriving in such numbers that the council had to move into larger quarters. About 150 persons altogether heard Chairman Bottom urge the outlying counties to appoint local coordinators, as localities around Hampton Roads had already done.

On the same day came a warning to Norfolk that it had indeed seen only the beginning of the boom. Congressman Harris announced in Washington that the President had just signed a bill appropriating another $16,000,000 for construction in the Norfolk area. Included were $4,875,000 for building quarters in the Navy Yard for crews of ships under repair and $3,850,000 to expand the receiving station at the Naval Base, so that it could take care of 5,500 more men.[16]

The Navy moved vigorously to protect its men from casualties at home. The appearance of six sailors at St. Vincent's Hospital on Thursday night, December 18, with tear-gas injuries brought to a head a situation that had been growing steadily worse. One of the "social clubs" operating in the county had adopted its own methods of preserving order. G. C. Shackleford, owner of the unpretentious little County Club, on Cottage Toll Road, better known as "Shack's Place," had possessed himself of a small arsenal of blackjacks and tear-gas weapons, which he and his employees used to quiet unruly sailors, or even those who might possibly get unruly.[17]

The injuries this time were so serious—one sailor was threatened with permanent impairment of his vision—that the Navy acted at once. The next night a large contingent of naval officers and members of the shore patrol got hold of several law-enforcement officers and swore out search warrants. The angry sailors surrounded the County Club and did not hesitate to use their axes when doors failed to open promptly.[18] Two months earlier "Shack's Place" had weathered a raid by A. B. C. agents without any serious interruption to business, but this time it was different. "Shack" was sentenced to a year in jail, and half a dozen of his

---

[16] *V-P*, December 17, 1941, pp. 22, 13.
[17] *V-P*, December 19, 1941, Part II, pp. 18, 1.
[18] *V-P*, December 21, 1941, Part II, p. 1.

employees went along with him for shorter terms.[19] The Norfolk County Circuit Court, in fact, was stung into action on the injunctions which had been pending before it for two months. All five of the "clubs" raided in October were handed restraining orders forbidding them to handle alcoholic beverages for the next sixty days.[20]

Progress meanwhile was being made on the Civilian Defense organization. A meeting of all city defense leaders on Thursday, December 18, made a little clearer the administrative pattern that was emerging. Coordinator Marshall had named Campbell Arnoux, manager of WTAR, and E. E. Bishop, manager of WGH, to represent the communication and transportation section; Clarence Robertson was directing industrial protection, and Louis Paret, demolition and salvage programs. T. David Fitzgibbon was chief of air raid shelters. S. H. Ferebee reported on the progress of the air raid wardens, and Police Chief Woods and Fire Chief Cannon stated that their respective auxiliaries were under training. Dr. A. B. Hodges, director of emergency medical services, announced that every doctor in the city had placed himself on call, and explained plans for organizing base hospitals and casualty stations in case of air attack. Dr. A. V. Crosby, chairman of the Norfolk Red Cross Chapter, showed how his organization's disaster program fitted into the emergency medical services.[21]

Coordinator Marshall assured Christmas shoppers that there would be no more practice blackouts until after the holidays, but the Army warned that there was to be no holiday for the Virginia Aircraft Warning Service. On the contrary, General McDonnell, head of the First Interceptor Command, sent instructions calling for "especial vigilance."[22] The importance of the information center was emphasized by the news that all the volunteers working there would have to be photographed and fingerprinted for identification purposes.[23]

The spirit of this first wartime Christmas in 24 years warmed

[19] *V-P*, December 25, 1941, Part II, p. 10. A jury subsequently reduced Shack's term to six months.
[20] *V-P*, December 31, 1941, p. 18.
[21] *V-P*, December 19, 1941, Part II, p. 18.
[22] *V-P*, December 21, 1941, Part II, p. 1.
[23] *V-P*, December 22, 1941, p. 16.

Norfolk's heart. Although there was no peace on earth, there was good will to servicemen. Sailors were amazed that Norfolk could be so kind and generous. Contributors were giving freely to the $90,000 Red Cross War Fund; almost one-third had been privately subscribed before the public campaign opened.[24] Two anonymous Methodist donors provided a free Christmas dinner for 100 sailors in the church recreation hall.[25] Security Storage had a magnificent Christmas party with roast wild goose and Virginia ham and "beverages of the season," to which the ticket of admission was two servicemen. Veteran Marines said they had never run across anything like this hospitality in all their experiences.[26]

Most important of all, the people of Norfolk opened up their homes. An announcement over the radio that the Navy Y had several servicemen who would like to spend Christmas in someone's home brought a response which overwhelmed Carol Tidball, women's activities secretary at the Y. Hundreds asked for sailor guests; one couple specified Southerners, so that the Civil War would not mar the Christmas spirit. So great was the demand that there were not enough servicemen to go around. Two prospective hosts, indeed, almost came to blows over the last two British sailors.[27] The bombs falling on Pearl Harbor seemed to have blown up the old Norfolk attitude toward the Navy.

[24] *V-P*, December 25, 1941, Part I, p. 3.
[25] *V-P*, December 25, 1941, Part I, p. 5.
[26] *V-P*, December 25, 1941, Part II, p. 10.
[27] *V-P*, December 27, 1941, p. 16.

12

CHANGING OF THE GUARD

As soon as the Christmas shopping season was over, Norfolk prepared for its second blackout of the month. This one, called by the Hampton Roads Defense Council, was to cover the entire region from Accomac to Emporia. Better results were looked for in Norfolk, since faults discovered in the snap drill of December 13 were being corrected. There was a definite time set for the blackout so that everyone could know when he was supposed to turn his lights out. Chief Air Warden Ferebee had managed to build up his staff so that there would be more wardens patrolling the streets, and there was now a city ordinance to back them up if anyone tried to resist their authority. Coordinator Marshall declared: "Our aim is to black this city out as black as ink. There will be no switches pulled, but air raid wardens will check to see that lights go out."[1]

On the Monday after Christmas at 8:15 P.M. all the sirens in the city burst loose. Norfolk was still relying almost entirely on the feeble blasts of the police cars and fire engines, but these were sounded for twelve minutes to give everyone a chance to hear them. Streetcars obediently came to a halt, and automobiles pulled over to the curb. The street lights went out, and stores and restaurants grew dark. Even the Navy Yard and the Base interrupted their urgent work to cooperate in the test. It took the city 25 minutes to get all its lights out, according to a flier from Langley Field who was inspecting the blackout. Even then a few lights glimmered at 3,000 feet, but above 10,000 feet, where the bombers fly, the city had vanished into the night.[2]

The air raid wardens out on the streets discovered fewer than twenty violations of the rules, most of them unintentional. De-

[1] *V-P*, December 29, 1941, pp. 14, 7.
[2] *V-P*, December 30, 1941, p. 20.

fense officials were pleased at the results of the test. "I was very much gratified with the effectiveness of the blackout," declared City Manager Borland. "What impressed me most is that we have reached the point where we are coordinated. By that I mean the Army, Navy, Civilian Defense workers, and the general public now work in coordination. This is essential—and it has taken time to reach the stage where we can work as we do. There are still some minor defects to be smoothed out, but we can say that we are getting thorough public cooperation."[3]

Coordinator Marshall was equally satisfied. He admitted the warning signals were not effective and would not be until the arrival of the steam sirens which had been ordered. Another problem raised by the blackout was the activity of self-appointed air raid wardens, who took it upon themselves to punish violators. Bricks were tossed through several store windows where lights had been left burning; one which shattered the window of a Granby Street cigar store set off a burglar alarm which whistled all through the blackout. A group of sailors tried to turn off the lights on a parked car and when they found the doors were locked kicked in the headlights.[4]

The best way to prevent this vandalism was to put a larger patrol force on the streets, and for this more volunteers were needed. Fortunately, the long-proposed registration of volunteers was at last getting under way. Dean Hodges had swung into action on the program immediately after Pearl Harbor and rushed through the printing of the necessary cards. An advance campaign had been waged to bring out the volunteers, with civic groups pressed into service to explain to the public the nature of the jobs to be filled.[5] The Sunday paper printed a copy of the registration blank, listing the services to be performed. Workers were needed for fourteen "Civilian Protection" tasks, including air raid wardens, auxiliary firemen and policemen, messengers, nurses aides, ambulance drivers, and telephone operators. Among the nine "Civilian Participation" jobs were clerical work, producing goods for the Red Cross, dancing with servicemen, and studying nutrition and home nursing.[6]

[3] *V-P*, December 30, 1941, p. 20.
[4] *V-P*, December 30, 1941, p. 20; *L-D*, December 30, 1941.
[5] *V-P*, December 27, 1941, pp. 16, 4.
[6] *V-P*, December 28, 1941, Part II, pp. 1, 3.

The morning after the blackout, teachers interrupted their holiday vacations to go back to the schoolrooms to enroll the registrants. Norfolk volunteers fell short of the ten thousand needed, as only 7,231 cards were filled out. This included some enthusiastic youngsters who showed boyish ambitions to be air raid wardens or auxiliary policemen and a few girls who thought that they would like to join road repair crews or the decontamination corps. One fourteen-year-old lad volunteered for the bomb squad, saying he had a bicycle which he could use in the work.[7] The cards were turned over to Mrs. W. MacKenzie Jenkins, just named head of the Civilian Defense Volunteer Office. Mrs. Jenkins recruited her own volunteers to sort the cards and found herself permanent quarters on the mezzanine floor of the Bankers Trust Building.[8]

The service most urgently in need of volunteers was the information center in the Post Office basement. Here was the heart of the whole civilian defense system, where the approach of enemy planes would first be detected, but this vital center was still being haunted by problems. Work there was unusually demanding, since the 'round-the-clock schedule created some inconvenient shifts and each volunteer was needed for four hours every other day. Although the small band of veterans of the October maneuvers were still sticking to their posts, only a thin stream of new recruits was coming to the registration office set up near the center. Those who did enlist sometimes found that they were pressed into service without any instructions and received conflicting orders as to when they should report for duty.[9]

The trouble once more was the unsettled responsibility. John Twohy, in charge of obtaining the volunteers, felt that he should assign the workers to a satisfactory shift in order to keep them on the job. The Army, interested in keeping the shifts evenly manned, transferred the volunteers to other shifts which they did not like. The result was that Twohy thought the Army was interfering with his recruiting campaign while the Army felt that the campaign was not getting satisfactory results.

When Twohy resigned after several weeks, Coordinator Mar-

[7] *V-P*, December 31, 1941, p. 18; January 1, 1942, Part II, p. 12.
[8] *V-P*, January 1, 1942, Part II, p. 12; January 11, 1942, Part II, p. 1.
[9] Letter of C. E. Gettinger to Marshall, December 23, 1941, reporting complaints of girls in his office. Civilian Defense: Complaints file, NWHC records

shall assumed the responsibility of straightening the matter out. The day after Christmas he went to New York to talk to Brigadier General John C. McDonnell, head of the First Interceptor Command, which included the Norfolk center. From the general he obtained a confirmation of his idea that recruiting and assignment of volunteers was a civilian function.[10] With this question apparently settled, Marshall held a conference with the Army officers and Twohy, but failed to persuade the latter to resume his job. Marshall then turned to George Loeb, who was chairman of the Norfolk Council of the American Legion. On January 12 Loeb reluctantly accepted the task and spent the next few days studying the problem.[11]

The first step was to get the names of the volunteers who had registered on December 30. The cards as originally printed had made no specific mention of the Aircraft Warning Service, and there might have been no volunteers for the information center had it not been for Lynette Hamlet. Examining the form as printed in the Sunday paper on December 28, she had noticed the omission and at once sprang to action. She had a thousand posters printed the next day and saw that they were put up in all the schools, the banks, and the stores. She talked to the principal of every school where registrations were being taken and instructed them to have the teachers write in Aircraft Warning Service on the cards.[12]

As a result of this activity several hundred volunteers had been enrolled, but their cards were not yet sorted out. At Loeb's request Mrs. Jenkins separated these volunteers' cards from the rest, and sent him a list of 76 names on January 17, adding 258 more a few days later. Loeb set to work methodically, charting the shifts with the number already working and the number needed at each hour. On January 20 he and Mrs. Jenkins conferred with Colonel John E. Barr, the new commander at the information center who had arrived the day Loeb accepted his appointment. Colonel Barr agreed that the Civilian Defense Volun-

[10] Marshall to McDonnell, January 27, 1942, Civilian Defense: Civilian Air Raid Warning file, NWHC records.
[11] Loeb to Marshall, March 6, 1942, Civilian Defense: Civilian Air Raid Warning file, NWHC records.
[12] Lynette Hamlet scrapbook, NWHC records.

teer Office should interview the registrants and refer them to the center.[13]

Unfortunately, interviewing could not begin before January 23, and when the volunteers did start arriving, they came at the rate of only three or four a day. Colonel Barr, impatient to build up his staff, decided to resort to other methods. He asked Dr. A. V. Crosby for the name of some capable woman leader, and Doctor Crosby suggested Lynette Hamlet, already working at the center. Miss Hamlet, busy with her school work, did not feel that she could take on this additional responsibility, and called a meeting of the heads of the women's organizations in the city to find some one else. The meeting decided that the person to handle the job was Lynette Hamlet. She at once devoted herself whole-heartedly to the assignment, going to the center every day after school and remaining there until two in the morning.[14]

The only shortcoming of this new program was that it was shoving the Civilian Defense officials out of the way. When Colonel Barr explained his plan to Marshall and Loeb on January 27, they decided to let the Army handle it, and Coordinator Marshall wrote a long letter to General McDonnell, throwing up his hands.[15] Two days later Mrs. Jenkins read an article in the *Ledger-Dispatch*, appealing to all persons who had previously volunteered to report directly to the information center. Deciding that her office was no longer expected to conduct the interviews, she sent all the names still remaining on her list to the center and gave up all responsibility in the matter.[16]

In spite of this disaffection, the new program brought in recruits more speedily. Miss Hamlet resorted to her time-tested methods of publicity with appeals in the papers and over the radio. Captain Lynn Farnol, publicity director of the First Inter-

[13] Loeb to "Jim," January 18, 1942; Loeb to Marshall, March 6, 1942; Mrs. Jenkins to Marshall, March 4, 1942. Civilian Defense: Civilian Air Raid Warning file, NWHC records.

[14] Lynette Hamlet scrapbook, NWHC records. The school board on February 12 granted her a leave of absence with pay for the rest of the term. *V-P*, February 13, 1942, Part II, p. 12.

[15] Marshall to McDonnell, January 27, 1942, Civilian Defense: Civilian Air Raid Warning file, NWHC records.

[16] Mrs. Jenkins to Marshall, March 4, 1942, Civilian Defense: Civilian Air Raid Warning file, NWHC records.

ceptor Command, brought down from New York the two women who had organized the center there to help in the drive for volunteers.[17] General McDonnell himself explained the organization and urged:

When Norfolk residents realize the urgent need of workers at the information center, I feel sure that they will volunteer immediately so that they will be properly trained should an air raid come.[18]

These pleas brought volunteers coming in droves to the registration booth in the basement of the Post Office building, which Miss Hamlet had staffed with members of her chapter of the American Association of University Women. The first week added 150 new recruits. Fifteen men taking a construction course at Kempsville signed up with their instructor for the unpopular 2:00–6:00 A.M. shift. One volunteer said: "In times such as these it is not the hours that are most convenient to us, but the hours when we can do the most good that we should work."[19] One intrepid 74-year-old woman appeared to volunteer for duty. When the solicitous registrar inquired about her health, she replied, "I can eat anything up to nails, and them with gravy on them."[20]

In spite of her age, this volunteer had the fighting spirit of the women of the information center. Day after day they reported for their assignment with faithful regularity. When principals complained that three nights a week was too much for school teachers, they took the matter up with Colonel Barr, who won the approval of the school board.[21] When the *Virginian-Pilot* suggested that a lighter schedule might make it easier to win recruits, three of the volunteers wrote scornfully:

. . . we are amazed at the suggestion because at a time like this . . . your paper had the effrontery to suggest that four hours every second day, an average of fourteen hours per week, is too much to ask of American women. . . .

We suggest an editorial berating our women, not sympathizing, for their utter lack of co-operation and their utter disregard for our country's

[17] *V-P*, January 31, 1942, p. 18.
[18] *V-P*, February 3, 1942, p. 16.
[19] *V-P*, February 8, 1942, Part I, p. 3.
[20] *V-P*, April 11, 1942, p. 18.
[21] *V-P*, February 13, 1942, Part II, p. 12.

plight. If it will cause injured feelings we say, "TO HELL WITH INJURED FEELINGS—THIS IS WAR!!!"[22]

While the information center was going through its throes of reorganization, Chief Ferebee's air raid wardens were being recruited up to full strength. On January 20 Mrs. Jenkins sent him a list of those who had volunteered as wardens on December 30.[23] Since nearly 2,000 had registered for this service, there were recruits to spare. An emergency training program was hastily organized in January with weekly meetings of all wardens in each zone to hear talks on some aspects of civilian defense.

Chief Ferebee was also successful in getting Norfolk housewives to advance spring housecleaning to January. He issued an appeal that attics be cleared of all inflammable material as a protection against fire bombs. Women set to work with a will to clean out their garrets, although they found their task delayed by sorting out forgotten keepsakes and looking through old magazines. One woman discovered a trunk which she had sent to the attic on her return from boarding school ten years before to stay until she would have time to unpack it. Others found toys and dolls discarded by children long since grown. Shoving sentiment aside, they resolutely carried them downstairs. For weeks the trucks of the Goodwill Industries were making 45 calls a day to pick up articles from attics.[24]

Citizens were busily preparing impromptu defenses for their homes. Buckets of sand to smother incendiary bombs were standard equipment. The sand was free, dumped on street corners by generous contractors, but one man found another unfilled need. He wrote to the city manager:

I wish to have some information in which I believe you could furnish me. All you hear now days is Blackouts and Air-raids and no one seems to no what to do. The information in which I wish to receive is to do with getting bags in which to fill with sand. The folks around the block all agree that if we could get some bags in which to fill with sand that we could fix a garage in which to go in case of alarm.

[22] V-P, March 7, 1942, p. 4.
[23] Mrs. W. Mackenzie Jenkins to Ferebee, January 20, 1942, in Civilian Defense: Air Raid Wardens: S. H. Ferebee file, NWHC records.
[24] V-P, January 13, 1942, p. 18; January 17, 1942, Part II, p. 1.

If the city would try to get bags for people that have ideas but don't know where to get the material I think it would be a good idea to suggest it to some one in which to get the idea across. Thank you.[25]

Gasoline dealers offered their cooperation in defense measures. Discovering that their unsuccessful effort to limit the hours of service stations now had a patriotic basis, they announced that they were renewing their campaign. Closing the gas stations down at night, they said, would make sure that their lights would be out in case of an alarm, would save essential electricity, and would permit 300 station operators to volunteer for defense duties.[26]

Meanwhile the whole Civilian Defense set-up was being re-organized at the top. The system had been hastily thrown together in the days after Pearl Harbor when there was no time to argue about finances or responsibility. At the meeting on December 8, at which Marshall had been appointed coordinator, he had handed City Manager Borland a letter outlining his financial needs. In the urgency of the moment he was told to go ahead and do the job, and his expenses would be paid.[27] The next day he got an office and a telephone from the Army, borrowed office supplies from the Hampton Roads Council, and hired a secretary and put her on the Defense Council payroll.

By January, however, difficulties developed. He received an eviction notice from the government on the grounds that his office was not a Federal agency and therefore could not be quartered on Federal property. Governor Price refused to approve his secretary's salary on the grounds that he was not an officer of the Regional Defense Council. At this juncture the coordinator turned to the one remaining source of funds. He wrote Colonel Borland:

...we have had no funds available for stamps, stationery, supplies, etc., that are necessary for the maintenance of the Coordinator's Office, nor has the very capable secretary been paid for her services, and I would appreciate it very much if you will let me know at your earliest convenience just what we may expect here and when the expenses which have already been authorized will be paid. . . .

[25] Gene E. Taylor to Borland, Civilian Defense: Air Raid Wardens: S. H. Ferebee file, NWHC records.

[26] V-P, Feb. 6, 1942, Part II, p. 14.

[27] Marshall to Borland, January 13, 1942. Civilian Defense: Financing file, NWHC records.

I am sure that you are aware of the embarrassing position in which the Coordinator's Office is placed by the complete lack of funds here for the small minor necessities of such an important work, and will look forward to hearing from you with some immediate relief.[28]

City Manager Borland, already hard-pressed to hold the city's rising expenses under the ceiling imposed by his pledge to keep the tax rate down, was not at all pleased to discover that the defense baby had been laid on his doorstep. Moreover, the coordinator, strictly speaking, was not a city official, since he had been appointed, not by the city manager, but by the Defense Council. Already potential problems of conflicting authority had arisen. On January 6 the coordinator had casually told the city manager that he was having the city's traffic lights painted to shield them in future blackouts and was planning to black out the lights on the fire boxes.[29] Although the friendly personal relations between Marshall and Borland prevented any disagreement, it seemed imperative that the city should have control over Civilian Defense activities.

Borland therefore obtained from Marshall a complete description of the existing Civilian Defense organization on January 16,[30] and the next day went to Richmond for a conference with like-minded officials from other cities. The group decided to present their ideas to the new governor, Norfolk's Colgate W. Darden, Jr., who was to be sworn in on January 21. The day after the inauguration they conferred with Darden and found him sympathetic towards their proposal that the regional councils be abolished and Civilian Defense functions turned over to the cities and counties. He suggested that a committee be formed to draw up a new bill for that purpose.[31]

Unfortunately, newspaper headlines the next morning gave the impression that Darden intended to scrap the entire Civilian Defense organization. Colonel Borland hastened to explain that there would be no change in the volunteers' set-up. "We will need all who already have volunteered their services and more,"

[28] *Ibid.*
[29] Marshall to Borland, January 6, 1942, Civilian Defense: Correspondence, Norfolk, file, NWHC records.
[30] Marshall to Borland, January 16, 1942, Civilian Defense: Correspondence, Norfolk, file, NWHC records.
[31] *V-P*, January 23, 1942, Part I, pp. 1, 7.

he said. "The principal difference will be that all supervision of
Civilian Defense activities will be under the direction of the duly
constituted civil authorities in the cities and counties of the state.
This is as it should be." There had been no discord between the
city and Civilian Defense, he declared, but a lack of coordination.
There would be no discord under the new plan, if he could help
it, he added, but there would be coordination.[32]

For the next month the Civilian Defense organization was in a
state of suspended animation. The drafting committee, headed by
Colonel Borland, on January 24 drew up a bill which placed control of Civilian Defense in the hands of local officials. In the cities
the chief executive was made director with the power to name a
coordinator as deputy if he so desired. The committee, made up
of local officials, wrote into the bill a provision that the state
should pay all the expenses, but at the Governor's insistence
financing was handed back to the cities along with the responsibility.

While the new bill was being whipped into shape and rushed
through the General Assembly, uncertainty still remained. Employees at the Regional Defense Council office in the Pender
Building at once started looking for new jobs with such success
that Dean Hodges had only four of his fifteen staff members still
with him when he closed up his office on February 28.[33] The passage of the new defense act on February 11 at last settled the
question of who was going to pay the bill. City Manager Borland
reluctantly asked the city council for an emergency appropriation
of $10,000 for Civilian Defense. Mayor Wood told his fellow
council members: "Well, gentlemen, this is right bitter medicine,
but we will have to take it. We must prepare for the defense of
our citizens."[34]

On the still unsettled question of the status of the present
Civilian Defense workers, the *Virginian-Pilot* spoke up with a
plea for immediate action:

In connection with City Manager Borland's statement to the City
Council that "some of the old organization of the Hampton Roads

[32] *V-P*, January 25, 1942, Part II, p. 1.
[33] *V-P*, February 26, 1942, p. 10.
[34] *V-P*, February 18, 1942, p. 18.

Regional Defense Council would be retained under the reorganization now under way under the new State law," and his further statement that "some of the employes of the old Hampton Roads Regional Defense Council will be retained," it is in order to emphasize what undoubtedly the City Manager understands: that these are matters which ought to be settled as quickly as possible. . . .

The *Virginian-Pilot*, which has great respect for the work already done, has high hope that under the new State plan of civilian defense the work will be done even better. But there ought not to be one hour's unnecessary delay in establishing whatever reorganization is deemed wise.[35]

The very next day Colonel Borland acted. He called a meeting of representatives of all the agencies charged with the protection of the area, including the Army, the Navy, the V. P. F., and Civilian Defense to discuss problems, and announced that the entire Civilian Defense organization from Coordinator Marshall down had been reappointed. He tried to smooth any still ruffled feathers by stressing that the reorganization had not been due to any criticism of the previous system, but "to give the leaders, the director, the coordinator and all other Civilian Defense officials complete legal authority for what they must do and give their acts the protection of the law." He declared:

We must forget any petty jealousies if any exist, we must prevent any petty jealousies, any lack of harmony in our jobs. . . .

The new law makes me director of civilian defense. I did not ask for it. This is war. We have a big job to do and there must be no misunderstanding about it. Each man and woman must know what he has to do. I want all those who have been serving to continue to serve. We cannot get along without you. . . .

You're in the Army now, so to speak, and with your help I'm going to make a success of this job. You will have to take orders and obey orders. There may be times when you think that they are wrong, but you must obey those orders. There must be no confusion. I want to know we are ready to act if a raid does take place, if bombs do fall.[36]

Harmony reigned at the meeting. Admiral Simons announced that even the Army and the Navy had perfected plans for co-

[35] *V-P*, February 19, 1942, p. 6.
[36] *V-P*, February 21, 1942, p. 16.

operation. Colonel Borland unwittingly reopened an old wound
by asking Colonel Barr if he needed any help at the information
center. Barr replied that he certainly did; he still had only 600
volunteers working and needed 1200. Many persons at the meeting were startled to learn that such a vital agency was so understaffed. The city manager, unaware that his Civilian Defense
organization had already washed its hands of this project, promised to get the needed recruits.[37]

The new defense director took one more step to promote harmony in the city. Acting under the authority of the new State
law, he named an advisory defense council, intended to represent
all races and creeds. Included were two prominent Negroes, P. B.
Young, editor of the *Journal and Guide*, and David Alston, labor
leader, as well as two Jews, two Catholics, and four white Protes-
tants. At the council's first meeting Colonel Borland told the
group that the enemy was trying to promote racial and religious
discord. He explained:

In picking this committee, I have tried to assemble ten men who
have but one thought and that thought is America; ten men who will
show the people of Norfolk that by our combined efforts we can help
win this war, and that the citizens of Norfolk can and will work side
by side in harmony with one objective.

This committee, I know, will subordinate all personal thoughts and
actions and keep foremost in their thoughts only those things which are
safe and in the best interests of all our people, regardless of race, creed,
or color.

My reason for addressing you in this manner is by reason of the fact
I feel that we are not taking this war seriously. The American people
do not take kindly to discipline, and our Government does not discipline.

We therefore must discipline ourselves, and we must be prepared for
all eventualities.[38]

Still unsettled was the question as to whether Norfolk's new
Civilian Defense system should walk alone. Governor Darden held
a conference with the Hampton Roads defense directors to determine whether there should be any agency to coordinate the communities. The Hampton Roads executives were unanimous in

[37] *V-P*, February 21, 1942, p. 16.
[38] *V-P*, March 7, 1942, p. 16; March 8, 1942, Part II, p. 1.

opposing any organization like the late and unlamented Regional Defense Council. They said that they preferred to develop the Civilian Defense program themselves. They were willing to accept a regional planning agency if the state would pay the bill, but the governor declared that the state could furnish no special favors to a single area.[39] The need for coordination was satisfied by an agreement to hold monthly conferences with the governor to discuss problems which required joint action.

[39] *V-P*, March 19, 1942, Part II, p. 12. These conferences were held from April to October, 1942, when they were abandoned.

13

MORE COMING

WHILE its civilian defenses were being reorganized, Norfolk waited nervously for the air raid which might come at any moment. On the first night of 1942 a shiver of excitement ran over the northern part of the city when the lights of the Naval Base suddenly went out without any preliminary alarm. Worries soon subsided when it was learned that the blackout had been caused by an unknown motorist who had smashed into an electric-light pole and cut off the power.[1]

Though no bombs fell, the war soon seemed to be moving right in on the city's front doorsteps. As Hitler unleashed his U-boat pack to snap at America's vital coastal supply lines in the middle of January, four ships were torpedoed in six days. The fourth vessel went down off the Carolina coast early on January 18, carrying with it a Norfolk sailor. That night thirteen survivors were landed at the Naval Base, and six of them were taken to the Marine Hospital.[2]

The next day a Latvian ship, one day out of Norfolk, was smashed by a German torpedo. By January 30 the Nazi wolf pack had claimed its fourteenth victim, the *Rochester*, sunk in a daylight attack off the Virginia coast.[3] Day by day the submarines took their toll of the coastal shipping, while the Navy tried desperately to organize a counterattack. One U-boat commander boldly surfaced almost within sight of Cape Henry light to shell a helpless tug towing two coal barges to Boston.[4]

[1] *V-P*, January 2, 1942, p. 9.
[2] *V-P*, January 20, 1942, p. 1.
[3] *V-P*, January 22, 1942, p. 22; January 31, 1942, p. 1; February 1, 1942, Part II, p. 1.
[4] This sinking occurred on March 31, 1942, but it remained under the cloak of Navy censorship until three years later. *V-P*, July 8, 1945, Part II, p. 1.

Soon "the survivors were landed at the Naval Base" seemed to be almost a daily line in the papers. Several times Nazi torpedoes found their mark in passenger vessels, bringing in civilian survivors in numbers too large for the Base to handle. One April day the Red Cross took a call from the Navy to learn that care was needed for 133 submarine victims and hastily set up quarters wherever it could find vacant rooms. When a second call came on April 23 the Red Cross was better prepared. Even though the message from Naval Intelligence routed officials out of bed at 4:30 A. M., by 8:00 A. M. all the needed supplies had been collected, and by 1:45 P. M. the first survivors were being admitted to the temporary quarters established in the Brith Sholom Center where cots had been set up and food was being served. Thirteen seriously injured passengers were rushed to the hospital.[5]

These testimonies of the nearness of the shooting war brought a sense of urgency to the people of Norfolk. The tempo of life speeded up as work went on, day in and day out. The new spirit brought a more enthusiastic response to the war drives. Frank W. Evans, placed in charge of the Victory Book campaign to gather books for servicemen's libraries, sent the Boy Scouts out collecting books and magazines. They came back bringing 7,000 books and 15,000 magazines to overwhelm the already overcrowded Public Library with the job of handling them.[6] The Community Chest came to an agreement with the USO and the Navy Relief Fund to join forces for a single campaign in April and worked so successfully that Norfolk was the first city of more than 100,000 population to pass its goal. The city gave a record total of $402,000 without the aid of any outside help to organize the campaign. As a result, collection costs fell to 3.6 per cent, less than half the expenses of the preceding year. The value of this joint War Fund experiment was so clear that it was to be adopted throughout the nation.[7]

The spirit of unity seemed to be suffering little damage from the minor irritants created by the submarine warfare. As early as January the sugar shortage threatened to interfere with an essen-

[5] *V-P*, April 26, 1942, Part I, p. 1, Part II, p. 1.
[6] *V-P*, January 11, 1942, Part II, p. 1; February 15, 1942, Part II, p. 3; conversation of the author with Miss Mary D. Pretlow.
[7] *V-P*, March 13, 1942, Part II, p. 12; May 14, 1942, p. 20.

tial routine. The local distributor announced that he was putting his customers on a monthly quota for Coca-Cola syrup. "At various times," he said, "you will be out of Coca-Cola, but there is nothing we will be able to do about it."[8] Grocery stores, limited by allotments based on 1941 sales, found themselves unable to supply the 1942 population. Small retailers refused to sell more than two pounds to a customer. Colonial Stores set up an informal rationing program, limiting purchasers to one pound of sugar for each dollar's worth of other groceries they bought, with a maximum of five pounds, and promptly got into trouble with the OPA. W. C. Pender, the company's general counsel, had to make a special trip to Washington to explain that the plan was not designed to increase the company's business but merely to cut down the sale of sugar.[9]

Restaurants tried to persuade their patrons to be careful with the sugar bowl. One eating place, allotted only ten pounds of sugar a day instead of its usual fifty, posted this information on the wall as a friendly hint. The owner complained that some customers were not satisfied with less than five spoonfuls in a single cup of coffee. Just to save the sugar, he was allowing only one cup of coffee to a person.[10] In one downtown drugstore, it was said, a heavy, impatient customer demanded three large spoonfuls in his coffee. When the waitress replied that she could give only two, he grew insistent. A smaller man, sitting on the next stool, got up and said, "You don't get any sugar, and you don't get any coffee, either, but you get this," and landed a right on the impatient man's face.[11]

Other foods were increasingly hard to get. Bananas virtually disappeared. In April a Federal inspector could find only fourteen in Norfolk, normally the state's banana center. These were priced at 75 cents, he said, when they would ordinarily have been worth only a dime. Coffee deliveries to retailers were cut by 25 per cent. Looking ahead, many persons began digging victory gardens, and the seed business boomed.[12]

[8] *V-P*, January 8, 1942, Part II, p. 14.
[9] *V-P*, January 21, 1942, p. 18; February 3, 1942, p. 16.
[10] *V-P*, January 29, 1942, p. 14.
[11] *V-P*, February 4, 1942, p. 7.
[12] *V-P*, April 23, 1942, p. 22; April 28, 1942, p. 1; April 29, 1942, p. 13.

More serious than dietary adjustments were the steadily increasing restrictions on the use of automobiles which threatened to disrupt the city's way of life. The freezing of the sale of all tires in December had been a grim warning of a treadbare future for the average motorist. For him the inauguration of tire rationing on January 19 offered little hope. James M. Wolcott, city tire administrator, told the tire inspectors who gathered to receive their instructions: "If the applying motorist is not a physician, surgeon, visiting nurse, or a veterinary, you can save your time and his by explaining simply that he is not eligible for tires or tubes." Even eligible drivers could get new tires only if their old ones were unfit for repairing or recapping.[13]

The technicalities of rationing brought Norfolk the first civil action undertaken by the OPA in the country. The Smith-Douglas Company filed suit against the Joynes Tire Company to compel delivery of a number of tires it had ordered the previous August but had never received. The OPA entered the case with a countersuit, claiming that such delivery would be a violation of its regulations, and succeeded in convincing the court that Smith-Douglas was not entitled to the tires.[14]

The difficulty of getting tires in legal ways set off a wave of tire thievery. Thirty-six tires were reported stolen in two days. In one case thieves jacked up a car and carried off a tire, not bothering with a purse on the seat containing a diamond ring. One car reported stolen was recovered with all four wheels and tires missing. Motorists scurried around looking for garages in which they might lock up their automobiles, but these were hard to find. Even a garage was insufficient protection, as Clerk of the Corporation Court W. L. Prieur, Jr., discovered one morning. When he went out to his garage, he found that thieves had piled concrete blocks under his car and carried off both rear wheels. The crowning insult came when someone stole the spare tire off James M. Wolcott's car. Tire Administrator Wolcott was not eligible for a new one.[15] The city acted to restrain the thieves by

[13] *V-P*, January 18, 1942, Part II, p. 1.
[14] *V-P*, February 15, 1942, Part II, p. 1. Smith-Douglas eventually obtained the tires when the injunction was dissolved.
[15] *V-P*, January 2, 1942, p. 18; January 5, 1942, p. 14; January 20, 1942, p. 18; March 13, 1942, Part II, p. 1; March 18, 1942, p. 20.

stiffening its ordinance regulating second-hand dealers. When the General Assembly made tire theft a felony, judges were quick to make the punishment fit the crime. Although the first two men to be sentenced under the new law got off with a one-year term, the next five averaged six years apiece.[16]

All types of tire-saving measures were attempted. City merchants appealed to customers to carry small packages to eliminate unnecessary deliveries and debated cutting regular delivery service to every other day. A group of Norfolk businessmen, living at Virginia Beach, chartered a bus to bring them to their offices. A dozen young men from Colonial Place bought bicycles and started pedaling their way to work every day. One enthusiast claimed he could beat the streetcars and the buses every time. The Ideal Laundry converted to horses and discovered a new hazard of war. The traffic on Hampton Boulevard frightened the animals so much that the company had to apply to the city council for permission to erect hitching posts. There was little likelihood, however, that the hitching post would replace the parking meter, a survey indicated. While there was still one horse-and-mule dealer and one harness maker left in the city, there was no one who could manufacture wagons or buggies.[17]

There was no escape from treadless tires by purchasing a new car, for new automobiles were already on the ration list. The Ford assembly plant in Newton Park operated on a cut-back schedule during January and then shut down. Auto salesmen, who had made as much as $1,000 a month in 1941, mourned the loss of their livelihood, while dealers looked around for some means of staying in business.[18] Motorists resignedly prepared to make their old cars last for the duration.

One more reason for leaving the car at home was the return of the gas shortage. In March Petroleum Coordinator Ickes put the service stations back on a 72-hour week as a conservation measure. Only too happy to have the regulation again in effect, the Tidewater Retail Gasoline Dealers Association promised to cooperate by observing the hours and selling as little gasoline as possible.

[16] *V-P*, January 14, 1942, p. 18; April 21, 1942, p. 20; April 23, 1942, p. 22.
[17] *V-P*, January 8, 1942, p. 20; January 18, 1942, Part II, p. 1; March 12, 1942, p. 20; June 24, 1942, p. 20.
[18] *V-P*, January 3, 1942, p. 16.

In April deliveries were placed on a quota basis, cut back one-third from 1941 sales. Even under limited hours, stations could not make these allotments last, and some were forced to close down before the end of the delivery period. Then it was announced that May deliveries would be cut 50 per cent and that a card rationing system would be introduced, limiting non-essential users to six gallons a week.[19]

Grounded motorists tried to fight their way on to the already crowded buses and streetcars. Every month the Virginia Electric and Power Company was registering a new high for its transit business and wondering how it could possibly haul any more passengers. Crowding was worst on the long line out Hampton Boulevard leading to the Naval Base. Men on their way to work waited hopefully for an approaching trolley, only to be passed up by the already jampacked vehicle. Sometimes as many as eight cars in a row went by without stopping. One Navy officer had to allow two and a half hours to cover the four miles between his home and the Base. VEPCO asked all persons who could walk to work not to use the streetcars and talked of requiring every passenger to show a work pass before he would be allowed to ride the Naval Base cars. Looking at the 2,000 automobiles still making the daily trip to the Base, the company tried to calculate how long it would be before these passengers would also have to take to the trolleys.[20]

The Navy called in R. W. Siver, a traffic engineer from New York, to survey the situation. He told the Navy to stagger its working hours to spread the traffic more evenly during the day. When he suggested that store and school hours should also be staggered, Colonel Borland and VEPCO officials replied that there was no immediate need. Siver agreed but added, "Soon it will be necessary."[21]

VEPCO had ordered fifteen new buses in January, but it did not hope for delivery before May. The company scoured the country, looking for second-hand streetcars. Although it bought trolleys in Pennsylvania and Texas, it could find only forty.

[19] *V-P*, March 19, 1942, Part II, p. 1; March 20, 1942, Part II, p. 14; April 19, 1942, Part II, p. 2; April 25, 1942, p. 1.
[20] *V-P*, March 28, 1942, p. 16; April 24, 1942, Part II, p. 12.
[21] *V-P*, April 24, 1942, Part II, p. 12.

Even they were little help, for there was no one to operate them. The company had employed 127 operators in February, 1940, and two years later had been able to boost that number only to 164 when it needed 250. VEPCO Supervisor J. L. Thomas explained the problem to a reporter. When he was asked, "Have any of the new drivers become lost?" he replied with a twinkle in his eye: "Not exactly. You see, we teach them first where Granby Street is, and then Main Street. So far, so good, but then they see the Confederate Monument and the Portsmouth ferry. 'Portsmouth,' they exclaim, 'that's where the Navy Yard is,' and that's about the last we see of them."[22]

Other businesses were having similar trouble. The demand for labor was so great that when two vagrants, brought up in Corporation Court, were given their choice of six months on the city farm or going to work, both found jobs within an hour, one at ninety cents an hour, the other at $1.20. City stenographers, paid $100 a month, were leaving for better jobs. The City Civil Service Commission debated lowering the requirements for the police force in an effort to find replacements. Hotels found their employees disappearing daily, and the new workers they hired demanded more pay and did less work. The Monticello discovered that its operating costs were up $10,000 a month over a year earlier. Domestic servants seemed to have vanished. One maid explained the shortage to a reporter: "Man, ain't no cullud women goin' work nowadays. All dere men got jobs, and 'ey figure it's dere time to rest up. Only reason I'm working is I'm a widder-woman. Other women might has to work when times is tight, but nobody but a pore widder like me slaves and mops when de men is bringin' it in on Sattidy."[23]

That the shortage had only begun was indicated by the Navy's plans for further expansion. Congress poured another 43 and a half million dollars into construction at the Base. The new Naval Base Hospital on the old golf course was to be doubled in size to accommodate 1,500 beds. The Air Station reached out across

[22] *V-P*, February 1, 1942, Part II, p. 1; March 20, 1942, Part II, p. 14; March 28, 1942, p. 16.

[23] *V-P*, January 22, 1942, p. 22; March 13, 1942, Part II, p. 12; April 22, 1942, p. 20.

Taussig Boulevard to take in another 500 acres.[24] The new base at Little Creek added another 1,761 acres of Princess Anne County to have room for its constantly increasing duties. South of the Naval Base the Navy opened Camp Allen as a training center for its newly-authorized Construction Battalions. Soon the new Seabee units were overflowing Camp Allen and had to move out to the property just acquired at Little Creek, now named Camp Bradford. On the old St. Helena reservation in Berkley the Navy was building barracks to house 1,500 men and a mess hall to feed 5,000 as a berth for men attached to ships undergoing repair in the Yard.[25]

Hustling to keep pace with this intensified activity was the construction of housing. The outbreak of war had made it imperative to get homes built immediately, regardless of what local toes might be tramped on. Before turning to government construction, however, the Navy made one final, futile effort to keep housing in the hands of private enterprise. Just ten days after Pearl Harbor the Navy called local builders and realtors together to explain the need. Representative after representative from Federal agencies once more made clear just how many homes were required and urged private builders to take on the job with the promise of every assistance.[26]

No amount of urging of present needs, however, could divert local thoughts from a grim postwar future. At a second conference two days later John Sears of the late joint housing committee once more saw the ghost city walking, and many others seemed frightened by the same spectre. The meeting asked for the compromise long favored by the Norfolk Housing Authority: demountable homes, which could be folded up and carted away as soon as the war was over. Lawrence M. Cox, director of the authority, declared: "We should protect the city for its value after the emergency."[27]

Another conference in January reached an agreement on de-

[24] V-P, February 7, 1942, p. 16. The 508.38 acres added made a total of 1,944.29 acres acquired by the Naval Air Station since June, 1940.
[25] V-P, March 1, 1942, Part II, p. 1; March 21, 1942, p. 16; May 24, 1942, Part II, p. 1; May 31, 1942, Part II, p. 9.
[26] V-P, December 18, 1941, pp. 26, 15.
[27] V-P, December 20, 1941, pp. 18, 6.

mountable housing. The government was to build 10,000 homes in the area, the magical figure so long chanted by Bruce Shafer. Although this was four times as many homes as had been put up in booming 1941, the pledge of the government to remove them as soon as they were no longer needed satisfied local financial fears.[28]

Before the month was out, a contract had been let for half of the ten thousand homes. Barrett and Hilp, a San Francisco firm which had learned the mass-production technique at Fort Leonard Wood in Missouri, was awarded the contract to build the five thousand homes on the Portsmouth side of the Elizabeth River. No time had to be lost searching for suitable locations, since prospective sites had been selected the previous fall by the State Planning Board, working in cooperation with the National Committee on Emergency Housing. By the middle of February the location of three proposed projects on the Norfolk side had been announced and by the first week of March contracts had been let for 5,700 units on these tracts.[29]

In spite of this flood of temporary housing projects, the Government had not abandoned private enterprise. A revision of the National Housing Act to permit FHA financing of homes intended for rent brought in more out-of-town builders with plans which would have stunned the joint housing committee a few months earlier. On Indian River work was started on a 650-house project, while 400 more homes were proposed for the old Simpson farm in Bay View. Biggest project of all was announced by Levitt and Sons, a Long Island firm which had been forced out of the quality home field by priorities. William J. Levitt, head of the firm, explained that he was starting a group of 750 homes but hoped to build three times that number before he was through. He assured local interests that the project would be well planned and would not become a ghost village after the war.[30]

[28] *V-P*, January 8, 1942, pp. 1, 7; January 9, 1942, Part I, p. 8. Shafer in the meantime had decided that Norfolk really needed 40,000 more homes. *V-P*, January 15, 1942, p. 6.

[29] *V-P*, January 28, 1942, p. 20; February 15, 1942, Part II, p. 1; March 1, 1942, Part II, p. 1; March 7, 1942, p. 16.

[30] *V-P*, January 17, 1942, Part II, p. 12; February 1, 1942, Part II, p. 1; February 4, 1942, p. 20. Levitt's statement was not as reassuring as it sounded. The building and loan associations had not been afraid that the new housing

Construction was also under way on all the other projects which had been debated in 1941. The Federal Public Roads Administration in December allocated a half-million dollars to widen Sewells Point Road, Taussig Boulevard, and Hampton Boulevard north of Lafayette River. Funds were also granted for the proposed Norfolk by-pass between the toll-free highway and Sewells Point Road. By February the State Highway Department was ready to let the contracts for these projects.[31]

The city decided to save three months on the construction of its second pipe line to Lake Prince by negotiating the contract instead of asking for open bids. With this shortcut it hoped to complete the new line by June or July instead of in the fall. The need for haste in the expansion of the water system had been underlined by a long winter drought which had lasted until March, bringing the level of Lake Prince down nine feet below normal. The only saving factor was a temporary winter reduction in the use of water which lowered daily pumping from 23 to 21 million gallons.[32]

To get more water into Lake Prince, the city used the old redwood pipe taken up from the Lake Prince line in 1940 to run a temporary line to Lake Burnt Mills, a mile and a half away. By March 12 the redwood was back in action, pumping eight million gallons a day into Lake Prince. For additional insurance the Federal Works Agency decided to build a twenty-mile pipe line of its own to carry 25 million gallons a day from the Nottoway River to Lake Prince. A plentiful supply of water now seemed assured in the near future.[33]

The dangerous situation in the hospitals forced a prompt decision on that question. On the last day of January Norfolk General Hospital was jammed with 272 patients; every room was full, single rooms were doubled up, and there were beds in the sun parlor. St. Vincent's had 208 patients, the largest number on record. Leigh Memorial's only vacant beds were in the maternity

would stand vacant in the postwar depression; their concern had been rather that people would vacate the old houses, on which they held mortgages.

[31] *V-P*, December 28, 1941, Part II, p. 1; January 13, 1942, p. 18; February 3, 1942, p. 16.

[32] *V-P*, January 7, 1942, p. 20: February 10, 1942, p. 15.

[33] *V-P*, January 7, 1942, p. 20; January 21, 1942, p. 18; March 8, 1942, Part II, p. 1; March 12, 1942, p. 12.

ward, and it had been filled to capacity for several months. An expansion program was quickly agreed upon by all local interests. Norfolk General and Leigh Memorial would each get a sixty-bed addition, while a new 200-bed hospital would be built on Granby Street in Talbot Park. This would be operated by St. Vincent's, which would turn over its old property to the city after the war. By April the FWA had allocated $1,807,775 to pay for this ex pansion.[34]

Work was also being speeded on the new auditorium. The city council met in special session in December to authorize payment of $245,000 for its share of the building in order that the Army could get construction under way, and on New Year's Day test piles were driven to locate the bottom of old Smith Creek and determine how deep the piling for the new building would have to be. On February 26 the bids were opened, and the city made the disappointing discovery that it was going to have to put up more money. The low bid was just under $600,000, whereas the estimated cost of building and furnishings had been only $525,000. The council resignedly voted another $175,000.[35]

While the new auditorium was going up, other recreational facilities were being provided for the sailors. The Salvation Army's USO center at Plume and Granby streets opened in February, the most elaborate center Norfolk had yet seen. It provided 125 beds, including twenty set aside for parents or relatives visiting servicemen. On the first floor was a large canteen seating eighty persons, with a recreation room on the seventh floor. The old City Hall auditorium became a full-time center with a Tuesday night dance added to the regular Saturday night feature. There were 350 pairs of roller skates to provide entertainment two nights a week, with other events scheduled the remaining nights of the week.[36] On March 15 the Smith Street USO was opened, at last providing a recreation center for Negro servicemen. In just a few more months, it seemed, all the problems would be solved.

[34] V-P, February 2, 1942; February 11, 1942, p. 18; March 29, 1942, Part II, p. 1; April 10, 1942, Part II, p. 12.

[35] V-P, December 27, 1941, p. 16; January 2, 1942, p. 8; February 27, 1942, Part II, p. 1; March 4, 1942, p. 18.

[36] V-P, February 8, 1942, Part II, p. 1; February 13, 1942, Part II, p. 12.

14

ELIMINATION OF ILLUMINATION

SETTLING the status of the Civilian Defense organization in
February at last enabled Coordinator Marshall to go to
work on perfecting his system. For months his staff had
been held together only by devotion to duty. He had retained his
office in the Federal Building only by pulling a few political wires
to get his eviction notice revoked; he had kept his secretary by
her hope that someone would eventually pay her salary. There
had been no money to rent halls to hold classes for training the
wardens or even to buy postcards to send them notices of meetings.[1]

Although the new arrangement provided the necessary funds
to carry on Civilian Defense, it could not create perfect cooperation. There were occasional misunderstandings between the director and the coordinator and sometimes even a definite disagreement over policy. In spite of these inevitable minor frictions,
however, the two men continued to work in relative harmony.

An indication of future relationships arose in February when
Borland and Marshall discussed the problem of publicity. Each
of the various Civilian Defense groups was handling its own public announcements, which sometimes contradicted each other and
created confusion. After their conversation the city manager sent
the coordinator a memorandum, stressing: "It is most important
that publicity be coordinated as well as other activities." Marshall
promptly replied that he already had someone in mind for this
task, adding: "I realize the necessity for the coordination of this
effort because I feel the public as well as the people who are
active in this service require a great deal of education along the
lines of civilian defense." Borland in alarm hastily sent back an

---

[1] Marshall to Borland, January 13, 26, 1942, Civilian Defense: Financing
file, NWHC records.

answer: "You misunderstood my letter. Please do not hire any-body for publicity. What I want to do is cut down publicity."[2]

Nevertheless, a few days later the defense director yielded to the insurance salesman's arguments and agreed to the appointment of Maurice E. Bennett, Jr., of the advertising department of the Norfolk Newspapers, as director of public relations. Colonel Borland even helped Coordinator Marshall persuade Paul S. Huber, president of the newspaper company, to release part of Bennett's time for the new job, and on March 13 Bennett's appointment was announced.[3]

The dynamic new director attacked his task with such enthusiasm that the part-time job soon became full time. All Civilian Defense agencies were instructed to clear any publicity stories through him, a policy acclaimed by radio stations and newspapers. The policy of coordination soon became so thorough that the managing editor of the *Ledger-Dispatch* feared it was extending to the censorship of news and firmly informed Marshall: "It is not our policy or intention to delay or withhold publication of any news of public interest to satisfy the vanity or to suit the convenience of any person or persons connected with civilian defense."[4] Coordinator Marshall quickly cleared up this misunderstanding, and no further difficulty with the newspapers developed.

In the meantime, the city's financial support was strengthening the weak spots in the defense system. Enough telephones could now be installed in the Federal Building office to permit the operation of a control center. This was the staff headquarters for the Civilian Defense army, where reports of damage by enemy bombs would be received and whence directions for aiding the victims would be sent. On March 10 a test of the new center was staged. Chief Air Raid Warden Ferebee directed his men to be out on the streets that night between eight and nine, ready to telephone in a report as soon as they saw a car bearing a white

[2] Borland to Marshall, February 28, 1942; Marshall to Borland, February 28, 1942; Borland to Marshall, February 28, 1942. Civilian Defense: Publicity file, NWHC records.

[3] Marshall to Huber, March 9, 1942, Civilian Defense: Publicity file, NWHC records; *L-D*, March 13, 1942.

[4] Tom Hanes to Marshall, May 8, 1942, Civilian Defense: Publicity file, NWHC records.

flag. The wardens cooperated by making 617 reports in an hour, setting the phones in the control center jangling every six seconds. The men seated around the control table quickly discovered the shortcomings of their new equipment. In the crowded space they bumped elbows reaching for the instruments and often found that they had picked up the wrong telephone. Coordinator Marshall decided that the phones should have lights to show which one was ringing. Moreover, he realized that the control center could not function properly in its cramped quarters.[5]

Fortunately, more adequate offices were available across the street in the VEPCO Building. On March 28 the control center and all the Civilian Defense offices moved into these new quarters. The biggest part of the moving was changing the telephones, as most of the equipment in the Federal Building office had been borrowed. Now the defense office at last received some furniture it could call its own. Raymond C. Mackay was placed in charge of the control center, and the other members of the general staff, who were to sit around the control table during tests or actual air raids, were brought into the new quarters and shown their duties. Early in April State Coordinator J. H. Wyse and his assistant, John J. Howard, visited the new center on an inspection trip and declared that it was "in fine shape."[6]

Now that a few of the earlier problems had been settled and the pamphlets sent out from Washington digested, the intended pattern of the Civilian Defense system was becoming clearer to those on the inside, if not to the general public. Coordinator Marshall's January dispute with the Army over the Aircraft Warning Service had ended with the Army in complete charge. Recruiting and assignment of the volunteers, however, remained in civilian hands. Next to the information center was the civil air raid warning center, which received signals from the information group and passed them on to the district warning centers located throughout the state, which in turn passed the word on to the local control centers. The CARW equipment was manned

[5] *V-P*, March 8, 1942, Part II, p. 1; Civilian Defense: Air Raid Wardens, Tests, file, NWHC records.

[6] Memo in Civilian Defense: Hampton Roads Regional Defense Council file, NWHC records; *V-P*, April 4, 1942, p. 16; Maurice E. Bennett to Joseph Leslie, April 27, 1942, Civilian Defense: Public Relations file, NWHC records.

24 hours a day by Norfolk volunteers, but it had by now been placed under the State Office of Civilian Defense since it served the entire state.

The Norfolk Office of Civilian Defense had thus been freed of all responsibility for any of the links of communication until the signal reached the local control center, which also served as a district warning center to relay the message to the local military installations and the nearby cities and counties. There were four signals in the standard code: the "yellow," which alerted the defenses; the "blue," warning that enemy planes were approaching and that defenses should be mobilized; the "red," meaning enemy planes were overhead and all lights should be put out; and the "white," or all clear. Frequent tests were made, using the "white" signal to avoid confusion. Each message was passed along to all the control points to test their readiness. To prevent any possible mix-up, Coordinator Marshall agreed with the local commander at the information center to substitute the letters, "A," "B," "C," and "D," for the respective colors when practices were called from the Norfolk warning center.

Under Director Borland and Coordinator Marshall were the commanders of the various defense units. First organized and best known of these were the air raid wardens. Chief Ferebee had been able to get his training program under way in February, and by the end of the month 1,800 wardens had received at least their first five hours of instruction. Also in the public eye were the auxiliary police, who were being given a rigorous course of training by the city police department. The fire department was instructing another group of auxiliary firemen. The fire department also had charge of the rescue squad, trained to dig victims out of fallen debris.

'Louis F. Paret, as head of the emergency public works department, was responsible for demolition and clearance and road repair. Also under his jurisdiction was the decontamination division, headed by W. A. Ryder, which had 58 instructors who had completed a thorough course in war gases and decontamination. Each of these instructors was to organize a squad of his own. Dr. A. B. Hodges, head of the emergency medical service, had established eight casualty stations and assigned doctors, nurses, nurses aides, and messengers to each one. Partial equipment had been supplied the stations by the Red Cross. In addition, two staff agencies, the drivers corps and the messenger service, had been set up to supply emergency transportation and communication.[7]

Although no total blackouts had been called since December, the city was growing perceptibly darker at night. Tests elsewhere had demonstrated what Norfolk had already learned, that lights left on in stores or over advertising signs could not readily be extinguished during a blackout. The U. S. Office of Civilian Defense therefore sent instructions to Richmond on February 28 that all unattended lights in metropolitan areas which could not be put out at a moment's notice were to be turned off at twilight. Governor Darden at once issued an executive order, giving these instructions the force of law. In Norfolk, City Manager Borland and Police Chief Woods promised full enforcement, and merchants tried to puzzle out the meaning of the order which would have been clear enough in less uncertain times. Many businessmen, confused by the term, "partial blackout," thought that they were supposed to turn off their advertising signs only on nights when blackouts were scheduled, and Governor Darden had to explain that the order meant every night.[8]

Close on the heels of the partial blackout came a new lights-out regulation which compounded confusion. The Army had decided that the glare of lights along the coast was outlining American ships at night as perfect targets for the lurking U-boats. In order to restore the cover of darkness to the ships Lieutenant General Hugh A. Drum, commander of the First Army Area and the Eastern Defense Command, asked the cooperation of all the governors of the Atlantic coast states in eliminating the illumination which was silhouetting the ships at sea. When Governor Darden received this request on March 11, he at once promised to do everything necessary as soon as he found out what that was.[9]

Norfolk, well inside the capes of the Chesapeake, saw little

[7] Maurice E. Bennett to Joseph Leslie, April 27, 1942, Civilian Defense: Public Relations file, NWHC records. This organization was in accordance with the national pattern recommended by the U. S. Office of Civilian Defense.

[8] *V-P*, March 1, 1942, Part II, p. 1; March 3, 1942, p. 18; March 5, 1942, p. 18.

[9] *V-P*, March 11, 1942, p. 18; Richmond *Times-Dispatch*, March 12, 1942, p. 8.

reason for concern over this new measure, but Virginia Beach was alarmed. Don Seiwell, secretary of the Chamber of Commerce there, went to Richmond to talk to Darden, discovered the Governor still knew nothing about the proposed regulations, and finally had to go to New York City for a conference with the chief of staff of the First Army. Returning with the reassuring news that the Beach would only have to turn off its neon signs and screen its shore lights, he left a memorandum of the Army's ideas with the Governor, who proceeded to draw them up into an executive order.[10]

On Saturday morning, March 21, Norfolk was surprised to learn that Darden's order extended the dimout inside the bay, reaching all the way to Willoughby Spit on the southern shore. Forewarned Virginia Beach was already at work dimming its lights, but Norfolk and Princess Anne County were too stunned to act. Since Colonel Borland happened to be out of town, Police Chief Woods sought excuse for inaction in the lack of any official communication direct from Governor Darden. The *Virginian-Pilot* scolded:

> We leave it to those trained in these legal refinements to say whether an order broadcast by the Governor instead of addressed to specific enforcement officials, is an order to be obeyed or merely an oration to be applauded. But the ghastly record of coastal ship-sinkings, we think, might have suggested to the Norfolk and Princess Anne police chiefs the wisdom of taking a chance on the order's legality. . . .
>
> The procedural issue will, of course, be cleared up without delay. . . . The Governor will have to send personal telegrams—maybe engrossed parchments—to the hesitant enforcement officers, and put the business on a protocol basis.[11]

The real issue, however, was not the legality of the order but its necessity. The Navy, which had the primary responsibility for fighting the submarines, seemed to have no intention of turning out its own lights at the Base and at Little Creek. With the Navy's brilliant floodlights glaring out into the night, there

[10] *V-P*, March 13, 1942, Part II, p. 12; March 17, 1942, p. 18; Richmond *Times-Dispatch*, March 17, 1942, p. 9.
[11] *V-P*, March 22, 1942, Part II, p. 1; March 23, 1942, p. 14; March 24, 1942, p. 6.

seemed little point in warning individual householders to pull down their shades. As Ocean View's Zone Warden, M. G. Duffy, reported to Chief Ferebee after an inspection trip: "The only comment that I wish to make is for you or some one in charge to start at the end of Willoughby and ride to Little Creek and take a look at all the U. S. Government places and then wonder what the public will say to having their places blacked out."[12]

Many people in Norfolk, moreover, including the city manager, did not believe that the lights at Ocean View were visible from the sea. Nevertheless, Colonel Borland ordered the police to study the situation. Police Captain M. H. House surveyed the Ocean View area and recommended that all neon signs be turned out, that lights reflecting on the bay be shaded, and street lights blacked out on the side toward the water. As an additional check, the city manager asked the Navy to make an inspection from the bay and suggest any further changes that might be needed.[13]

Since no requests came from the Navy, the matter seemed settled. Meanwhile, however, the Army had decided that its request for civilian cooperation was not getting satisfactory results. Without bothering to complain to local officials, it ordered Third Corps Area headquarters at Baltimore to prepare a strict set of regulations. On April 29 Norfolk was startled to read in the morning papers that Major General Milton A. Reckord, commander of the Third Corps Area, had just issued a new dimout order, which included not only Ocean View but also downtown Norfolk as well as Portsmouth.[14]

The city was dumbfounded by this latest development. Borland and Marshall promptly went to Richmond to ask the Governor what it was all about, but found that Darden knew no more than they did. Brigadier General Don E. Scott, local Army commander, reported that he had received no information yet. The operators of the amusement park at Ocean View wondered if they would have to close up at night. When a reporter asked the Navy Yard whether it would obey the Army's dimout order, he received

[12] Duffy to Ferebee, March 23, 1942, Civilian Defense: Air Raid Wardens file, NWHC records.

[13] House to Chief John F. Woods, March 23, 1942, copy in NWHC records; V-P, March 24, 1942, p. 18.

[14] V-P, April 29, 1942, p. 20.

an "emphatically negative answer." Strict compliance with the rules, a spokesman explained, would seriously hamper the Yard's production.[15]

On May 1, the day after the Reckord proclamation was supposed to go into effect, the order was officially received in Norfolk, but it failed to make clear what lights needed to be turned off. Just to make matters more complicated, State Coordinator Wyse announced in Richmond that he had received a wire from the Navy reporting that the existing dimout was entirely satisfactory. Colonel Borland decided to ask the Army and the Navy to make observations and decide what lights were to be extinguished. "We don't want to go off half-cocked," he declared, "turning off lights right and left without knowing whether it is actually necessary to turn off these lights. We do want to do our part, however, and if the Army and Navy will tell us where we are wrong, we will do our best to make things right."[16]

Fortunately, signs of cooperation between the land and the sea forces at last appeared. Enforcement of the Reckord proclamation was suspended for the time being, and General Reckord appointed Brigadier General Rollin L. Tilton, head of the Chesapeake Bay Sector Command, to work out an agreement with the Navy on standard dimout practices.[17] The Navy inshore patrol, accompanied by members of the Army's Internal Security Force, made several reconnaissances and reported that Norfolk's lights were not likely to silhouette passing ships. The only spot in the city where excessive illumination was noted was in East Ocean View.[18]

Although these reports indicated that Norfolk was nearly dim enough, General Tilton went ahead with the drafting of his new regulations. To cooperate with him in this task, the Governor appointed a special committee at his May meeting with the Hampton Roads defense officials. This group met with Tilton on May 26 and promised that they would correct any violations

[15] *V-P*, May 1, 1942, Part II, pp. 12, 1.
[16] *V-P*, May 2, 1942, p. 16.
[17] Telegram, Major S. T. McCloskey to J. H. Wyse, May 1, 1942; mimeographed copy of memorandum, General Tilton to General Reckord, May 7, 1942. VOCD records.
[18] Copy of letter, Tilton to Commanding General, Third Corps Area, May 9, 1942; Colonel F. T. Bonsteel to Borland, May 15, 1942. Civilian Defense: Blackouts file, NWHC records.

disclosed. The general, it was understood, would submit his plan to the committee for study before it was formally issued.[19]

From the Army itself, General Tilton received less cooperation. After trying unsuccessfully to obtain instructions from Eastern Defense Command headquarters in New York, he decided to go ahead on his own. He then submitted his new set of regulations to both New York and to Third Corps headquarters and waited for approval. The new rules were a distinct disappointment to the Hampton Roads officials, as they made no modification in the original order and in fact extended the dimout as far inland as Suffolk. Colonel Borland entered a protest, declaring that putting out all the neon signs in the city of Norfolk struck him as "a little drastic and unnecessary."[20] In spite of this general opinion, the committee of Hampton Roads officials unanimously agreed to accept the proposed regulations. Enforcement was suspended until the Army should formally issue the new rules.[21]

Fortunately there was no such lack of coordination over the rules governing blackouts. The city had held its two December drills before there had been any opportunity to draw up a set of regulations. Then the reorganization of the Civilian Defense structure had delayed action, while Colonel Borland waited for an agreement on uniformity in the Hampton Roads area. Uniformity was at length obtained when Governor Darden on April 20 issued a standard set of rules for the entire state. Colonel Borland immediately ordered thousands of copies of the Governor's order printed for public distribution.[22]

The new rules provided a complete code of instructions on proper blackout behavior. They reaffirmed the standard signals, a fluctuating siren blast for the alarm and a steady tone for the all clear. They prescribed rules for vehicles, pedestrians, schools, hotels, motion picture theaters, and even dogs and cats. The

[19] Memorandum, Colonel Alan L. Hart to Governor Darden, May 26, 1942, VOCD records; Marshall to Darden, June 19, 1942, Civilian Defense: Blackouts file, NWHC records.

[20] Borland to Tilton, June 18, 1942, Civilian Defense: Blackouts file, NWHC records.

[21] Tilton to Borland, June 22, 1942, Civilian Defense: Blackouts file, NWHC records; memorandum, Colonel Alan L. Hart to J. H. Wyse, June 27, 1942, VOCD records.

[22] V-P, April 26, 1942, Part II, p. 2.

Governor's order also required both a blackout and a daylight drill every month in Norfolk and other vital areas of the state.

The city's Civilian Defense workers prepared to go back into action. Chief Air Raid Warden Ferebee tested his men to see whether they were ready. After notifying them to expect a drill sometime during the week, he sent out a surprise call on Tuesday night. Zone wardens called their section wardens, who called their senior wardens, who in turn passed the word on to the block wardens. The notice reached 1,745 out of a possible 2,700. Since several hundred wardens at meetings or still in training were not called, Chief Ferebee considered this a fairly good record.[23]

Approval was obtained for a blackout of the entire south side of Hampton Roads on May 18, the first in more than four months. At 9:02 P. M. the newly-arrived sirens went into action for the first time, and in two minutes the forewarned public had lights out or blackout shades drawn. Darkness reigned all over the south side, as even the Navy Yard and the Base took part in the blackout. Automobiles, streetcars, and buses came to dead stops. The city was wrapped in unaccustomed silence, even on East Main Street. One group of servicemen did burst into song, but they were quickly silenced by the shore patrol. The biggest problem was the sailors, who insisted on roaming the streets in their gleaming summer whites. Several of them kicked in the window of a building on West Bute Street where lights were showing. Another group threatened to smash the window of a shoe repair shop where a neon light had been left on but finally compromised by tearing down the awning and hanging it in front of the offending gleam. Elsewhere officers were able to persuade would-be window-breakers to leave the glass alone by pointing out that the owners would be fined.

So efficiently did the volunteers do their job of halting traffic that some defense officials found it difficult to get to their posts because they were stopped so often. Wardens on 18th Street had trouble with one café which refused to turn off its lights even after the auxiliary policy had been sent for. Ocean View had a special problem, as Zone Warden Duffy reported to Chief Ferebee: "I would like to have you talk to Bill Aycock in regard to

[23] *V-P*, April 29, 1942, p. 13.

the Army Officers Club and the Enlisted personnel of the Army in Ocean View to find out why they do not turn their lights off as everyone else does." On the whole, however, cooperation was excellent. Coordinator Marshall announced that a mere twenty violations had been reported, only fifteen of which were real infringements.[24]

On Thursday night of the same week the Civilian Defense system held another drill to test its readiness for actual disaster. To avoid disturbing the public, no blackout was called and the sirens were not blown. Instead local radio stations interrupted their programs at 8:12 P. M. to announce: "Test maneuvers for Civilian Defense, Norfolk, Virginia, commence immediately." The heads of the emergency services at once hastened to their posts at the control center, while other volunteers prepared for their duties. Fourteen section wardens stared at sealed envelopes, waiting for the arrival of the time marked on the outside. At that moment they ripped open the envelopes and reported the imaginary disaster in the message to the control center, which dispatched the necessary aid.[25]

In Lakewood, Section Warden Emery Cox notified the center at nine o'clock that a bomb had damaged the Preston home, and fifteen seconds later dispatched a messenger to summon first-aid trained neighbors as well as a nurse and doctors. In two more minutes the neighbors had reached the scene. The fire department and a salvage car, dispatched from the control center, arrived over the Lakewood bridge at 9:12, only to learn over the car radio a minute later that the bridge had been theoretically blown up eight minutes before. A Red Cross car, sent from Granby High, was detoured around the impassable bridge and arrived at 9:36. Nurses aides carried the "victims" to the car, but here a bit of confusion developed. The squad leader tried to call the high school to learn whether the victims should be taken there, but discovered information would not give him the school's unlisted number. Then he called Red Cross headquarters and was told to take the wounded to the school. When they arrived, how-

[24] V-P, May 19, 1942, p. 18, May 20, 1942, p. 18; C. E. Wright to Ferebee, May 19, 1942, M. G. Duffy to Ferebee, May 19, 1942, Civilian Defense: Blackout Incidents file, NWHC records.

[25] V-P, May 22, 1942, Part II, p. 12.

ever, the building was dark, and the victims had to be taken back home with their imaginary injuries untreated.[26]

The following Monday, just a week after the blackout, Norfolk had its first daylight drill, in accordance with Governor Darden's order. At 11:00 A. M. the sirens sounded the beginning of a half-hour test. A note of realism was added when the Army moved armored trucks, bearing fully-armed soldiers, into the downtown section. The soldiers threw a ring around the Federal Building and set up an emergency communications system. Most pedestrians promptly obeyed the rules by taking shelter, and those who hurried on were soon brought to a stop. One motorist refused to halt, insisting that he had to catch the Little Creek ferry. Some people violated the regulations by hanging out of windows or remaining in doorways. A shoe clerk used his time to advantage by selling defense stamps to persons who had taken shelter in the store. In the residential districts air raid wardens, absent at work, turned their duties over to their wives. In Stockley Gardens women wardens took care of the women sunning their babies there by escorting mothers and children to the basement of the Ghent Methodist Church.[27]

The experiment with women wardens proved quite successful, and Chief Ferebee decided to enroll women for daytime service as a regular policy. He insisted that they be given the same training as their husbands and receive credentials and insignia. The sirens, however, were not doing their job. Even though four more had been added to the original eight, wardens still found many people who had never heard the alarm. Ferebee declared: ". . . I cannot emphasize too strongly the sense of helplessness the wardens have when they depend on a warning system that is as faint as ours now is."[28] To correct the difficulty the city ordered still more sirens and settled down to a monthly routine of air raid tests.

[26] W. Fred Bonney to Ferebee, May 25, 1942, Civilian Defense: Blackout Incidents, NWHC records.
[27] V-P, May 26, 1942, p. 18.
[28] Ferebee to Marshall, June 4, 1942, Civilian Defense: Blackout Incidents, NWHC records.

15

PLENTY OF NOTHING

NORFOLK had never known a summer like the summer of 1942. It set new records for being hot; it set new records for being dry; and, worst of all, it set new records for being crowded. None of the promises that had bloomed in the spring had yet borne fruit, and every old problem seemed intensified. For a year there had been no more room for any newcomers, and yet they continued to arrive. How they managed to find a place to sleep was a mystery. Clerks in rental agencies developed a hard shell of indifference to protect themselves from the home-seekers who mobbed their offices. One reporter who tried his luck received only a cold stare and a polite rejection. "We don't take names, ever," the young lady said. "All our apartments are leased, and there's really nothing this agency can do for you, really nothing at all. You might come back in October." At a home where an apartment had been advertised for rent he met a lady who was bored but patient. "There was a vacancy here," she told him, "a third-floor apartment we furnished with some of our older things and some nice things we bought, but some people had waited up for the paper to come out, and they rushed right over and were so insistent I rented it to them without waiting for anyone else. The phone has been ringing until I had to take the receiver off. I wish I could help you, but that's the way it is."[1]

This scene was repeated day after day. Hopeful househunters waited for the appearance of the first edition of the morning paper and then dashed madly off for any advertised vacancy. Pleas by late sleepers for applicants not to call before ten were ignored by the homeless, who started their door-knocking at dawn.

[1] Robert H. Mason, "Vignettes of Norfolk in Wartime," *V-P*, March 12, 1942, Part II, pp. 12, 7.

Would-be renters came by the hundreds, sometimes with babes in arms, pleading for the apartment. Long after the weary landlord had posted a notice, "Apartment already rented, sorry," optimists with no faith in signs continued to ask for the vacancy. Some pleaded in wistful disappointment for at least a chance to see what they had missed and heaved rapturous sighs over a few shabby rooms. Desperate home-seekers turned to advertising: "Ten Dollars reward for a clue or information telling us where we can get a place to live, unfurnished, for likeable 30-year-old wife and two well-behaved children, boy 8, girl, 10; husband be out of town for a year."[2]

Single men usually had to be satisfied with half a bed, sometimes for only half a day, as bed rooms operated in shifts like their occupants. Exigency made strangers bedfellows. One warworker, who reported that his roommate had stolen his wallet, had to confess that he did not know the fellow's name.[3] Workers at the Navy Yard turned their troubles over to the Yard's housing coordinator, E. S. Smith, who received letters by the hundreds. One of them read:

I called your office this morning to see if you would help us find some place to move. I would be well satisfied to have a trailer. After explaining my reasons to the office girl I was told to write you a letter.

Sometime ago I wrote you about getting a house. At that time there were three extra people living with me. Now there are 4 people less, as my mother located elsewhere and a week ago I lost my little girl. She died of pneumonia.

I explained to you in my first letter the condition this house is in and someone is always sick as this house is very drafty, full of holes in the floors and doors. The toilet room is always wet due to leaky plumbing which has been that way for years according to a previous tenant. The sink drain is bursted under the house and water stands under the kitchen all the time and the floor is always damp.

When my baby died I had my rent in my pocket but fearing something would happen I held it and the day my baby was buried I explained to the agent and asked him to wait one week as I had no insurance on my baby and it took every cent I had for the doctor and undertaker. Mr. Abbott (the agent) said it would be all right so just as soon as I

---

[2] *V-P*, June 27, 1942, pp. 18, 9.
[3] *V-P*, August 7, 1942, Part II, p. 16

had paid it out he got a court order to make us move instead of waiting as he had promised.

So I must have a place by next week the 11th or I will just have to leave the Navy Yard and go back home. I can't find a place anywhere.

I would be truly grateful if you could just find me a trailer to live in until I can get one of your houses. There is just myself, wife, one baby 3 years and one aged 2. I'm not angry with the owner of the place but the health department should force him to make it a decent place to live in.

Since coming to Norfolk a year ago I have been unable to locate a place where I could stay permanently and it is very expensive to keep moving about. I don't owe anyone a cent for rent except for this past month here which I am perfectly willing to pay.

I'll be anxiously waiting to hear from you and hope you will be able to help me as I like my work and only ask for a chance to take care of my family.[4]

Negroes inevitably fared worst of all. Decent homes in Norfolk's colored section had been few and far between even before the boom; except for the 300 in Oak Leaf Park, virtually none had been added since. A survey undertaken just after Pearl Harbor by the Norfolk Housing Authority disclosed appalling conditions. Of 199 housing units only four were considered standard. In 49 units two or more families were living. In one-room units as many as five persons were living; two-room apartments held up to seven persons, while twelve persons crowded into some three-room quarters. Baths were shared generously, in one instance by as many as seventeen families. One ten-room house had ten apartments.[5]

An even worse situation was uncovered by the Family Welfare Association in June. The association found six houses in which 161 persons were living at a total rent of more than $350 a week. In one room seven persons were existing. The man and his wife slept in one single bed, while their four children slept in the other. The wife's younger brother had an Army cot to himself. In the small hall bedroom next door a man, his wife, and two grown sons shared one three-quarter-size bed; neighbors could not figure out how they slept. In another house forty persons had as their only sanitary facilities two tubs and two toilets, one of which would

[4] "Norfolk, Va.," *Architectural Forum*, 76: 366–72 (June, 1942).

[5] Norfolk *Journal and Guide*, December 27, 1941, p. 16.

not work. The houses were all thick with flies, and the cellars were full of water.[6]

As people sought frantically for places to live, economic pressure shoved rents skyward. From April, 1940, to November, 1941, rents in Norfolk jumped 13.7 per cent, the second largest increase in the country. By March, 1942, they were 19.5 per cent above the pre-war level and were still climbing.[7] The Fair Rent Committee was deluged with "innumerable, almost continual complaints," according to Chairman W. C. Pender, most of them protesting against roominghouse operators. One woman with three children complained that she was paying $40 a month for three rooms and had to furnish heat for her own and the next-door apartment. The rent a year earlier, she said, had been only $22.[8] In most instances increases ranged from $10 to $20 a month, although the rent on one Portsmouth dwelling rose from $26.50 to $75.[9]

The Navy Yard, losing 500 workers a month because of the housing situation, appealed to Governor Darden to act under the new rent control bill passed by the General Assembly. The OPA meanwhile ordered Norfolk rents returned to April, 1941, levels within sixty days. Chairman Pender of the Fair Rent Committee welcomed this assistance in his task, although he felt there should be some adjustment formula to provide for equalizing rents of that date for comparable quarters. Real estate men in general accepted the idea of control and pledged their support to eliminate gouging. They protested, however, against setting the ceilings at April, 1941, rates. For leased properties this date was in the middle of the rent year, which meant that rents then had been set in October, 1940, before the boom had fairly got under way. Feeling that they were entitled to reasonable increases, the real estate men asked the OPA to change the ceiling date to October, 1941.[10]

The deadline for the OPA's sixty-day notice arrived on May 1 without any evidence of voluntary compliance. The OPA there-

[6] *V-P*, June 25, 1942, pp. 22, 13.
[7] *V-P*, February 25, 1942, p. 18, reporting a *Business Week* survey; *Domestic Commerce*, June 4, 1942, pp. 3–6. The second figures are based on 1935–39 averages, probably slightly lower than April, 1940, levels.
[8] *V-P*, March 3, 1942, p. 18; March 19, 1942, Part I, p. 6.
[9] *V-P*, June 16, 1942, p. 18.
[10] *V-P*, March 3, 1942, p. 18; March 19, 1942, Part II, p. 12; May 9, 1942, p. 16.

fore moved in and appointed Claud P. Brownley, Jr., rent director for the Hampton Roads Defense Rental Area. Landlords were warned that they could be compelled to refund three times the overcharge, with a minimum of $50. Controls went into effect on June 1, although the registration of housing units was not held until July. By August the OPA started on its enforcement campaign, bringing suit against the operator of a group of tourist cabins in the Tanners Creek district.[11]

A few landlords complained about this government interference with free enterprise. One rugged individualist declared:

The ability to rent one's house is a property right, and should not be taken from the owner without compensation. If the government wants to see lower rents here for the duration of the war, for the benefit of its employes, it should compensate the owners for their losses in not being able to rent their houses in their way, and itself rent out the houses on a lower basis.

It seems strange for Uncle Sam to send in special police from the outside to tell us what rents our houses are worth and to put us in jail if we do not act in accordance with their views.

In the opinion of the writer, if dwellings here were rented by public auction instead of privately larger rents would prevail than those now shared by property owners.

The owners are morally and legally entitled to the rentals offered them for houses by the divinely ordained law of supply and demand.[12]

Such opinions were rare, however. The Norfolk Real Estate Board confined its opposition to the date chosen for the ceiling. Although it hired a lawyer to present its case, the OPA refused to make any concessions.[13]

Even though rents were being pulled down to earth, homes were no easier to find. All the thousands of homes that had been projected in the spring were still unbuilt, and the builders were snarled in red tape and priorities. After the Defense Housing Coordinator had begun the program in January, a new consolidation wiped out that office in February and created a National Housing Agency in charge of all projects. The new NHA found

[11] V-P, May 29, 1942, Part II, p. 12; August 18, 1942, p. 18.
[12] V-P, June 27, 1942, p. 4.
[13] V-P, July 26, 1942, Part II, p. 1.

that the War Production Board would grant no priorities for housing servicemen's families, and the 1,800 homes for enlisted men scheduled for erection west of Cottage Toll Road, fell under the ax. The WPB tried to turn the war-workers' housing projects into barracks, but the NHA finally convinced it that homes were needed as well as dormitories. Meanwhile, the Barrett and Hilp firm which had contracted in January to build 5,000 homes near Portsmouth in 150 days had to wait 111 days before the Government would even let it start.

The contracts which had been let in February for the prefabricated village on Broad Creek Road and the Negro housing project had to be cancelled. Not until June was a new contractor found for the Broad Creek group. A Washington firm moved in, bogged down, and quit, and then the project had to be turned over to local builders. The men who were putting up the private homes had troubles of their own; there was no lumber, no wire, no plumbing. Then in May the WPB suddenly stopped work altogether with a new restriction order. Levitt's, with only 200 of its 750 homes finished, laid off half its crew. The Norfolk Housing Authority looked for kerosene lamps for Roberts Park because no wiring for electricity was available. Completed homes stood vacant because there were no furnaces or no sewer pipe. Although the WPB promised that it would soon allocate the necessary materials to finish all the scheduled houses, it was a month before the builders could get back to work again.[14]

While work on the defense homes proceeded under handicaps, other projects came to a complete standstill. A WPB order in May eliminating all unnecessary public works using critical materials wiped out the still unstarted elementary school on Granby Street. The fate of the Negro school in Campostella trembled in the balance, but it was finally saved. The Army, given the decision on the new auditorium, decided to complete it by substituting reinforced concrete for the critical steel girders. The old contract had to be cancelled, however, and the bare foundations baked all through the summer. Not until August was a new contractor found.[15]

[14] V-P, May 28, 1942, p. 20; June 3, 1942, p. 20; June 4, 1942, p. 11; Richmond Times-Dispatch, June 4, 1942, p. 19; L-D, June 27, 1942, p. 3.
[15] V-P, May 24, 1942, Part II, p. 1; June 25, 1942, p. 22; August 23, 1942, Part II, p. 1.

Work on the new water lines also ran into priority troubles, and meanwhile a dry spring was shrinking the water supply. City Manager Borland announced that the situation might become critical, and the *Virginian-Pilot* asked for advice:

How is a householder, nursing his lawn or even his victory garden to know how much he can use the garden hose without deserting his obligation to the war burdened community? Maybe it is better that the zinnias die than that the water in the city lakes sink to disturbing levels.

Some guidance is needed from the City Hall. If the time has come to conserve water, we should have a statement to that effect from the city authorities, together with some indication as to the extent to which water conservation should be carried. The present period of drought is the time for such a clarification. Nobody knows how long the drought will continue. Nobody knows whether good citizenship and responsibility to the war effort requires one to spare the hose or to use it.[16]

The city replied with a water-saving ordinance providing a fine for the use of a hose to sprinkle lawns or gardens or to wash cars and windows. Nature cooperated with an all-day sprinkle to save the withering gardens, but water consumption fell only from 23 million to 22 million gallons on the first day of the water ordinance. In spite of the rain the city had only enough water to last for four or five months.[17]

The state geologist offered the public instructions on how to drill wells, which in Norfolk fortunately was easy. All one had to do was to drive a pipe—if he could get a pipe—fifteen to twenty feet into the ground. Even Portsmouth, still nettled over the unneighborly way in which Norfolk had tried to force through action on the sanitation district and the Elizabeth River tunnel, offered to lend some of its water, and Norfolk replied by giving a dinner for the Portsmouth city officials. Before the new pipe line had reached the Portsmouth connection, however, the city discovered its generosity had been too impetuous, as investigation disclosed that it had no water to spare.[18]

The city sank test wells around Lake Prince, looking for water to fill up the half-empty lake. The FWA rushed work on its pipe

[16] *V-P*, May 7, 1942, p. 6.
[17] *V-P*, May 13, 1942, p. 12; May 17, 1942, Part II, p. 1; May 20, 1942, p. 18.
[18] *V-P*, June 11, 1942, p. 20; July 11, 1942, p. 16; July 22, 1942, p. 4; July 29, 1942, p. 18.

line to the Nottoway River and promised that by mid-September it would be able to pump from the Blackwater River to a spot where the water would flow into Lake Prince. By this means it hoped to furnish fifteen million gallons a day to Norfolk. Then the rains came, drenching Norfolk rains, flooding the streets. In fifteen days of August more rain fell than in any full month on record previously. Victory gardens came back to life, the lakes filled up, and the water shortage was over.[19]

Not so easily ended were other shortages which complicated life in the hectic summer of 1942. Coffee had become scarce when retailers were put on delivery quotas 25 per cent below their 1941 sales. An appeal to adjust these figures in accordance with the growth in population in the last year won WPB approval for a 35 per cent increase and ten weeks later the OPA issued the necessary authorization.[20] Local bakers had their basic quota of sugar upped from 70 per cent to 120 per cent by the local rationing board for the same reason, but the state rationing office ruled that the local board had no authority to grant such increases. Congressman Harris carried the fight to the OPA headquarters in Washington but found himself battling a stone wall. The baffled bakers were forced to stop making cakes entirely and had to cut down on pies.[21]

The sugar problem for the individual housewife was simpler. The arrival of rationing in May ended her harried search from store to store for a bag of sugar. Women stood in line to register for their families' ration books at the schools, as the men had already gone through one registration. Some registrants were down to their last bowlful, while others had as much as 100 pounds, but all were now made equal. Each person was to get half a pound a week thereafter.[22]

A week after the sugar registration came the promised gasoline rationing. Applicants were placed on the honor system in stating their needs and were granted A, B, or C cards, allowing three, six, or nine gallons a week respectively. A special X card, granting

[19] *V-P*, July 30, 1942, p. 18; August 14, 1942, Part II, p. 12; August 15, 1942, p. 16.
[20] *V-P*, April 28, 1942, p. 1; May 19, 1942, p. 18; July 31, 1942, Part II, p. 10.
[21] *V-P*, April 29, 1942, p. 13; June 7, 1942, Part II, p. 1.
[22] *V-P*, May 5, 1942, p. 17.

unlimited gasoline, was reserved for certain essential groups. A great deal of confusion attended the issuing of the new cards. The operator of a hot-dog hand cart had to be told that he could refuel his stove without a card. Some who wanted more than the maximum of nine gallons a week permitted by the C card crowded into the ration board's office to demand an increased allotment. Others who needed more were given X cards by the volunteer registrars, although they were not eligible to receive them. Board Chairman Wolcott had to ask for the return of the incorrectly issued cards and found himself overwhelmed by the prompt response.[23]

The only sign of reduced travel on May 17, the first Sunday after rationing went into effect, was that fewer North Carolina cars were noticed in town, and a week later the traffic was unusually heavy. Although it was not a hot Sunday, thousands drove to the beaches or just drove. Gas dealers on reduced quotas limited their sales to out-of-town cars but soon forgot to punch the cards of their regular customers. By the middle of June this artificially inflated demand was draining some stations dry, and by June 27 more than half the service stations in the city were closed. An emergency appeal by the Navy brought a 15 per cent increase in basic quotas from the Office of the Petroleum Coordinator to keep Norfolk automobiles rolling.[24]

Meanwhile a more effective system of gasoline control was on the way. This system, which went into effect on July 21, provided a book of coupons, which had to be surrendered in exchange for gas. The dealer then had to turn in the coupons to obtain additional supplies of gasoline. Each motorist obtained his basic A book from the volunteer registrars, then filed his application with the ration board for a B or C book according to his needs. Dealers were no longer troubled with gasoline quotas, since they could obtain as much gasoline as they could sell.

Even though there was now plenty of gas for Norfolk's war workers, the new system brought no relief to the city's transportation system. In an effort to take some of the strain off the Hampton Boulevard line to the Naval Base, City Manager Borland ordered two-thirds of the stops eliminated. The absent-minded

---

[23] *V-P*, May 15, 1942, Part II, p. 12; May 16, 1942, p. 16; May 21, 1942, p. 20.
[24] *V-P*, May 17, 1942, Part II, p. 1; May 18, 1942, p. 14; May 25, 1942, p. 14; June 28, 1942, Part II, p. 1.

suffered inconvenience on May 15, the first day of operation under the new order. Passengers waiting at the eliminated stops shook their fists at the motorman who passed them up. Those on the car pushed the button frantically as they sailed on past their usual corner. Women shoppers were surprised and indignant when the trolleys failed to stop for them. One man, noticing a woman heavily laden with bundles passed up by three cars, decided he had better tell her that the cars did not stop there any more. He was rewarded for his courtesy by an angry reply: "You're no gentleman or you would have told us that the cars didn't stop at this corner instead of standing there like a dummy and let us miss three of them."[25]

Eliminating the stops speeded up service so much, however, that a girl on the first car got to work fifteen minutes early and had to wait for her boss to let her in. Gradually trolley-riders abandoned their grumbling and accepted the walk of an extra block or two. Soon the system was extended over the rest of the city, and half of both car and bus stops were eliminated. The Bay View bus line was discontinued to improve service elsewhere.[26] Ferry transportation was also speeded up by the erection of a third landing dock in Portsmouth.[27]

Taxicab service was likewise expanded to take care of growing transportation needs. The taxi company was authorized to add 25 cabs to the 75 it was already operating. The city council also approved the licensing of 64 more for-hire cars to make a total of 117 of these meterless independents. Still cabs were hard to find. Often passengers arriving on the Baltimore boat or at the bus station discovered that there was not a single taxi waiting. The cab company explained that nearly half its vehicles were laid up for lack of tires. The independents, with no obligation to provide service, were not bothering with the small change to be picked up by hauling visitors to hotels.[28]

Many of the for-hire cars, it appeared, were developing a specialized service, shuttling sailors and civilians between downtown Norfolk and the lurid night spots in the county just east of

[25] *V-P*, May 18, 1942, p. 16.
[26] *V-P*, June 24, 1942, p. 20; June 30, 1942, p. 18.
[27] *V-P*, July 5, 1942, Part I, p. 5.
[28] *V-P*, May 13, 1942, p. 18; June 11, 1942, p. 20; August 13, 1942, p. 20.

the city line. One group of independents was economizing on gasoline and rubber by insisting on a full load of six passengers each
way. This earned a profitable $12 for the round trip, plus a cut
from the house for the driver who brought in the business.[29]

The popularity of the clubs and cabins around Cottage Toll
and Sewells Point roads was being increased by the renewed war
of the police against prostitution inside the city limits. Ever since
the closing of the segregated district in January, 1941, the police
had been arresting prostitutes periodically, but the quarters for
women in the city jail, intended for a maximum of 45 persons,
were soon overflowing. The court therefore could merely impose
the customary $25 fine and suspend the jail sentence. Since many
out-of-town girls, hearing of the easy money to be picked up in
Norfolk, had arrived to swell the number of the exiles from East
Main Street, not to mention the boom-happy youngsters who
retained their amateur status while plying the profession, the
police had been able to do little more than make a gesture of
enforcement.

In the spring of 1942, however, the Navy, concerned over an
increase in venereal disease infection among its personnel, suggested that more vigorous enforcement was advisable. Colonel
Borland ordered that all women violating their suspended sen-
tences were to be rearrested and placed in the city jail, regardless
of the fact that it was already crowded. This new policy resulted
in driving many of the prostitutes out into the county and created
a dangerous situation in the jail. During the heat wave in July as
many as 110 women were jammed into the prison quarters. They
had to sleep doubled up in the 45 single beds, with the overflow
spreading floor mattresses in the halls and even on the stair
landings. Jail authorities admitted conditions were cruel and in-
human, but were powerless to do anything about it.[30]

The city could not transfer the women to its prison farm since
it had no facilities there for white women and did not feel that it
should go to the expense of providing them to meet a problem that
had been created largely by outsiders. Colonel Borland tried to
secure the cooperation of the state by asking the State Commis-

[29] *V-P*, August 13, 1942, p. 20.
[30] *V-P*, July 17, 1942, Part II, p. 18.

sioner of Public Welfare, Dr. William H. Stauffer, for more room at the State Farm for Women at Goochland, saying:

I feel that Norfolk should be given extra consideration in the allotment of space in the State institution by reason of the fact that these women have come here from all over the United States, as well as from other towns and cities in this State.

As the great majority of these women, therefore, are not legal residents of Norfolk and are here solely by reason of the military establishments in this area, I do think that the State should help us solve this problem.[31]

More than a year before Norfolk had been promised help to meet this situation. When Charles P. Taft had visited the city on March 28, 1941, he had declared that Norfolk would receive enough money to establish a quarantine hospital for women with venereal disease. The city had been by-passed, however, in the detailed plans worked out by the Office of Defense Health and Welfare Service. The ODHWS after a survey of the situation had decided that State action was more appropriate and recommended that the State apply for the grant. A committee of State officials had then made another survey in September, 1941, and decided to apply for funds to expand the State Prison Farm at Goochland and settled all the administrative details in time to submit the application on January 15, 1942. By that time most of the good ideas of 1941 were falling under the priorities ax, and after two months the Federal Works Agency had decided that the project would have to be deferred for the present.[32]

Now that the need was so urgent, a new approach to the situation was called for. Federal, State, and local officials, along with military representatives, met in Colonel Borland's office and agreed unanimously that something should be done to provide quarters for the unfortunate women in the city jail. It was suggested that demountable buildings from one of the abandoned CCC camps might be transferred to Goochland to provide emergency shelter. On July 19 Governor Darden sent State officials to Washington to get the Army's permission to take over the

---

[31] *V-P*, June 26, 1942, Part I, p. 11.

[32] *V-P*, February 24, 1943, p. 20; statement of John J. Hurley, field representative, Social Protection Section, ODHWS, in *Hampton Roads Investigation*, pp. 346–348.

CCC buildings. Back through channels came the answer: The Army had no intention of giving up any of the CCC camps because it might need them sometime. The ODHWS went to work to polish up the Army brass. Police Chief Woods was summoned to New York City to take part in a conference with the ODHWS and came back on August 8 with the reassuring news that the Army had agreed to surrender two of the CCC camps in Virginia and that the Federal Government would establish a detention home to care for a thousand prostitutes.[33]

Prostitution, of course, was only a minor phase of the over-all police problem. The over-burdened police force, at a rock-bottom minimum when the boom began, was not expanding along with the population; in fact, it was actually decreasing because of the difficulty in finding replacements for the men who left. Fortunately, crime did not increase at the same rate as the population, even though newspapers occasionally talked of a crime wave.[34] Another factor staving off disaster was the responsibility of the Navy for keeping order among its thousands of sailors swarming over the downtown streets.

The Navy, however, was falling even farther behind than the city in meeting this responsibility, even though the Fifth Naval District had taken every step authorized by naval regulations. In May, 1941, shortly before Admiral Taussig retired as commandant, he had tried to make the shore patrol more effective by giving it a permanent skeleton organization. The shore patrol previous to that time had had no regularly assigned personnel except a chief petty officer who came on every evening at five o'clock to post the sailors who had been given patrol duty for that night. Under the new plan a half dozen chief petty officers were assigned permanently to shore patrol duty so that a watch could be kept in the city police station 24 hours a day. In addition twenty petty officers from the Base were detailed for a thirty-day period of shore patrol duty. This semi-permanent group supervised the ship's men, who were still given patrol duty only for one night at a time.[35]

[33] Hurley statement, *op. cit.; V-P*, July 9, 1942, p. 20; July 18, 1942, p. 16; August 3, 1942, p. 6; August 9, 1942, Part II, p. 1.

[34] *V-P*, July 13, 1942, p. 14; August 30, 1942, Part II, p. 1.

[35] "History of the Naval Shore Patrol, Fifth Naval District," in U. S. Armed Forces: Naval Shore Patrol file, NWHC records.

These new patches on the Navy's old, traditional system of casual policing covered up some of the worst of the holes. The permanent, and even the semipermanent, officers stayed on the job long enough to get acquainted with patrol problems. Each evening, as a new shore patrol group came on duty, the new men were given strict instructions for their night's assignment. Nevertheless, most of the old weaknesses of the system were still apparent. The patrol continued to be lenient with shipmates, and there were seldom enough men to cover all the trouble spots. Even when arrests were made, the complaining witness was likely to be off at sea when the charges were heard.

With both civil and naval police shorthanded, vice threatened to get the upper hand. "Waitresses" in East Main Street taverns, working on commission, boosted sales by promising servicemen "shack-up" dates after closing time if they bought seven-dollar bottles of champagne. When the tavern shut its doors, half a dozen sailors would show up for a date with the same girl, and in the ensuing brawl the waitress would escape alone. Men who were lucky enough to take a waitress home often found they had been unlucky instead, as the health card she was required to have proved no guarantee against venereal infection.

In the dark alleys leading off East Main Street lurked even more hazardous temptations. Negro girls tried to pick up a pitiful quarter by enticing sailors back into the shadows. Panders and pint-peddlers solicited customers for their wares. Navy men who yielded to temptation often paid dearly, as the alleys concealed thugs ready to cut, beat, and rob any sailor who fell into their hands. Assaults on servicemen in one section between Church and Fenchurch Streets became so common that the entire area had to be placed out of bounds.[36]

Realizing the seriousness of the situation, Admiral Simons appealed to Washington for permission to organize a permanent shore patrol. The Navy Department in June turned down this proposal to break with naval tradition and rejected it again in July. A conference on the subject in the city manager's office on August 10 decided to try a new channel. Colonel Borland went to Washington himself to talk to Secretary of the Navy Knox about it. After he had reported the results of his conversation at a second meeting on August 18 and the conference had wired an appeal for aid to Secretary Knox, the Navy at last agreed to assume the responsibility for police protection. An officer from the Bureau of Naval Personnel came to Norfolk to discuss the subject with Admiral Simons, and on August 24 the permanent patrol was approved.[37]

[37] Testimony of Lt. Col. J. H. Bain, March 23, 1943, *Hampton Roads Investigation*, p. 56.

16

HOT UNDER THE COLLAR

ONE of the most annoying things about living in Norfolk in the hot summer of 1942 was the sensation of being in a vast goldfish bowl, with the whole world staring. The newspapers and magazines of the nation had discovered the city as a horrible example of wartime crowding, and it seemed as if every journal in the country was carrying an article about Norfolk. *Collier's* had started the parade in March with a semi-fictional article, "Norfolk Night," by Walter Davenport. Davenport, who had intended to do the conventional story on housing, got sidetracked into the more sensational side of the city's night life. He described a neatly-curtained "girlie" trailer camp, surrounded by a red, white, and blue stockade, and mentioned another camp where the girls had Hollywood signs over the doors of their trailers, like *It Happened One Night* and *All That Money Can Buy*.[1]

Norfolk greeted this story with little more than a raised eyebrow in spite of its lurid details. In fact, most people seemed interested to read about a side of the city's life of which the average person knew little. A reporter estimated Norfolk's reaction:

It was a collective shrug of the shoulder. It meant, "Well, what of it? Norfolk and its environs know sin in its milder and more understandable forms. But, after all, this is a seaport town. Show me another such place, comparable with this, that reveals less sin."

Salty comment came from a well-known public official who has touched many ports in many lands. . . .

"Of course, Norfolk is sinful," he said. "Why shouldn't it be? Far be it from me to advocate sin. In the first place, I'm too old; in the second, I'm reformed, and reformed people are pretty well determined in their opposition to the sins they have enjoyed. . . ."

[1] Walter, Davenport, " Norfolk Night," *Collier's*, March 28, 1942, pp. 17, 35, 38, 39. There had been at least two prewar articles, in the *Survey Graphic* and *McCall's*.

Nobody disagreed with the charge that Norfolk and its environs are a little sinful—in fact, very sinful, sometimes. But where's the story? What's all the squawk about? Ain't it a great seaport? Ain't this the home base of the Atlantic Fleet? If you got all the sin out, where would be the honest-to-goodness sailors?[2]

By summer, however, shoving and sweltering were lifting tempers higher, and Norfolk greeted an article in the June issue of the *Architectural Forum* with a howl of protest. The story taken as a whole was an accurate and fair account of the housing problem in Norfolk. It pointed out that the Navy had failed to take the need for housing into consideration in its preliminary plans for expansion, that the Navy's requests for housing, when made, got tangled up in Washington red tape and confusion, and that local interests had opposed expansion for fear that surplus housing would be left after the war. Nevertheless, when the *Virginian-Pilot* reprinted the article and thus gave it wider circulation than it would ever have had in the pages of a professional magazine, many Norfolkians grew even hotter than the weather.

Part of the complaints arose from the fact that an editor had lifted the phrase, "confusion, chicanery, ineptitude", from the article to place it in the heading, conveying the impression that Norfolk was full of crooks, although the story made it clear that the "chicanery" referred only to a minority of rent-gouging landlords. Moreover, civic pride was offended by statements that "Norfolk is not much of a town," with an "air of decrepitude" and an "overwhelming impression of apathy and decay." Most important of all, local toes were tramped on by blunt references to "a town controlled by a small group of men who had a heavy stake in keeping things the way they were . . . a group that considered FHA 'unsound' because it eliminated eight per cent second mortgages."

Norfolk, proud of its recent face-lifting, resented the emphasis on the lingering shabbiness. As one architect said, "This writer makes Norfolk seem to be nothing but a dump; it blames the town for what it hasn't done, but says nothing about the good things we have done."[3] Major Francis E. Turin, of the Norfolk

[2] *V-P*, March 22, 1942, Part II, p. 1.
[3] *V-P*, June 19, 1942, Part II, pp. 12, 6.

Advertising Board, true to his duty of upholding the city's reputation, offered to supply the *Architectural Forum* with pictures of Norfolk's architectural gems to refute the charges of decrepitude. Even the *Virginian-Pilot*, which had started the whole rumpus by publicizing the story, criticized the writer:

> Gross exaggerations creep into his account of trailers parked on "the lawns of old mansions," of "lines" forming at the movies at 10:30 in the morning, of sky-rocketing food prices, of stores and restaurants that "have given up the pretense of trying to provide service for their customers." And by dint of completely ignoring certain of the city's physical aspects that are admirable, the portrait-painter represents Norfolk as a Rip Van Winkle kind of town over-whelmingly given over to "apathy and decay" save when war touches its magnificent harbor and electrifies the city's hardened arteries.[4]

Other groups promptly washed their hands of the responsibility for the housing crisis which had been imputed to them. One local real estate man, V. H. Nusbaum, declared:

> The wholesale condemnation of the Navy, real estate men and banks is unjust, unwarranted and improperly placed by a distant spectator who turns out to be a magazine reporter. . . .
> In the first place the only local body which loudly opposed housing were a few building and loan association officials.
> Emphatically they were not the Real Estate Board representatives for they have never opposed any sound building project in Norfolk to my knowledge.
> Secondly, in our experience of locating 2,000 housing units in Norfolk the naval officials we contacted were very influential and cooperative in distinctly stating the local housing needs to the builders and F. H. A. officials. . . .
> I do not know what the local banks did to encourage the building program except the Investment Corporation of Norfolk, a local mortgage institution, which has cooperated at every opportunity with the builders and F. H. A. The Richmond office of the F. H. A. could not have been more cooperative than Mr. Barksdale and Mr. F. A. Van Patten. Any curb on activities here was placed by Washington officials. It also came from the War Production Board, who either wisely or otherwise made it difficult through orders, red tape and delay to get sufficient material to complete over 1,000 housing units almost ready for occupancy.

[4] *V-P*, June 21, 1942, Part I, p. 6.

In order for the people to know and hear from one actively engaged in the housing business—do not let anyone blame the Navy officials here or the Norfolk Real Estate Board. If it had been left to these gentlemen, Norfolk would have been adequately housed by now.[5]

At the Norfolk Real Estate Board, on the other hand, Otto Hollowell, who had been named in the article as a man who denied the existence of a housing shortage in 1940 and who in 1942 still believed the shortage was much exaggerated, preserved a superior calm:

A careful reading of the story, I believe, would give few persons occasion to be unduly upset. The magazine quite obviously wanted a sensational story and that's what they got, and that in a nutshell covers the incident. . . .
The board has always maintained that the Federal Government should build temporary housing for temporary workers. It is downright stupid to ask this community to stand a financial loss that should rightly be spread throughout the nation as a part of the war cost. I, for one, see no reason why the banking and realty interests should feel they have been badly treated by the story.
Strictly personally, and with the best of feeling, I was quite amused that the young man, who spent about 15 minutes with me while making his whirlwind survey should find me "confused" about the local housing problem. Our position has, as an examination of the daily press will reveal, been steadfastly consistent that the Federal Government should provide such temporary housing as the war effort requires.[6]

The *Ledger-Dispatch* absolved everybody of responsibility, even including the city government, which no one had blamed. Admiral Simons, whose remarks about "sabotage" in the fall of 1941 had been quoted in the article, tried to pour oil on the troubled waters by declaring: "By and large I am now satisfied with the efforts being made here in connection with housing."[7]

Protest was futile to stem the tide of journalists sweeping over the city. A feature writer for *PM* and a journalist from the *American Mercury* arrived to make a quick survey. *Business Week* and even the staid *Domestic Commerce* analyzed Norfolk. When a reporter from Baltimore appeared on the scene, the *Virginian-*

[5] *V-P*, June 20, 1942, p. 9.
[6] *V-P*, June 20, 1942, p. 9.
[7] *L-D*, June 20, 1942, p. 6; *V-P*, June 26, 1942, Part II, p. 12; Part I, p. 13.

Pilot sighed wearily, "The *Sun* Also Rises."[8] Even though all the
reporters tried to be fair, they inevitably emphasized the sensational side of the story and spread all the embarrassing details
of Norfolk's predicament before the nation's eyes. It was bad
enough to be reminded of such unpleasant facts as that two or
three Negro homes collapsed every winter, but it was still worse
to have the truth exaggerated by occasional slips. *PM* reported
that the city had 75 cabs, while the Baltimore *Sun* declared that
there were "only 350." The *Sun* converted desk-bound Admiral
Ben Moreell into a "naval hero"—perhaps the reporter was thinking of the housing war—and produced the astounding misstate-
ment that the city budget for 1942 was 700 per cent larger than
the 1941 figures.[9]

Occasionally some visitors managed to find a good word to say
about Norfolk. A Massachusetts Congressman, Pehr Holmes,
inspecting the city with a House subcommittee, said: "We have
been impressed by the class of housing units which have been
erected here, both in Federal and private projects. They measure
up to a higher standard than we have seen elsewhere. The people
also appear to take a great pride in their homes and we noticed
nice landscaping and shrubs around many new houses."[10] A Canadian writer managed to make Norfolk's crowding sound thrill-
ing instead of irritating:

> Since the war began, I have seen a lot of war effort and bases of one
> kind or another. But nothing like what I have seen here in this region
> around Hampton Roads in back from the mouth of Chesapeake Bay.
> . . . At the yards and bases of this mighty region I have found a sense
> of energy, human and mechanical, that I have not felt since I was in
> Russia in 1932 towards the end of the first five-year plan. Here also I
> have found boom and creation comparable only to that of Florida in
> 1926 when men created a paradise out of mangrove swamps.

[8] Henry R. Lieberman, "Inside Norfolk—Pearl Harbor of the Atlantic,"
PM, Magazine Section, June 20, 1942, pp. 3–7; J. Blan van Urk, "Norfolk—
Our Worst War Town," *American Mercury*, February, 1943 (this story was
based on a visit in June, 1942); "What's a War Boom Like?" *Business Week*,
June 6, 1942, pp. 22–32; W. Cornell Dechert, "Wartime Dislocations in Norfolk
and Baltimore Areas," *Domestic Commerce*, June 4, 1942, pp. 3–6; *V-P*, September 1, 1942, p. 6.
[9] Baltimore *Sun*, August 16, 1942, pp. 1, 7; August 17, 1942, p. 1.
[10] *V-P*, March 29, 1942, Part II, p. 1.

... Compared to this, eastern Canadian ports I have visited in war-time were quiet backwaters. I wish I could convey to Canadians the might and meaning of this Virginian ant-heap of naval and air activity. To me the promise of it spelled victory for our side.[11]

The Canadian, however, was almost alone in appreciating the accomplishment. Even the people of Norfolk seldom reflected on the progress that was being made, preoccupied as they were with what had not yet been done. So many unpleasant things had already happened that they were ready to believe the worst of the future. It was easy to accept the rumors of May that military authorities would prohibit the usual escape to the beaches from the summer heat. A Fort Story officer put this fear to rest with the not entirely reassuring announcement: "If the bathers don't mind stepping in oil, and if they can stand seeing a body wash ashore now and then from some ship blown up by the Germans, it's all right with us."[12]

This grim warning was realized with unexpected detail a few weeks later. As thousands lay on the sand or dipped in the ocean at Virginia Beach on Monday afternoon, June 15, and idly watched two tankers moving against the horizon five miles out, they were startled by an underwater explosion, quickly followed by another, and stared in astonishment as one of the ships slowly sank beneath the surface while the other came to a halt. The excited onlookers, their number growing constantly, watched while patrol planes dropped depth charges, other planes flew out from shore, a blimp appeared, and Navy craft scurried back and forth across the surface looking for a submarine. As the Coast Guard brought in the body of a man who had been killed by the explosion, a breathless hush fell over the crowd, brought face to face with a casualty of the war.

Although the damage had actually been caused by mines and there was not a German U-boat within miles, hundreds of watchers, intent on the exploding depth charges, thought they saw a submarine blow up and disappear beneath the surface. Imagination was magnified by repetition until scores of people were ready to swear that they had seen a submarine appear and shell the

[11] Frederick Griffin in the Toronto *Star Weekly*, quoted in *V-P*, May 24, 1942, Part II, p. 1.
[12] *V-P*, May 22, 1942, Part II, p. 12.

tanker, and one person even declared that a shot had just missed the Cavalier Hotel.[13]

Newspapers held back any mention of this event until they were sure it was not covered by the cloak of security regulations, which had already reduced Norfolk to the anonymity of "an East Coast port" in all dispatches concerning the submarine warfare, and it was not until a full day later that the story was published. The result of this silence on an event which everyone knew had happened was that people wondered how many other disasters were occurring of which they had not been told. Norfolkians lent credulous ears to the story that an Axis submarine had been captured with Bond Bread among its stores or that the sailors carried stubs of local movie tickets in their pockets. A derelict iron tank became a German submarine, which was reported beached on the shore at an indefinite location which moved all the way from Willoughby Spit to Virginia Beach. One excited rumormonger even fired a torpedo into the Cape Charles ferry.

Rumors like these were slippery and hard to catch up with. Public denials failed to kill them, and their source was elusive. When a reporter tried to track down the grounded submarine, he found many people who said they had heard the story from a person who had actually seen the sub, but when the supposed eyewitness was tracked down, it always turned out that he had heard the story from some one else who had actually seen the submarine. It was easy to disprove the story that a vessel had been stopped off Morehead City by a German U-boat commander, who had taken the captain on board and told him: "You must have a filthy bottom, should have it scraped. You're one hour and 32 minutes late." The captain named in the story denied it, but the rumor merely fastened itself to another captain.

In one case the newspapers did manage to catch up with the rumor. When a telephone call came in, asking about a submarine that was being towed through Hampton Roads, the paper sent its reporters out to see what was happening. The newsmen arrived in time to discover that the "submarine" was a tow of logs —and also to see curious crowds of "eyewitnesses" lining the shore.[14] Nevertheless, in spite of every refutation, the rumors lived

[13] *V-P*, June 17, 1942, p. 1; *L-D*, June 27, 1942, p. 14.
[14] *L-D*, June 27, 1942, p. 14.

on and fastened themselves on the minds of the people so firmly that years after the war Norfolkians would still repeat tales of submarines captured or ships sunk in the Chesapeake or in Hampton Roads, all of them vouched for by some untraceable eyewitness.

A more vicious type of rumor threatened to throw the city into a panic. Stories circulated before each blackout that Negroes were planning to take advantage of the darkness to make a mass assault on the whites. This dangerous gossip rose to a hysterical climax just before the blackout scheduled for Tuesday, August 18. The rumor started that Negroes were buying up ice picks in preparation for an attack on the whites, and the story gathered circumstantial detail as it traveled. The Saturday before the scheduled test a responsible white businessman telephoned the *Journal and Guide* editor to report that he had just been told that colored people in the last three days had purchased 300 ice picks at one downtown hardware store. The rumor created so much excitement that the newspapers and the police undertook an investigation of its truth.

Two days after the blackout the facts were published. The *Journal and Guide* in a careful inquiry had failed to find any colored persons with any knowledge of plans to make trouble or of any desire to make trouble. The only Negroes who had heard of the ice-pick story were those who had been told about it by some white person. No store had noticed any unusual demand for ice picks or any other potential weapon. The nearest the police had come to tracking down the source of the story was to find one man who said he had heard it from four women at a bridge table.[15]

City Manager Borland issued a public denunciation of the rumors:

In every single case, Norfolk police officers and Federal Bureau of Investigation agents were called on to trace the source of the rumors. In not one case did they find any foundation for such reports. However, they were spread about all over the city, often by good but unthinking citizens.

And that was just what the enemy wanted us to do. That was falling for his propaganda, which was designed to disunite the people of this country. Our people should put a stop to spreading idle rumors.

[15] Norfolk *Journal ana Guide*, August 22, 1942, p. 1; *V-P*, August 20, 1942, p. 6, August 27, 1942, p. 20.

The Negro population in the City of Norfolk as a whole is law-abiding and patriotic. I am in daily contact with the leaders of the Negro race, and I know this to be true.

There are to be no race riots in Norfolk or any other kind of riot. My advice to all the people is to stop gossiping.

I am convinced clever enemy propaganda is back of all the rumors which have been circulated here, and it is the duty of patriotic Americans of all races to put an end to them.[16]

There was, of course, no evidence that enemy agents had been responsible for propagating the rumors. Explanation enough was provided by the apprehensive atmosphere of Norfolk, which could readily magnify an occasional assault by a Negro on a white person into a racial conspiracy. Housewives, harried by the inevitable difficulty of finding and keeping good servants when better-paying jobs were so plentiful, had imagined the existence of an Eleanor Club. Negro maids were supposed to have formed this organization to demand the right to use the front door or to refuse to cook late dinners or to disrupt some other long-standing servants' custom.[17] This story had originated long before the war in a dislike in certain quarters for the New Deal in general and Mrs. Roosevelt in particular, but Norfolk's nervous tension was giving it new currency.

While these rumors were killed by the glare of publicity thrown upon them, there was much concern over the dangerous racial situation of which they were a symptom. Tempers snapped easily in the exasperating summer of 1942, and incidents which would normally have passed unnoticed were exaggerated into angry quarrels. Some Negroes asserted their rights with insolence, and some whites arrogantly tried to put them in their place. Trouble was most frequent on the crowded streetcars and buses. Negroes, required by law to move to the back, had to push through the packed whites to get there. Irritated bus drivers sometimes vented their pent-up annoyances on the Negroes. One bus driver arbitrarily ended his run five or six blocks before his scheduled destination at a colored housing project, forcing his passengers to walk the rest of the way. Another bus operator, seeing only three

[16] *V-P*, August 20, 1942, pp. 22, 14.

[17] Norfolk *Journal and Guide*, August 22, 1942, p. 1; *V-P*, August 20, 1942, p. 6.

colored persons left on his vehicle at the next to the last stop, demanded: "You niggers move to the back seat." When one man failed to move, the bus driver detained one of the passengers and had him arrested. The man was acquitted when it was revealed that he was one of those who had moved.[18] Fortunately, leaders on both sides showed patience and common sense. The *Journal and Guide* promised:

Let's treat each other as human beings, with certain human rights, right here in Norfolk and Portsmouth, and there will be complete unity and accord; and as far as colored people are concerned, there is no cause for concern that Hitler's agents would be able to make the slightest impression upon them.[19]

Colonel Borland showed a commendable broad-mindedness for the chief executive of a Southern city. He appealed to the whites in one talk:

Do not let anyone draw you into an argument because a man's skin is black or his religion is something or other. This is no time—and no time is the right time—for racial or religious intolerance, especially not in Virginia. If anybody says anything about something being good or bad because of racial or religious reasons, it's a good time to tell him where to head in.[20]

The city relaxed its rigid rule against Negro policemen enough to train and swear in a large number of colored auxiliary police, swearing in one group on the very night of the August 18 blackout. As a further measure of conciliation, Colonel Borland called a meeting of 38 representative Negro citizens, who were assured by Governor Darden that he was convinced that there would be no disturbance of the friendly relations existing between the races.[21]

Friction between black and white was only one form in which Norfolkians expressed their resentment against accumulating annoyances. In this sweltering summer everyone appeared to be

[18] *Journal and Guide*, July 25, 1942, p. 23.
[19] *Journal and Guide*, July 25, 1942, p. 23.
[20] *V-P*, March 25, 1942, p. 20.
[21] *V-P*, August 20, 1942, pp. 22, 14; September 19, 1942, p. 16.

angry at everyone else. When the stores at Admiral Simons' request agreed to stay open on Thursday nights to give war workers a chance to shop, the clerks complained at the loss of a free evening. When the experiment was abandoned after a month's trial, the war workers charged that the clerks in several stores had banded together to be impudent to the night shoppers to discourage them.[22]

War workers also feuded with each other. A "Weary War Worker" denounced the social clubs which were ruining his rest, declaring:

> They start about bedtime (for defense workers) giving the community 40 different kinds of plain and fancy hell-raising, making more noise than a Commando raid, and this brawling, cursing, horn blowing, yelling, and juke box cacophony, continues until almost daybreak. With the windows open during the hot nights, there is no escape from this unnecessary bedlam, and the good citizen drags out of bed when the alarm rings, feeling any thing but ready for the day's effort to help win the war.[23]

This complaint brought a loud snort from "A Non-Weary War Worker" on the night shift, who wanted the clubs kept open for his own entertainment. "Non-Weary" picked up a familiar brick to hurl back at "Weary":

> I will bet my shirt he is from North Carolina, as this town is packed full of them, and they are the only ones that I have heard that complain about everything here. Why don't they go back to their quiet State and leave Virginia to her Virginians and others that are satisfied with noises that prevail in all boom towns?[24]

None of these quarrels, however, could equal in intensity the perennial argument between Norfolk and the Navy, which blew loudly out into the open. All the pushing and the shoving and the sweltering, which snapped civilian tempers so abruptly, brought even sharper responses from the sailors, who did not have the civilian's option of staying or leaving. The *Virginian-Pilot* wisely offered a safety-valve for all this discontent by opening up its

[22] *V-P*, June 7, 1942, Part II, p. 1; June 25, 1942, p. 6.
[23] *V-P*, September 17, 1942, p. 6.
[24] *V-P*, September 21, 1942, p. 4.

letters column to the sailors, who promptly proceeded to use and abuse this privilege. One angry tar wrote:

> Norfolk has a reputation and a name that wouldn't look good in a cheap pulp magazine. Among sailors the world over, there are two places that they don't want to go ashore—Norfolk and San Juan. It is quite understandable.[25]

They complained that the Norfolk movie theaters, unlike those in most other cities, did not offer reduced prices to servicemen. They declared that clerks in stores and waitresses in restaurants passed them up to take care of civilians. They growled about 40-cent cokes and 50-cent beers. They dug up the hoary tale about restaurants that had a special set of menus with higher prices for servicemen and revived the World War I story about signs that said: "Sailors and dogs keep out." They said that Norfolk drivers with empty cars passed them by when they attempted to hitchhike into town. Most of all, they complained that Norfolkians greeted them with cold stares instead of friendly handclasps.

There was an embarrassing foundation of fact underneath this superstructure of sensation. Service in stores and restaurants was unquestionably poor, as businessmen frankly admitted. One department store manager said of his clerks: "We get 'em third rate, develop 'em into second rate, then lose 'em."[26] Sailors, however, were probably treated no worse than civilians. Although a few mercenary waitresses may have ignored servicemen in favor of higher-tipping civilians, most of the imagined discrimination was merely the result of a long and irritating wait for service, which was imposed on everyone, in or out of uniform.

Prices were undoubtedly high. Even though the 40-cent cokes and the 50-cent beers were found only at the swank night clubs, many places were charging 10 cents for soft drinks and 25 cents for bottles of beer, nearly twice the pre-war level. Many other prices were rising at the same rate. The bacon-and-egg breakfast at the drug-store counter, for example, which had cost 15 cents in 1939, was now 35 cents. Retailers tried to justify such advances by pointing out the higher cost of labor, but the basic reason, of course, was the normal operation of the profit motive, now con-

---

[25] Letter from "One of Many Laughing Sailors," *V-P*, August 18, 1942, p. 6.
[26] "What's a War Boom Like?" *Business Week*, June 6, 1942, pp. 22–32.

sidered unpatriotic profiteering. Inflation took bigger bites out of
the sailor's pay only because it was smaller than the check
carried home by the average civilian.

The serviceman's indignation at Norfolk's high prices, however,
was heightened by the absence of the special price concessions to
men in uniform to which he was accustomed in other towns.
Although the baseball park did admit sailors at half-price, this
exception was so insignificant that it was overlooked in the general
controversy. Sailors were quick to conclude that the failure to
offer reduced rates was another demonstration of the mercenary
motives of Norfolk businessmen. The fact of the matter, however,
was that special rates to servicemen would have been too expensive
a courtesy for the Norfolk theater-owner to offer, since sailors
often provided half the local audiences. As one taxi-driver explained, "If we give the gobs a rake-off on movie tickets, none of
us civilians could get in."[27]

The criticism that stung the deepest was the charge that Norfolk
was hostile to servicemen. This feeling had its roots in Norfolk's
prewar reputation as a bad liberty port, which had spread
throughout the Navy, with the result that sailors arrived in the
city expecting to dislike it. Looking for cold shoulders, they easily
found them, especially since Norfolk did not consider a man in
uniform such a delightful novelty as he was in other cities.

Norfolkians were struggling to revise their traditional attitude
toward sailors, but the adjustment was slow and difficult. Even
though they knew that the wartime Navy was made up of men
from every walk of life, even though they themselves had sons in
service, they could not entirely free themselves from old habits
of thinking. Girls brought up to avoid sailors found it difficult
to be friendly, and those who did go out with Navy men often
had to conceal the fact from their parents. In the circumstances
it was not surprising that there were never enough girls at the
service dances, seldom more than one for every four men. One
sailor complained:

Those girls who are there are either adolescents, five or six years the
sailor's junior, or matrons 10 to 15 years his senior, taking 20 to 22 as

[27] Henry R. Lieberman, "Inside Norfolk," *PM*, Magazine Section, June 28,
1942, pp. 3–7.

the average Navy man's age. And most of the girls, when they dance with a sailor, make him feel like some bowing, scraping medieval serf receiving a favor from the lady of the manor.[28]

Two boys from Mississippi said: "'. . . the girls evidently thought we were foreigners, Japs or something, as they sure did stay away from us."[29]

The girls and their parents, however, were gradually overcoming this aloof and condescending attitude, especially since the outbreak of the war. Granby Street on Saturday night presented obvious evidence that many sailors were finding dates. In fact, one observer thought that the trend would soon reverse the older prejudice so that girls would be ashamed to be seen with a man not in uniform.[30] The churches generally extended a welcoming hand to visiting servicemen, and many of them organized special entertainments to make the sailors feel at home. Members of the congregations often invited them home to dinner. The city offered the use of the Ocean View golf course on weekdays.

The biggest improvement since the summer of 1941 had been in the expansion and multiplication of the recreation centers. There were now eight USO centers operating in the city in addition to the one supported by the Lutheran church. The Navy tried to eliminate some of the anti-Norfolk feeling among its men by publicizing these developments. An article addressed to the entire Navy declared:

Several years ago if you were transferred to Norfolk all your friends gathered around to offer their condolences and you wondered what you had done to deserve such a horrible fate. Norfolk has long been notorious in the Navy as "bad liberty," and "bad duty." In this desert of nothing-to-do the only oasis was the Navy Y. But there've been some changes made, and you men who have been away from Norfolk for a year or so are due for a pleasant surprise, as far as entertainment facilities are concerned, when you come this way again.[31]

[28] Letter from "The Kid from Jersey," *V-P*, September 1, 1942, p. 6.
[29] Letter from John R. Henderson and Thomas Williams, Richmond *Times-Dispatch*, February 24, 1942, p. 10.
[30] *V-P*, May 29, 1942, Part II, p. 12.
[31] Mary Ellen Newcomer, "There've Been Some Changes Made," *Our Navy*, Mid-July, 1942, p. 16.

The *Woman's Home Companion* also tried to reassure mothers and sweethearts who might have been alarmed by the flood of articles emphasizing Norfolk sin with a glamorizing story about the wholesome entertainment being provided in the city.[32]

In spite of all these developments Norfolk was still not doing a good job of welcoming its visitors because it could not. Like everything else in the city the USO centers too were overcrowded. There was no solution for any problem in 1942's torrid summer; the only consolation was the promise that next year things would be better.

[32] Nancy Hale, "A Sailor Named Bill," *Woman's Home Companion*, July, 1942, pp. 42–43.

17

DRILLS IN THE DARK

EVEN the Civilian Defense organization was affected by the hectic summer. There was confusion over the failure to receive the long-promised arm bands and helmets to identify and protect the defense workers. Hopes were raised early in June by the announcement that 2,740 steel helmets were on their way to Norfolk, enough to equip the air raid wardens, if not the rest of the defense staff. The blackout on June 17 came and went, however, without any sign of the tin hats. Finally on June 30 Director Borland wrote to Washington to find out where the missing equipment was.

Wardens overwhelmed their superiors with protests about their difficulties in identifying themselves until the zone wardens decided to leap over all the customary channels and go directly to the top. Sixteen of the defense leaders, acting as Norfolk citizens, addressed a letter to President Franklin D. Roosevelt, with a copy for Governor Darden, declaring:

The men and women who have undergone training to protect the City of Norfolk want to know why their repeated requests for helmets, to say nothing of gas masks, have been met with only vague promises—promises and more promises. The defense workers are trying to carry on, but the situation is discouraging.[1]

Response to the letter was unexpectedly prompt. The very next day word arrived from the director of the U. S. Office of Civilian Defense, James M. Landis, that an order for the helmets had been given an Ohio firm, which had been expected to ship them on June 2. At the same time George Hope Taylor, procurement officer for the Norfolk OCD, learned that the helmets had been shipped on July 7 and could be expected shortly.[2]

[1] *V-P*, July 11, 1942, p. 16.
[2] *V-P*, July 12, 1942, Part II, p. 1.

When the arm bands still failed to arrive, one lowly warden decided to emulate his superiors. He explained:

I am a plain buck private air warden who applied to the block warden for a sleeve band, for identification purposes. General Block Warden said he would report the matter to Sergeant Section Warden who, in turn, would see Lieutenant Zone Warden, who would go to Captain City Warden, who would lay the request before Major Area Warden, who would—here I was lost in the air.

Having gone through the buck-passing experiences of 1917–18, I perceived that the air warden run-around was simply a 1942 version of the old army game, so what th' hell! C'est la guerre!

But I have learned recently, that the rules air warden superiors have been teaching their subordinates the superiors themselves have been skipping. The zone wardens and others near the shavetail rating, having grown impatient at the non-delivery of some 2,000 helmets for air wardens, cut the red tape. They, in one breath, exonerated every official in Virginia, charged the blame for non-delivery squarely to Washington, went over the heads of all Virginia officials, and wrote directly to the President of the United States that they wanted action, too sweet—or something.

Probably it was the expectation of zone wardens and others who told the President they wanted service, pronto, that he would lay aside the Atlantic Charter and the six billion dollar tax bill details, to rush the bottom-up basins to one of a dozen cities in urgent need of them. And that gives me an idea.

Nobody in Norfolk—even in Virginia, is blamable for the non-delivery of my sleeve band. I exonerate all State and city officials. I will write direct to President Roosevelt, suggesting that I shall like action. . . .

When I grow too old to dream I'll have this to remember: Even as the gallant zone wardens heroicly [sic] did their part in the Battle of Helmets, I, too, did my bit in the Battle of Sleeve Bands—1942.[3]

Confusion reached a new high in the preparations for the June 17 blackout. Chief Warden Ferebee had been planning an hour's maneuver for his men for June 4 when he learned that the State OCD had scheduled a state-wide blackout for June 17. He and Marshall then decided to hold the maneuver during the blackout to lend greater realism. A few days later, however, it was learned that the total blackout would last only half an hour. Marshall therefore decided to ask for permission to extend the blackout in

[3] Letter of "Private Knight Ayre," *V-P*, August 8, 1942, p. 4.

Norfolk to a full hour to allow time to complete the planned incidents.

After failing to locate Colonel Borland, Coordinator Marshall called up Richmond on Wednesday, June 10, and talked to John J. Howard, the State Air Raid Precautions Director. Howard agreed to let Norfolk have the full hour blackout. A few minutes later Colonel Borland, in Richmond on business, dropped in at Howard's office. The Norfolk city manager, who believed in keeping blackouts to a minimum, was surprised when he learned of Marshall's telephone call and declared that he did not want the blackout extended. Somewhat confused, Howard wrote to Marshall the next day:

> While this office will continue to make every effort to cooperate with any local council, we must know that requests for such radical changes have been agreed upon by those in charge of that particular council. Therefore as it stands now, your air raid test will last only thirty minutes.[4]

By Friday Marshall had a chance to talk to Director Borland. Although disturbed over the confusion, Borland yielded to Marshall's arguments and agreed to call State Coordinator Wyse's office and give his consent to the hour blackout. Howard, still puzzled, telephoned Marshall to find out what was going on. When he learned that the director and the coordinator were at last in agreement, he agreed to grant permission for the extension. The next morning, however, Marshall found on his desk Howard's letter of Thursday, which said the blackout would be for only half an hour. Now thoroughly confused, the coordinator sat down and dictated a long letter to Borland, reviewing the whole story in full detail. Fortunately the city manager had already received a later letter from Howard, authorizing the hour blackout, and the matter was at last cleared up.[5]

[4] Howard to Marshall, June 11, 1942, Civilian Defense: Blackouts file, NWHC records. Howard wrote to his chief, J. H. Wyse: "There is, however, one condition in the State which it is not in my power to correct. I mention the lack of coordinated effort between the Director and the Coordinator in the City of Norfolk. There seems to be some misunderstanding in that City." Howard to Wyse, June 13, 1942, VOCD records.
[5] Howard to Borland, June 12, 1942, Marshall to Borland, June 13, 1942, Civilian Defense: Blackouts file, NWHC records.

The public was just as muddled by the blackout announcement as were the defense chiefs. This first drill to be called from State headquarters complicated the rules by providing for two types of blackout, the "strategic," which was to last all night, and the "total," which, it was now agreed, would be for one hour in Norfolk. The dusk-to-dawn test was the idea of Army brass of the make-the-civilians-feel-the-war school. The Norfolk defense officials, who had tried out this idea a week after Pearl Harbor, were vigorously opposed to the plan and registered a protest against it with State Coordinator Wyse.[6] An all-night blackout could not be enforced on the naval installations nor on the numerous other war activities in the area. So many exceptions would have to be granted, as Marshall pointed out, that the darkening would be ineffective and many individuals would see little use in putting out their lights while the sky was still lit up by the bustling war plants. Moreover, the existence of two different sets of rules was confusing. When the strategic blackout began, lights were to be turned out, but traffic could proceed with auto headlamps on low beam. At the signal for the total blackout all traffic was to halt, pedestrians would seek cover, and air-raid conditions would prevail. The all clear would permit autos to move again, but lights were to remain off.

The blackout turned out better than was expected, however. The public accepted the idea without complaint. Most people simply went to bed when dusk fell about nine o'clock and got a good night's rest for once. Sailors who were caught on a halted Naval Base trolley during the total blackout also used the opportunity to catch up on their sleep. The only misunderstanding over the rules resulted from a last-minute revision. Original instructions to the wardens had stated that cars must have the upper half of their headlight lenses painted to move during the strategic blackout. A belated concession to the public had made the use of the low beam all that was necessary, but there had been no time to notify the wardens of this change except through the newspapers. Some wardens therefore followed their original orders and told bus drivers to turn off their lights, and several of the bus drivers insisted on obeying the company's instructions to keep them on.

[6] Borland to Marshall, April 28, 1942, Marshall to Borland, May 2, 1942, Marshall to Wyse, June 11, 1942, Civilian Defense: Blackouts file, NWHC records.

Other problems cropped up in the communications system. A mistake in the signals from the warning center started Portsmouth's blackout eighteen minutes early. Norfolk County, on the other hand, never got the signal at all, but sounded the alarm anyhow when the Navy Yard signals went off. The civilian defense staff, literally sweating out their problems in their sweltering VEPCO office, discovered that their telephone lines could not handle the wardens' calls. One warden had to spend twenty minutes trying to get his message through. Violations were scarce, as arrests were now being made. One merchant was fined for failing to turn off his lights, and three persons were given a stiff $100 penalty for exceeding the fifteen-mile speed limit in force during the strategic blackout. Colonel Borland warned that other drills must be expected. "We do not enjoy having these tests," he said," not any more than the people who are hardest hit by them. But the State Office of Civilian Defense and Federal officials feel they are necessary to train our people to meet actual air raids if they occur."[7]

On June 29 Norfolk held its second daylight drill in compliance with the Governor's executive order requiring monthly practices. At 11:30 a. m. the sirens sounded over the south side of Hampton Roads, and two minutes later Granby Street was completely cleared of moving cars and pedestrians. The traffic on the Berkley Bridge stopped so promptly that both lanes were blockaded and emergency vehicles could not get through. L. Snyder's store on Church Street was prepared for its air-raid guests with a program of entertainment to while away the waiting time. As pedestrians took shelter in the store, they were invited to join in group singing and also to take part in a quiz show with prizes for the right answers.

Downtown office workers this time refrained from hanging out the windows, but shoppers persisted in huddling in the store entrances, where there would be danger from shattered glass if bombs should fall. Many firms annoyed Coordinator Marshall by repeated calls asking to be excused from the test. He gave a firm no to all requests, including one from a produce dealer who objected to having his potato-loading interrupted. An Ocean View woman, hanging up her Monday-morning wash told the warden to go about his business when he asked her to go inside the house, and the police had to be called to persuade her that air-raid drills were more important than her laundry. Many parts of the city still could not hear the sirens, even though two more had been added to the twelve used in May, and Colonel Borland ordered an additional four. Otherwise the drill went off so satisfactorily that Marshall declared, "If I were asked to put my finger on an outstanding fault, I can tell you frankly it would be hard to do so."[8]

The July practices were a double-barreled affair, both coming on the same day. The noon-time drill went off with smooth efficiency, but the blackout that night created complications because the exact time of the alarm was not announced in advance. As a result, absent-minded moviegoers left lights burning behind them at home, and some persons forgot to turn off lights in stores or on advertising signs. Wardens discovered new occupational hazards when one had a dog sicked on him by an angry householder and another had a knife pulled on him. Coordinator Marshall, thumbing through a stack of complaints, demanded better cooperation:

> There are still too many people who view these air raid tests with indifference and contempt, and who are unwilling to obey the orders of wardens who have been appointed to help and correct them. Norfolk is one of the country's most likely targets for enemy aerial attack, and the people of the city have just got to take these tests more seriously.[9]

Hard on the heels of this drill came the news that Norfolk was in for another all-night blackout, or, to be more exact, from 8:30 P.M. to 1:00 A.M. Colonel Borland lost no time in registering another protest with State Coordinator Wyse:

> Far be from me to question any order emanating from proper sources ... but as one sensible human being to another, we are overdoing the blackout business.
> ... I know that the public is not going to re-act favorably very much longer to these five, six, seven hour and all-night tests. The weather is extremely hot and will remain so, certainly throughout the middle of September. There are numerous industries here that must operate and consequently they will be going full blast with lights on, but the poor

[8] *V-P*, June 30, 1942, p. 18.
[9] *V-P*, July 17, 1942, Part II, p. 12.

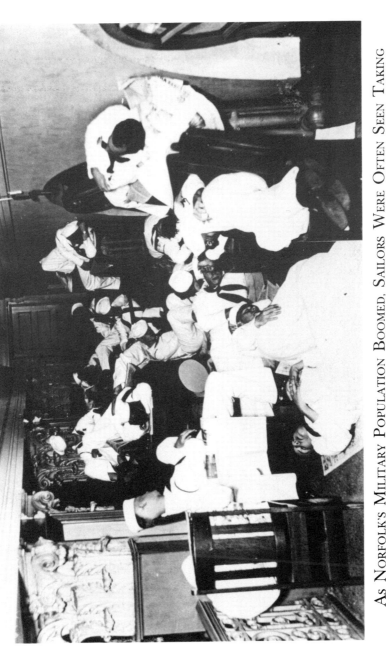

As Norfolk's Military Population Boomed, Sailors Were Often Seen Taking Catnaps In Public. (Borjes Collection.)

Women Filled In a Variety of Jobs for Men Who Shipped Out to war – Including Truck Drivers. (Borjes Collection.)

At the USO on Smith Street, Soldiers and Sailors Could Jitterbug Away the Cares of Wartime. (Borjes Collection.)

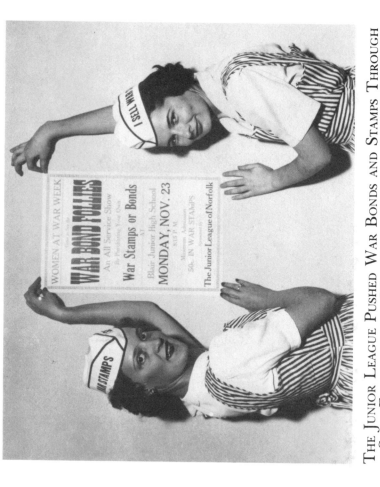

The Junior League Pushed War Bonds and Stamps Through Such Events as the "War Bond Follies" at Blair Junior High. (Borjes Collection.)

Norfolk's Citizens Got a Chance to Inspect a Captured Japanese Submarine, on Display on Freemason Street. (Borjes Collection.)

German Prisoners of War Were Put to Work at the Weaver Fertilizer Co. Plant. (Borjes Collection.)

Capt. Charles H. Hall of the 99th Fighter Squadron (Center Front) Was the First Black Aviator to Shoot Down an Enemy Aircraft. He is Surrounded, Left to Right, by Capt. Maurice Johnson, Lt. Willis H. Fuller, Lt. Price D. Rice and Capt. Herbert E. Carter. They Spoke at a Rally at Booker T. Washington High School. (Borjes Collection.)

HOMECOMING: A NORFOLK FAMILY FESTOONED ITS HOME TO GREET A RETURNING WAR VETERAN. (BORJES COLLECTION.)

Demonstration Air Raid Shelter Erected on the Courthouse Lawn During the Civilian Defense Rehearsal of October, 1941

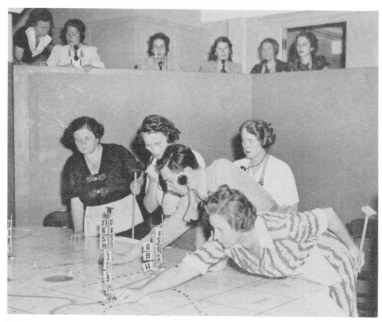

VOLUNTEERS AT THE INFORMATION CENTER PLOT THE
COURSE OF PLANES FLYING OVER VIRGINIA

Norfolk's Japanese Aliens Are Rounded up by the City Police at the News of the Attack on Pearl Harbor

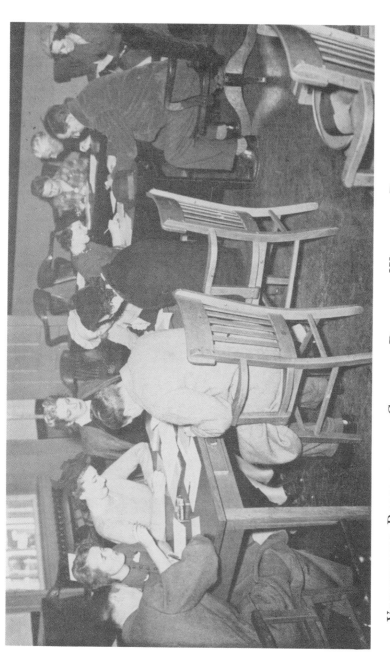

VOLUNTEERS REGISTER FOR CIVILIAN DEFENSE WORK ON DECEMBER 30, 1941

The General Staff of Norfolk's Office of Civilian Defense Gather in the New Control Center, April, 1942

TRAFFIC HALTS ON GRANBY STREET DURING NORFOLK'S FIRST DAYLIGHT DRILL, MAY, 1942

The First Battalion of the Virginia Protective Force Joins in an Armistice Day Parade

School Children Gather Waste Paper for the Scrap Drive

BENMOREELL, THE NAVY'S HOUSING PROJECT FOR ENLISTED MEN

FINISHING WORK ON LIBERTY PARK, ONE OF THE PREFABRICATED PROJECTS

MEMBERS OF THE PERMANENT SHORE PATROL DISPLAY
THEIR THREE UNIFORMS

THE NAVY FIGHTS FIRES SET OFF BY THE EXPLOSION OF SEPTEMBER 18, 1943

SAILORS CROWD INTO THE CANTEEN AT THE SALVATION ARMY USO

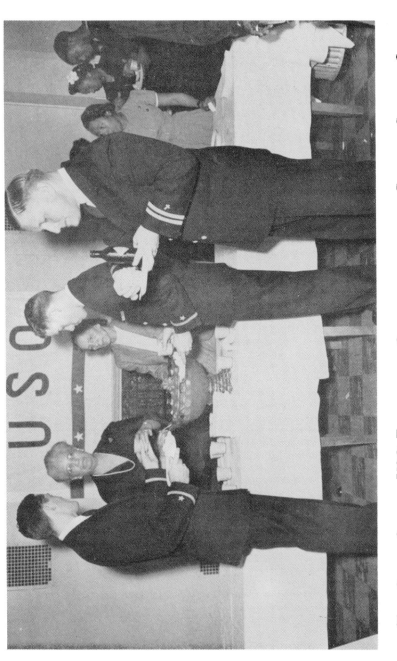

The Smith Street USO Entertains Officers from the Carrier Shangri-La

Sailors are Entertained at a Salvation Army USO Party

Norfolk Offers a Welcoming Hand to Servicemen

old public must either sit in darkness or stay cooped up in a room with all the windows shut down in order to keep the lights from shining in the streets. This office is receiving calls from people who have sickness in their families and it makes it extremely difficult for them. Furthermore, the proper operation of cars during blackouts is hazardous. It is needless for me to say anything further. I just cannot help entering this protest in the interest of public safety and public morale.[10]

Once again, however, the public was unexpectedly compliant. No one protested the repetition of the state-wide strategic blackout on the night of August 18. Civilian Defense workers tested their coordination by handling a series of 28 prepared incidents. Medical workers were dispatched to handle three gas "casualties" at the Monticello Hotel, and other crews were sent to take care of bombs supposed to have fallen in Algonquin Park near Governor Darden's home, now occupied by Coordinator Marshall. There were also several unscheduled incidents. Three calls came in for ambulances to meet real emergencies, and one warden telephoned that he was locked in a house and needed a rescue squad to get him out. Civilian cooperation was good. No one forgot to turn his lights off, since the strategic blackout kept him from turning them on in the first place. Stores that were still open closed up at 8:30, and only the restaurants had to carry out special blackout arrangements. Only two arrests had to be made, one for failure to take cover, the other for reckless driving. Both were made by auxiliary police, now functioning with full authority in blackouts.[11]

Meanwhile, the first change in the Norfolk OCD high command had taken place. Chief Air Raid Warden Ferebee, who had been the first man to join Coordinator Marshall in the almost forgotten days of September, 1941, found that the death of his brother and business associate in June was throwing so much of the burden of the business on his shoulders that he could no longer attend to his defense duties, and regretfully decided to resign. Marshall named his assistant, George Bowers, as his successor. Bowers plunged

---

[10] Borland to Wyse, July 20, 1942, Civilian Defense: Blackout Incidents file, NWHC records.

[11] *V-P*, August 19, 1942, p. 18; August 20, 1942, p. 14. The August daylight drill was held on August 14 without incident.

into his new job with energy, launching a series of inspections of section posts, followed by a series of conferences to discuss problems. He enforced the rule that every warden had to secure his fingerprinted identification card from police headquarters and complete his first-aid training before he would be issued one of the newly-arrived helmets. Each section was expected to establish post quarters and equip it as a first-aid center, as many of them had already done.[12]

It was time to get the warden system in its best working order, since there were to be no more announced drills. One test that came without warning was the result of an accident. On August 25 a slightly confused telephone operator, receiving the customary "red flash" test signal over the Army's communication system, routed it to the Norfolk warning district instead of to the civil air raid warning center, which was supposed to receive it. The warning district automatically began passing the flash along to control centers, and sirens screamed in Norfolk and Portsmouth before the error could be corrected. The all clear sounded in Norfolk within two minutes, but the fact that the Portsmouth alert was still being blown created confusion. The coincidence of a single plane flying over the city, followed by a group of planes, made the unheralded alarm seem authentic. Everyone downtown promptly forgot all the rules about not using the telephones and jammed the pay stations to call home to make sure families were safe.[13]

A more intentional surprise was held on September 11 as a demonstration for a couple of major generals who were inspecting the city's defenses. At the sound of the sirens the startled public followed instructions and sought shelter without question. Hollywood's John Payne, arriving at City Hall to see Mayor Wood and open a war bond drive, was shown to the basement instead. All the defense officials got to their posts at the control center in the VEPCO building within ten minutes.[14]

Surprise blackouts, however, were more of a problem. Although the State OCD did announce that there would be a test sometime from October 5 to October 12 and made it easy by holding the drill

---

[12] Mimeographed instructions to section wardens, undated, "OCD 158," Civilian Defense: Air Raid Wardens Bulletins file, NWHC records.

[13] *L-D*, August 25, 1942; *V-P*, August 26, 1942, pp. 20, 13.

[14] *V-P*, September 12, 1942, p. 16.

on the first night of the period, dozens of people forgot to turn off their lights before they left home. Marshall termed this carelessness "thoroughly disgusting," and Police Court Justice Clyde Jacob got tough with violators. Nineteen storekeepers each received $25 fines, and no excuses were accepted. Pleas of operators that clerks had failed to obey their instructions to turn the lights out were of no avail. One merchant said that he had not made up his mind whether he would pay the fine or not, but the information that he would have to go to jail until he did pay brought a prompt decision.[15]

A daylight test also called by the State for October 21 created more complications. Advance notice of the date was sent out to the various defense officials, and Coordinator Marshall attempted to arrange for the cooperation of the Army and the Navy. He found, however, that the military authorities were going to be extremely busy with certain important troop movements that week and would not be able to cooperate in a test until the week following. Coordinator Marshall telephoned State Coordinator Wyse and asked that the date be changed, but Wyse reassuringly reminded him that a daylight drill would not interfere with troop movements, as the Army and the Navy would not be halted by the air raid wardens.[16]

Nevertheless, Norfolk did not have an air raid drill on October 21 after all. On that day a smoldering five-year-old dispute suddenly flared up and disrupted the city's transportation system. Back in 1937 VEPCO had encouraged and recognized a union of its employees, requiring all of its workers to join and pay dues to this Independent Union of Employees. Workers in VEPCO's transportation division, however, denounced this organization as a company union and called in the Amalgamated transportation workers to organize them separately. The Amalgamated appealed to the National Labor Relations Board in 1938, which ordered the independent union dissolved. The I. U. E. then fought a protracted battle through the courts until the Supreme Court late in 1941 handed the matter back to the NLRB for reexamination. Regarding this as a victory, the Amalgamated had voted to strike on Feb-

[15] *V-P*, October 6, 1942, p. 20; October 17, 1942, p. 18.
[16] Marshall to Wyse, October 17, 1942, Wyse to Marshall, October 17, 1942, NWHC records.

ruary 16, 1942, but had unanimously agreed to call off the strike at the request of the U. S. Conciliation Service until the War Labor Board could act. The WLB held hearings on the dispute and turned it back to the NLRB, which on September 24 again ordered the I. U. E. dissolved. The I. U. E. with the encouragement of VEPCO management kept the merry-go-round spinning by again appealing to the courts and in the meantime complicated the issue by offering to affiliate with the Utilities Workers Organizing Committee of the CIO. At this point the weary bus drivers, who had been pushed and cursed by the public all summer, finally lost patience with management and the government and voted in favor of a strike.[17]

The actual strike, which started at 4:00 A. M. on Wednesday morning, caught the city by surprise. Many first heard the news when their maids called to say: "If you want me, you'll have to come and get me; there's a strike on." Less than half of the scheduled streetcars and buses went into operation. The Navy rounded up all available transportation and sent buses and trucks out through the city to gather up its workers. City Manager Borland called Governor Darden and got permission to cancel the scheduled air raid drill, and sent police out to the car barns to prevent violence, which never developed. The strike, in fact, was as peaceful as anyone could ask. The strikers waited in a store near the car barns, hoping that they could go back to work in time to get the school children home through the rain which was falling. When a telegram from the War Labor Board arrived shortly before three, urging them to go back to work, they voted almost to a man to call off the strike and rushed out to the dispatcher's office for car assignments.[18]

The strikers would have been even more unhappy over their protest demonstration if they had known the true significance of the urgent activity at the Naval Base. The previous Sunday Norfolkians had stared curiously at an unending stream of military vehicles which flowed up Hampton Boulevard while police shunted civilian traffic into side streets. Everyone knew that something big was happening, but only a few realized that the Army

[17] *V-P*, January 8, 1942, pp. 20, 12; February 14, 1942, p. 18; February 17, 1942, p. 14; October 16, 1942, Part II, p. 12.
[18] *V-P*, October 22, 1942, pp. 1, 7.

was embarking in Hampton Roads the largest and best-equipped landing force that had ever sailed from American shores under the command of a major general named George S. Patton, Jr. On the very day of the strike the loading was being completed. Fortunately the incident caused no interference, and Patton's men left Hampton Roads on October 24 to make their scheduled rendezvous on November 7 with the rest of Eisenhower's army off the coast of North Africa.[19]

While the convoy was still on the Atlantic, Norfolk defense officials tried to iron out the last wrinkles in the defense system. Since the city had reported to the State OCD that it was ready to have the Army call surprise drills at any time, it was assumed that the only tests called thereafter would be those considered necessary by the Army. On this basis Coordinator Marshall was able to win an agreement from the military authorities that they would cooperate in all future drills. The promise was made in a conference in Marshall's office with Army and Navy officials, including one familiar figure in unfamiliar garb, Lieutenant Commander Raymond B. Bottom, now representing the Fifth Naval District Security Office. The service authorities also said that they would see that servicemen obeyed the regulations in future blackouts.[20]

At the same time the Navy renewed a promise to coordinate its air raid signals with the rest of the area. At each drill civilian confusion had resulted from the fact that the Navy sounded its sirens on the blue signal—the preliminary alert which warned of the possible approach of enemy planes—as well as on the red, while civilian sirens sounded only on the red. Persons living near the Navy Yard or the Naval Base usually put their lights out when they heard the Navy sirens and then mistook the civilian alarm for the all clear and switched their lights back on. Although it was true that the wailing note of the alarm was a different sound from the sustained tone of the all clear, the average civilian had never learned the distinction.

One of the daytime woman wardens in Larchmont, in fact, went to her post on hearing the Navy alarm and ushered everyone to

[19] For the story of the loading of the task force, see John R. Kilpatrick, "The Sailing for the Invasion of North Africa," in William Reginald Wheeler, ed. *The Road to Victory* (Newport News, 1946), I, 65–72.

[20] *V-P*, November 3, 1942, p. 18.

shelter. When the city alarm sounded, she accepted it as the all clear. She was on the way to the store in her car when she was stopped by another warden who informed her that the air raid was still on.[21] At night the problem was even more serious with people switching their lights on when they should have been switching them off. An additional complication was the difficulty of hearing the city sirens, especially in the winter with the windows closed. One harassed Berkley warden described the problem in vigorous language and original spelling:

On our last test, we were in a meeting some one went out side and heard the alarm. I my self started up Liberty st. from Fauquir to Main st. all lights burning up stairs and down Many houses with two familys had to go up on 2nd floor to get the lights out.

by the time I had reached Main. st. So. Norfolk or the Navy yard sounded out and all turned lights back on. so half of the time was gone before I could go from house to house worning people Thats too long to wait to get out lights, isn't it?

We must have some warning system we all can hear in side or out with out guessing, and I wonder why Norfolk Ports mouth and Navy yard and So. Norfolk couldn't come on at the same moment so there won't be any mistakes. it will be too late if the emeny is near to go back over and over to tell people to turn out lights test not over yet.

I had told people if not sure watch st. lights. by the way they didn't go out for 10 or 12 minutes, we called So. Norfolk sub. station and told them to pull the switch. So as a wordon I am not finding fault, I want to be a good wardon and do the very best for every one, but if we have to give the warning by telling people from house to house, it will be over before some find out. We over here can hear the Navy yard, but they have always been coming on at different times and sounding the all clear sooner than the City did, except this last test, when they did black out they stayed for the whole time.

I am sure you understand what I mean, you see a light on, we hurry and knock or hollow they say I am sorrow we didn't even know there was a black out on. Wehere as if we had the assurance they did known, the we could and would report ever one who had lights showing out side.

Other words as long as we just tell them turn out your lights please, we will never have a black-Black out.[22]

[21] James Elliot to Richard M. Marshall, June 30, 1942, NWHC records.

[22] Dewey F. King to Marshall, November 14, 1942, Civilian Defense: Air Raid Wardens, Zone 1, File No. 2, NWHC records.

One other problem still unsettled was the authority for calling blackouts. At the beginning of the year this responsibility had been entirely up to the localities; next the State had required the localities to have monthly practices; then the State had begun calling the drills. Norfolk had been putting up a fight for home rule in blackouts on the grounds that the city was in a better position to cooperate with local military authorities than was the State. The issue was raised at the final meeting of Governor Darden with the Hampton Roads officials, held in Norfolk on October 26. Colonel M. C. Woodbury, the current commander at the information center, then suggested that the problem of military cooperation might be solved by letting the Army call the air raid signals. The Army would assume this responsibility whenever the Governor certified that the defense system was ready for surprise blackouts.[23]

The Governor therefore agreed to certify the Hampton Roads area as prepared and announced that tests thereafter would be called by the Army. When no drills were called for a month, the rumor circulated in Norfolk that the Army had refused to accept the certification because certain other Hampton Roads communities were too poorly organized. The truth of the matter was that the Army had refused to accept a part of the state, and Governor Darden was not yet ready to certify the entire state. In the meantime word arrived from the State OCD that local practices were no longer to be held and that the State would soon call a surprise blackout of its own. Coordinator Marshall, who had understood at the October meeting that the State would give up its control over air raid drills, declared: ". . . seeing all of these statements in the papers has gotten me so confused that I don't know whether I am coming or going."[24]

In spite of the coordinator's confusion the surprise test, when it came on December 3, went off smoothly. The defense staff in Norfolk had some useful assistance from a cold wind, which swept practically everyone off the streets before the sirens sounded. The biggest problem revealed was the continued violation of Governor

[23] Marshall to Darden, November 28, 1942, Civilian Defense: Correspondence, Richmond, file, NWHC records.
[24] *Ibid.*

Darden's partial blackout order, which required that all unattended lights must be put out at night. City Detective Phil Adams in City Hall looked out to see the floodlights still burning on the parking lot across the street. When an employee said he could not turn them off because the station was locked up, the detective got a .22 rifle and shot the lights out. A colored auxiliary policeman smashed in the door of a store on Church Street in order to turn off the lights inside. Authorization to employ force if necessary had been granted to the wardens and the auxiliary police several months earlier, but this was the first time it had been used.[25]

Businessmen were learning to be more careful, however. Only seven merchants were fined for leaving their lights on, compared with nineteen during the last test, and one of these pleaded extenuating circumstances. The sirens had sounded while the Ames and Brownley annual banquet had been in full swing on the windowless third floor of the department store, and no one had noticed them. Finally, during a lull in the party, someone heard the air raid warden pounding on the front door downstairs, and store officials scurried around trying to turn off all the lights. Absentminded householders this time also received fines instead of warnings, but only seven had slipped. Highly embarrassed was a retired vice admiral who had left a hall light burning upstairs when he went off to a church supper. The admiral paid his fine without a protest, saying simply, "I slipped . . . and I'm mortified." Also red-faced was an air raid warden who had been taken unawares by the siren and had dashed away so rapidly that he had forgotten to turn off his bathroom light.[26]

There would be less trouble with forgotten lights in the future, since most of them were now to be kept turned off under the dimout regulations, which at long last were to be enforced. The dimout situation, apparently settled by the preparation of General Tilton's rules in June, had instead reached new heights of bureaucratic confusion. At the Governor's monthly conference with Hampton Roads officials on July 24 the group had discussed the dimout proposal. Portsmouth's City Manager Arthur S. Owens

[25] *V-P*, December 4, 1942, Part II, p. 12.

[26] *V-P*, December 12, 1942, p. 20. The *Virginian-Pilot* showed a bit of absent-mindedness itself by forgetting the initial "f" when it referred to the admiral as the "most frank defendant" and had to apologize next day.

protested that it was silly to ban night baseball unless the Navy Yard lights were also to be shaded, but other officials agreed to accept the regulations. Governor Darden therefore decided to issue the new rules as an executive order, even though no formal approval had yet come from the Army.[27]

The Governor's new order went into effect at midnight on Sunday, August 9. All unnecessary exterior lighting, such as advertising signs, was to be turned off, while essential outside lights were to be shaded so that no rays would show above the horizontal. The order incorporated General Tilton's proposal, which was merely an interpretation and elaboration of the rules issued by General Reckord from Baltimore on April 28, which had been theoretically in effect since that date but had not been observed by anyone, including the U. S. Army. The Governor's proclamation, however, made the regulations the law of the State with the police responsible for their enforcement. The police, nevertheless, were as reluctant to act under this new executive order as they had been under the one issued in the spring. Norfolk's Chief Woods declared: "I am not going to order my men to make wholesale arrests for violations of these dimout regulations until I am sure what constitutes a violation and what doesn't."[28]

Enforcement was thrown into further confusion when Portsmouth's city manager told a reporter that night baseball had been exempted from the dimout ban. The careful newsman checked the story with Governor Darden and found that Darden had obtained permission from General Reckord for the ball parks to operate at night.[29] Since the ball parks furnished more sky glare than any non-military operation in the area, there was protest from other businessmen against turning out their lights. Finally, after a conference with the Hampton Roads officials, Governor Darden agreed to a modification of his original order, permitting show windows to be lit, and allowing any exterior lighting, including baseball fields, if the lights were properly hooded.[30]

Understanding that these new provisions would be formally issued as amendments to the original executive order, Police Chief

[27] *V-P*, August 15, 1942.
[28] *V-P*, August 11, 1942.
[29] *V-P*, August 15, 1942.
[30] *V-P*, August 22, 1942, p. 16.

Woods waited for two months for something to happen. At last he discovered that the Governor was contemplating no further changes. Declaring forthrightly, "Norfolk has been muddling along on this dimout business too long now, and it is time to take some action," he ordered the police to start warning merchants that dimout enforcement would soon begin. The surprised Church Street merchants asked Chief Woods to send someone to explain what the dimout rules were. The chief came himself but had to confess that the rules baffled even him. He said he was clear about two things: all outside advertising signs had to be turned off, and all inside lights had to be put out when the store closed.[31]

When the storekeepers asked how much light they could keep in their windows to let the public know they were open, he replied that the order said the light should be kept to a "minimum," but that he could not say just what the minimum was.[32]

Meanwhile, the Army after months of gestation was about to produce what was intended as a clarification of all these problems. On November 16 First Army headquarters issued a new set of dimout regulations, which attempted to put the original order into precise and enforceable terms. For the benefit of the public the exact engineering terminology of the order was explained in practical language. All of downtown Norfolk, Portsmouth, and Suffolk were to be included in the dimout. Illumination in store windows was to be reduced to a mere 5 or 10 per cent of the usual brilliance. Auto headlamps were to have their upper halves shaded. All exterior lights were to be well hooded so that the source of light could not be seen at any great distance. This order effectively barred night baseball but made the regulation seem more just by including not only the Army camps but even the Navy Yard within its scope.[33]

Unfortunately the channel-conscious Army again ignored channels in issuing the order. Instead of sending out advance copies to defense officials and others who would be responsible for its enforcement, First Army headquarters without prior warning an-

---

[31] Even on these two he was not entirely clear. The first provision had been modified by the Governor's announcement of August 21, and the second was part of the partial blackout order, not of the dimout.

[32] *V-P*, October 18, 1942, Part II, p. 1; October 23, 1942, Part II, p. 12.

[33] *V-P*, November 23, 1942, p. 16, November 25, 1942, pp. 24, 10.

nounced the new regulations in the newspapers. A week later General Reckord's Third Service Command explained the new rules in detail to the papers but still did not send a copy to even the State Office of Civilian Defense. Coordinator Marshall spent a few frustrating days trying to get hold of the new rules. He talked to Colonel Woodbury, commander at the information center, and arranged to fly with him to Richmond for a conference on November 25. On the scheduled day the punctual colonel waited five minutes for Marshall, decided he had changed his mind, and flew off without him, leaving the tardy coordinator fuming at the airport a few minutes later.[34] Returning to his office, Marshall called up State Coordinator Wyse and found that there was nothing to discuss about the dimout anyhow, as copies of the new regulations had not yet arrived in Richmond.

As days passed without any further word, Coordinator Marshall's impatience grew. On November 28, two days before the order was to take effect, he told a reporter, "As far as I am informed, the new regulations are merely hearsay."[35] To his good friend Governor Darden he poured out his resentment at the Army's handling of the affair:

If some civilian pulled a similar trick on the Army he would probably be court-martialed and shot.

It would appear that the one person, or persons, not having information with reference to the new dimout order are those who are supposed to enforce the law.

I have never yet received a call, an apology, nor an explanation of any kind from Colonel Woodbury. This is the most remarkable incident of this kind I have ever known, and this, taken with everything that has happened recently in connection with the Army makes me feel it would be remarkable if the public is able to understand anything that is going on....[36]

The Governor reassured him that copies of the new regulations were at last on their way to him and explained with characteristic tact, "Why the Army should have released them before they

[34] *V-P*, November 25, 1942, p. 22; Darden to Marshall, November 30, 1942, Civilian Defense: Correspondence, Richmond, file, NWHC records.

[35] *V-P*, November 29, 1942, Part II, p. 1.

[36] Marshall to Darden, November 28, 1942, Civilian Defense: Correspondence, Richmond, file, NWHC records.

were sent to the respective cities is beyond me, but after all the important thing is to attempt to get along as best we can, notwithstanding the confusion and the apparent lack of coordination."[37] Like a good soldier, Marshall promptly forgot his annoyance and proceeded to enforcement. He had the regulations published in the papers and called on the public to comply. Three weeks later, however, many persons were still taking the new order no more seriously than they had the old. Colonel Borland ordered the police to begin issuing warnings to be followed by arrests for persistent violators.[38]

So long had this complicated controversy raged that everyone seemed to have forgotten the original purpose of the dimout. Defense Director Borland told the public: " . . . these dimout regulations have been put into effect to safeguard the life, limb, and property of the people of Norfolk in the event of any enemy action such as air raids, sabotage, et cetera. . . . "[39] Perhaps even the Army no longer remembered that the only reason ever given for turning down Norfolk's lights was to eliminate the sky glare which outlined ships as targets for enemy submarines. For, if there had ever been any such justification for dimming downtown Norfolk, by the time the order was actually enforced the U-boat menace was being conquered, and the regulation was no longer necessary.

[37] Darden to Marshall, November 30, 1942, Civilian Defense: Correspondence, Richmond, file, NWHC records.
[38] V-P, December 20, 1942, Part II, p. 1; December 22, 1942, p. 20.
[39] Statement by Borland, December 30, 1942, NWHC records.

18

MOBILIZED FOR OFFENSE

ONE reason for public cooperation in air raid tests was the astounding energy of the public relations office in Civilian Defense. At Maurice Bennett's desk in the VEPCO office ideas were constantly popping, and most of them were soon translated into action. Not content with the preparation of routine news releases, Bennett was constantly sighing for new forms of publicity to conquer. He organized a speakers' bureau, and supplied the speakers with background material, lectures, and even instructional films. He prepared and presented a daily radio program, persuading both local stations to give him time on the air. He planned such ingenious stunts as having a circular folded into each copy of the New York *Sunday News* delivered in Norfolk. He talked the local printers into promising to print circulars for him without charge. His plea for money to buy the necessary paper met with an emphatic no from Colonel Borland, but even that doughty defender of the taxpayers' funds eventually surrendered.[1] Soon the public relations director had persuaded VEPCO to donate free space for Civilian Defense posters in every streetcar in the city.

One of Bennett's original ideas was a public opinion poll. He obtained some forty women volunteers who each week asked the public such questions as, "Is your home prepared for an air raid?" or "Are you now engaged in defense work?" Forty-three representative sections were laid out in the city, according to scientific sampling principles, and an interviewer assigned to each one. The volunteers learned that 98.8 per cent of the population believed Civilian Defense was necessary and 15 per cent thought the war would end in 1945.[2] As the polls closed, Bennett's imagination

[1] See Civilian Defense: Financing, and Civilian Defense: Public Relations, files, NWHC records.

[2] The stories ran every Friday in the *Ledger-Dispatch*, May 8–July 17, 1942; see Civilian Defense: Publicity file, NWHC records.

conceived a rumor clinic to put to rest the various rumors circulating in the city.

The scheme which offered most scope for Bennett's talents, however, was one suggested by the State OCD. When Coordinator Wyse urged each locality to hold a Town Meeting for War, the Norfolk public relations man laid plans for a spectacular show. Nothing less than Foreman Field's 18,000 seats was big enough to contain the Bennett vision. Artists designed for him a stage fifty feet wide and 54 feet high with tall red, white, and blue pylons at either end and a sphere bearing the "CD" emblem in the center. From lumbermen and building contractors he wangled the materials and labor necessary to build it. The Army lent huge searchlights to be placed behind each pylon to extend them high into the sky.

As a principal speaker for the first night he obtained Governor Colgate Darden, making his first formal appearance in his home town since his inauguration, with Congressman Winder Harris to serve as moderator. He secured Colonel Malcolm Stewart, then commander at the information center, Admiral Simons, Colonel Borland, and Coordinator Marshall to serve as a panel of experts to answer questions from the audience and set up a board of censors to screen the questions in advance. He arranged for a motor cavalcade all the way from City Hall for the visiting dignitaries, while the Red Cross women and the Civilian Defense workers were to march in. He planned for four choirs, four bands, and a drum and bugle corps. Waves of publicity flowed over the newspapers.

The meeting on August 6 went off in magnificent splendor, if not quite according to advance announcements. Only two bands showed up, and the projected curtain of light behind the stage was not finished in time. Half the seats in the stadium were left unfilled in spite of every effort to round up a crowd. Those who came were well rewarded, however. They saw an impressive parade of Civilian Defense workers with banners flying and heard Governor Darden discuss the problems created by the war. They also listened to the answers to many of the questions they had handed in, the real purpose of the meeting.[3]

After the ambitious planning of this first meeting anything else was bound to be anti-climactic. Bennett, reached out boldly for

[3] *V-P*, August 7, 1942; *L-D*, August 7, 1942.

big-name speakers, snared Leon Henderson, head of the OPA, but failed to capture Soviet Ambassador Maxim Litvinoff. He had to be satisfied with an English lady who had once been a member of the British cabinet and the well-publicized Navy hero, Lieutenant Commander John D. Bulkeley. Even the utmost in Bennett showmanship, however, could not bring busy Norfolkians out to town meetings. Crowds dwindled at each successive meeting, and Commander Bulkeley's talk was rained out entirely.[4]

Meanwhile Coordinator Marshall was becoming curious about the nature of the independent little empire which was growing up about the public relations office. Endowed with his own secretary and stationery, Bennett was pouring forth ideas too rapidly to keep his superiors informed about what he was doing; sometimes Coordinator Marshall first heard about one of these new projects through the newspapers. Too impatient to wait for ordinary mail, the publicity director was running up a bill for long-distance calls and telegrams, which was making an alarming hole in the limited defense budget. Called in for a conference with the defense chiefs, Bennett was asked to clear his publicity through Marshall's office in the future and to cut down his expenses.[5]

Thoroughly impressed by the value of Bennett's ebullient energy, Marshall arranged to retain his services. Since the publicity man's leave of absence from the Norfolk Newspapers was expiring on December 1, Colonel Borland agreed to his appointment as a full-time employee of the Civilian Defense office with the city paying his salary. The high-flying public relations director, however, felt restless with his wings clipped and decided to return to his newspaper post instead. Marshall regretfully accepted his resignation, and a peaceful calm descended on the Civilian Defense office.[6]

[4] See Civilian Defense: Town Hall Meetings file in NWHC records. Leon Henderson spoke on August 21, Miss Margaret Bondfield on August 27, and Commander Bulkeley talked over the radio on September 10. A fifth meeting with four ministers speaking was held on September 29.

[5] Marshall to Bennett, November 9, 1942, Civilian Defense: Public Relations file, NWHC records.

[6] See Civilian Defense: Public Relations file, NWHC records. No other director was ever appointed. Three successive secretaries, Anne Bundy, Patricia Bamman, and Mrs. Zelda Covich, were in charge of public relations until the office was discontinued June 30, 1944.

One campaign to which Maurice Bennett had devoted a great deal of his effort was the salvage drives. Publicity, in fact, had been the chief function of the Committee for Conservation and Salvage when it was first organized in February, 1942. The committee had devoted itself to encouraging the public to save waste paper and scrap metal instead of throwing them away. These materials could be sold to the junk dealers by anyone who wished. For those who did not want to bother the Scouts collected waste paper, while the firemen accepted any metal left at the firehouses.[7]

As shortages became more acute, more intensive scrap drives were required. By the middle of June, with new supplies of reclaimed rubber needed to span the gap until synthetic rubber plants could be built, President Franklin D. Roosevelt proclaimed a national rubber drive which stimulated the public imagination by transforming old overshoes into new tires. The plan called for individuals to turn in all their old rubber at gasoline stations, where they would be paid a cent a pound. Service stations would collect from the oil companies, which in turn would be reimbursed by the government. The program was formulated so hastily that there was no time for working out the procedure in detail before the drive began on Monday, June 15. Some cautious dealers insisted that they would not pay anyone for scrap rubber until they knew where the money was coming from, and Mayor Wood urged citizens to hold on to their old tires for a few days until instructions came through. One service station owner, Alton B. Edelblute, a little more reckless, said he would pay for the rubber, adding, "If the government doesn't reimburse me, oh, well, what the hell. It won't be more than ten dollars, and I guess we can afford that to win the war."[8]

Within a few days all the dealers had equipped themselves with scales borrowed from their bathrooms or bought from junkmen, and were handing out pennies for rubber. Enthusiastic youngsters, inspired by the profit motive, searched every likely and unlikely corner. The Berkley branch of the Norfolk Boys Club fished more than a ton of old rubber out of the Lafayette River.[9] Biggest haul of all was the worn-out tires used as fenders on the harbor barges.

[7] *L-D*, February 10, 1942; *V-P*, February 18, 1942.
[8] *V-P*, June 15, 1942, p. 14.
[9] *V-P*, July 11, 1942, p. 16.

The Southern Materials Corporation alone contributed 100,000 pounds of old tires from its 75 barges, the largest individual contribution in the state. This gift sent the city's total soaring to over a million pounds.[10]

Somewhat overshadowed by this emergency campaign was a three-day drive by the Norfolk salvage committee. Plentiful advance publicity, Bennett-engineered, asked the public to put out all their old scrap on the curb on the day it was to be collected in their area. Businessmen lent trucks while the Boy Scouts gathered up the junk on the curbstones.[11] In three days the Scouts picked up over sixty tons of metal.[12] A month later the salvage committee tried another tack with a drive to get store scrap. The Norfolk Lions undertook a one-day campaign, signing up 250 downtown merchants to a pledge to clean up every possible salvage item in their stores. The first 57 to report their job finished had turned up over sixty tons of scrap iron and steel and 21 tons of old rubber.[13]

The biggest campaign of all began on September 21 as the United Scrap Drive under the sponsorship of the newspapers. The Norfolk papers outdid themselves in an effort to make the public scrap-conscious and to clear the last possible bit of junk out of every basement and attic. Scrap wardens were delegated to knock on doors and tell people what to do with their trash, and the papers printed salvage stories every day.

The young and the old got out the scrap. The youngsters of Benmoreell formed Commando and Ranger teams to see which could find the most metal, and the Rangers came out on top when they found two old cars which they tore apart. The Boy Scouts brought in 140 tons. An Ocean View resident, aged 84, who had been too old to fight in the Spanish-American War, did his part in the current conflict by contributing a ton of metal he had been accumulating for the last 27 years. Norfolk's last surviving Confederate veteran, T. N. Mayo, remembered a muzzle-loading shotgun he had acquired just after the Civil War and brought it up out of the basement to toss on the scrap pile. The Business and Pro-

[10] *V-P*, July 19, 1942, Part II, p. 1.
[11] *L-D*, June 29, 1942, pp. 1, 13.
[12] Undated *L-D* clipping in Civilian Defense: Salvage, Clippings, file, NWHC records.
[13] *V-P*, July 30, August 13, 1942.

fessional Women's Club collected nearly half a ton of old iron by a "scrap party" and manned a truck themselves to haul it in.

Even the animals did their part. Seven elephants offered their services to drag old autos to the junk pile. A goat wore a sign, declaring, "No ifs, ands, or butts—dig out your scrap!" and dropped a tin can on the scrap heap. A Scotch terrier named Mac gave up his personal fire hydrant, which had stood in his front yard since the city had discarded it several years before.

The Customs House contributed two large anchors which had long decorated its front, and the five old cannon which stood at the Naval Base entrance also went off to war. When the managers of two local industries said they did not have time to look for scrap, Cochairman Tom Hanes reported them to State Headquarters, and a special investigator was sent out from Richmond to look into the matter. Altschul's cleaned out its scrap so thoroughly that it had to borrow some for a window display. The drive ended on Saturday, October 17, with a scrap matinee held by the movies, which brought in another 22 tons. When the final figures were tabulated, Norfolk was credited with 108 pounds per capita, more than its quota, an excellent record for a city with so many busy citizens.[14]

While these spectacular campaigns captured the public imagination, salvage needed a steady pressure behind it to keep waste materials moving to recovery depots. To provide that pressure Coordinator Marshall discovered another human dynamo in the person of George Russ, after the first two salvage chairmen had found themselves unable to spare sufficient time for the work. The new chairman set up a full-time office in the quarters of his own business, with a full-time paid secretary and telephone, and a special letterhead listing every conceivable kind of salvageable article.

Since the metal scrap drive had flooded all the local junkyards, Russ teamed up with Maurice Bennett to launch a publicity drive for the feminine departments which had been added to the salvage campaign. Women were urged to turn in their old silk and nylon stockings to be converted into powder bags, and collection depots were established at the local stores. Housewives were instructed

[14] *V-P*, September 19, 1942, p. 16; September 25–October 18, 1942; October 20, 1942, p. 8; Civilian Defense: Salvage Clippings file, NWHC records.

on how to save the fat left over from their cooking instead of pouring it down the drain. When they had filled a can with grease, they were told to take it to their meat dealer, who would pay them for it.

A more complicated organization was required for the third task assigned the ladies. To meet the demand for tin, blocked off by the Jap hold on the mines of Malaya, the United States had embarked on the expensive job of salvaging the thin coating of tin from old cans. Housewives were asked to keep the tin flowing to the detinning plants which had been established by properly preparing each discarded can. Pictured instructions showed how simple it was to remove the top and bottom from each can and then tramp it flat. Collection was undertaken by the city trash trucks, each of which had a special compartment for the prepared cans.

The campaign got under way with the usual headaches. The harried restaurants did not want to take the time to prepare their cans. Housewives complained that they could not find any of the rotary-type can openers and the knife-type was too much trouble. Those who had carefully cleaned their cans were indignant when careless trash collectors tossed them in with the other trash. Chairman Russ, concerned about his unfilled freight cars, surveyed the city dump and found many thousands of tin cans rusting there. To increase cooperation he urged that the city pass a tin-can ordinance, making it a misdemeanor to throw away a tin can, which the council was to enact in January, 1943.

The job of making direct contributions to the war effort, as exemplified in the salvage campaigns, represented a side of civilian defense totally unrelated to air raid protection. This type of work had been the major purpose of the old regional councils, but the shock of Pearl Harbor had forced all local coordinators to concentrate on building up their protective organizations. As early as April State Coordinator Wyse had attempted to revive the contributory side of the program by urging the appointment of local chiefs of Civilian Mobilization to head up the various functions not directly related to protection against air raids, such as encouraging the planting of victory gardens or training in home nursing and nutrition.[15]

[15] Memorandum, Wyse to local defense coordinators, April 21, 1942, Civilian Defense: Civilian Mobilization, 1942, file, NWHC records.

Although Norfolk had handed all these functions except the volunteer office and the salvage committee over to already existing community organizations, Director Borland and Coordinator Marshall named Frank S. Sager, head of the Norfolk Council of Social Agencies, as chief of Civilian Mobilization, in compliance with Wyse's request, although no one quite understood what the duties of the new chief were. The job, in fact, was so completely forgotten that Chief Sager forgot his title and thought he was "welfare warden," and three months later Borland and Marshall were again debating whether he should be named chief of Civilian Mobilization.

One reason for the revival of this interest in July was the appointment by the State OCD of James F. Nicholas as supervisor of Negro Civilian Defense activities. Supervisor Nicholas began inquiries about Negro activities and on July 17 came to Norfolk for a conference on the subject. Both Borland and Marshall were receptive to his ideas, as they were interested in increasing interracial harmony. The Negroes already enrolled in Civilian Defense work had put up a complaint about their identification cards, which contained descriptions which they resented, such as "wooly hair" or "maroon eyes." A month earlier Coordinator Marshall had received an angry call from Publisher P. B. Young, Sr., of the *Journal and Guide* on this subject. Marshall explained that these cards were being issued at police headquarters, where the customary police terms were being used, but promised to have the practice changed.[16]

The fact that there were already two Negro representatives on the defense council helped promote harmony, but there was still no colored person in any administrative capacity in the defense organization. Borland and Marshall therefore agreed to name a director of Negro Civilian Mobilization, who would attempt to increase colored cooperation with Civilian Defense. To fill this post they appointed Horace G. Christopher, secretary of the colored Y. M. C. A. The *Journal and Guide* applauded "the wise move of Norfolk's civilian defense chiefs in further integrating colored citizens into the city's preparation for any emergency," and urged

[16] Young to Marshall, June 26, 1942, Civilian Defense: Negroes file, NWHC records.

Negroes to show their approval by volunteering at the new director's office.[17]

The whole concept of Civilian Mobilization, however, was still so nebulous that even the ingenious Maurice Bennett could say nothing more about it than was contained in the memorandum which had come from Richmond months earlier.[18] Not until Larry H. Hardiman, Jr., took over did the position expand to its intended limits. Chief Hardiman made contacts with all volunteer organizations whose work was connected with the war effort and formally associated them with his office. Cooperation served to multiply their accomplishments. Hardiman, for example, was able to help the Norfolk nutrition center by finding it proper offices, by providing it with publicity through the OCD public relations office, and by getting the Boy Scouts to distribute pamphlets for it. He also formed a new group to face the problem of child care. A new Lanham Act had granted Federal funds to establish day nurseries in war centers so that mothers with small children might be able to accept defense jobs. The new committee discovered that Norfolk had 1263 mothers who would go to work if they had some place to leave their 1500 children. The group therefore arranged to apply for the baby-sitting money.[19]

One part of the Civilian Mobilization program which was not carried out in Norfolk according to the national pattern was the block leader organization. The block leaders were supposed to be the feminine counterpart in Civilian Mobilization of the masculine air raid wardens in Civilian Defense. Just as the block warden prepared the houses in his area for a possible enemy attack, so the block leader was to help the homes in her section by visiting her neighbors and showing them how they could aid the war effort. Norfolk's masculine defense chiefs, however, refused to concede that women could do this job better than men. Although the U. S. Office of Civilian Defense recommended, Governor Darden asked, State Coordinator Wyse urged, and Director Borland requested,

[17] Undated clipping from *Journal and Guide*, Civilian Defense: Civilian Mobilization, 1942, NWHC records.

[18] See story in *L-D*, July 23, 1942.

[19] Hardiman to J. H. Wyse, December 14, 1942, Civilian Defense: Civilian Mobilization, 1942, file, NWHC records.

Coordinator Marshall and his staff stubbornly insisted that the air raid wardens could do everything the block leaders could do. State Supervisor of Civilian Mobilization Mary Marks reminded them that men were too busy to take part regularly in campaigns, that they had little enthusiasm for door-to-door visiting at the end of a day's work, and that housewives might not be impressed by a man's discussion of nutrition problems, but Norfolk stuck by its guns.[20] The fact of the matter was that in labor-scarce Norfolk women were almost as busy as men and had little more time for visiting, and the men at the head of the Norfolk OCD shuddered at the thought of trying to find 2,500 more women volunteers.

Norfolk's conversion of air raid wardens into block leaders was in a way symbolic of the change that had already come over the Civilian Defense program. In the harried hours after Pearl Harbor, when no one had known where the next bomb would fall, protection had seemed paramount, and the contributory services had been shoved aside. By the end of 1942, however, the United States had recovered the initiative, as attested by the landings on Guadalcanal and in North Africa. The shift to the psychology of offense was already marked among Americans at home who were beginning to feel that a contribution to help win the war might be as important as a practice blackout. The new spirit was evident in a year-end meeting of all the defense officials, called by Colonel Borland. While the city manager stressed that the war was not over yet and that the air raid wardens must remain on the alert for a possible attack, he laid the emphasis for 1943 on such programs as teaching better nutrition, establishing child care centers, and collecting scrap.[21]

[20] Mary Marks to Borland, December 21, 1942, Civilian Defense: Civilian Mobilization, 1942, file, NWHC records.
[21] *V-P*, December 11, 1942, Part II, p. 12.

19

A LIMIT TO EVERYTHING

SOMEHOW or other Norfolk still seemed able to find room for more people. The newcomers were living in trailers by the thousands, in garages and even in converted chicken houses, existing in the hope of getting one of the still unfinished new homes. Older Norfolkians had moved over to make more room. A survey by the Census Bureau in August, 1942, revealed that only one city residence out of five still had any surplus living space left in it. More than two-thirds of the city's homes were packed to capacity, with at least three persons to every four rooms, while one out of every nine had more than three persons to every two rooms. The survey indicated that there were 5,100 potential bedrooms being used as spare rooms or studies, but more than 1,100 of these were available for rent.[1]

Government housing authorities did their best to mobilize these last few nooks and crannies for war. They appealed to the public to sacrifice privacy for patriotism, pointing out that each room rented would provide one more worker at the Navy Yard or the Naval Base. They offered to lend the necessary money to any owner to convert a large home into small apartments. Then, to eliminate any possible risk, they offered to lease any suitable building, pay all the conversion costs, and turn it back to the owner at the end of the war. As a final persuasion, they threatened to invade what seemed to many the last refuge of private property by talking about requisitioning rooms, if it should become necessary.

In spite of every resource the ultimate in crowding was finally reached, and there was room in Norfolk for not even one more.

[1] *V-P*, September 23, 1943, p. 20; U. S. Bureau of the Census, "Survey of Occupancy of Privately Owned Dwellings in Norfolk."

In October, 1942, for every new person who came to town some one else had to leave to make room.[2]

This situation would have resulted in a dangerous employment crisis if a glimmer of hope had not been offered by the fact that the long-delayed housing projects were at last nearing completion. Nearly 15,000 homes were scheduled to be finished in the Norfolk area in the last four months of 1942. Private builders, winning the battle of priorities, sold or rented 2,000 homes during September and October and started 2,700 more.[3] Contractors on the public housing projects had a tougher time fighting their way through government red tape. On the Portsmouth side the experienced Barrett and Hilp firm was moving with amazing speed now that it was started at last. It set up a prefabricating plant in a fertilizer factory at Money Point, converted an old hosiery mill into barracks for its employees, and even provided pinto ponies to move its engineers about the site when mud made the ground impassable for automobiles. The contractors on the Norfolk side had to move more slowly while they learned how to do the job. The parts for their houses were fabricated outside the city and shipped in, some coming from as far away as Alabama. By November all the builders were in high gear, and houses were being finished at the rate of 200 a day.[4]

To make these new houses do the most good in increasing war production, the National Housing Agency established a War Housing Center in Norfolk, replacing the old Homes Registration Office set up in 1941. The new center was to continue listing all available housing, public as well as private, and would also act as a central renting agency for all public housing. Vacancies in these projects would be assigned only to war workers with preference going to persons who had just arrived. This last-come, first-served policy was adopted to help recruiters bring new people into the area with the promise that a home would definitely be waiting for

[2] Oliver C. Winston, "Public War Housing in the Hampton Roads Area," *Virginia Municipal Review*, XX, 295–312 (November, 1943).

[3] *V-P*, October 28, 1942, p. 18.

[4] Report of Milton Fischer, acting regional representative of the National Housing Agency, *V-P*, November 18, 1942, p. 22. The 200-a-day figure includes houses in the 5,200-unit project in Newport News.

them.[5] It was estimated that the Norfolk area would need to find another 26,000 war workers by the summer of 1943, more than enough to fill all the scheduled housing.[6]

By the end of 1942 there was still a great deal more promise than fulfillment in the housing picture, but the dawn seemed to be breaking. The 230 homes for Negroes in Roberts Park were finished and fully occupied before Christmas. Hundreds of people were living in Broad Creek Village homes, even though there were neither streets nor sidewalks. A newspaper boy and his dog got stuck so fast in the mud there that they had to wait until a neighbor came along to pull them out.[7] Liberty Park, the other prefabricated project, was ready to admit its first Negro families. Two hundred trailers were being brought in at Lewis Park, across Hampton Boulevard from Benmoreell, and the prospective occupants were waiting impatiently for a chance to move in. Twenty-five of the trailers were to be of the expandable type, where seven could sleep—or two could live; the rest had room only for four persons. The Lewis Park dormitories were a complete failure, however. There were 400 vacancies in their 428 rooms. Likewise, the Tucker dormitories for Negroes at 41st Street and Powhatan Avenue were only half full. Planning had failed to provide restaurants within walking distance of the dormitories, and the workers found it more important to be sure of a place to eat than of a place to sleep.[8]

Other problems seemed on their way to solution. Work was started on the new Granby Street hospital in October, halted in December, and then started again.[9] The new auditorium, its proposed steel girders now transformed into reinforced concrete beams, was once more going up; by the summer of 1943 it promised to provide at last some adequate space for entertaining the servicemen. Admiral Simons announced that he was planning a Fleet Recreation Park on Hampton Boulevard, with athletic fields and an indoor recreation center, where sailors could have off-Base

[5] *V-P*, September 27, 1942, Part II, p. 1; December 3, 1942, p. 20.
[6] *V-P*, October 28, 1942, p. 18.
[7] *V-P*, December 11, 1942, Part II, p. 12.
[8] *V-P*, December 3, 1942, p. 20.
[9] *V-P*, November 10, 1942, p. 22; December 8, 1942, p. 22; December 11, 1942, Part II, p. 12.

relaxation without flooding the downtown section.[10] Already in service was the new Taussig Gymnasium in the Navy Y, which could seat a crowd of 400 for a basketball game.[11]

The sailors warmed slightly toward the civilians as the weather cooled. The newspapers reminded them of many little courtesies Norfolk had been showing the Navy, which had hitherto been overlooked. The garden clubs, for instance, had been taking turns in decorating the Navy Y lobby every week end since spring. Norfolk amateurs had started the Troupers Club early in 1941 and had been putting on shows for a dozen military posts in the area ever since. The Epworth Methodist Church was putting on parties for servicemen every Wednesday night with a WPA orchestra provided by the City Recreation Bureau.[12]

No one thought, however, that the city was doing all it should or could to meet its responsibilities toward the servicemen. As a step in this direction the city council named a Norfolk Advisory Recreation Commission, with Tom Hanes as chairman, to study the problem. Colonel Borland asked the commission to prepare a report on what recreational facilities were available in the city, as, he said frankly, he did not know. He told them to recommend the broadest possible recreation program, "consistent with the amount of money available." Fred Stewart, head of the City Recreation Bureau, urged that the city should itself finance some entertainment to make the servicemen feel that they were welcome in Norfolk. The first step in coordinating the activities already under way was a formal Thanksgiving dance in the Shrine Temple, sponsored by all the USO's, which brought out 1,500 servicemen and 400 girls. To make up for the shortage of dancing partners, 350 girls volunteered for the Victory Belles, a newly-formed organization.[13]

Another important change in the sailors' recreation was foreshadowed by the organization of the permanent shore patrol in September. The sailor on liberty had always been free of any

[10] V-P, August 30, 1942, Part II, p. 1.

[11] V-P, December 6, 1942, Part II, p. 2.

[12] V-P, October 18, 1942, Part IV, p. 6; October 20, 1942, p. 8; November 22, 1942, Part IV, p. 3.

[13] V-P, November 3, 1942, p. 6; November 5, 1942, p. 22; November 6, 1942, Part I, p. 6; December 20, 1942, Part IV, p. 3; December 27, 1942, Part II, p. 7.

supervision other than that of his friendly shipmate on temporary duty; the new patrol was to be made up of permanent policemen, efficient in their duties. Most of the new recruits came from civilian police forces. The man in charge of recruiting was the Norfolk police captain who had rounded up the Japs on Pearl Harbor Day, now Chief Petty Officer Ted Miller, and the head of the new force was Roanoke's chief of police, James Francis Ingoldsby.

Group by group, the new recruits took over the shore patrol as they completed their training. They had to fight their way into control of the situation, and sometimes there were a couple of dozen of them in the hospital at the same time. They gave as good as they got, however, and gradually the sailors learned to respect, if not to love, the Navy cops. One more chapter was added to the Norfolk legend in the Navy's annals; it was the city where the shore patrol did not take liberty literally.[14]

Just two weeks after the first contingent of the new force went on duty, the shore patrol gave a dramatic demonstration of its new authority. One of the Navy's big problems was the clubs and cabins which flourished beyond the city limits. The clubs, operating outside the law, were frequently the scene of violence. Drunks broke into fights; sailors denied admission burst in the doors. Club operators, warned by Shack's fate the previous Christmas, had not again dared to resort to his rough-and-ready measures to preserve order. Moreover, the clubs served as pick-up spots for the girls from the nearby tourist cabins, which were being used to solve the recreation rather than the housing problem.

The Navy was concerned over these sex centers because of their interference with efficiency. Reports showed that 75 per cent of the venereal disease infections which made a sailor unfit for active duty had been acquired in the county clubs and cabins. Although Admiral Simons had declared these places out of bounds, the old shore patrol had never been able to keep all the hot spots covered. The new force secured the cooperation of the city police, who were authorized by the city charter to act a mile beyond the city limits, far enough to reach the center of the county night life at the intersection of Sewells Point and Cottage Toll roads.

Early in the morning of Sunday, October 18, the two police

[14] *V-P*, September 10, 1942, p. 13; September 24, 1942, p. 24; *Time*, February 21, 1944, p. 70.

forces struck suddenly at this crossroads, rounding up 115 persons who had been occupying the Southern Cabins, Shack's Cabins, and Timkin's Cabins. The shore patrol loaded 53 sailors into trucks to be taken back to their ships, while the city police had two buses waiting for their prisoners. Of the fifty women hauled into police court many were recognized as faces once familiar on East Main Street, and Justice Jacob went through the motion of sentencing 37 of them to a year on the jampacked State prison farm. A number of the others, who were not known as professionals, were let off lightly. Mrs. Shackleford was released when she explained that she was not operating Shack's Cabins, even though the license was in her name. The place, she said, was being run by a Negro hired man until her husband got out of jail. "Cato" Bennett, the owner of the Southern Cabins, claimed he was a misused man since he had supposed the couples who rented his cabins by the hour were legally married, and decided to reform his business by converting the cabins into housing for more legitimate war workers.[15]

A few weeks later the shore patrol was back at the same spot, this time in company with A. B. C. agents in a drive against the clubs. They hit the lavish High Hat and the Southern Club, as well as the Cotton Club and Tinytown in Princess Anne County. When an A. B. C. agent testified that the High Hat had presented the roughest scene he ever encountered, the Norfolk County Court ordered both it and the Southern closed for a whole month.[16] In addition the local tavern keepers were called together by the Brewing Industry Foundation and reminded of their duties to respect the law. Lieutenant Ingoldsby told them they should call his shore patrol if a sailor drank too much or was picked up by a prostitute.[17]

While progress was being made in solving all these problems, nothing could be done about the fuel and food shortages which Norfolk shared with the rest of the country. Norfolk usually felt each rationing restriction first and worst, since quotas were always based on 1941 sales and readjustments to take care of increased population came belatedly. Sugar, coffee, and gasoline had all

[15] *V-P*, October 19, 1942, p. 14; October 20, 1942, p. 20.
[16] *V-P*, November 7, 1942, p. 16; November 14, 1942, p. 18.
[17] *V-P*, November 13, 1942, Part II, p. 14.

passed through that stage, and now it was the turn of meat. All meat packers were ordered by the OPA to reduce their slaughtering of beef during the last quarter of 1942 by 30 per cent and to make a 25 per cent reduction in pork butchering. Packers naturally paid little attention to the reduction during the first months of the quarter, then by the end of November suddenly discovered that they had used up their quotas and appealed to the OPA for a new allotment.

The shortage was worse in Norfolk, not only because the quotas did not take the increased population into consideration, but also because Norfolk had a relatively low ceiling price on meat, and packers shipped to more profitable markets. On the other hand, many small packers ignored both quotas and ceilings, slaughtering whatever cattle they could find and selling the meat for whatever they could get, which was plenty. Following the usual appeal from Congressman Harris in Washington, the OPA sent representatives to look into the matter. Thomas A. Willett, spokesman for the food dealers, declared that the Norfolk area had only 30 per cent of the beef and pork it needed. Tripping over his mathematics in his alarm, he asserted local quotas were "easily 150 per cent short of what would be normal."[18] The OPA took the problem under consideration.

Meat would soon go under formal rationing, it was promised; so would canned goods. In November coffee was rationed on the cup-a-day basis. Ration board duties had changed unrecognizably since the day in January when James Wolcott had agreed to take charge of apportioning tires to civilians. The administration had been transformed, too, from a group of volunteers operating as a remote branch of the Office of Civilian Defense into a full-time, paid staff under the direct control of the OPA. Volunteers, however, continued to furnish daily assistance to the regular clerks, and the unpaid ration board members gave hours of their time to act on the flood of applications for bicycles, tires, typewriters, and canning sugar. In August Wolcott and his fellow board members resigned because, it was announced, they had been unable to devote sufficient time to the work. On the recommendation of Colonel Borland, State OPA Administrator J. Fulmer Bright ap-

[18] *V-P*, November 24, 1942, p. 22; December 13, 1942, Part II, p. 1.

pointed a new board, headed by retired Admiral Frank H. Brumby.[19]

The ration board office in the north end of the old municipal building was the most harried spot in all of Norfolk. Irritation at worn-out tires, dry gas tanks, or empty sugar bowls was naturally vented on the ration board. Few could be calm-minded enough to remember that the rationers were merely doing their best to apportion the available supplies as fairly as possible. Then, too, OPA headquarters had a remarkable knack for increasing this irritation by the way it handled the situation. It required, for instance, that each motorist surrender all the tires he owned in excess of five per car and that he should crawl around his car to take down the serial numbers of all the tires remaining. After that experience the car owner went to the ration board and found that the OPA had forgotten about Norfolk's increased population and failed to send enough of the necessary blanks. In order to see that everyone got his fair share of fuel oil, it insisted that each home owner measure all his floor space—at the same time ignoring the much fairer indicator of cubic space—record how much oil he had used the previous winter, and then go through a series of complicated calculations which defied mathematicians.

It was small wonder that many people forgot that the ration board's function was to see that everyone got gas who needed it and believed that the board's chief pleasure was in denying gasoline to needy applicants. One day the staff ran out of blanks for filing the serial number of tires, blanks for applying for fuel oil, and blanks for asking for more gasoline. Growing tired of explaining to each new arrival that they were just out of the necessary forms and of being bawled out for their pains, the staff with misguided inspiration decided to close for the day and lock the door. Annoyed applicants continued to come, tried the door, saw the clerks sitting inside ignoring them, and began pounding. As the angry crowd grew outside, the frightened clerks shivered inside at the rattling door until someone called the police for protection. The board decided to remain open next day even if there were no forms.[20]

In December the OPA managed to throw the entire city into confusion over the fuel oil situation. Norfolk with its thousands of

[19] *V-P*, August 6, 1942, p. 20; August 12, 1942, p. 20.
[20] *V-P*, November 21, 1942, p. 16.

oil burners and kerosene-using space heaters would have been a tough job for the ration staff to handle even if they had not been tangled up by the fuel formula. Working day and night, they still could not get the coupons handed out. The OPA allowed oil users to buy on credit for the time being, promising to turn the coupons over to the dealer when they were received. Then on December 11 when there were still thousands in Norfolk without coupons, the OPA suddenly ordered all credit deliveries stopped. Admiral Brumby, chairman of the ration board, met the emergency by writing out authorizations to the local oil companies to continue deliveries anyhow. An OPA official in Washington announced that such local action was illegal, and the national oil companies telegraphed their local branches not to recognize it. When one oil company refused to deliver oil to the Portsmouth ferries, the ferry superintendent called up Congressman Harris, and Harris and Senator Byrd got the OPA to promise to do something. Meanwhile, Amoco had delivered oil all through the day on Admiral Brumby's authorization, but quit at five when it heard from the company's headquarters. The Colonial Oil Company refused to deliver all day, received the Brumby authorization about 4:30, called up the company's Chicago office, and resumed deliveries. The small dealers, not bothered with the details, got inventory coupons from the ration office, exchanged these for oil from the large dealers, and went ahead selling on credit.[21]

The ration board chairman issued a desperate appeal for volunteers, to come in and help get the coupons out. "We can use any person who volunteers, even if they can only use a pen or a pencil to address an envelope," officials said. Volunteers came to work all day Sunday, and the office had to stay open nights for another week, but eventually the coupons went out. It was just in time, for the following Sunday snow fell all day, closing the churches, and the thermometer dropped to eleven on Monday morning, closing the schools.[22]

The weather could hardly have chosen a more opportune time to halt traffic, for it had been impossible to buy gas over the weekend. At noon on Friday, December 18, the OPA temporarily pro-

[21] *V-P*, December 12, 1942, p. 20.
[22] *V-P*, December 13, 1942, Part II, p. 1; December 14, 1942, p. 14; December 22, 1942, p. 20; December 22, 1942, p. 10.

hibited the sale of all gasoline except for emergencies. The announcement created little excitement in Norfolk, although most drivers took the precaution of filling their tanks before noon. Those who were tardy benefited from the fact that many service station operators managed to avoid hearing about the order until the middle of the afternoon or later. Then the OPA office started sending out investigators, and the stations got strict. One Navy Yard worker had to take a service station attendant from South Norfolk into the rationing board to convince him that it was all right to sell war workers gasoline under the emergency clause.[23]

One more straw was piled on the burdened camel's back with the shortage of Christmas cheer. The A. B. C. stores, faced with the difficulty of getting whiskey, tried to stretch out their supplies by limiting sales to a quart instead of a gallon and changing the closing hour from 10:00 P. M. to 6:00 P. M. As a result, eager purchasers clogged the stores. An almost steady line of sailors and civilians formed in the West Main Street dispensary from opening to closing time. One week end just before Christmas, the North Carolina liquor stores were closed as a preliminary to rationing, and North Carolina customers piled into Norfolk. The rumor spread that Virginia stores were about to be shut down, sending local purchasers to get their supplies in time. The Main Street store was jammed with sailors who insisted that they were going to get the whiskey they had come to buy, regardless of the legal closing time, and the manager had to get the shore patrol to help him shut his doors.[24]

Most people in Norfolk, however, had learned to submit more or less resignedly to the inevitability of line-standing. There were lines everywhere—at the movies and the restaurants, at the post office and city hall, at the bus stations and the railroad ticket offices. One fellow with tired feet, standing in the line at the city tax window, moaned, "Lawd, lawd, stan' in line to git yo' money, and den stan' in line to give it all away."

"I had several hours off and nothin' much to do," an ensign from the Naval Base related, "so I headed to Norfolk for an evenin' out. I hitched a ride with a gent from Little Creek, and stood in

---

[23] *V-P*, December 19, 1942, p. 1.

[24] Robert H. Mason, "It's Stand in Line...," *V-P*, December 13, 1942, Part II, pp. 1, 4.

Ocean View with some other people until two or three street cars rocked on by. After 'while, though, 'long came one with enough room for me to squeeze in. Well, I got to Norfolk, but by the time I'd stood in one line to get a check cashed and in another line to get a little crock of likker, my leave was near 'bout up and I had to head back to quarters."

A worried hostess in a dining room said, "I know the people standing up waiting for tables get mighty tired, and I know the people eating ruin their digestion trying to hurry up so someone else can have their seats. I'm afraid the people won't come back and the dining room will lose money, and I'm afraid that more will come and that everyone will be more uncomfortable."[25]

The climax to all this crowding came in the days before Christmas. For months people had been saying, "Why, it's just like Christmas Eve downtown; the stores and streets are so crowded." Now it was Christmas Eve, and there were more people than ever before. Thousands of shoppers surged through the stores, stripping their shelves bare of anything that looked like a Christmas gift. Candy, perfume, even handkerchiefs, disappeared. Lines an hour long stretched in the A. B. C. stores, and some went patiently back again to the foot of the line for a second quart. Others thought it was quicker to take a couple of empty suitcases to Washington or Baltimore and bring back a supply for their friends. Turkeys were plentiful in the city markets, but at prices that ade housewives gasp with indignation.

Thousands of persons used every conceivable means of leaving Norfolk to get home for the holidays. Long lines of cars waited at the gates at Little Creek for ferry after ferry. Coaches were jammed until the aisles were impassable before the train could pull out of the station. Buses ran doubleheaders and tripleheaders, and still there were standees holding on to the baggage racks. Departures lagged so far behind that schedules were forgotten. Some families arrived to spend Christmas with a husband or son who could not get home. One Navy wife reached the Navy Y with a Pekinese dog, a Persian cat, and eleven cents. She did not know whether her husband was in Norfolk or not, but he might

[25] Robert H. Mason, "It's Stand in Line...," *V-P*, December 13, 1942, Part II, pp. 1, 4.

be, and Mrs. Addie L. Benton, the Y's husband-hunter, found him for her.

There was no peace on earth, but for the moment good will toward men reigned in Norfolk. A Navy chief put on a red suit, false whiskers, and a benign face to play Santa Claus for 1,200 children at Benmoreell, whose fathers were somewhere on the Atlantic. The Gray Ladies and the Junior Red Cross carried gifts to the torpedoed seamen convalescing at the Marine Hospital. Norfolk people by the hundreds invited servicemen who could not get home to share their Christmas dinners, sometimes to sit in the place of a son who was away in service—sometimes in the place of a son who would not be coming home.

It was not a very merry Christmas by any standards. Still, Norfolk for the first time since Pearl Harbor had a brief respite. Even the Navy Yard let its weary workers take a day off on Christmas. They had to be back to work the next day, which was Saturday, but the stores took a long week end. It was the quietest Saturday Norfolk had seen in many months. Those who came downtown had the strange experience of riding in half-filled buses and walking along a deserted Granby Street. It was enough to arouse nostalgic memories of the good old days, before the United States had discovered Hampton Roads, when Norfolk was calm, comfortable, and complacent.[26]

[26] *V-P*, December 24, 1942, pp. 20, 13; December 25, 1942, pp. 20, 17; December 29, 1942, p. 18.

20

WINTER OF DISCONTENT

As Norfolkians sat up in New Year's Eve parties to make sure that 1942 actually departed, they wished each other a Happy New Year in the fervent hope that 1943 was bound to be better. Shortly, however, they were feeling that 1943 might be even unhappier. The gasoline crisis, which seemed to have been solved before Christmas by slashing the value of "B" and "C" coupons by 25 per cent, was suddenly back again. Weather was holding up the movement of tank cars to the East, and stepped-up military demand was draining off reserve supplies. Gasoline and fuel oil distributors were put on quotas of 40 per cent of their 1942 deliveries by the Petroleum Administration for War in order to protect these reserves.

On the OPA was imposed the unpleasant duty of cutting down the rationed allotments to meet these new figures. The day after New Year's shivering oil-burner users learned that their fuel, already reduced by one-third from normal quantities, would be slashed another 10 per cent. There was cold comfort in the news that non-residential users would be cut back 25 per cent. Even this reduction was insufficient, and by the middle of January many Norfolk distributors had nearly reached the end of their monthly quotas. A big freeze in the city's homes was averted only by shifting all the available tank cars to fuel oil instead of gasoline.[1]

This move kept the home fires burning but only intensified the gasoline crisis. The gas situation was more difficult to handle, because the OPA's rationing system had again broken down. OPA regulations, drawn up in large part by intense young pa-

---

[1] *V-P*, January 3, 1943, Part II, p. 1; January 16, 1943, p. 14. Shivering residents were warned not to light up their gas ovens, since the city's gas supply was made from the scarce fuel oil. *V-P*, January 4, 1943, p. 12.

triots who had spent more time studying administration than human nature, were designed to be carried out by an idealistic, self-sacrificing public. Rules were drawn up in Washington to give theoretical fairness and were handed down to the local board members, who were supposed to follow them precisely, regardless of any hardship which might be created by this arbitrary action.

The board members, being human, naturally interpreted the rules much more liberally than they were supposed to to ease the local situations, especially since there was no limit on the amount of gasoline which each board could grant. On top of this inflation of the rationed demand, was piled the black market. Most of the black market flourished on stolen coupons. The ration boards, not yet impressed with the great value of these little OPA coupons, had been quite casual in handling them. Clerks could steal coupons by the thousands without anyone being the wiser.[2] Legal coupons, in fact, floated around so cheaply on the black market that it did not pay the counterfeiters to produce the readily-duplicated stamps.

In the emergency the OPA could think of only one way to plug the leak into the black market. To restrict the flow of gasoline to absolutely necessary channels, the rationing agency decided to embark on the dubious experiment of trying to regulate the use of the gasoline. At noon on Thursday, January 7, therefore, an OPA edict banned the use of automobiles for non-essential purposes. "If it's fun, it's out," was the simple rule announced by OPA officials. The people of Norfolk promptly offered their cooperation in saving gasoline. Miss Elizabeth Jernigan Bell, secretary of the current group of debutantes, immediately cancelled a dinner party scheduled in her honor. The Kiwanians and the Junior Chamber of Commerce called off their ladies' night parties. Downtown parking lots operated on a skeleton basis during the day and closed up entirely at night, as Norfolkians stopped driving to the movies. Sales of used cars came to a complete stop, and operators of drive-in restaurants led a lonely life.

[2] A sailor in Norfolk, for example, who was attached first to the ration board at the Naval Base and later to the downtown board, sold coupons worth 50,000 gallons of gasoline without arousing any suspicion by his superiors. The theft was accidentally uncovered by the city police in making an arrest on another matter. *V-P*, January 21, 1943, p. 18.

Both State and city police promised their cooperation in enforcing the ban and turned into the ration board the license numbers of all cars parked near pleasure spots.[3] So many people seemed to take up walking that the OPA was forced to put shoes on the rationing list on February 7.

As the initial patriotic cooperation was rubbed away by the inconvenience of squeezing into crowded streetcars, people soon began grumbling about the OPA, but they were able to take out part of their peeve on an almost equally unpopular set of letters, A. B. C. The Alcoholic Beverage Control Board, at last forced to adopt a rationing system, stirred the anger of its thirsty customers by the way it handled the plan. The news that each registrant would have to pay a 25-cent fee rankled enough, and that was followed with the announcement that the stores in the Tidewater area, where registration would be heaviest, would not stay open at night, like the stores elsewhere in Virginia, on account of dim-out regulations. As a result, the scheduled week of registration ended on January 30 with thousands of Norfolkians still without their ration books.[4]

At last the A. B. C. Board decided that some emergency action was necessary. It continued the registration in the stores for three more days and decided to conduct night registration in the courthouse, which was presumably dimmed out properly. Dozens of volunteers showed up to speed the process, but the A. B. C. clerks would not permit them to issue the ration books, since they had not been sworn in as State employees. Restricted to filling out the application blanks, the volunteers soon got so far ahead of the clerks that they went home in disgust.[5]

On February 4 the A. B. C. clerks went back to selling liquor during the daytime, ending a thirteen-day dry spell, but the night registration continued. Governor Darden finally satisfied the A. B. C. Board's conscientious scruples by pointing out that the members of the V. P. F. had taken an oath of allegiance to the State and could therefore be trusted to hand out the ration books. With the help of the V. P. F. and other volunteers, regis-

[3] *V-P*, January 7, 1943, p. 1; January 8, 1943, Part II, p. 12; January 10, 1943, Part II, p. 1.
[4] *V-P*, January 23, 1943, p. 14; February 2, 1943, p. 16.
[5] *V-P*, February 2, 1943, p. 16.

tration went on at night in the courthouse and in four new
offices which were opened. All through February a flood of applicants continued to appear with no sign of let up. Finally the A.
B. C. Board hired 342 emergency workers and opened up four
more offices during the first week of March in the hope of winding
up the job. Still the applicants came, and the Board decided to
continue registration in the old city hall for another week. A
month later the city hall office was still handling 200 applicants
a day.[6]

Food as well as drink was a problem. An OPA ukase in January
banned the sale of sliced bread, and for six weeks people hunted
for mislaid bread knives or bought new ones, and tried to relearn
the technique of producing a slice that would fit in the toaster.
Then, when practice was beginning to make perfect, the bakers
were allowed to put their own slicers back into action. Although
ragged toast was only a temporary affliction of the breakfast
table, Norfolkians were still starting the day wrong by being
reminded of the rationing of sugar and coffee. On top of this
came restrictions on the butter and the breakfast bacon, with
the announcement of Ration Book No. 2.

Registration for this, at least, was not accompanied by the
protracted inconvenience of getting an A. B. C. book. As a preliminary the housewife had to count all her cans of food, remember
how many pounds of coffee she had had on hand last November,
and fill out an application blank listing all the members of her
family. Then she took the blank and all the family's sugar ration
books to the nearest school, where the teachers and volunteers
supplied by the Civilian Defense Volunteer Office gave her Ration
Book No. 2. In the process both books were "tailored" by the
removal of stamps for excess coffee or cans.

The use of the new books required a preliminary education in
the point system. The blue stamps were designed for use with
processed (canned, dried, or frozen) foods, which went under
rationing March 1. Each can was assigned a point value, scaled
according to the relative scarcity of the various fruits and vegetables, and the housewife had to budget her 48 points per month
just as she budgeted her dollars. In spite of the complexity of the

[6] *V-P*, February 6, 1943, p. 16; February 25, 1943, p. 22; March 3, 1943, p.
20; April 14, 1943, p. 18.

new system it got under way with a minimum of confusion. One woman showed up at the checking stand the first day with more than 48 points worth of food. When the cashier reminded her that she had only 48 points to spend, she pointed out all the stamps remaining in her book and had to be told that the rest were not yet valid. Another customer, who handed over her stamps and started to leave, was embarrassed by the reminder that she had to pay in cash as well as coupons. A sailor brought a can of pears up to the stand and was told that he would have to have a ration book. "Oh, hell," he complained, "this damn war is getting worse and worse."[7]

By the time the red stamps were required for the purchase of meats and fats four weeks later, Norfolkians were ready to welcome the arrival of rationing. The imposition of slaughtering quotas in the fall of 1942 had thinned out the meat counters ever since. The only thing that prevented a meat famine was the existence of a thriving black market. Tidewater farmers killed four times as. many hogs as in the previous season and sold them for fat prices. Truckers picked up hogs and cattle in Danville or North Carolina, slaughtered them in a field or a shed, and hauled the carcasses in, uninspected and ungraded, to sell whole to restaurants or small groceries. The prices charged by the meat-leggers forced the small store owner to boost his own prices well above the ceilings.[8] Norfolkians prudently bought up every ounce of point-free meat that was available on Saturday night, March 27, and hoped that the arrival of rationing on Monday would bring an adequate supply of meat at ceiling prices.[9]

Meanwhile, right in the middle of the enforcement of the pleasure-driving ban and the issuing of Ration Book No. 2, Norfolk's ration board had blown up in a front-page explosion. Almost from the first there had been friction between the local board and the State OPA office in Richmond. Part of the difficulty lay in the fact that the board was grossly overworked, since it was caring for the entire city, several times the population handled by the average local board. Slight relief had been offered

[7] V-P, March 2, 1943, p. 16.
[8] Based in part on a statement by J. W. Luter, president of the Smithfield Packing Company, V-P, March 4, 1943, p. 20.
[9] V-P, March 28, 1943, Part II, p. 1.

in August, 1942, when the membership was increased from four to six. In addition, a second, all-Negro board had been established in December with five members headed by Horace G. Christopher. Although the new board was eventually to take a large part of the colored population off the shoulders of the white board and even to care for a number of white persons who found its uptown offices more convenient, the State OPA office had not yet got around to supplying it with either supplies or staff.[10]

The basic disagreement, however, was over policy. While ration boards everywhere had been liberal in interpreting the regulations, Norfolk had felt that its special position entitled it to even more consideration. Norfolk's allotment, therefore, had tended to be as liberal as the regulations allowed, and on occasions the local board had even used its discretion to revise the regulations to meet local needs. In May, 1942, for example, the ration board had itself authorized an increase in the sugar quota for bakers in spite of the fact that it had no such authority, and in December Admiral Brumby had on his own responsibility overruled an order issued by the Washington headquarters of the OPA.

This independent attitude had been frowned upon in Richmond and had led to the resignation of the first rationing board in August, 1942. The State office had requested Chairman Wolcott's resignation, and the other members had resigned in protest. To avoid arousing a public controversy over the issues involved, the official announcement stated that the resigned members had been unable to give sufficient time to the work of the board, and the ex-board preserved a dignified silence. Inevitably, of course, the new six-man board recommended by Colonel Borland was soon following the same independent policy.

Also continued were the same casual administrative methods, which were regarded in Norfolk as friendly service and in Richmond as careless negligence. Placing great confidence in human nature, the board made no check of its clerks or its coupons. To one Negro volunteer, Clarence Edward Stokes, who had offered to help in the issuing of the kerosene stamps, a supply of stamps was given. He took the stamps to his home and acted as a one-man rationing board for his people. He issued the stamps to those

[10] *V-P*, December 19, 1942, p. 16; *Journal and Guide*, December 26, 1942, p. 1, February 13, 1943, p. 1; Negroes: Rationing file, NWHC records.

who needed them, even delivering them in person when necessary. When people who had not received their sugar ration books came to him, he acquired a supply of them to distribute. The astounded OPA investigators who uncovered this distributing system arrested the unfortunate volunteer, unable to believe that the ration board could have been so trusting.[11]

A check-up of the local board from the State office in January disclosed so many departures from the approved routine that it brought Henry L. Caravati, State organization executive, to Norfolk. Personalities soon clashed so violently that Caravati on January 25 demanded the resignation of Mrs. Mary Ann Briggs, chief clerk of the board, Chairman Brumby, and the two members in charge of gasoline and fuel oil. The admiral, however, stubbornly refused to strike his colors under fire, and the others stuck by him. After nearly two weeks of impatient waiting, Caravati sent word to the non-resigning members on Friday, February 5, that unless they would submit their resignations at once, he would announce their dismissal to the newspapers. Again he received a firm refusal.

Caravati therefore immediately sent out dismissal letters to the three board members. Next morning he conferred with an indignant Colonel Borland, who had made a special trip to Richmond earlier to intervene in the affair, and then announced the action to the newspapers. He attempted to play down the news by saying that the services of the board members had been terminated because in the future the work would be so heavy that almost full time would be required of the members. This was the same excuse that had been used in the August resignations, but this time the ousted members were as angry as Caravati and did not hesitate to speak out.

As the news spread through the city, all Norfolk blazed in resentment at the apparently arbitrary action. Fellow board members pointed out that the announced reason was ridiculous, since the three men fired had been the hardest working persons on the board, and submitted their own resignations. On Monday the city was without a ration board, and the volunteers who had been helping out in the office went on strike. Only one of the usual ten to fifteen showed up to work. Two others came in to announce

[11] *Journal and Guide*, February 13, 1943, pp. 1, 10.

that they would no longer give their services. A regional OPA officer from Atlanta, in temporary charge, began frantically calling up all over the city, asking for help. The Red Cross Motor Corps refused and telephoned Colonel Borland to tell him of their action. When the city manager reminded them that people needed gasoline and sugar, no matter what happened, they reported for duty, declaring that they were working "for the people of Norfolk, not for the OPA officials in Richmond. We are just as indignant," they said, "about what has happened as we ever were."[12]

Efforts to get at the real reasons for the dismissals were unrewarding. The *Virginian-Pilot* conducted a long-distance inquisition of State Administrator J. F. Bright and learned only that the board members had been asked to resign "because things were not going well in the rationing office." Pressed for details, he merely reiterated that the work was "not going smoothly." Congressman Harris asked General Bright to come to Norfolk on Saturday to hold a hearing on the charges against the ousted members. The city council met in special session to send a telegram asking that the members be reinstated pending an investigation. When General Bright wired back that the dismissed men would not be reinstated, the entire board met with Colonel Borland and declared that they would not accept a public hearing before an official who had already judged the case.[13]

Colonel Borland spent two hours in conference with General Bright in Richmond on Wednesday but came back with no comment. On Saturday T. Nelson Parker, chief OPA attorney, came to Norfolk, instead of General Bright, and spent the entire morning in a private meeting with the ex-board-members and Colonel Borland and Congressman Harris, while reporters waited outside. The newsmen were rewarded only with an uncommunicative communiqué, which stated that "a full, free and frank discussion" had been held and that General Bright was "expected to take some action reflecting the results of this meeting."[14]

The State administrator, however, was conveniently on vaca-

[12] *V-P*, February 7, 1943, Part I, p. 1; February 8, 1943, p. 1; February 9, 1943, p. 1.

[13] *V-P*, February 8, 1943, p. 1; February 9, 1943, p. 1; February 10, 1943, p. 20.

[14] *V-P*, February 14, 1943, Part II, p. 1.

tion and remained silent. This delaying action proved effective, for rationing had been brought almost to a standstill. One member of the old board, E. M. Moore, had been prevailed upon to remain to approve as many applications as he could, but the signature of two members was required for allotments of automobiles, stoves, and typewriters. In the emergency Colonel Borland reluctantly accepted the acting chairmanship to keep business moving and began persuading other citizens to assume the unpopular burden. By Saturday, February 20, the city manager had obtained a full board of seven members, and for the first time in two weeks the Norfolk ration board was able to function properly.[15]

Norfolk's surrender brought a temporary truce to the battle with Richmond. Colonel Borland declared that the investigation has disclosed nothing "which in any way reflects on the character, integrity and honesty of purpose" of the dismissed rationers, which no one in Norfolk had doubted for a moment, and that was the final statement on the dispute. There was some consolation, however, in the news that Norfolk would soon have a district OPA office of its own and would thus become independent of General Bright's forces.

[15] *V-P*, February 21, 1943, Part II, p. 1

21

MOSES AND IZAC INVESTIGATE

W HILE Norfolk was having its troubles with one branch
of the Federal Government, it was unexpectedly offered
somewhat belated assistance by another. In February
Secretary of the Navy Knox wrote Governor Darden that his
attention had just been called to an article in the *American
Mercury*, describing Norfolk as "Our Worst War Town," and
suggested that the State and the Federal Government should
cooperate with the city to solve the problems described.[1] The
Mercury story was sensational enough to cause alarm, but Norfolkians wondered curiously how Secretary Knox's attention-caller
had missed the equally lurid articles of the previous summer. The
undisclosed explanation was that the Secretary had read something else besides the magazines, but that he was not talking
about it.

This undercover literature was a report prepared by a committee headed by New York City's Park Commissioner Robert
Moses. Investigators for the committee had been in Norfolk in
November, 1942, gathering information from city officials and
Navy officers. Although the report covered a number of Navy
towns, it found conditions in Norfolk worst of all. Its most
important recommendation for improvement was that a central
committee of the heads of the various Federal agencies be set up
in Washington, with a special representative in each of the congested areas to expedite the clearance of needed measures. This
Secretary Knox had decided to put into effect, and he had already
drawn up the necessary executive order for the President's signature. He was somewhat handicapped, however, because the report
was so outspoken in its criticisms of all concerned that the Secretary was trying to keep its very existence a secret.

[1] *V-P*, February 21, 1943, Part II, p. 1.

Accepting Secretary Knox's invitation, Governor Darden went to Washington on Monday, February 22, and conferred with him there, along with Senator Byrd and Congressman Harris. The discussion centered on the chief problem with which the State had been concerned, providing a place to keep the women who were still crowded in the Norfolk jail.[2] The promise of speedy action which Chief Woods had brought back from New York City in August, 1942, had been tripped up by red tape. In the six months since, the project had been booted back and forth between Washington and Richmond while bureaus argued at cross purposes. Little more than a month after Governor Darden had been notified that the Army would turn over the CCC camps, the heads of his health, welfare, and corrections departments had agreed on a plan to operate the proposed institution. It was proposed that the one camp be moved to the site of the other at Green Bay in Prince Edward County. Under the supervision of the corrections department a quarantine hospital would be established with provisions for vocational training to prepare the prostitutes to earn their living in a more legitimate way.

By September 17, 1942, the application for Lanham Act funds to operate the institution had been drawn up and signed by the Governor. The application was turned over to the U. S. Public Health Service, which ruled that it did not meet the necessary requirements, since the proposed camp was more of a prison than a hospital. The ODHWS promptly urged that something be done at once to meet the crying need. After a month of conferences the FWA called another meeting of all officials concerned on November 6. Governor Darden himself attended and agreed to let the FWA make whatever changes were necessary to meet the Lanham Act requirements. More conferences finally resulted in a grant of $105,000 to operate the institution on February 11, 1943. The Governor, however, had decided by now that it would be impossible for the State to maintain the camp under the revised terms of the grant and suggested to Secretary Knox that it would be better for the Federal Government to assume the entire responsibility.[3] Since this was the only announced result of the

<hr/>

[2] *V-P*, February 23, 1943, p. 1.

[3] *V-P*, February 23, 1943, p. 1; statement of John J. Hurley, field representative, ODHWS, in *Hampton Roads Investigation*, pp. 346–348.

conference, headlines featured it as a "vice clean-up" measure, although Knox's interests were actually much broader. The executive order he had prepared was designed to aid in solving all the local problems of the congested production areas, with vice being a distinctly minor problem. At this point, however, Congress got wind of the Moses report. The House Committee on Naval Affairs called in Secretary Knox and had a chance to look at the confidential document. Behind locked committee doors Congressmen examined the criticism of their constituents and promptly dismissed the report as biased and unfair. Secretary Knox was asked to hold up his executive order until a special subcommittee of the Naval Affairs group could conduct its own investigation of the Navy towns.[4]

A month later the Congressional committee started its study of the crowded Navy ports by spending a week in the Hampton Roads area. A familiar figure in the group was Congressman Harris, but the most attractive member was Mrs. Margaret Chase Smith, Congresswoman from Maine. The committee spent two days touring the naval installations, the housing projects, and the "bad lands" on Cottage Toll Road. Mrs. Smith made a personal inspection of the women's quarters in the city jail, jam-packed as usual. She was shocked at the youth of the girls, one of whom was only fourteen. Although she found few beds and no sheets, she said that conditions were not as bad as she had expected.[5]

"We come with an open mind," said subcommittee chairman Edouard V. M. Izac, of California. "We realize you have been trying to cope with a multitude of problems created by the war and national defense for two years. We want to hear what you have been doing and what you think the Federal Government might do to help."[6] That was the kind of invitation the people of Norfolk welcomed. High officials and plain citizens turned out to tell the committee their troubles and to offer criticisms and suggestions.

The committee heard the story of the new hospital on Granby Street: how it had been approved, then delayed, started, then

[4] *V-P*, February 23, 1943, p. 1; February 24, 1943, p. 20.
[5] *V-P*, March 27, 1943, p. 16.
[6] *V-P*, March 23, 1943, p. 18.

stopped, knocked down to two stories, to one story, then raised again to three, and was now to be halted again while the WPB had another survey made. They learned that the completion of the seventy-bed extension to the Negro Community Hospital was being held up by lack of priorities, while work on the sixty-bed extensions at Norfolk General and Leigh Memorial had only just been started for the same reason. Admiral Taussig, appearing as head of the Hampton Roads Sanitation District Commission, complained that his sewers had not even had a chance to meet the WPB ax because they were still being held on an FWA desk.

The investigators heard that, although the Richard A. Tucker School in the Oak Leaf Park section had just been completed, the WPB had cancelled the white school in Bay View under the ruling that schools must be operated in two shifts before new buildings could be allowed. The Negro schools near Roberts Park and Liberty Park, they were told, were already on two shifts, although the latter development was only half occupied. When the committee asked why schools had not been built along with the homes in the big housing projects, they learned once more that the WPB had refused to approve such facilities originally.

The Congressmen listened to complaints about the food. The wife of a chain-store manager protested about high prices, and a welder in the Navy Yard took the day off to tell about his troubles in the restaurants. Admiral Simons explained how his sailors on liberty, piled on top of the crowded civilian population, swamped the downtown eating places, while the scanty food allocations to the area discouraged the opening of new restaurants.

All the other old headaches were rehearsed—the undersized USO's, the crowded streetcars, the inadequate taxicab service. There was virtually unanimous agreement that there was no local responsibility for any of the problems. The transportation officer at the Naval Base, Lieutenant R. W. Siver, did suggest that VEPCO might have shown more enterprise in recruiting women operators for its vehicles, but Vice President Throckmorton explained that the company had had to equip restrooms first, and that familiar goat, the WPB, had failed to authorize priorities until recently.

In spite of all the complaints, however, the committee was surprised to learn that conditions were not as bad as painted in the Moses report. Vice, which had been featured in the preliminary headlines, had dwindled away to a minor problem. While dens of sin still flourished in the county, the aid of the permanent shore patrol had enabled Police Chief Woods to get the city dives under control. The Navy's venereal disease rate had been cut from 107 per 1,000 in January, 1941, to 37 in January, 1943, and two-thirds of these infections had been picked up outside the Norfolk area.[7] The major need remaining was a place where the city police could put the women after they had been arrested.

By spring sailors were promised more places to go. Admiral Simons' Fleet Recreation Park on Hampton Boulevard would soon be ready, even though the Navy Department had made him cut its proposed size in half. There the sailor could enjoy liberty, free from the environment of the Naval Base, without crowding into the downtown area. The admiral also proposed to keep some of his men off Granby Street by attracting them to Ocean View Park. He arranged for new operators to lease the property from VEPCO, add new concessions, and open the park in April, six weeks early. Moreover, the big USO auditorium, designed to provide all kinds of mass entertainment, was scheduled to be finished by early summer. There was enough water at present, and the city's new line to Lake Prince would at last be completed in June. The new Norfolk by-pass had been opened to military traffic in November and would be ready for the public by July.

Best of all, the housing problem at last seemed on its way to solution. The big housing projects of Broad Creek Village and Liberty Park, along with Alexander and Douglass parks on the Portsmouth side, after battling with priorities all summer and the weather all winter, were now at last nearing completion. As the streets were paved and the yards were seeded with grass, the sea of mud in which the homes were floating would disappear. Schools, already in operation in converted homes on the projects, would be moved to regular school buildings as soon as they could be finished. Stores would be added to make it possible to buy groceries without an irritating bus trip.

Future building was unlikely to be harassed by the problems which had plagued construction in 1942. The National Housing

[7] *Hampton Roads Investigation*, p. 308.

Agency, established in February, 1942, had now been in existence long enough to have its administrative channels dredged out so that applications could move smoothly through. The War Production Board had agreed to grant all priorities in a single package so that builders could get the necessary materials as they were needed. The somewhat impractical demountable idea, which had plagued contractors the year before, was now to be abandoned in favor of a new form of temporary construction.

The new temporary buildings were backed by the same promise as the demountables, that they would be removed as soon as the war emergency had passed. As an extra guarantee that they would not remain as postwar slums, the government leased rather than bought the land. All were of the same general type, two-story, frame buildings, containing one-bedroom, furnished apartments, the type for which the demand was greatest. Just below the city line, in South Norfolk, near the Navy Yard, builders would soon be starting on the Admiral's Road Apartments with 400 units, while work was already begun on 344 more homes for white couples in the Commonwealth Apartments on 25th Street. For Negroes 124 similar apartments were being added at Roberts Park, while Carney Park with another 224 was going up in Titustown, where part of the slums created by the emergency housing of World War I had to be torn down to make room for World War II.

The most remarkable thing about the Izac committee's investigation was that it was followed by action. Congressman Harris, assigned the task of preparing the report on the Hampton Roads area, immediately went to work and managed to incorporate virtually everything he had been trying to put through for the last two years. Of the eighteen recommendations made by the committee only one was not carried out, a proposal that the Navy establish downtown messhalls, which Admiral Simons ruled was impractical.[8] On all other points the Navy hastened to obey the instructions of the House Naval Affairs Committee.

To reduce the crowding, the Navy Department promised to assign no more activities to the area. The Navy, in fact, had for

[8] The recommendation that Norfolk be granted funds to provide quarters for white women on the city farm was not carried out, but the later establishment of a venereal disease hospital in the city answered this need in part. Many of the other points were not carried out exactly as recommended.

some months been engaged in moving activities out. The Chaplains School had been moved from the Naval Base up the Peninsula to the College of William and Mary, and the Seabees had been transferred to Camp Peary in the fall of 1942, submerging hapless Williamsburg in the process. Part of the activities of the Naval Air Station were transferred to a new station at Patuxent, Maryland, and the Naval Training Station was closed down.[9]

The Navy agreed to double the size of the shore patrol and began a recruiting program to find another 300 men, including fifty Negroes. The shore patrol went further to help out the city's badly depleted police force, which was down to 194 men and could attract no new recruits at the $138 a month starting salary. Nine shore patrolmen were assigned to ride in the city's scout cars, releasing nine city policemen for other duties.[10]

Other Izac committee recommendations were carried out through the agency of the President's Committee on Congested Production Areas under the direction of Corrington Gill, with R. S. Hummell as the committee's representative in the Hampton Roads area. The naming of this body, as recommended in the Moses report, had been held up in February by the intervention of the Congressional group, but was carried out in May after the Izac investigators had partially completed their inquiry. Although the President's Committee was entirely independent of the Congressional committee, it helped to carry out some of the latter's suggestions.

Approval of the proposed new schools crossed Washington desks in record time. An elementary school was started at Broad Creek Village in addition to the combined elementary and high school already under way there, and an elementary school was authorized for Liberty Park.[11] The WPB dropped its suspicion that some of the new hospital facilities were not really needed, and work on all of them was carried through to completion. The Procurement and Assignment Service, charged with recruiting doctors and nurses for the armed forces, agreed to let Norfolk keep all the medical personnel it had left.

[9] *V-P*, April 4, 1943, Part II, p. 1. The NTS, however, was replaced by a new Destroyer Escort School.
[10] *V-P*, May 11, 1943, p. 18; Chief Woods's testimony, *Hampton Roads Investigation*, p. 165.
[11] *V-P*, May 29, 1943, p. 16.

The food problem was met in part by obtaining priorities for a large restaurant near the new auditorium. The War Food Administration and the OPA decided to establish a reporting system to keep track of impending shortages so that new supplies could be allocated before a crisis occurred. This system, of course, could not provide all the food Norfolk wanted, in view of the developing national shortages, but it held forth some promise of equality of treatment in the future. The psychological change that this action symbolized was probably one of the most important outcomes of the Izac investigation. Norfolk was no longer to be regarded as the nation's step-child, neglected and scolded for its shortcomings. Now, like Cinderella, it was to be lifted from the ashes and given, if not a pumpkin coach, at least some special consideration.

With all these steps to make Norfolk a better place to live accomplished or promised, the way was at last paved for the recruiting program which was intended to bring workers into the district by the tens of thousands. In April there were 8,000 homes waiting for them in the Hampton Roads area, with 2,000 more scheduled to be finished each month until summer. Although all of these were to be reserved for the newcomers, even more accommodations were needed. The Census Bureau surveyed the city again and found a little more breathing space than it had the previous August. Nearly twice as many homes were now occupied to less than capacity; the Census Bureau estimated that, if every home were packed to capacity, 20,000 more persons could be squeezed into Norfolk's private residences.[12]

To get the maximum use out of all this available space the campaign to persuade more people to rent rooms was pushed with renewed vigor, even though Frederick Gutheim, field representative of the National Housing Agency, said that residents of the area had already responded "magnificently." More appeals were

[12] Capacity is three to six persons in a four-room home. The percentage estimates for the three surveys made by the Census Bureau were:

	August, 1942	April, 1943	May, 1944
Vacant	1.0	0.8	1.1
Below capacity	20.1	38.3	43.1
Capacity	66.9	48.2	47.0
Overcrowded	11.4	12.7	8.7
Not reported	0.6		0.1

Percentages were based on an estimated 45,000 privately-owned dwelling units.

made for properties which might be leased to the Government for conversion into apartments. Coordination was the watchword of the day, and the War Housing Centers in the three major Hampton Roads cities were placed under a Home Use Director, Miss Harriet Tynes, who was to supervise all housing mobilization.[13]

Labor recruiting was also coordinated. The offices of the Virginia State Employment Service, which had become the United States Employment Service in January, 1942, were a year later placed under the Hampton Roads Area Office of the War Manpower Commission. The new WMC office called a conference of employers and labor representatives in the region on January 5, 1943, and named a Management-Labor Committee of eight members to serve as an advisory council. The new plan was supposed to call for coordinated recruiting; each employer would submit his estimated needs for the next six months to increase his work force and replace those lost through the draft and for other reasons, and the WMC would then plan the recruiting.[14]

The program started off with a fanfare of publicity. Since it was cheaper to train women for war jobs than it was to build houses for workers brought into the area, a recruiting program was decided upon. There were 30,000 women available in the Hampton Roads area, it was estimated, and WMC set to work to get half of them into war jobs. One committee was set up to canvass all the housing projects and try to persuade women to enroll in training courses. Another group, headed by Major Turin, was appointed to publicize the new drive.[15]

Women in industry were nothing new in Norfolk. Shortly after Pearl Harbor the Navy Yard had diffidently announced that it would hire 26 women in its shops, and a year later there were over a thousand women there, operating cranes and welding ships. The Naval Air Station had likewise trained feminine mechanics to repair its planes.[16] One of the first civilian employers

[13] *V-P*, April 11, 1943, Part II, p. 1.
[14] *V-P*, January 6, 1943, p. 16; Area Office, War Manpower Commission, "History, War Manpower Commission, World War II, Hampton Roads Area."
[15] *V-P*, January 7, 1943, p. 18.
[16] Marie F. Beggs, "Women at Work," *Know Norfolk at War*, August, 1943, pp. 33, 34.

to abandon masculine prejudices was John Twohy's Transit Mixed Concrete Corporation. In June, 1942, a husky Marine sentry at the Naval Base gasped in surprise when he checked the pass on a concrete-mixer truck and looked up to see the curly-headed driver.[17] VEPCO bowed to necessity and put women on its street-cars in January, 1943.

One way to get more women into war jobs was to provide a way of caring for their children. Larry Hardiman's child care committee had got its program under way in December, and the school board applied to the FWA for the funds to operate four day nurseries. The school board was somewhat taken aback when the grant was announced in February, as it turned out that the FWA expected the city and the working mothers to pay for half the costs. The school board reluctantly voted to establish one day nursery in J. E. B. Stuart School on an experimental basis, decided to close it after poor attendance the first week, then discovered a $14,000 surplus in its budget and voted to open two more instead. By June there were four day nurseries, taking care of 71 children.[18]

These 71 mothers, unfortunately, were only a drop in the 15,000-woman bucket the WMC was trying to fill. Childless women did show up at the USES office to ask for work, but in nowhere near the needed numbers. Those that did apply often ran into prospective employers unwilling to take the necessary time to adapt a man's job to woman's capacities or simply too steeped in traditional prejudice against women to accept them in their shops. Recruiters beat the bushes to flush out more men, extending their drive to the Valley and beyond the mountains. Norfolkians were startled to learn that there were now more people coming to the city from West Virginia than from North Carolina.[19] Still there were not enough men. The Navy Yard's

[17] Mary Gwynne Campbell, "These Women Trade Teas and Frills for Ten-Ton Trucks—And Man's Pay," *V-P*, June 28, 1942, Part IV, p. 3.

[18] *V-P*, February 21, 1943, Part II, p. 1; February 26, 1943, Part II, p. 12; March 12, 1943, p. 22; April 23, 1943, Part II, p. 12; June 6, 1943, Part II, p. 1. By the end of the year there were five centers in operation, caring for 150 children, and a sixth was opened in the fall of 1944, providing for 250 children in all. *V-P*, September 27, 1944, p. 10.

[19] *V-P*, March 19, 1943, Part II, p. 10. At least one West Virginia recruit never reached the Navy Yard. He got off the C. & O. train in Newport News,

payroll reached a peak of 43,000 in February but never got any closer to its goal of 55,000. Instead it started slipping down again. New arrivals came in scarcely fast enough to replace those who quit or were drafted.

The housing projects stopped keeping their homes empty, waiting for workers who did not arrive. A new worker became any one who had moved into the area since June, 1941. Residents did not need even to hold a job in war production; employment in a "locally-needed" industry, such as transportation, was sufficient. Levitt and Sons' sprawling Riverdale development became virtually surplus before it was finished. Large display ads announced that homes were available to war workers. Soon the ads took on a prewar flavor, proclaiming Riverdale the coolest spot in Norfolk County, blazoning cheap rents, $33 a month including water. Non-war-workers were invited to rent the homes. Even a voluntary rent reduction, unheard of in wartime Norfolk, to $29 a month failed to fill the 1600 homes. Its concrete bathtubs, its coal ranges, its remote location proved insuperable handicaps. Bill Levitt turned the project over to a local agent, took a commission in the Navy, and abandoned housebuilding for the duration.

Employment programs had to be recalculated to meet the new situation. The United States had learned that its manpower, like its raw materials, was not inexhaustible. In 1942 Norfolk had been able to drain off surplus labor from other areas; by 1943 the surplus had disappeared, sucked up by mounting war production everywhere and by the draft. Single men in non-essential jobs had come close to satisfying Selective Service quotas during 1942. The extension of the draft to boys of eighteen and nineteen filled the quotas for the first two months of 1943, but from there on married men had to be called. By fall it would be necessary to draft fathers, and dependency would no longer be a factor in deferments.

Since the nation was scraping the bottom of the manpower barrel, the only resource was to make more use of what was

---

stared curiously at the soldiers and sailors piling into the C. & O. steamer for Norfolk. The ship and the water were too much for the mountaineer. Suspecting that he was being tricked into going overseas, he got back on the train and returned to West Virginia, *V-P*, May 31, 1944, p. 16.

already available. On February 9, 1943, a WMC order required employers in critical labor areas, including Hampton Roads, to go on a 48-hour work week, beginning April 1. This regulation had little effect in Norfolk, since the war plants were already on a 48-hour week and most of the establishments which were not were excluded from the provisions of the order. More effective was the new plan set up by the Navy Yard in June. Abandoning all efforts to reach its 55,000 goal, it prepared to get along with the 40,000 it was able to hold. This number, it decided, could be handled in two shifts instead of three. Under the two-shift system the working day could be lengthened to nine hours instead of eight, and the worker could be allowed 45 minutes for lunch rather than the hasty twenty minutes he had had before. The extra hour would permit employees to have most of their Sundays free. The average work week, however, would be raised from 51 hours to 56.[20]

Another program was set up to eliminate the waste caused by labor turnover. Irresponsible workers often drifted from one job to another, quitting when they felt like it and showing up again when they felt like it. Dismissals were ineffective discipline when there was another job around the corner. Employers too contributed to the problem by soliciting workers regardless of the job they already held. Shipyards actually injured their own production by pirating each other's welders. To bring these practices under control, the WMC office drew up an employment stabilization program which was approved by its Management-Labor Committee.

This program provided for a complete job-freeze all over the Hampton Roads area, the first time this step had been taken in the nation. No person was permitted to hire anyone for any purpose unless he could present a statement of availability from his last employer or the USES. The WMC admitted, however, that it had no intention of checking up on housewives who hired maids without a written release. Persons in certain critical occupations, such as welders, could not be hired at all unless they had been cleared through the USES office. No recruiting or advertising outside the area could be done without the approval of the USES, and recruiting for the Navy Yard and all other civil

[20] *V-P*, June 19, 1943, p. 16.

service posts was to be handled entirely by the U. S. Civil Service Commission. The regulation also included an optimistic statement that no employer should discriminate because of sex or race.[21]

The freeze was not quite a solid one. A man who was dissatisfied with his job and could not get a release from his employer could apply to the USES for a statement of availability. If the USES considered his reasons for leaving satisfactory or felt he could make a greater contribution to the war effort in some other job, it would grant the release. If it refused, the worker could appeal to a special appeals panel. If even that failed, he could still quit and get a new job after thirty days of idleness. Newcomers to the area could obtain a statement of availability from the USES. In the first week there was a rush to try out the new system. The USES offices in the Hampton Roads area received 782 applications for statements and granted 549 of them, about 400 to new arrivals in the region.[22]

As the novelty of the new plan wore off, people soon discovered that, like many other regulations in effect, it had no provision for its enforcement. Those who quit the Navy Yard and left the area could find jobs elsewhere legally; if they wanted to remain in town, there were plenty of employers who did not bother to ask about releases. While the program thus failed to stop the drain of labor away from the Yard, the restrictions on recruiting reduced the flow of newcomers to the area. The original recruiting program, however, was modified to permit the Navy to join the Civil Service Commission and the USES in the search for new workers and finally the Navy regained its independence. In October the stabilization program was revised to require inter-area releases; that is, a worker who left Hampton Roads could not be employed elsewhere until he had obtained a release locally, and a man who left an essential job elsewhere could not be employed in the Hampton Roads area until he obtained his release. The period of enforced idleness for a person without a release was extended from thirty to sixty days.[23]

[21] *V-P*, April 18, 1943, Part II, p. 1, Part I, p. 10. The job-freeze originally included only some occupations, but it was broadened two days later to cover all employment.

[22] *V-P*, April 29, 1943.

[23] *V-P*, October 17, 1943, Part II, p. 1; October 31, 1943, Part II, p. 1; Area Office, War Manpower Commission, "History, War Manpower Commission, World War II, Hampton Roads Area," pp. 31, 39.

The new agreement was more satisfactory to the Navy, since the restoration of its independent recruiting started the employment curve back up again. October saw a net gain of 1,423 workers in the area in spite of the fact that 1,202 were lost at the same time. There had been 3,565 new arrivals but 940 of these had been ordered to return home because they had not been able to obtain the necessary releases.[24] The program thus offered discouragement to job-jumpers and restrained over-enthusiastic recruiting. There was some question whether it did not waste more labor through its penalties than it saved through its stabilization measures, but the lack of any enforcement program made the question academic. Workers and employers found it easy to evade the rules when it was inconvenient to obey them.[25]

[24] *V-P*, November 13, 1943, p. 14.

[25] A similar program was tried during World War I. In March, 1918, a District Board of Control for War Construction Activities was set up in Norfolk to coordinate construction activities. Men were recruited by various agencies, but the Board of Control attempted to redistribute workers according to their need. On August 1, 1910, the recruiting of common labor throughout the nation was placed in the hands of the United States Employment Service. There is no report available on the success of these agencies. Bureau of Labor Statistics, U. S. Department of Labor, *The Impact of War on the Hampton Roads Area*, Part II, pp. 24, 35.

22

PLEASURE PROHIBITED

BY the spring of 1943 Norfolk had the promise of the Izac committee that it would get a fair share of everything, but the trouble was that by now even a fair share looked mighty small. While Norfolk had battled its way through that hectic year of 1942 without enough of anything but sailors, the rest of the country had been living off its accumulated fat. Now that the fat was used up, equality was to be achieved by cutting the other parts of the nation down to the level to which Norfolk had become accustomed. From now on its misery would have company.

Rationing of food under the point system appeared to be only a minor hardship. A couple of pounds of fresh peas replaced the rationed can of peas at the expense of a few more cents and a few more minutes of preparation. Unrestricted fish and poultry proved fairly satisfactory substitutes for rationed beef and pork. So carefully, in fact, did Norfolkians manage their blue and red stamps that they caused a last-minute rush to get them spent before the first group expired on April 30.[1] The chief effect was to send prices soaring on the non-rationed commodities. Just after processed foods were rationed, cucumbers sold for thirty cents each in the city market; two years earlier they had been advertised for five cents. Oranges in 1941 had been less than four cents a pound; now they were nearly six. Three pounds of spinach then had cost nineteen cents; now one pound sold for twenty.[2] Rising prices brought price ceilings, and price ceilings brought new black markets. One Saturday in June chickens had disappeared from the city market by noon. The Eastern Shore poultry which had formerly supplied Norfolk, dealers explained, could no longer be bought at ceiling prices.[3] Eastern Shore onions and cabbage fol-

---

[1] *V-P*, May 1, 1943, p. 16.
[2] *V-P*, March 12, 1943, p. 22.
[3] *V-P*, June 20, 1943, Part II, p. 1.

lowed the chickens into the black market. Soon ceilings were being virtually forgotten.

The gasoline crisis of January had meanwhile vanished without notice. During January most people had patriotically put up with the temporary inconvenience of leaving the car in the garage. By the time evasions of the pleasure-driving ban had become general in February, Norfolk had lost its rationing board and had no enforcing agency. Then in March, as improving weather conditions brought more gasoline to the East, the new OPA Administrator, Prentiss Brown, cut "A" rations in half and dropped the unpopular enforcement measures. Put on his honor to use gasoline only for essential purposes, everyone adopted his own interpretation of what was essential to him.

As supplies of gasoline seemed plentiful again, the existence of the honor system was quietly forgotten. Shipments to the East Coast, however, continued to be low, and the black market continued to rob the legitimate supply. Oil companies dipped into their reserves to make up the difference. Their stocks by the middle of May had dwindled to 27 per cent of normal, while a 40 per cent reserve was necessary to keep dealers supplied. Farmers in the Northeast complained that they could not get gas to run their tractors. At this moment a flood in the Mississippi broke the "Big Inch," which was already in operation over part of its route, and reduced prospective supplies even more. Petroleum Administrator Ickes promptly ordered the OPA to cut civilian use, and the OPA reluctantly dusted off its only weapon against the black market, the pleasure-driving ban.[4]

At noon on May 20 non-essential motoring was banned once more along the East Coast south to the North Carolina line. Again the State and city police both promised their cooperation in checking on violators. The OPA too threatened more stringent enforcement by doubling the number of investigators that had been used during the winter. Norfolkians were impressed with the seriousness of the situation by the news that three of the five big oil companies in the city were entirely out of gasoline and another had only one day's supply.[5]

Would-be cooperators called the uninformed city police to ask for interpretations of the rules. A father inquired whether it

[4] *V-P*, May 20, 1941, p. 1.
[5] *V-P*, May 22, 1943, p. 16.

would be all right for his son to use the car for a final week end before his induction into the Army. One woman wanted to know if she could drive to see her mother on the other side of town. "I know three or four short cuts, and the way I go it'll take only a teeny bit of gas," she coaxed. Another much distressed woman wanted permission to drive "Fritz" to the veterinarian for a vaccination against distemper, since it was too far for the dog to walk and he was not allowed to ride the streetcar. "Will it be all right for me to drive my car to church?" one uncertain caller asked. "It's not a pleasure trip; I'm going there to get married." One question the police gave up on came from an earnest young man who asked: "A certain man is riding my wife around in his car, and I want to know can't he be picked up for pleasure riding."[6] Shortly the OPA had prepared an interpretation of the new regulations, which showed that all the inquirers at police headquarters had been seeking pleasure except the prospective bride.[7]

The Office of Defense Transportation stepped in to slash the commercial use of gasoline by a 40 per cent cut applied to all "T" rations. All retail delivery of such "luxury" items as beer, soft drinks, ice cream, and magazines was prohibited. All other deliveries were greatly restricted; the laundryman could ring only twice a week, and the milkman could call only every other day.[8] Norfolk at last received a mark of special favor when the ODT required only a 20 per cent cut of the city's bus mileage.[9] Even this was a severe hardship where the bus service was already far from adequate, but VEPCO managed to meet the situation by removing buses from the off-hour schedules. By spreading out the crowding the impossible was accomplished, and room was made for the grounded motorists.

Buses leaving the Union Bus Terminal and the new Greyhound Bus Station were permitted to continue running the extra sections they had long been operating, but the extra buses were not allowed to depart for Washington, D. C., or Washington, N. C., until every seat was taken. The Norfolk Southern prepared to take

[6] *V-P*, May 23, 1943, Part II, p. 1.
[7] *V-P*, May 23, 1943, pp. 26, 13.
[8] *V-P*, May 24, 1943, p. 1; May 25, 1943, p. 1.
[9] *V-P*, May 24, 1943, p. 14.

emergency steps to get Norfolkians out to the beckoning beaches. It planned to substitute the less satisfactory but more economical rail buses for the highway buses it was required to take off the Virginia Beach run. The company also decided to restore regular passenger-train service to the Beach over the week-end.[10]

As Norfolk gas stocks were held near the danger point for days because of floods hampering tank-car shipments from the West, most people loyally obeyed the pleasure-driving ban, even though it grew daily more irksome. Only about 300 possible violations were discovered in the Norfolk area by the OPA investigators in the first ten days. By Decoration Day, a warm, pleasant Sunday, however, many yielded to temptation. The State Police stopped over 250 cars on the roads to the beaches, only to learn that the drivers had excuses ready. Many were out to decorate graves, even though they had no flowers with them. Others were on their way to visit sick relatives; the police were surprised to learn there were so many sick people in the area.[11]

A special hearing panel of the local rationing board was named to handle the reported violations. As those summoned appeared to state their cases, a number of irregularities were incidentally discovered. Motorists turned up with loose stamps, which they were not supposed to have. Some persons had "C" books who were not eligible for them. One member of the panel, Oscar F. Smith, was surprised that persons who had applied for "B" or "C" coupons intended entirely for essential driving had been granted so much gas that they could waste it on pleasure trips. OPA Administrator Prentiss Brown had already tried to meet that situation by reducing the value of all "B" and "C" coupons by one-sixth in order to squeeze out some of the water.[12]

Some of the violators who appeared were as frank as the sailor who handed over an empty A-book without a protest, explaining, "I knew when I got this notice that my car would be of no use to me, so I sold it." Most of the others had excuses which were valid, or at least plausible. The hearing panel was handicapped because the OPA investigators were out looking for new violations instead of being present at the hearings to present the charges on

[10] *V-P*, May 25, 1943, p. 18.
[11] *V-P*, May 31, 1943, p. 20.
[12] *V-P*, June 2, 1943, p. 24; June 9, 1943, p. 22.

the old ones. The panel was forced to accept the proffered explanation, as it did in most cases, or else hand out a relatively light penalty.[13]

Evidence that there was still a great deal of voluntary compliance was to be seen at the beaches. Instead of driving, would-be bathers piled on to the Norfolk Southern's restored passenger train. The original three passenger coaches had grown to six by the last week-end in June, and that Sunday eight coaches were packed to capacity. Even the Fourth of July week-end brought relatively few cars to Virginia Beach. In town, however, evasions began to be more common. Autos were seldom found in front of a movie, but a block or so away in either direction the streets would be parked full. A basket of groceries permanently on the back seat served as confirmation for the excuse that the driver was just on his way home from market. The OPA investigators gradually abandoned their hopeless fight, and on August 31 this was officially acknowledged,[14] just in time for the Labor Day week end. The news that OPA agents would no longer be checking license tags brought the largest crowd of the season to Virginia Beach.

Meanwhile the passengers who had been forced to squeeze on to the buses in that sweltering June were offered some relief. Acting on the recommendation of the Izac committee that an expert draw up a plan to improve the local transportation system and impose it on the community regardless of local opposition, the ODT had sent Felix E. Reifschnider to make an extended study of the situation in Norfolk and Portsmouth. The over-all service obviously could not be improved without reducing service in some sections, and Colonel Borland warned in advance that sacrifices must be expected. Rumors that the plan called for cancellation of the Edgewater and the Larchmont bus lines ran through the city, creating alarm.

The plan, as actually announced, proved to be not nearly so sweeping. The Atlantic City bus route was the only one abolished, and it was combined with another route. Most of the changes consisted of shortening the routes at either end. At the downtown end all the buses, instead of looping to Main Street or Church Street,

---

[13] *V-P*, June 8, 1943, p. 18.
[14] *V-P*, June 28, 1943, p. 14; July 5, 1943, p. 14; July 6, 1943, p. 14.

were to turn back on Randolph Street to City Hall Avenue. The biggest cuts on the uptown ends were on the Edgewater and Fairmount Park lines, although the upper end of Fairmount Park was to be served by a trolley instead.[15] Unfortunately newspaper accounts of the new plan emphasized the compulsory nature of the new plan. Reifschnider told reporters that he had not consulted the local city councils or VEPCO about the proposed changes. "We don't care whether they like this or not," he declared. "We want the councils to approve the changes but if they don't, we will put them into effect anyway." These words created a loud explosion on the other side of the river, where the cancellation of the Sixth Avenue bus line had tramped on some important toes. Portsmouth's City Manager Arthur S. Owens denounced the ODT's action as "Hitlerian." A group of American Legionnaires, headed by Major Turin, rallied to fight for Norfolk's freedom from arbitrary controls. Colonel Borland and the local ODT representative, Maclin Simmons, tried to pour oil on the troubled waters by explaining that Reifschnider had really been very cooperative and that his words had been misunderstood.[16]

When the city council met on Tuesday to consider the new plan, Major Turin indignantly told the group that the ODT's job was to supply the city with more transportation, not to take it away, and called on the city not to surrender any of its rights. Colonel Borland in reply said that the Government in Washington was his government, right or wrong, and that he wanted the city to cooperate in every way possible with the ODT to save tires and gasoline. He also told the council that the city would get 7,000 more bus miles per week as soon as the plan went into effect. Since it seemed that there was little the city could do to interfere with the plan in any case, the council adopted the ratifying ordinances. At the same time the council resolved to send a strong protest to the ODT over its failure to consult with the council in advance and also to ask the ODT to study the protests against the new system to see if something could be done about them.[17]

Week after week every meeting of the city council was overwhelmed with protests from people on the uptown ends of the

[15] *V-P*, June 19, 1943, p. 16.
[16] *V-P*, June 19, 1943, p. 16; June 22, 1943, p. 6.
[17] *V-P*, June 23, 1943, p. 22.

shortened bus routes, especially in Edgewater and Larchmont. Fairmount Park residents did not like the new trolley service, and some people had to walk as much as a mile. VEPCO Vice President Throckmorton said that the protests to his company were not coming from war workers; many persons, in fact, were chiefly concerned because their servants quit as a result of the new bus routes. Nevertheless, the council sent an ultimatum to the ODT, demanding an immediate investigation. The ODT promised a resurvey and at length made several minor readjustments, but Larchmont and Fairmount Park were to be denied relief until the end of the war.[18]

The sacrifices required of these sections, however, benefited the rest of the city. The new system speeded up the service and allowed buses to make more runs. More seats were to be seen than there had been for years. Navy Yard workers also received improved transportation. As recommended by the Izac committee, the Navy in June put on a boat to provide direct service from the ferry slip on Commercial Place to the Navy Yard, eliminating the roundabout bus trip through Portsmouth. For those who drove their cars, the Navy Yard Cooperative acquired a parking lot near Commercial Place.[19]

The gasoline crisis meanwhile had revived an old issue when the operators of for-hire cars licensed in the county asserted that they were compelled to waste gas and tires because the city made them return to the county empty after they had delivered passengers in the city. This problem had its roots in the war boom, which had made fantastic profits possible from the operation of cabs. The city had increased its own for-hire cars to 117 in 1942, in addition to the 100 orthodox taxicabs, and was doing as well as it could with its inadequate police force to keep their operators under control. Pointing out that Norfolk was "getting a mighty bad name" on account of the for-hire cars, Colonel Borland had to set to work in January to draft a stricter ordinance for their control. As adopted by the council, the ordinance limited their charges to 25 cents for the first mile and 10 cents for each succeeding half mile, the same rates the taxis were allowed to charge, and required

[18] *V-P*, August 4, 1943, p. 20; September 29, 1943, p. 22.
[19] *V-P*, June 29, 1943, p. 18; July 12, 1943, p. 14.

them to install meters, but the meters failed to arrive and the ordinance had to be suspended.[20]

If the city for-hire drivers had a bunch of bandits among them, those licensed in the county seemed to include persons experienced in every form of crime. The county had no regulation of any kind, permitting anyone who paid his license fees to operate, and many persons had recently entered the business who, not satisfied with the easy money to be made by legitimate high charges, had taken on such profitable sidelines as "rolling" drunken sailors or operating a house of prostitution on wheels. In the fall of 1942 the city police had started to crack down on these county drivers by enforcing the ordinance which prohibited cars not licensed by the city from picking up passengers inside the city limits.

Since the city cars could pick up passengers in the county, the county drivers, legitimate and illegitimate alike, regarded this as unfair discrimination. A carload of angry operators one night forced a city taxi off the road after it had taken on some sailors at Camp Bradford and ordered the sailors out. Other complications arose from the cab shortage. One of the larger operators in the county complained that a group of sailors who had entered one of his cars in the city were so angry when they were told to get out that they broke the windows in the car when they slammed the doors.[21]

When the county for-hire operators appeared before the city council on June 1 and appealed for the right to pick up passengers in the city, the council was so impressed by the inadequate cab service in the city that it asked the city manager to investigate the situation. Colonel Borland reported that he was opposed to granting the county men's application because 75 per cent of the for-hire cars' trips would be for non-essential purposes, which were now prohibited, and because it would be impossible to prevent the county cabs from hauling passengers entirely within the city limits. The council then proposed to meet that problem by authorizing the licensing of 150 of the county cars by the city with the same rights as the 117 city cars already granted permits, but discovered that would not be permitted by the ODT. The final de-

[20] *V-P*, January 13, 1943, p. 18; February 24, 1943, p. 20; June 9, 1943, p. 22.
[21] *V-P*, June 9, 1943, p. 22.

cision was to permit 150 county cars to pick up passengers in the
city for county destinations at fourteen specified points, including
the stations and the hospitals, after they had obtained a special
permit from the city.[22]

In an attempt to keep the car operators purged of the worst
element the council also adopted an ordinance making revocation
of the permit mandatory for conviction of a felony, engaging in
prostitution, or dealing in drugs. At the insistence of Councilman
George Abbott overcharging was also included in this list of offenses. In the absence of the still delayed meters the for-hire cars
were required to post their rates and to adhere to the new scale
of charges. A few of the more turbulent city operators tried to
force a strike against this interference with free enterprise when
the regulation was enforced in August, but cooler heads soon reflected that, without a meter, the passengers would seldom know
whether or not they were being overcharged.[23]

Meanwhile this pleasureless summer was having a strange effect
on many of the people who had newly come to Norfolk. Stirred,
perhaps by the self-destruction on which the world seemed bent
they seemed to be swept into violence and sudden death. Girls,
lonely and unhappy, tried to kill themselves. A girl from West
Virginia jumped from the Portsmouth ferry; a few days later
another was pulled back by a Navy chief. Two eighteen-year-old
girls from Radford, both married and separated from their husbands, on their way home from a dance, decided to leap, although
one was stopped. An Illinois woman's attempt to end her life resulted in ludicrous tragedy when she slipped into the shallow
waters at the foot of Freemason Street and floundered about
helplessly until two men pulled her out.[24]

Unbalanced servicemen seemed bent on dealing out death to
others. A sailor, quarreling with a pervert friend in a hotel room,
strangled him with his own necktie. An eighteen-year-old Marine
deserter stabbed an elderly acquaintance who provoked him. A
soldier was said to have beaten in the skull of a Navy Yard
worker with a beer bottle. A nineteen-year-old sailor, living with

[22] *V-P*, June 2, 1943, p. 24; June 9, 1943, p. 22; June 23, 1943, p. 22.
[23] *V-P*, June 30, 1943, p. 20; August 14, 1943, p. 14.
[24] *V-P*, July 16, 1943; August 2, 1943, p. 16; August 3, 1943, p. 18.

a sixteen-year-old wife, horrified the city by cold-bloodedly murdering two policemen who had caught him in a robbery.[25] These were the darkest parts of a picture which seemed to be growing steadily blacker during the summer. There was occasional ruffianism in the city. A sailor glanced at a young civilian mailing a letter in the post office one day, said, "You look like a draft dodger to me," and promptly knocked him down. The roughest incidents, however, occurred in the wilderness of vice on Cottage Toll Road. At the much-raided High Hat Club, now renamed Merry Gardens, sailors were accused of putting their hands on someone else's girl and a riot started, in which the unfortunate girl lost most of her clothes and had to be taken to the hospital. The manager, George Rohanna, restored order by firing his revolver into the floor, accidentally hitting one of the sailors in the foot. A few nights later a group of fifteen sailors besieged the Merry Gardens. They started throwing bricks into the place while the people inside replied with whatever missiles were available. When the sailors tried to break in the door, a man named George Cohen came out firing his revolver. The sailors disappeared, but one of the stray shots hit an innocent Coast Guardsman who had just arrived.[26]

This festering boil came to a head with another brawl on Saturday night, July 24. Three sailors that night started out for their customary week-end celebration by equipping themselves with a quart of liquor. When they had disposed of that, they hired a cab to go to the Casablanca, a dance hall near Edmund's Corner. On the way they stopped at one of the many spots where liquor was sold illegally to get another quart. When the second quart had also vanished, the sailors left the dance hall. Noticing a car outside, they asked for a ride back to town. The civilian occupants of the auto told them in vigorous language that the car was already full. Slamming the door, the sailors walked away to a cab and crawled into that. Meanwhile, Charlie C. Van Horn, who had had his foot in the door when it was slammed, decided to go over to the cab and express his opinion of sailors in general. One of the Navy

[25] *V-P*, June 23, 1943, p. 20; July 3, 1943, p. 18; July 15, 1943, p. 28; August 3, 1943, p. 14.
[26] *V-P*, July 21, 1943; August 3, 1943, p. 18.

men, W. J. Evans, thereupon got out and knocked Van Horn down. Back on his feet, Van Horn landed a haymaker which knocked the sailor down so hard that, as was later discovered, his skull was fractured. Another of the sailors then came out to the aid of his friend, and the civilian went down. Outnumbered, Van Horn backed up against a car and pulled his knife. When Evans lurched in regardless, the out-flung weapon pierced his throat. Dropping to the ground, he said in a surprised voice, "I've been stabbed." Less than an hour later the sailor was dead.[27]

The Norfolk County police conducted a prompt investigation of the murder and in eight hours had arrested Van Horn. They rounded up ten civilian witnesses and asked the shore patrol to locate the other two sailors who had been involved. In the meantime, Deputy Sheriff Frank Wilson released the story as he had heard it from the civilians, which placed all the blame on the sailors and made it appear that Van Horn had been acting in self defense. Rear Admiral Herbert F. Leary, however, who had replaced Admiral Simons as commandant of the Fifth Naval District on June 1, was distinctly dissatisfied with the investigation. He pointed out that several material witnesses to the crime had been released without any assurance that they would be present for the trial and that the police were making no effort to find out how Evans' skull had been fractured, an injury which was not explained in the story told by the police.[28] To some Navy men it looked as if the county police did not consider it very much of a crime to kill a sailor.

Admiral Leary promptly determined on drastic action to meet the situation. On Friday, July 30, a dramatic order placed large sections of Norfolk County out-of-bounds to Navy personnel. The banned areas included all the highways leading into Norfolk and Portsmouth from the west—U. S. 58 into Portsmouth, the toll-free highway, and Campostella Road—as well as the Cottage Toll Road section. Navy men who lived in the prohibited areas were allowed to stay there, but the ban covered every business place in the forbidden zone. Burly shore patrolmen turned back sailors who attempted to enter peaceful grocery stores or barber shops.[29]

[27] Reconstructed from varying accounts of witnesses reported in *V-P*, August 3, 1943, p. 18.
[28] *V-P*, July 26, 1943, p. 16; August 1, 1943, Part II, p. 1.
[29] *V-P*, July 31, 1943, p. 14; August 3, 1943, p. 18.

On the surface, Admiral Leary's order seemed like a bit of in-excusable petulance, as the disagreement over the handling of the Evans murder scarcely justified a sweeping blockade of the county's business. This new dispute, however, was only the latest in a long series of incidents which had created friction between the Navy and the county. The disagreement had its roots in the normal Navy-civilian irritation, which was perhaps stronger in the county, where the night spots brought out the worst elements among the sailors. This was intensified by the county's jealousy of the city, which steadily cooperated with the Navy. When the shore patrol had taken the city police along on its raids of October, 1942, the county officials had not concealed their feeling that the city should stay inside its own territory. The shore patrol had then planned raids in cooperation with the county police, but dis-covered that the vice dens had usually cleared away all the evidence of their iniquity before the raiders arrived. By February the Navy men had decided not to let the county officers in on their prospective raids.[30]

The reluctance of the county police to interfere with any of the minor forms of crime had long been notorious. City Chief Woods had long taken it for granted that he could expect no cooperation from the county officials in suppressing prostitution or gambling. The State police had experienced the same indifference late in May in the course of an accidental raid on the Pelican Club. A State policeman, out with an OPA agent checking violators of the pleasure-driving ban, had entered the Pelican to talk to the owners of the cars packed outside and found himself in the middle of a gambling den. When the State police called the county officers to ask them to come out and take over, they were told that they had started the raid and they could finish it. One county officer did appear on the scene, but he said he would rather not help, since it was out of his territory and his participation might cost him his job.[31]

The county police even failed to cooperate with members of their own force. One zealous volunteer from Norview had been

[30] *V-P*, February 24, 1943, p. 20. The announcement created much excite-ment at the time, as its vague wording sounded as if the shore patrol would no longer cooperate with the city police.

[31] Statement of Captain R. C. Barham, Virginia State Police, *V-P*, March 2, 1944, p. 14.

commissioned a special officer early in 1942. When he discovered a dice game going on in the Merry Gardens, with thousands of dollars on the table, he called Deputy Sheriff Frank Wilson to ask for help in making the arrests. Wilson told him that such work was not part of his job. Still taking his commission seriously, the Norview man arrested the owner of a confectionery store for operating a pinball machine. His career as a policeman thereupon came to an abrupt end.[32]

This benevolent attitude of the police was not inspired entirely by a desire to allow the sailors a chance to enjoy drinks, dames, and dice. The dives were naturally expected to use part of their profits to buy insurance against interference. While the rates for "Norfolk County insurance" were unknown, it was general knowledge that at least two of the county officers owned several of the night spots. This combination of graft and vice was too common in United States communities to be worth noticing in normal times, but it stood out in glaring contrast at the moment in the area, when the cities had cooperated with the Navy in its clean-up drive.

Even if the county's spirit had been willing, however, its flesh would have been too weak. In 1940, with a population of 35,000, it had had a police force of nineteen men to cover the wide semi-circle of territory surrounding Norfolk and Portsmouth. Inadequate then, the same force now had to patrol a section in which the population had doubled and the problems had tripled, with its only assistance coming from some volunteer special officers. Piled on top of that was an impossible organization. Each officer was restricted to his own district in the county. The police were appointed, not by the sheriff, nominally the chief law enforcement agent, but by the judge of the circuit court. The only central command that existed was that exercised informally by Deputy Sheriff Frank Wilson.

Spread over the whole problem was the tangled maze of Norfolk County politics, which enmeshed the whole police force. It was the custom for the judge to take the advice of prominent politicians in making his appointments. The incumbent Judge, A. B. Carney, had taken office in 1940 with the backing of the faction led by

[32] Statement of Fred Ryder, *V-P*, March 2, 1944, p. 14.

County Delegate James N. Garrett, but had recently fallen out of favor with that group. The men on the police force thus owed their original appointment to the Garrett faction but for the future would have to look to Judge Carney. To top off the confusion, Judge Carney fell seriously ill and for some time scarcely knew what was going on.

This was the situation into which the Navy had jumped with both feet. A commandant who had been longer in the district might have been more hesitant to act with such impetuous vigor, but Admiral Leary's order at least assured some action because it was hitting the county in a vital spot—the pocketbook. Businessmen moaned that they were losing thousands of dollars a day, and for-hire operators sat disconsolately in their idle cars. The only one who seemed to like the Navy order was old County Sheriff A. A. Wendel, who bumbled that he had been trying to get the Navy to take this step for a long time.[33]

Governor Darden, taken by surprise, promised to investigate. He said he had conferred some months previously with Navy officials on what the Navy said were the "deplorable" conditions in Norfolk County and had offered to help then, but had heard nothing further from the Navy. He wired Judge Carney that conditions required immediate attention and was told in reply that no action was needed. "Service men are well regarded here but are shown no preference," the judge telegraphed back. "Conditions in Norfolk County are reasonably good, and police force is doing a good job." County Delegate Garrett seized the opportunity to make political hay by placing the blame squarely where he wanted it. "If the bad conditions exist," he wired the Governor, "it is clear that our local enforcement and prosecuting agencies are either unable or unwilling to function."[34]

Governor Darden conferred with the Navy officials and agreed that conditions were "certainly serious if what I have been told is true." A private investigation revealed that most of the facts were correct, but there was little the Governor could do. He recommended that a special grand jury be called to look into the situation. A.B.C. agents began a series of raids on several of the night spots in cooperation with the shore patrol, hitting the Fairmount

[33] V-P, August 1, 1943, Part II, p. 1.
[34] V-P, July 31, 1943, p. 14; August 1, 1943, Part II, p. 1.

Social Club and the Fairmount Billiard Parlor. A raid on the Norfolk County Athletic and Social Club caught the members engaged in the athletic activity of picking up dice. Three county officers joined the A.B.C. men in a raid on the Sportsman's Club with a mysterious aftermath. When Officer H. L. Gardner returned to the station after taking the whiskey and the slot machines to the county jail, he found the tires slashed on his car parked outside the station and the coats he had left inside ripped to pieces, even though another county officer had been inside the station all the time. By an odd coincidence, it was rumored that this other officer had a financial interest in the Sportsman's Club.[35]

Direct negotiations between the Navy and the county were blocked by Judge Carney's stubborn insistence that all was well. Commonwealth's Attorney A. O. Lynch, the one county official who had shown much concern over the situation, obtained the judge's promise that he might not reappoint all the policemen after the first of the year and took this concession to the Navy without results. At length the September grand jury began investigating conditions, and Admiral Leary used that as an excuse for ending the awkward situation by lifting the out-of-bounds order.[36]

[35] *V-P*, July 31, 1943, pp. 14, 7; August 2, 1943, p. 16; August 17, 1943, p. 18; August 21, 1943, p. 14; March 5, 1944, Part II, pp. 1, 2.

[36] *V-P*, August 12, 1943, p. 22; September 15, 1943, p. 20.

23

PRACTICE MAKES PERFECT

B Y the beginning of 1943 the Civilian Defense system was reaching its peak. There were enough air raid sirens scattered about the city so that almost everybody could hear the alarm with the windows open and the radio off—twenty bought or borrowed by the city and 22 on Navy property inside the city limits.[1] Equipment for the volunteers was arriving in veritable floods: 4,700 steel helmets, enough to put tin hats on all the air raid wardens, the auxiliary firemen, the auxiliary policemen, the bomb squad, the rescue squad, the demolition and clearance squad, the emergency public works crew, and even the salvage volunteers. Almost as many gas masks arrived at the same time; Chief Air Raid Warden George Bowers arranged a training school to teach the workers how to use these protective devices. On the way were 6,668 hand-pump fire extinguishers, almost enough to put one in each block in the city.[2]

The morale of the volunteers was still high in spite of the fact that the threat of enemy attack seemed to be growing more and more remote since the landings in North Africa last November. Wardens moved, resigned, or were drafted, but the ranks were kept full through promotion and recruitment. Sections with more vigorous leadership had established section posts in converted garages or even specially erected buildings. With money raised by the local wardens, they were furnished with telephones, sand bags, stirrup pumps, first-aid kits, and any other equipment that seemed appropriate. The block wardens of the section held regular

[1] C. V. Bulls, "Air Raid Siren Installations," Civilian Defense: Histories, NWHC records. Location of these sirens was a problem, since each had a separate switch and had to be placed where there was someone on duty 24 hours a day.

[2] *V-P*, February 17, 1943, p. 10; August 3, 1943, p. 14.

meetings there, and the section posts often became neighborhood clubs. When the new Richard A. Tucker School was occupied in January, 1943, the Negro wardens of Berkley moved into the abandoned, decrepit old school building. They painted and repaired the structure, made it a well-equipped section post, and incidentally used it as a much-needed recreation center for the area.

The section meetings served as the only training for the wardens, as the instruction program had fallen by the wayside. After the preliminary training of the wardens early in 1942 had been completed, Dr. E. Ruffin Jones of the Norfolk Division had been placed in charge of training schools. He spent the rest of the spring recruiting teachers to serve as instructors, and when the summer vacation was over, arranged for a three-day training school for the instructors. He then reported that he was ready to start his classes, but by that time Coordinator Marshall and his staff felt that the 25-hour course prescribed by the Federal Government was too much to expect of the volunteers. Doctor Jones then condensed the work into a ten-hour course, but that too seemed to be too much. Coordinator Marshall suggested as a compromise that a list of speakers be prepared on whom the air raid wardens could call for instruction on specific topics. The list was prepared, but no one ever called for any speakers, and the training program was laid quietly to rest.³

Much more thoroughly trained were the two groups of auxiliary firemen and policemen, who had all been given an intensive course in their work by the respective city departments. The police, sworn in as officers, were authorized to make arrests on their own during blackouts. They were assigned the duty of guarding the Civilian Defense office in the VEPCO Building. A few found such regular duty too demanding, but most of them were proud of their job and stood by to help the police in their regular routine. The Negro unit under Auxiliary Police Lieutenant W. P. Thorogood rendered especially good service. Over the Fourth of July week end they were assigned to control the crowds boarding the busses headed for City Beach. An ancient prejudice went by the board when the city issued them sidearms for their task. So well did they perform their assignment that many predicted the city would

³ E. Ruffin Jones, "History of the Civilian Defense Training Schools o Norfolk, Va.," Civilian Defense: Histories file, NWHC records.

eventually admit Negroes to the regular police force. On another occasion they earned praise from Chief Woods for their help in capturing two murder suspects.[4]

An even prouder group were the auxiliary firemen under the direction of Henry Cowles Whitehead. Training had begun at each of the city's fire stations on January 7, 1942. Twice a week thereafter the amateur firefighters showed up at firehouses for drills, using the city's obsolete equipment. On November 17, 1942, diplomas were awarded to the 175 persons who had completed the course. In the midst of the "commencement" exercises a three-alarm fire broke out, and the graduates rushed forth to demonstrate their newly-acquired skill by helping the regular firemen. The regular drills did not cease with graduation, but the auxiliaries turned to the problem of acquiring their own equipment. The skid pumps already received from the U. S. Office of Civilian Defense were unsatisfactory, since they were too heavy to be loaded on a truck after the alarm sounded and it was impossible to find trucks on which they could be kept permanently. The arrival of a shipment of front-end pumps, however, presented a challenge. These resembled conventional firefighting equipment much more closely, and they had to be mounted permanently on trucks.

The group at Station No. 12 decided to beg, borrow, or buy a truck of their own. They found an old one, overhauled it thoroughly, mounted their pumper on it, and by March were putting on a public demonstration. The ten other companies, not to be outdone, determined to follow suit. In December the eleventh auxiliary fire truck was dedicated by Company No. 2, the Negro group. The skid pumps were also converted to practical use by mounting them on trailers which could be hitched behind a car and hauled to the fire. The helmets and gas masks sent by the U. S. Office of Civilian Defense were followed by coats, fire hose, ladders, axes, shovels, and ceiling hooks. Almost as well equipped as the regular firemen, the volunteers stayed in trim by continuing their weekly drills. When the city firemen went out on call, the auxiliaries moved into the station to stand wistfully by waiting for an emergency alarm which never came.[5]

[4] *Journal and Guide*, July 17, 1943, p. 16; *V-P*, October 6, 1943, p. 20.
[5] Civilian Defense: Fire Department, Newspaper Articles and Bulletins file, and Civilian Defense: Histories file, NWHC records; *Journal and Guide*, December 18, 1943, p. 6.

So pleased was Coordinator Marshall with the progress of his organization that he decided to show it off to the public. Asking his department heads to get their groups into shape for an inspection, he invited over a hundred representative local citizens and other persons interested in Civilian Defense to join him in an inspection of the Norfolk organization on Sunday afternoon, May 2. For many of the guests the tour was an education, as the general public had only a hazy idea of how Civilian Defense operated. They saw the warning center and the control center in the VEPCO Building with volunteers manning the bewildering array of telephones. They saw the maps on the wall at the south end of the room, ready to mark up air raid damage as it was reported.

Specially chartered buses hauled them to visit air raid wardens' posts and casualty stations and to such little known groups as the Red Cross's food and housing unit in Meadowbrook School, ready to provide relief to air raid victims, and the gas decontamination station set up in Norfolk Division. The casualty station at the Memorial Methodist Church in Berkley, equipped entirely by neighborhood donations, was particularly impressive with its operating room that would have done credit to a hospital. The visitors were shown the work being done by the Negro wardens to put the old Tucker school into condition. At each stop the volunteers were on hand, ready to demonstrate the work they were prepared to do.

Best show of all was provided by the firemen at the end of the four-hour trip. They brought out one of their newly-converted trucks, painted a gleaming fire-engine red. Volunteers, clad in their new blue coats, leaped off, connected their hose, and in a few minutes had a stream of water playing down 44th Street. A bit of unscheduled excitement was provided when a real fire alarm sounded and the auxiliaries had to clear away their hose in a hurry to let the city engine out of the fire house. The wailing sirens of the regular engines provided an appropriate accompaniment as the volunteers jumped back on to their trucks and dashed home to their respective stations. The visitors returned to their buses, quite satisfied with their trip. State Coordinator Wyse, down from Richmond for the occasion with his aide, John J. Howard, declared: "The setup here is all one could expect it to be. Everyone concerned deserves congratulations."[6]

[6] *V-P*, May 3, 1943, p. 12; *L-D*, May 3, 1943; Civilian Defense: Inspection Trip, and Civilian Defense: Histories files, NWHC records.

One point not visited on the inspection tour was the information center, which had lost all connection with Civilian Defense after the blow-up in January, 1942. Lynette Hamlet, named auxiliary captain of volunteers by the Army, had assumed responsibility for recruiting and training the volunteers, and a publicity campaign brought the number working on the boards to nearly a thousand, enough to operate satisfactorily along with the soldiers assigned to duty there. The training course set up by the Maury teacher, who was still putting in a half day at the school, gave each newcomer adequate instruction before she went to duty.

In the meantime the Army decided to go ahead with its plans to put the volunteers into uniform. They were told that they could live at home, working eight hours a day at the center. In April 175 applied for enlistment. The number was weeded down to 25, and by the time they were called in June only ten were willing to go. A recruiting campaign finally brought the number of those who would join the Women's Army Auxiliary Corps back up to 73.

Lynette Hamlet went off to Des Moines for training as a WAAC in July, leaving the volunteers in charge of two paid Civil Service employees. By September she was back in uniform as a WAAC officer, still at her old job of commanding civilians. As the WAAC's continued to arrive, however, Colonel M. C. Woodbury, by then the commanding officer, decided to simplify his command by dispensing with the volunteers. Civilians were gradually relieved from duty during the last six weeks of 1942, and the WAAC's took over entirely on December 31.[7]

Just five weeks later the volunteers were suddenly recalled to duty. Colonel Woodbury had discovered that the new WAAC's he was supposed to get were being assigned to other duties in the Army and that some of his own staff were being transferred elsewhere. Once more the volunteer organization had to be rebuilt. Some of the furloughed workers returned; others liked their vacation from the demanding four-hours-every-other-day duty so much that they stayed away permanently. Another recruiting drive was put on, this time under the direction of the Army. A big Sunday night meeting was held in the old city auditorium and appeals for help at the information center were delivered by two distinguished visitors, Mrs. Edward V. Rickenbacker and Major

[7] Hamlet, Lynette: Aircraft Warning Volunteers file, NWHC records.

Robert T. Jones, better known as "Bobby" Jones, golfing champion of the 'Twenties.[8]

By August the Army had gone half-way back to an old idea. The volunteers were enlisted in the Army Air Force Aircraft Warning Corps, sworn in to their unpaid jobs and authorized to wear a uniform. Many of the veterans were still sticking to their jobs; Mrs. Royden E. Wright had more than 2,000 hours of service to her credit, while 45 others had passed the 1,000-hour mark. New recruits were scarce, as there were only 639 volunteers at work.[9]

All the Civilian Defense teams were finding it increasingly hard to keep their line-ups at full strength during 1943, as the prospect of the big game ever being played kept becoming more and more unlikely. Nevertheless, they kept up their practice scrimmages faithfully and went to work to learn a new set of signals the coaches had handed them. One of the problems encountered everywhere during 1942 had been that so many people failed to hear the sirens, that the wardens found it impossible to get the lights out in the five minutes of grace allowed. The Army had experimented in New York City with an audible blue signal as a preliminary warning to the public. After the blue signal the same conditions prevailed as during the strategic blackout of the summer of 1942; lights were put out, but there was no restraint on the movement of pedestrians and traffic, as there was after the red signal. In order to provide the blue signal, the sustained blast formerly used for the white, or all clear, was transformed into a blue and the all clear was announced over the radio and by turning on the street lights.

Satisfied with the results of the New York experiment, First Army headquarters decided to put the new signals into effect in January, 1943, throughout the Eastern seaboard. As soon as Coordinator Marshall received his instructions about the new system, he began finding fault with it. The public would not be able to tell the two signals apart, he felt, and even if they did, they would be utterly confused in remembering what each one meant. Moreover, the wardens would not hear the all clear over the radio and would

[8] *V-P*, February 7, 1943, Part II, p. 1; March 15, 1943, p. 12. The information center moved out of the Federal Building to more spacious quarters in the Wainwright building about March 1.

[9] *V-P*, August 15, 1943, Part II, p. 1.

not know when the air raid was over. After putting these criticisms into a telegram to General Hugh Drum, commander of the First Army, he changed his mind about sending the wire and decided to give the new signals a chance.[10]

In order to give the public a chance to get acquainted with the new signals the first tests were announced in advance. A daylight practice throughout the state was called for February 17. Coordinator Marshall published a full-page advertisement in the local papers, explaining the changes, and prepared a program for the radio stations. With customary Norfolk originality he revised the instructions slightly by providing that the street lights would be turned on during the daylight drill to indicate the blue signal and turned off on the all clear, thus providing a visible, if not an audible, all clear.

The people of Norfolk proved surprisingly good pupils. When the sirens let loose their two-minute steady blast at 10:50 A. M., they went on about their business, as they were supposed to do in daylight after the blue. When the wailing red sounded ten minutes later, pedestrians took cover and cars began to stop. Before the wardens and the police could get everyone halted, the blue signal at 11:05 permitted traffic to move again. The worst traffic problem was caused by motorists who got confused and stopped on the blue, piling up cars behind them. The all clear given over the radio at 11:15 was also missed by many. Coming between programs, the announcement got lost among the commercials.[11]

Once more Coordinator Marshall drew up his objections to the new system, this time in a communication through channels to State Coordinator Wyse. He recommended that the state go back to the old system with three two-minute blasts, instead of one, to sound the alarm, so that everybody would have a chance to hear it. Wyse took the matter up with the Third Service Command, although, as he added, "I have my doubts about getting any action, as the Army is very reluctant to make changes after they have once established procedure."[12]

[10] Unsent telegram to General Hugh Drum, January 26, 1943, Civilian Defense: Correspondence, Richmond, file, NWHC record.

[11] *V-P*, February 18, 1943; memorandum in Civilian Defense: Correspondence, Richmond, file, NWHC records.

[12] Marshall to Wyse, February 19, 1943, Wyse to Marshall, March 6, 1943, Civilian Defense: Correspondence, Richmond, file, NWHC records.

Meanwhile an announced night drill was called for March 5, and Norfolk seemed to know what to do about the new signals in the dark. Lights went off on the first blue at 8:50 p. m., stayed off through the following red and blue, and came back on only when the radio announced the all clear. The single hitch occurred when VEPCO waited for a message from the OCD to turn the street lights back on, while the warning center thought they would get the signal over the radio. It was eight minutes after the all clear before the streets were lit again. Third Service Command now ordered a surprise test, and the State OCD called that on March 17. Norfolk once more handled the blackout in routine fashion. This time the street lights again provided the only hitch, by not going out for seven minutes after the blue sounded.[13]

Satisfied with the results of this test, State Coordinator Wyse at last certified the state to the Third Service Command as ready for the Army to call the drills. This meant that future tests would be announced over the flashing lights of the CARW equipment. This equipment had been employed to send out practice whites to the district warning centers of the state, including Norfolk, but the Army had refused to permit its use for the State's drills. Now that the Army was taking over, a standard phraseology was to be required, and Norfolk lost a little more of its independence.

Early in 1942 Coordinator Marshall after a conference with the current commander at the information center had agreed to use letters instead of colors when calling a practice from the warning center in order to prevent confusion. Warnings from the Norfolk district thus went out: "This is a practice blackout. A," instead of "This is a practice blackout. Yellow," the formula used by all the other warning centers in the state. The State OCD had suggested several times that Norfolk ought to conform with the rest of Virginia; now the Army was about to issue an order.

Alarmed at the cumbersome confusion the new Army order might create, Coordinator Marshall and Civil Air Raid Warning Officer J. Branham Cooke decided what the proper phraseology should be and told John J. Howard of the State OCD their opinions. Howard called up regional OCD headquarters in Baltimore and found that the new phraseology was exactly what Marshall had recommended. Sending the new instruction cards on to the

[13] Civilian Defense: Blackouts, Incidents, file, NWHC records.

Norfolk coordinator, Howard added hopefully: "I trust that you and Cooke can agree that the wording will go out as issued."[14] Norfolk accepted the new wording and used it thereafter. Colors took the place of the "A, B, C, D," system, which had become confusing anyhow when the new signals converted it into an "A, B, C, B, D" system.

Meanwhile the Army seemed to be in no hurry about calling a test, and the State OCD decided to hold a few more practices of its own. Unable to use the CARW signals, the State officials tried to maintain the surprise element by calling the warning centers just an hour before the blackout was to start. Coordinator Marshall had no idea there was to be a drill until the yellow was called to him at his home at 8:35 on April 27. The girls in his office, however, had found out early in the afternoon when officers from Naval Intelligence, which had received advance warning from the State, dropped in to find out what time the test was scheduled.

The blue signal at 8:54 caught many people downtown and sent them scurrying to get home before the red at 9:09. The second blue at 9:44 demonstrated that a number of persons had forgotten their lessons as lights came back on in many places. A number of forgotten lights stayed on all during the blackout, which was not surprising, since many lights had been carelessly left on even when the blackout was announced in advance. Art Lewis's Carnival, which had lost most of its brilliance to the dimout, went completely black for an hour and five minutes, while thousands of customers waited patiently for the all clear.[15]

Another surprise test called by the State OCD on May 19 caught the Norfolk Tars in the ninth inning of a scoreless tie with Durham, and the fans who waited an hour in the dark went home unrewarded, because by the time the blackout was over, the dimout had begun. Residents kept their lights off until the all clear was heard, but this time some of the wardens got mixed up and tried to move pedestrians off the street on the blue. Several of the siren operators also got confused and blew all red signals, instead of two blues and a red. Norfolk Civilian Defense suffered its first

[14] Howard to Marshall, March 30, April 5, 1943, Civilian Defense: Warning Signals file; Marshall to Howard, March 31, 1943, Civilian Defense: Correspondence, Richmond, file, NWHC records.

[15] V-P, April 28, 1943, p. 20; L-D, April 28, 1943; Civilian Defense: Blackouts, Incidents, file, NWHC records.

casualty during the test when Auxiliary Policeman Sidney Wein-raub was hit by a car and received a broken leg.[16]

The signs of confusion prompted Coordinator Marshall next morning to renew his campaign to have the signals changed. He wrote Howard: ". . . not only I but all of the members of my advisory group, the heads of departments, the public and the Press, and, in fact, every one in Norfolk and without exception so far as I know, are violently opposed to the present arrangement and would like to see it simplified and changed." He wanted longer siren blasts and fewer of them, he said, as well as some audible all clear. When the *Ledger-Dispatch* criticized the new signals, he cut out copies of the editorial and sent it to regional and U. S. OCD officials. He wrote to other local coordinators and urged them to join him. Finally he called on the Governor to enlist in his crusade against confusion, but the Army remained obdurate.[17]

Meanwhile new forms of confusion had appeared. Early in the morning of June 19, unidentified planes were reported on the board at the information center. The blue was ordered sent out over the CARW equipment as a preliminary alert. Since this was the first time the blue lights had ever flashed and no test was expected at such an hour, there was confusion in the Norfolk warning center. It took the volunteers on the warning phones more than twenty minutes to get all their calls through, and it was as long before the street lights were off and the sirens sounded in the city. Civilian Defense personnel tumbled out of bed and went to their posts until the all clear came through and the street lights went on again at 3:15 A. M., after the mysterious aircraft had turned out to be friendly.[18]

Four days later airplanes were again over the city in a realistic test staged by the Army. As planes soared over head and search-light beams hunted them out, the Army's chemical warfare service added the "smoke-out" to the blackout and the dimout by spread-ing artificial fog over the city. The blue signal came on at 7:59

---

[16] Civilian Defense: Blackouts, Incidents, file, NWHC records.

[17] Marshall to Howard, May 20, 1943, and other letters, Civilian Defense: Warning Signals file, NWHC records.

[18] Civilian Defense: Blackouts, Incidents, file, NWHC records. In Suffolk someone forgot to turn off the streetlights, and the wardens were up most of the night because there was no way to tell them the all clear had been given.

P. M. in midsummer daylight, and the street lights went on as customary in daytime drills. The red signal at 8:28 in the gathering dusk created a real problem, because the lights were supposed to go out on the red but turning them off in daytime meant an all clear. After a little delay the lights went out. Coordinator Marshall had trouble with his own air raid wardens, who held up two members of his staff on their way to the control center until he dispatched a police car to pry them loose. There were the usual cases of confusion and forgotten lights, but the chief sufferer was the Navy Yard, which did not especially appreciate the protection the Army had given it. The two-and-a-half-hour blackout cost the Navy Yard 30,000 man hours, it dolefully reported.[19]

As a result of the test Coordinator Marshall decided to abandon his experiment with the use of the street lights for daytime drills and renewed his one-man campaign to have the old signals restored. The only sign of any weakening on the part of the Army was news from Baltimore that General Reckord had announced that State OCD's had been authorized to adopt an audible all clear if they wished. Several weeks later State Coordinator Wyse declared he could do nothing until he heard from General Reckord. Salt was rubbed in Norfolk's wounds by the report that Virginia was satisfied with the current signals and wanted no change. At length in August the blocked channels of communication were opened, and Virginia announced that the all clear would be given by a short blast on the siren of not more than 45 seconds.[20]

The new all clear was tested out in a surprise drill on the night of August 17. The 46-minute blackout brought few reports of violations, and only a few wardens stopped traffic during the blue period. Coordinator Marshall thought the new method of sounding the sirens to indicate the end of the blackout a decided improvement, although he still clung to his opinion that the original warning system had been much more satisfactory.[21]

The August test, however, brought on a new battle with the Army over the blacking out of war plants. In September, 1942,

[19] Civilian Defense: Blackouts, Incidents, file, NWHC records.

[20] *V-P*, July 30, August 5, 1943. When First Army headquarters found out about the 45-second signal a month later, it ordered the sound reduced to 15 seconds. The Norfolk OCD thereupon adopted a 30-second signal.

[21] Civilian Defense: Blackouts, Incidents, file, NWHC records.

Third Service Command excused the industries on its master responsibility list from further participation in air raid drills. Coordinator Marshall had promptly denounced the proposed exemptions, declaring they "would make a complete farce of a blackout in Norfolk." As a result of this and other protests, Third Service Command had changed the order into a recommendation that the State OCD's not require important war plants to black out for more than ten minutes, but a month later replaced the recommendation with an order that war plants could not be required to black out for more than five minutes.[22]

Undisturbed by these complicated and confusing directives, Coordinator Marshall had continued to insist that every plant in the area obey the same blackout rules he was enforcing on everybody else and had hitherto been successful in obtaining their cooperation. In the August drills, however, Welding Shipyards had taken advantage of the Army's concession and stopped work on the tankers they were building at the Army Base for only five minutes. When Marshall notified them that they were expected to blackout for the full period of the test, they explained that the Army had exempted them, but he insisted that he was granting no exceptions.

On the shipyards' appeal to Third Service Command, Lieutenant Colonel Roland W. Sellew, officer in charge of such problems, assured the Army Base company that they were entirely correct in their position. Back through channels to the Norfolk OCD office came orders that the shipbuilders should not be interfered with. For a week Coordinator Marshall thought over the problem and finally decided to go directly to the top. To General Milton A. Reckord, head of the Third Service Command, he sent a long explanation of his views, declaring:

> The Welding Shipyards. . .is the only company that has felt it necessary to go any further after this office has explained its views in the matter. In their case we feel that they have met neither the requirements for blacking out, other than pulling main switches, nor for dimming out. Since this particular concern adjoins the Naval Operating Base, which is always properly blacked out for the duration of all signals, it would, according to our best judgment, be a farce to excuse them.

[22] J. H. Wyse to Marshall, October 1, 1942; Marshall to Wyse, October 3, 1942; instructions from Third Service Command, October 19, November 21, 1942, Civilian Defense: Industrial Plant Protection file, NWHC records.

In view of the fact that the Commanding Officers of such vitally important Military establishments as the Norfolk Navy Yard and the Naval Operating Base consider that blackouts are sufficiently important to cause their establishments to remain in total darkness for the entire blackout period, we believe you will agree that it is illogical and unwise to permit a small, relatively unimportant plant to remain lighted, except for a five minute period, especially when such a plant immediately adjoins such an establishment as those mentioned above.

In consideration of the above it is respectfully requested that you personally rule upon this very important matter, and that we be advised of your decision in the matter.[23]

Coordinator Marshall's logic fell an easy victim to Army routine. The letter was referred to the regional OCD headquarters in Baltimore and back—through channels—came the reply: Mr. Marshall should note that the exemption of the shipyard had been ordered by General Reckord, and that the matter was out of his jurisdiction. Furthermore, Mr. Marshall should realize that communications with the Commanding General should be sent through the State OCD.[24] Still convinced that he was right, the Norfolk coordinator ignored the instructions from Baltimore and once again told the shipyard firm that he would grant no exceptions. Again Welding Shipyards wrote to Colonel Sellew for confirmation of the previous exemption, and again it was confirmed by the colonel, who by this time was growing tired of the matter. OCD's regional headquarters wrote to Coordinator Wyse a little testily: "You, no doubt, have notified Marshall on this case and he certainly should have it by this time. I hope that we can count this matter closed now."[25]

Norfolk, however, at last did win one battle with the Army. The dimout regulations, postponed all through 1942, had been finally ordered into effect with all their rigor at the beginning of 1943. Although neither Defense Director Borland nor Coordinator Marshall believed in the necessity of the dimout, both went ahead with its enforcement. The police were told to check violations in the

[23] Marshall to Reckord, September 9, 1943, Civilian Defense: Industrial Plant Protection file, NWHC records.

[24] Colonel Henry A. Reninger, Acting Regional Director, to J. H. Wyse, September 15, 1943, Civilian Defense: Industrial Plant Protection file, NWHC records.

[25] Colonel Henry A. Reninger to J. H. Wyse, October 19, 1943, Civilian Defense: Industrial Plant Protection file, NWHC records.

downtown area while the wardens kept an eye out in the residential districts. The police showed plenty of patience. Not until January 22 was the first offender fined, a restaurant owner who had persistently failed to turn off his neon sign. A few more fines brought generally good compliance from the downtown business places, and Granby Street at night was shrouded in gloom. Householders were shown even more lenience. They were given only warnings until April, when Coordinator Marshall announced that arrests would begin.[26]

Baseball teams complied with the regulations by starting their games in the daylight and finishing them under the lights in the hour of grace allowed after sunset. Ocean View Park, however presented a special problem. Unlike downtown Norfolk, it had turned its lights down in the spring of 1942, and Manager Cecil T. Duffee presumed that the park was dim enough. Coordinator Marshall and a VEPCO lighting expert told him about April 1 that he would have to make changes to comply with the new regulations. Manager Duffee kept turning out more lights and inviting Marshall to return for another inspection, until the coordinator finally ordered him to erect a baffle in front of all the lights on the concessions on the seaward side. The tangle of leases involving the concessions created an argument over who was responsible for the baffle, and nothing was done within the five days Marshall had allowed for starting work on it. The coordinator therefore asked Police Chief Woods to close every unbaffled concession, and the park then put up a temporary baffle to shield its lights.[27]

Hot nights brought a problem, and the OCD took a full-page advertisement in the papers to show householders how they could keep their windows open and the lights on at the same time. An enforcement drive began against motorists who had failed to paint out the top half of their headlights, and the first fines were handed out to violators in July. The problem was complicated by the fact that just across the city line there was no effort at enforcement. One OCD officer in the Tanners Creek District began to prepare charges against offenders, but he was told not to file them until

[26] V-P, January 23, 1943, p. 14; February 18, 1943, p. 20; April 4, 1943, Part II, p. 1.

[27] V-P, May 15 1943; Civilian, Defense: Ocean View Lights file, NWHC records.

after the election. When the election was over, he was informed that the charges were too old.[28]

Disgusted with the difficulty in obtaining compliance, Coordinator Marshall waited hopefully for some word that the Army would abandon its unpopular regulation, which was causing traffic accidents without accomplishing anything. In July he learned that the Army was discussing some modification of the rules. The Army, however, was also drawing up plans for a national semi-dimout to save electricity, which might be put into effect at any time. The Third Service Command, therefore, felt that it would be too confusing for it to proclaim a modified interim dimout, only to have that followed by a new set of semi-dimout rules, and therefore preferred to keep the existing regulations until the Army made up its mind definitely.[29]

After three more months of suspended animation Marshall grew tired of waiting. Undismayed by his recent defeats by the Army, he led a delegation of Norfolk citizens to Richmond on October 20 to appeal to the Governor to do something about the dimout. At Governor Darden's direction Coordinator Wyse got in touch with General George Grunert, the new head of First Army and Eastern Defense Command in New York. To Norfolk's amazement, bureaucracy ground into action. Within a week, the Army, the Navy, the War Production Board, and the Office of Civilian Defense had all agreed to end the compulsory dimout. Instead, everyone was asked to cooperate in a new voluntary semi-dimout, or brownout, to save fuel. Quite willing to let somebody else make the suggested sacrifice for a change, Norfolk celebrated in a wild spree of lighting.[30]

Coordinator Marshall promptly reminded the public not to get confused about their lights; although the dimout was gone, blackouts were still to be expected. As if to reenforce his warning, Third Service Command staged a drill the following night at 8:15. Lights flickered out obediently as the sirens sounded. Coordinator

[28] *V-P*, May 20, 1943, p. 12; July 21, 1943, p. 22; Civilian Defense: Dimouts, General, NWHC records.
[29] Raymond H. Zeller, Senior Lighting Engineer, 3rd OCD Region, to J. H. Wyse, June 30, 1943, Civilian Defense: Ocean View Lights file, NWHC records.
[30] *L-D*, October 21, 1943; *V-P*, October 24, 1943, October 28, 1943, p. 20.

Marshall went to the top floor of the VEPCO Building and was quite pleased with what he could not see. The only bright lights were across the river in Portsmouth. Third Service Command now decided to switch signals. On November 17 it ordered the blue signal given at 8:41 A. M. Civilian Defense personnel started to their posts, and, when the sirens blew again at 9:02, wardens automatically began shooing pedestrians off the street. Some argued that the sirens had given only a short blast, which meant the all clear, but the wardens replied that it must have been the red, because the red was supposed to follow the blue. Coordinator Marshall finally asked the radio station to announce the all clear all over again so that everyone would get the signals straight, and wrote another letter to Richmond demanding that the old alarm system be restored.[31]

Even though the defense volunteers still got confused when called to duty by the sirens, they functioned efficiently in other emergencies. Several times they had been given an opportunity to use their training to meet disasters unconnected with enemy action. The big fire in the Hoffer Brothers Furniture Store on Main Street on December 15, 1942, had tested several of the defense agencies. While four of the fireboats recently provided by the Coast Guard to protect the waterfront pumped water on the flames, auxiliary firemen and policemen joined the shore patrol in keeping back the crowds. The Red Cross brought out its new mobile canteen unit, presented by the carpenters union, a day ahead of its dedication to serve coffee and sandwiches to the firefighters, and two Red Cross motor units stood by with ambulances to take care of any casualties.[32]

Other Civilian Defense workers mobilized again to meet disaster on July 7, 1943. Construction workers at Camp Bradford that afternoon began falling severely ill from contaminated sandwiches eaten at lunch. As one worker after another began dropping off, a call was put into the Red Cross for help. The Red Cross called Dr. A. B. Hodges, chief of the emergency medical corps, and told him that he should prepare to receive 200 patients. Doctor Hodges

<hr>

[31] *V-P*, October 30, 1943, p. 14; November 18, 1943, p. 22; Civilian Defense: Blackouts, Incidents, file, NWHC records; Marshall to Howard, November 18, 1943, Civilian Defense: Correspondence, Richmond, file, NWHC records.
[32] *V-P*, December 16, 1942, p. 20.

notified Dr. A. K. Wilson at St. Vincent's Hospital to set up the emergency ward prepared in the hospital basement. M. C. Messick, chief of the OCD drivers corps, was called upon to provide trucks to bring the necessary cots and mattresses from the warehouse to the hospital, and 45 minutes later they arrived with Coordinator Marshall leading the way. The medical staff assigned to duty at the St. Vincent's casualty station reported promptly, as did the volunteer nurses aides. The staff, in fact, appeared much faster than did the sick workmen, and soon there were three attendants to every patient. The 33 patients who were brought in, however, benefited from the emergency preparations. Although there were not enough hospital holders in Norfolk to give them all the intravenous injections they needed, they received the injections through the ingenious device of suspending the bottles from coat hangers hooked over the steam-pipes on the basement ceiling.[33]

A group of Negro wardens and auxiliary police saved several lives by emergency action when a Navy flier crashed into a home in Titustown on August 15, 1943. Although both plane and house instantly burst into flames, several wardens rushed up and dragged to safety a passenger in the plane who had been thrown clear by the crash. They then ordered all the nearby homes evacuated and stood by to preserve order until the fire department arrived to extinguish the blaze.[34]

None of the defense volunteers, however, were called upon to meet the greatest disaster that had befallen Norfolk since the dirigible *Roma* crashed at the Army Base on February 21, 1922, killing 34 of its crew. At 11:01 A. M. on September 15, 1943, Coordinator Marshall raised his head from his work at a very loud report which shook the building, but his secretary dismissed it as thunder. A few minutes later he had occasion to call his assistant coordinator, James H. Wood, who asked him what he was doing about the explosion. Marshall then learned that there had been a tremendous blast out at the Naval Base, although no one knew any of the details. A moment later Doctor Hodges called to ask if he should mobilize the emergency medical corps.

Coordinator Marshall immediately tried to get in touch with

[33] *V-P*, July 8, 1943, pp. 20, 15; Civilian Defense: Histories file, NWHC records.
[34] Civilian Defense: Histories file, NWHC records.

Captain E. M. Woodson, Base security officer, but the regular telephone system was jammed with inquiries. He then called over the direct line used by the warning center for air raid tests and left word to have Captain Woodson telephone him. The captain was called from the scene of the disaster by a "walkie-talkie" and told the coordinator that the Navy would be able to take care of the situation. If the need should arise, the civilians would be summoned. Marshall then told the emergency medical corps to stand by.

Meanwhile, in the initial excitement of the explosion, a call had somehow gone out over the police radio that police, doctors, and nurses were needed. Impulsive volunteers of all kinds rushed out to the Base to offer their services and complicate the Navy's task. Captain Woodson called the Norfolk OCD in great annoyance to find out who was responsible for sending out the unneeded volunteers but was assured that the coordinator's office was not to blame.[35]

The explosion, it was later discovered, had occurred when several depth bombs, slipped partially off the trailer on which they were being hauled, and were detonated by the heat as they were dragged along the concrete road. The tons of explosives set off totally destroyed several buildings and killed 24 persons, with fatal injuries to four others. Ambulances from all over the Hampton Roads area were mobilized to carry the 250 wounded to hospitals. One Willoughby ferry came over entirely loaded with ambulances from Fort Monroe. The police cleared Granby Street and Hampton Boulevard of traffic to let the ambulances rush through. The Portsmouth ferries left as soon as they had loaded two or three ambulances on their way to the Naval Hospital, and one of the boats which was laid up for repairs was pressed back into temporary service.[36] Spectators staring at the speeding ambulances gave silent thanks that at least they were not likely to be called out again by an enemy attack.

[35] "Explosion," Civilian Defense: Histories file, NWHC records.
[36] *V-P*, September 18, 1943, p. 1.

24

THEY ALSO SERVED

Just as Colonel Borland had predicted for 1943,[1] the emphasis was shifting from civilian defense to what might have been called civilian offense. The multitude of volunteer activities designed to aid the war effort fell into the domain of Larry J. Hardiman, Jr., as chief of Civilian Mobilization. New ideas for increasing these activities were to spring up constantly in the Washington hotbed; even Richmond would occasionally sprout an original idea. A stream of instructional memoranda forwarded these inspirations to Norfolk where Marshall and Hardiman accepted them with enthusiasm or buried them discreetly in the files.

The employment office for all the new campaigns as well as the old was the Civilian Defense Volunteer Office, still under the chairmanship of Mrs. W. MacKenzie Jenkins. On thousands of cards her staff kept the names of men and women willing to devote their spare time to regular or occasional duties. The CDVO had furnished recruits for all the protective services early in 1942 and stood ready to help out in any emergency. It supplied the volunteers who aided in the liquor rationing registration and maintained a permanent group of unpaid workers at the ration board. In the summer of 1944 it was even to recruit boys and girls to pick peaches and apples in Virginia's orchards when the fruit threatened to go to waste for want of the usual farm labor.

The production of food was the concern of another of the groups under the Hardiman wing. The idea of increasing the food supply by promoting the raising of victory gardens had been passed on by the State OCD to the local coordinators early in 1942, but had been submerged under what then seemed more pressing matters, as far as Civilian Defense was concerned. The

[1] *V-P*, December 11, 1942, Part II, p. 12.

local Federation of Garden Clubs, however, hearing about the program through the national federation, took it up with enthusiasm and in November 1942, held a victory harvest show of their products in Foreman Field. The gardeners thought about setting up a committee of related groups, although they did not realize that their project had any connection with Civilian Defense.

Since the Norfolk OCD was likewise unfamiliar with the ladies' work, Larry Hardiman started work independently on the victory garden committee he was told to organize. Naming D. E. Hopkins as chairman, he brought together members of the Federation of Garden Clubs and the Horticultural Society to form a committee to promote the planting of gardens. When a few months later someone remembered to invite the president of the Federation to join the committee, that officer was somewhat surprised to learn that the OCD had taken over her program but promised to cooperate.[2]

The victory garden committee estimated that 30,000 gardens were planted inside the city in 1943 and that home gardens increased the vegetable supply of the area by 50 per cent. For 1944 the new committee chairman, Frederick Heutte, prepared to encourage even more gardening. Lectures and radio talks were given to instruct the novice. An experiment at Lafayette School in 1943 was expanded into a city-wide plan. For each school that wanted to grow food for its own lunchroom the city would prepare the ground and provide free soil and fertilizer.[3]

Closely associated with the victory garden committee was the campaign for better nourishment. The Norfolk Nutrition Committee, headed by Dr. Raymond Kimbrough, with the aid of the OCD, was able to make Norfolk as nutrition-minded as any city in the country. The group started off 1943 by holding a two-day "Foods for Victory" school in January. This went off so well that a monthly "Health for Victory Club" was started the following month. Each month the instructor, Mrs. Horace Woolf, director of VEPCO's home service department, handed the members a complete set of well-balanced menus for the month. The Health for Victory Club expanded into three separate groups, whites,

[2] Mrs. Charles Day to L. J. Hardiman, April 14, 1943, Civilian Defense: Civilian Mobilization, 1943, file, NWHC records.
[3] *L-D*, March 8, 1944.

Negroes, and a special section for the Red Cross Canteen. In June a series of weekly canning classes were held to preserve the food coming out of the victory gardens. In November a second "Foods for Victory" school was held, followed by another series of club meetings. A nutrition refresher course for dietitians in school lunchrooms and elsewhere was also held in the spring of 1944. Canning was made easier by the purchase through the OCD of forty pressure cookers, essential to the safe canning of vegetables. These were placed in various sections of the city and rented out to persons who needed them.[4]

Hardiman's groups had still other responsibilities for the community's health. The Civilian Defense blood bank, created originally as a reserve against air raids, passed over to his side of the organization when the stored plasma seemed more needed for ordinary civilian emergencies. For the classes in home nursing, conducted by the Red Cross, Hardiman's only responsibility was to enlist students. When the emphasis shifted to training nurses aides to help the understaffed hospitals, it was still the Red Cross's job, but when the demand came for men to serve as volunteers in hospitals, Hardiman took over the job of finding the men.

There was some question at first as to whether the Civilian Defense responsibility for the community's health included venereal disease. This problem, unlike most of the other programs, was the result of local inspiration. Doctor Kimbrough, noticing what the cooperation of OCD had done for his nutrition committee, approached Coordinator Marshall in the summer of 1943 with the idea of working on the control of venereal disease. Although Marshall looked with disfavor on the suggestion, he later went along with Doctor Kimbrough and Kenneth Miller, field representative of the American Social Hygiene Association, to confer with Colonel Borland. Defense Director Borland suggested that the OCD should cooperate with the other interested agencies.

A meeting of representatives of various agencies was called for August 31, but so many people were sick or out of town that nothing was decided. Instead, a steering committee was appointed to arrange for another public conference, which got postponed

[4] Civilian Defense: Civilian Mobilization, 1942, 1943, 1944, files, NWHC records.

indefinitely. At length the steering committee got together and agreed to ask Alex H. Bell to serve as chairman. After the customs collector had been persuaded to accept the post, the steering committee approached the question of venereal disease control on September 29 and decided that the first thing to do was to find a place to put the infected women. The group agreed that the only place available was old St. Vincent's Hospital which would be turned over to the city when the new Granby Street building was finished. When Colonel Borland was asked about the problem, he said that the city could turn over the building for that purpose to the U. S. Public Health Service but that the city could not accept responsibility for caring for the women because it could then never get rid of it.[5]

Several members of the committee then went to Richmond to confer with Governor Darden over the project to have the State operate the proposed hospital, which had again been revived, but discovered that no agreement had been reached. Finally Federal agencies decided to operate the project. The National Housing Agency agreed to turn over to FWA the Tucker dormitories at Lamberts Point, which were nearly empty anyway. The Federal Works Agency remodeled the buildings to transform them into a quarantine hospital with facilities tor treating 45 white women, 30 Negro women, 19 white men, and 16 Negro men. The converted structures were turned over to the U. S. Public Health Service to operate as the Hampton Roads Rapid Treatment Venereal Disease Hospital in June, 1944.[6] With the use of penicillin, just becoming available to civilians, the hospital could cure, or at least render non-infectious, most cases in less than a week.

At the same time the city health department greatly increased its facilities to care for persons who could not be sent to the hospital. The one city clinic operating in July, 1943, was joined by six others, and the investigating staff was increased from one full-time and three part-time workers to four full-time and eight part-time. The field staff turned up so many previously undiscovered cases that the average number of cases handled by the

[5] Memorandum in Civilian Defense: Venereal Disease file, NWHC records.
[6] Memorandum in Civilian Defense: Venereal Disease file, NWHC records; V-P, December 11, 1943, p. 14; June 4, 1944, Part II, p. 1.

city clinics rose from 90 a month early in 1942 to 350 a month two years later. In addition, an average of 150 a month were being referred to private physicians.[7]

Meanwhile, Alex Bell's committee turned to the second phase of its job, breaking down the taboos which had long prevented discussion of the problem and educating the public on the dangers of venereal disease. The steering committee called a meeting on April 11, 1944, of more than a hundred representatives of all the agencies concerned in the problem. The group heard some startling figures. Doctor Kimbrough cited Selective Service records which showed that six men of every hundred called up for induction in the city had venereal disease. He said that syphilis cases reported in Norfolk in 1943 had increased 31 per cent over 1942, gonorrhea by 185 per cent. Seven of every ten women committed to the city jail in the last eight months had been infected. Rear Admiral J. J. A. MacMullin, medical officer for the Fifth Naval District, said that Norfolk was the worst spot in the nation for venereal disease.[8]

The Norfolk Venereal Disease Control Committee, which was formed at this meeting, arranged for subcommittees to attack the problem from all angles. A social protection committee was named to study the whole question of prostitution and its control and prevention, while a social hygiene group was charged with the investigation of means of checking juvenile delinquency. A special publicity committee went to work on ways and means to get the problem before the public. In November, 1944, a well-planned publicity campaign started into action. Leaflets were placed in the pay envelopes of every industrial plant showing the dangers of venereal disease. Newspaper advertising, radio programs, billboards, and cards in the streetcars and buses all urged the wisdom of a blood test. Even department store windows featured the latest fashion in health protection. The city health department offered to make blood tests of all the employees of any firm that requested it. In some areas of the city the investigators

[7] *V-P*, September 3, 1944, Part II, p. 1; "The Venereal Disease Control Program of Norfolk," in Civic Clubs and Organizations: Norfolk Venereal Disease Control Program file, NWHC records.

[8] *V-P*, April 12, 1944, p. 14.

went from door to door offering to make blood tests. For all who were found to be infected, free treatment was offered at the city clinic for those who could not afford a private physician.[9]

Other public information programs originated in the U. S. Office of Civilian Defense. Norfolk had successfully sidestepped the block leaders idea, which was designed to set up a channel of communication into every American home, but that was no great loss, since the State office received no further assignments for them after the first few months. Although the wardens, who had been asked to take over these jobs, did not go calling on every lady in the neighborhood, as the block leaders were supposed to, they did manage to carry out several campaigns in which their sex was not a disadvantage. Notable was one they undertook right in the middle of the first pleasure-driving ban in January, 1943, to promote car pools. Wardens who had found it a little awkward explaining point rationing to housewives were much more at home talking to their husbands about automobiles. They found out who was driving where and when and then matched up those who could ride together. The wardens reported that they had visited 24,642 homes, or just about half the residences in the city, and had established nearly 4,000 new car pools. People without regular hours were given "Share-A-Ride" stickers for their cars to indicate their willingness to pick up anyone who was waiting for a streetcar.[10]

Norfolk did agree to participate in another publicity organization projected about the same time as the block leaders. There was to be a national committee coordinating all the agencies of publicity at the national level, with similar coordinating committees at the state and local levels. Thus, at the push of a button in Washington, well-planned, coordinated publicity campaigns on any given subject could overwhelm the public and insure automatic cooperation. Coordinator Marshall took to the idea as soon as he heard about it and at once set to work forming an information committee for Norfolk. He brought J. Linwood Rice, assistant state coordinator, down from Richmond to explain the

[9] *V-P*, November 12, 1944, Part II, p. 1; November 19, 1944, Part II, p. 1; Civic Clubs and Organizations: Norfolk Venereal Disease Control Program file, NWHC records.

[10] Civilian Defense: Civilian Mobilization, 1943, file, NWHC records.

purpose of the new organization at the committee's first meeting. All the members promised to cooperate and waited for their instructions. Growing restive after a month, Marshall wrote to Rice to find out what the committee was supposed to do next. Rice's polite answer could not conceal the fact that the coordinated publicity idea had been a still birth.[11]

Some eight months after the information committee had been buried quietly, Norfolk was again asked to take part in a publicity drive to protect war secrets. This program had begun in June, 1943, with an experimental campaign in Richmond and 28 other cities over the nation to see what Civilian Defense could do to educate the public to the danger of spreading military information inadvertently. The success of this test led to the appointment of state committees to continue the campaign with local committees in areas designated as "critical." The program got under way in Norfolk on October 26 when John J. Howard and J. Linwood Rice of the State OCD came down from Richmond to discuss the idea with Coordinator Marshall and representatives of the FBI and Army and Navy Intelligence.

Marshall at once went to work on the program, calling a meeting of representatives of all the publicity agencies in the city on November 17. The group agreed to put on an intensive two-week campaign beginning December 1, with continuous publicity thereafter. The telephone company had already agreed to put up warning posters in all its telephone booths on that date and to send out folders with its bills. VEPCO promised to put specially prepared posters on the front of all its streetcars and buses. Posters went up on all the ferries, in the theater lobbies, and in the stores. Horace Christopher and Thomas W. Young sent out announcements to all the colored ministers to be read from their pulpits. All the air raid wardens were given instructions on the need for keeping secrets. Newspapers warned the public about the dangers of loose talk, and WTAR presented the same story in dramatic form.

Much of the campaign failed to come off because of the lack of time for preparation, but Norfolkians received a fairly good

[11] Marshall to Rice, February 17, 1943, Rice to Marshall, February 19, 1943, memorandum, September 15, 1943, Civilian Defense: Information Committee, NWHC records.

education on the harm which might come from casual comments. Another meeting of the committee was planned for after Christmas to renew the drive, but other things intervened. A reminder from Richmond in February, 1944, about the increasing importance of protecting military secrets in the coming pre-invasion months brought the reply that tentative plans were being made for further intensification of the drive. The plans never got beyond the tentative stage, and the committee did not meet again. Further directives from Richmond were filed with the others and forgotten.[12]

One of the projects which helped to bury the security of war information program was the "I-Meeting Day" program conceived by the State OCD. The plan called for meetings in every Virginia community on the day of the forthcoming invasion of Europe, or "I-Day," as it was then known. The purpose of the program was to call for a rededication to the war effort through meetings to be held at eight o'clock on the night of I-Day, where audiences would be given pep talks about buying war bonds, collecting scrap, or obeying price ceilings. To keep the Civilian Defense touch, the message, "This is I-Day," was to be delivered through the warning centers to every control center in the State, and the news would then be proclaimed to the public through ringing church bells or using any other audible signals, "EXCEPT THE PUBLIC AIR RAID WARNING SIRENS."

The instructions were passed on by Defense Director Borland on March 28 to Coordinator Marshall, who discussed the plan with several of his staff members and found numerous faults in it. He thought the day of the invasion would be a poor time to talk to people about saving tin cans or taking care of their health. It would be impossible to get out a crowd on such short notice, and the ringing of bells sounded too much like a celebration. The idea was filed away as another Richmond brainstorm until a week later Colonel Borland brought up the subject. He pointed out that the idea had the Governor's backing and that it was therefore up to Norfolk to do something about it.

[12] See Civilian Defense: Security of War Information file, NWHC records. When mat and proof for a suggested story on the subject arrived from Richmond in September, with the recommendation that it be submitted to the local papers and then returned, Coordinator Marshall's efficient secretary noted: "Do nothing about this and in ten days . . . return to Mr. Wyse."

About the same time Campbell Arnoux, manager of radio station WTAR, came to Marshall with an idea he had for blowing the sirens to wake up the public, if the news should come during the night, since the radio stations were planning to go on the air the moment the flash arrived. Marshall, who in the meantime had decided that the meetings should be religious in nature, joined forces with the radiomen and asked WTAR representatives to join him in a committee with ministers representing the various church groups in the city. The ministers all agreed that the churches should have special services at eight o'clock on the evening of the day of invasion. The committee also agreed to ask Governor Darden's permission to blow the sirens, as Arnoux had suggested.[13]

The program was elaborated at another meeting a few days later. WTAR was to notify the OCD as soon as the station went on the air. The Norfolk sirens would be sounded as well as those in Portsmouth and Virginia Beach, as these communities had decided to join the celebration. The churches were to be open all day for prayer, and a minute of silent prayer would be observed all over the city at 11:00 A. M., while all activities came to a halt. The sirens would again give the signal for this. At 8:00 P. M. the church services would be held, as originally scheduled, and at the same hour the movies would interrupt their show to flash a special prayer on the screen.[14]

The well-laids plans, however, ran into many tribulations. Although Governor Darden agreed to the blowing of the sirens, he said he would have to get the approval of Third Service Command. When Third Service Command turned down the proposal, the Governor appealed to Eastern Defense Command and received the same rejection. Once more baffled by the Army, Coordinator Marshall determinedly decided to blow the police sirens and the fire engine sirens and all the other sirens in town which the Army could not control. A few days later he met further opposition when Howard and Rice dropped in from Richmond and suggested that many people might object to being awakened by the sirens. A few minutes afterward A. E. Parker, who was in charge of the

[13] Memorandum, April 13, 1944, Civilian Defense: I Meeting Day in Virginia file, NWHC records.
[14] Memorandum, April 18, 1944, Civilian Defense: I Meeting Day in Virginia file, NWHC records.

program in Portsmouth, called up to say that Portsmouth had decided to drop part of the program and that he was so disgusted he was ready to quit. Feeling equally disgusted, Coordinator Marshall wrote the Governor that he would like to call the whole thing off.[15]

Even the home folks took up the criticism. Both the local papers on the same day blasted the siren proposal. "If this plan is permitted to go through," said the *Ledger-Dispatch*, "it will be the first time, at least of recent record, in which the people of this community or any other community have been called to prayer by police and fire sirens." The *Virginian-Pilot* commented: "It invests the concept of prayer for Divine intercession—a solemn and contemplative communion—with a hippodromic bedlam of noises associated in the public mind not with the idea of quiet communion but with the idea of celebration—as at the birth of a New Year."[16] Surveying the city's ministers, the *Virginian-Pilot* found support for its opposition to the blowing of the sirens, although the preachers who had acted with the committee tried to explain the decision.

In spite of all this opposition the apparently incongruous program fulfilled its original purpose. At 3:54 A. M. on the morning of June 6, 1944, the police and fire sirens sounded all over the city, summoning the people to listen to the news. Those who were within hearing range woke up and turned on their radios—or decided to finish off a good night's sleep and let the news wait until morning. After the excitement of listening to the broadcasts from the invasion beaches of Normandy had quieted down, people turned to prayer. All day long men, women, and children filed into the city's churches and bowed their heads to pray for the safety of their loved ones, and that night large crowds turned out for the special services. As Coordinator Marshall had predicted, religion, rather than patriotism, dominated the feelings of the people on the day which Norfolkians would remember as "D-Day."[17]

The coming of D-Day meant no slackening in the most durable

[15] Marshall to Darden, April 29, 1943, Civilian Defense: Correspondence, Richmond, file, NWHC records.
[16] *L-D, V-P*, April 27, 1944.
[17] See Civilian Defense: I Meeting Day in Virginia file, NWHC records.

of all the Civilian Defense programs. The salvage office under George Russ had lost the high-pressure publicity campaigns which had characterized it in 1942 and settled down to routine tasks. Carrying on despite a fire which destroyed the building which housed his business and the salvage office in January, 1943, Russ kept the day-in-and-day-out campaigns going. He checked on the activities of his silk stocking chairman, Victor Wertheimer, until that campaign ended in September, and helped his fat salvage chairman, J. W. Field, see that the butchers took the housewives' saved grease. Tin cans had to be collected, hauled, loaded, and shipped to the detinning plant at Pittsburgh, Pennsylvania.[18]

The scrap metal campaign was revived in March, 1943, when the Boy Scouts undertook a door-to-door canvass of the city to gather any junk that had been uncovered during spring housecleaning. Norfolk, they learned, had been thoroughly cleaned out the preceding fall. In three weeks they dug out less than a quarter of a million pounds, when their goal had been a million and a half. Thereafter the salvage group made no organized effort to dig up scrap, but saw that whatever metal was reported found its way to the junk dealers.

Another comeback was made by the waste paper drive, which had been so successful nationally early in 1942 that it had jammed up the waste paper yards and left many Civilian Defense groups with piles of paper that had to be wasted. In the fall of 1943 the word again went out that waste paper was needed to supply the mills. The first idea tested in Norfolk for collecting paper was to use the air raid wardens. Each section post was asked to organize the children of the neighborhood to bring all the old paper they could find to the post, where it could be collected in large enough quantities to make it worthwhile to send a truck. Trophy cups were offered to the sections with the best record to stimulate interest.[19]

Since this system brought only isolated responses, a new method was inaugurated in January, 1944. Larchmont School on its own initiative had collected fourteen tons of paper through its students,

[18] See Civilian Defense: Salvage, General, file, NWHC records. Total tin shipments from the city were 681.502 gross tons, for which the city received $5,698.26.

[19] V-P, November 16, 1943.

and it was suggested that the plan be made city-wide. Within a month the schools were refusing to take any more paper because there were no trucks available to haul away the huge piles already gathered. In the meantime, the paper shortage was already making itself noticeable to the public. Paper bags were getting scarce, and it took a watchful eye to find facial tissues in the stores.

Impressed by the emergency, people saved their paper, but no collection system was available. The OCD obtained the offer of a volunteer paper collector, but the multitude of calls soon overwhelmed him. Then the Junior Chamber of Commerce offered a new plan. The Jaycees agreed to borrow trucks and spend a Sunday gathering all the available paper. On April 23, 1944, some fifty volunteers swept into action with eighteen trucks and during a hectic fourteen-hour day loaded eight box cars with the paper left out on the curbs.[20] After another strenuous Sunday in July, the Jaycees received reinforcements. The Coast Guard Auxiliary offered to join in the campaign, and the Army and the Navy furnished trucks. The new waste paper team kept the city's contributions flowing smoothly to the mills thereafter.

Most important of all the groups of volunteers not associated with Civilian Defense was the American Red Cross. Although working closely with Coordinator Marshall's organization, the Red Cross carefully preserved its traditional independence. Like the Red Cross chapters everywhere, the Norfolk group knit sweaters, wound bandages, made baby shirts, and filled ditty bags; nearly 16,000 local women took part in these activities. Norfolk's special position, however, imposed many extra duties on the local chapter, and it expanded far more rapidly than did the city. The Motor Corps, which in 1939 had only nineteen members, rose to 175 three years later, operating three ambulances and a station wagon. All of them were trained in mechanics, first aid, and military drill. The canteen group, organized in 1939, had nearly a thousand workers by 1943 and served more than 115,000 meals that year. In 1939 there were fifteen Gray Ladies, visiting the sick in the U. S. Marine Hospital; by 1942 there were 150, spending nearly two hours a day at the new Naval Base Hospital and the Marine Hospital. The 520 nurses aides trained by the Red Cross spent more than 100,000 hours helping out the city's

[20] *L-D*, April 4, 1944; *V-P*, April 24, 1944, p. 10.

understaffed hospitals. Mrs. Howard A. Flagge alone put in more than 2,800 hours in the hospitals.[21]

Norfolkians responded to the call to give their money as well as their time. In each of the war loan drives the city went over the top after an enthusiastic campaign by local volunteers. The city also launched a drive in March, 1943, sparked by Major Francis E. Turin, to sell $37,500,000 in bonds to pay for a cruiser to be named the *U. S. S. Norfolk*. The drive was completed in July, although the proposed cruiser was to be cancelled by the end of the war. The cruiser campaign launched one of Norfolk's most energetic bond salesman on his career. Sam Sutton, immigrant from Russia who owned a small confectionery store on Park Avenue, arose in a meeting of the Anglers Club to make his first public speech. So persuasive was his talk that he sold more than $7,000 worth of bonds that night. Impressed by his success, he abandoned his business for two weeks to sell a half million dollars worth of bonds. Later sales put him above the million mark.[22]

Even more outstanding was the work of another European immigrant, Elias Codd, who operated a delicatessen on Princess Anne Road. He started out by selling war stamps during a national campaign to push these through grocery stores. Then he decided to branch out by selling war bonds to his customers, taking their money and standing patiently in line to get the bonds for them. Even when his sales had mounted to the hundreds of thousands, he objected to receiving any publicity, but when he had sold $600,000 worth, a reporter friend printed the story over his protests. The resulting publicity brought him so many new customers that he was able to sell $3,000,000 worth of war bonds and received national recognition as one of the country's outstanding bond salesmen.[23]

The people of Norfolk also responded to the calls for charity. The Norfolk United War Fund, caring for the Community Fund, other city charities, and virtually all the war relief agencies except

---

[21] See report of the Norfolk chapter in Civic Clubs and Organizations (General): American Red Cross file, NWHC records.

[22] *V-P*, April 15, 1943, p. 24; Frank Sullivan, "America's Leading War Bond Salesmen," *Know the Navy and Norfolk*, August, 1944, p. 184.

[23] Banking and War Finance file, NWHC records.

the Red Cross, never had any trouble in exceeding its quota by a generous margin. In four wartime drives it raised two and a quarter million dollars, sending more than a million of the sum to war relief agencies.[24] The Red Cross War Fund drives likewise always reached their goals.

[24] See the excellent history of the War Fund in Civic Clubs and Organizations (General): Norfolk United War Fund file, as well as three scrapbooks kept by the Fund, in the NWHC records.

25

MORE FUN

I N March, 1943, just before the Izac committee arrived in Norfolk, the Advisory Recreation Commission made the report for which it had been asked when appointed the previous November by the city council to survey all the recreational facilities available and to recommend improvements. The commission offered several suggestions for showing the city's good will toward the visiting servicemen. It urged that the City Recreation Bureau set up a canteen for enlisted men and a club for officers, for whom no recreation at all had been provided in the city. It also asked that the Recreation Bureau set up a headquarters for distributing free tickets to servicemen; operators of movie theaters and promoters of sports events would be willing to supply 2,500 free passes a week. Modest as these proposals were, they foundered on the hard rock of the budget; the city council appropriated no money to pay for them.[1]

In spite of the failure of this attempt, the tide had already turned. By the spring of 1943 sailors were beginning to find it a little easier to have fun. At Ocean View the Catholic USO started a beach club to help out the badly overworked club operated there by the Navy Y, and the Jewish USO set up a similar center farther out, on the beach at Lynnhaven. Ocean View Park opened nearly two months early, and its enlarged concessions offered a counter-attraction to the East Main Street entertainments. By June the original section of Fleet Recreation Park was thrown open, and work had been started on the expansion which was to double its size. The USO's also improved the summer by holding a series of outdoor dances in Lafayette Park. All these uptown activities served to keep thousands of the sailors off the sweltering streets downtown, although there were still enough there to

---

[1] *V-P*, March 24, 1943, p. 20. The Recreation Bureau did organize an information center for officers, staffed by volunteers, in the lobby of the Monticello Hotel.

make Navy men ask plaintively, "Isn't there some small town near here where I could go and not have to see a million gobs around me?"

The biggest improvement of all was the completion of the long-delayed auditorium. In the arena of the new building on Saturday, May 15, the Army District Engineer, in charge of the construction, formally turned the keys over to the Federal Works Agency, for whom it had been built. FWA passed the keys on to the Federal Security Agency, which had authorized the construction, and FSA handed them on to the USO, which would operate the building. The city, which was to receive the keys after the war was over, at once set to work to acquire the neighboring property in order to provide appropriate approaches and landscaping.

On Saturday, July 31, the weekly dances moved from the old city hall out to the arena of the new building and went on a regular Tuesday and Saturday night schedule. The USO management committee, headed by Richard D. Cooke, needed several more months to find entertainment to fill both the arena and the theater of the new building on a regular basis. The committee adopted the policy of admitting all servicemen free to the dances and allotting a large number of free tickets to other events for distribution to men in uniform. Civilians were admitted to the auditorium, unlike the other USO centers, so that the money they paid for the tickets would cover the cost of the entertainment. Civic groups like the Norfolk Forum, the Community Concerts Association, and the Norfolk Symphony Orchestra were allowed to hold their events in the theater on the condition that they set aside part of the tickets for free distribution.

The biggest problem was trying to keep both the arena and the theater in constant operation. During the fall amateur or professional boxing became a Friday night feature at the arena, and professional wrestling shows were put on Wednesday nights. Along with the dances, this kept the arena going four days a week with basketball games on many of the off-nights. The theater was a greater problem, since the fifteen or twenty civic entertainments scheduled for it were only a step towards keeping it going. The committee finally agreed to lease the theater to William L. Wilder, owner of a local movie chain. Wilder was to provide movies and stage shows there every day no other event was scheduled. Free tickets would be allotted for distribution, and all servicemen would be admitted at half-price.

The first stage show under the Wilder management opened on January 28, 1944, and all 1,900 seats in the theater were filled at both performances. In addition to the traveling entertainers the theater boasted a permanent seventeen-piece orchestra and a twelve-girl chorus, the Centerettes. The theater thus restored to Norfolk a type of entertainment which had vanished shortly after Pearl Harbor. Because of the lack of air-conditioning the stage shows were given up during the summer of 1944, but the opening of a new burlesque theater in Ocean View Park took up the gap by providing a different type of flesh show for the sailors.

The provision for suspending the movies on nights civic events were scheduled caused some difficulties. The expense of maintaining the movie staff during an idle night was a burden on the operator, and sailors who had come downtown to see a song-and-dance show were sadly disappointed to learn that there was a lecture on instead. Moreover, the arena still had some dark nights. The management committee therefore decided to shift all the civic concerts to the arena, where twice as many people could be accommodated. This brought some grumbling, since the arena was much better designed for a wrestling match than it was for a symphony concert.[2]

The awkward architecture of the arena, however, did not dampen the enthusiasm of the crowds that turned out for whatever events were staged there. Radio's "Grand Ole Opry" gang brought out civilians and servicemen in such numbers to hear their hill-billy music that the huge arena could not hold them. Even though an extra show was staged to take care of the overflow, there was a near-riot among the disappointed listeners.[3] For those who preferred a different type of entertainment the management committee obtained such an array of talent as had not been seen in Norfolk for many years. The San Carlo Civic Opera Company, Jeanette MacDonald, Grace Moore, Lawrence Tibbett, and Fritz Kreisler all appeared at the arena in a single year, in addition to the Camel Caravan and many others.[4]

The opening of the new auditorium permitted the USO center

[2] *V-P*, March 24, 1944, p. 18.
[3] *V-P*, March 24, 1944.
[4] *V-P*, February 4, 1945, Part II, p. 4.

in the old city hall to be transformed into something more nearly adequate to the city's needs. After being closed down for the remodeling it swung back into action on December 10, 1943, just three years and three days after the little band of Norfolk volunteers had pressed it into service as one of the first servicemen's recreation centers in the nation. A new floor on the auditorium provided a permanently available skating rink while the rest of the second floor was turned over to other forms of recreation. Here a sailor might lunch at the snack bar, play ping pong, write a letter, try a hand at finger-painting, have a gift wrapped, or read a hometown newspaper.[5]

Even more significant of the warming relations between Norfolk and the Navy was the gradual awakening of many civic groups to their responsibility. In December, 1942, the Pilot Club assumed the burden of equipping and operating a "Pilot House" as a recreation center in the basement of the Salvation Army USO. Members of the club provided refreshment and entertained servicemen there at weekly parties.[6] The Sons and Daughters of Liberty set up a "Liberty Cookie Barrel" at the Salvation Army USO and undertook to keep it full of home-made cookies. When the organization disintegrated, Mrs. Peggy Koons organized her friends to take over the job.[7] Some 150 local women joined the Norfolk Women's Council of the Navy League, which was formed in January, 1943, and undertook the task of supplying hostesses at Fleet Recreation Park as well as setting up a Navy League House to provide quarters for women visiting enlisted men and establishing a commissioned officers' club.[8]

The Masons opened up a full-time recreation center on Freemason Street, financed and operated by the order itself. The Presbyterians set up a Hospitality House in Ocean View, and the Episcopalians operated one at the Church of the Good Shepherd in Meadowbrook. Other churches, like the Park Place Methodist and the Second Presbyterian, held regular parties twice a week

[5] V-P, December 11, 1943, p. 14.
[6] "History of Pilot Club War Activities," Civic Clubs (Women's): Pilot Club of Norfolk file, NWHC records.
[7] V-P, July 4, 1943, Part II, p. 10; Entertainment: Private Entertainment, Mrs. Peggy Koons file, NWHC records.
[8] Entertainment: Norfolk Women's Council of the Navy League of the United States file, NWHC records.

for servicemen. Sailors were invited to join in the Little Theater productions and to play with the symphony orchestra. Officers and enlisted men mingled at the bimonthly parties given by Mr. and Mrs. Albert V. Crosby, and rank was left at the door when music lovers gathered in informal sessions at the S. H. Ferebees.

Much credit for the civic awakening went to Tom Hanes, *Ledger-Dispatch* editor. Undiscouraged by the ignoring of the recommendations made by his Recreation Commission in March, he returned to the battle in October after a six weeks' cruise on an American warship. Aboard ship he talked to hundreds of sailors and from them heard so many complaints about Norfolk that he soon learned not to mention where he was from. On his return he became a one-man committee to arouse the city's conscience. Speaking to one organization after another, he told them in plain terms what sailors thought of Norfolk and pointed out that the city's evil reputation, spread throughout the country, would come back to haunt it in post-war years.

At last he stirred the Kiwanians to action. The group voted to establish an inter-club committee to investigate and correct the conditions which were arousing criticism from the Navy men. On October 21 this Norfolk Citizens' Committee was organized with Edwin E. Bibb as its head. An Army officer, Lieutenant J. E. Caswell of the Norfolk Fighter Wing, appeared to rehearse the servicemen's complaints. Clerks and waitresses were insolent, he reported; cab-drivers overcharged their passengers; and the dance halls collected 55 cents, plus a service charge, for two bottles of ginger ale. Unfortunately, these complaints were voiced just as often by civilians as by servicemen, and there was very little that could be done about them.[9]

Nevertheless, the committee resolutely turned to attacking every possible problem. Its subcommittee on transportation discovered with surprise that it had no problem; the sailors were having no trouble getting into town any more. The committee attacked the problem of high prices by appealing to the OPA for a price ceiling on beer. The movie theaters volunteered to give away a thousand free passes a week. Joe and Frank Phillie's confectionery store on Granby Street started a little goodwill mission of its own by surprising servicemen on Thanksgiving Day. Some

[9] *V-P*, October 8, 1943, p. 24; October 22, 1943, p. 22.

1,500 men and women in uniform were handed checks as usual that day, but, when they attempted to pay for them, the cashier told them everything was on the house.[10]

As a demonstration of Norfolk's friendliness toward the Navy, the committee launched plans for a mammoth, all-day Christmas party at a cost of more than $50,000. There was to be a football game in the afternoon, boxing and wrestling matches, big parties at the Palomar and the Hague Club, and hundreds of smaller parties in private homes. A few weeks later, however, the head of the entertainment subcommittee reported that he had heard nothing but criticism of the proposal and recommended that it be cut down to a more modest size. Plans for a big dinner ran into a snag when it was pointed out that servicemen would get a better dinner in their own mess halls than would most civilians. It was finally decided to let the hospitality on Christmas Day be in private hands. On Sunday, the day after Christmas, the Kiwanians put on a free canteen in the new arena with turkey sandwiches, coffee, cokes, and cakes for every serviceman that showed up. Local talent provided a stage show and a carol sing in the new theater after the supper.[11]

All of these activities had been concentrated primarily on the white enlisted man, who made up the vast majority of Norfolk's uniformed population, but there were many special groups with special needs. Service women were admitted to most of the USO's on the same basis as men, and they had their own special center just across the street from the Central YWCA. Colored sailors, however, were barred from all the white USO's except at the new auditorium, where they were admitted on the same segregated basis as civilian Negroes. For recreation they were supposed to seek the Negro USO on Smith Street, which was adequate and attractive enough as a building, but which had been located in one of the worst slum sections of the city on a poorly paved street with a yard on which no grass would grow. Hostesses were few and far between, because many mothers would not permit their daughters to go through the dark and dirty streets to reach the building.

[10] *V-P*, October 24, 1943, Part II, p. 1; November 23, 1943, p. 20; November 16, 1943, p. 18; January 13, 1944, p. 14.

[11] *V-P*, October 30, 1943, p. 14; November 23, 1943, p. 20; December 19, 943, Part II, p. 1.

Although few whites realized it, the same friction between sailor and civilian prevailed in the Negro part of the city as in the white sections. Negro sailors, like the whites, got drunk and brawled with civilians. Negro night clubs had so much trouble that they refused to admit a man in uniform unless he was vouched for by a civilian member. One Norfolk Negro, back home in uniform, had the door of his own club slammed in his face when he tried to enter it. Since Negro civilians had few entertainment spots to boast about, Negro sailors had even less. The *Journal and Guide* pleaded for action, but its colored audience was helpless, and its white neighbors failed to hear.[12]

A luckier group were the British sailors, who were as popular with Norfolk civilians as they were unpopular with their American counterparts. From the time the first British uniforms had appeared with the arrival of the *Illustrious* in May, 1941, the people of Norfolk had gone out of their way to be friendly with their English cousins. The first organized activity to entertain them developed after the arrival of the *Queen Elizabeth* for repairs in the Navy Yard in September, 1942. Mrs. Robert M. Hughes and a group of her friends then organized a British Leave Service to provide out-of-town entertainment for sailors on leave. Chairmen were appointed in various sections of Virginia to find homes willing to take the men in for a week or ten days. Mrs. Hughes carefully sorted out matching personalities and saw that the guests got off on schedule. The same group served as a committee to turn the old house at the foot of Freemason Street into the Union Jack Club. Ladies joined members of the crew of the *Queen Elizabeth* in getting the grounds into shape; Mrs. M. L. T. Davis, Jr., Norfolk's well-known poet, put as much energy into pushing her wheelbarrow as she did into her verse. After the opening of the Union Jack Club in 1943, the British tars had a recreation retreat where they were safe from the gibes of American gobs.[13]

Almost a forgotten group were the Navy officers. Most of them, of course, had adequate incomes and lived in their own homes with their families, with no more need for special consideration than civilians in the same circumstances. There was, however, many a lonely young ensign with no family and little money, in

[12] *Journal and Guide*, October 23, 1943, p. 8; March 11, 1944, p. 3.
[13] Mrs. Robert M. Hughes, "British Leave Service," British Interests in Norfolk file, NWHC records.

the same position as the enlisted man, but barred from the USO's which were open to the ordinary sailor. He had no other refuge than Bachelor Officers' Quarters until the women of the Navy League opened the club for officers of the United Nations navies in the old Talbot home on West Freemason Street just after Christmas of 1943. Unlike the other clubs, this was on a strictly bring-your-own-girl basis. A group under Mrs. Elias Etheridge also opened an information bureau for officers in the lobby of the Monticello Hotel, where waiting officers could relax on the concrete benches which had replaced the upholstered chairs of prewar days.[14]

In a similar position but even more neglected was the civilian war worker. On the Portsmouth side there was a special USO center to care for the civilians in the Navy Yard, but in Norfolk there was only what money would buy—beer gardens and movies, or the less legitimate pleasures beyond the city line. Single men living in a furnished room, or half a furnished room, had as much need of recreation as any sailors had. Shortly after the Izac committee report pointed out this deficiency, the joint USO's held a special "All-Star Celebrity Night" show in the old auditorium, and 1,800 war workers filled the hall for the free show.[15] After this gesture the USO's returned to their job of trying to take care of the sailors, and the war workers went back to taking their entertainment where they could find it.

One more group which needed consideration was the wives and children of servicemen. Both the YWCA-USO and the Navy Y had taken an interest in the problems of those who were already settled in the area and furnished any necessary aid. The biggest difficulty, however, was with those who came to visit or to stay with a husband stationed in the area. Early in 1942 when priorities seemed about to strangle American industry, the WPB had decreed that no more housing would be built for servicemen's families. Families were expected to stay home or take the consequences. Instead, they did not stay home and they visited the

[14] V-P, January 2, 1944, Part II, p. 1; Entertainment: Norfolk Women's Council of the Navy League of the United States, Officers' Information Service Bureau files, NWHC records. The Monticello information office was set up at the request of the City Recreation Bureau.

[15] V-P, May 10, 1943, p. 14.

consequences on every Army or Navy town in the country. In they came—lonely, innocent wives, young mothers with babes in arms, burly matrons with a pack of children—and dumped their problem on the city's lap. The Navy Y took one wing away from the sailors and assigned it to the use of the women and children; the Salvation Army USO made some of its few beds available. Yet these scarcely made up for the hotel rooms taken over by the armed services.

The Navy League House, opened in July, 1943, was a help in providing overnight housing for women. The Travelers Aid posts in each of the bus and railroad stations furnished advice to each new arrival. Another important aid was the USO information center, opened on the first floor of the old city hall in October, 1943. Although the center answered questions on almost every conceivable subject, its most important task was to locate rooms for rent. It set up a central agency for registering all available rooms in the city for temporary stay, the first time such a service had been provided, although the War Housing Center had long acted as a central bureau for permanent housing. Pathetic stories about a family with two children who had to spend two nights in their car or the twenty-year-old wife who sat up all night in the station with her three-month-old baby just to see her husband after a year's separation—tales like these brought the offer of rooms until sometimes there were more than enough.[16]

Another group which began to fare better was the seamen of the merchant marine. On March 1, 1943, the United Seamen's Service took over the York Hotel as a residence for torpedoed sailors who were awaiting new berths. On December 17 this service was moved to the Hotel Fairfax, which was renamed the U. S. S. Fairfax Residential Club. Volunteers served here as elsewhere to provide games, dances, and other entertainment. The United Seamen's Service also took over the Prince George Hotel to provide similar service to colored seamen.[17]

Last but not least among those whose recreation was being considered was the plain, ordinary civilian resident of Norfolk.

---

[16] See Travelers Aid scrapbook, NWHC records.

[17] *V-P*, March 1, 1943, p. 12; Entertainment: U. S. S. Fairfax Residential Club, NWHC records. The Norfolk club was the first to be set up inside the **United States.**

The Norfolk Advisory Recreation Commission in its report in March, 1943, had pointed out that recreation facilities for civilians had been diminished while the population was growing. The end of the WPA in January, 1943, had terminated the supervision formerly furnished at the city's playgrounds. The USO had taken over the auditorium, the Army had taken over the softball field in Lee Park and part of Lafayette Park. It was an indication of the gradual development of the city's attitude that the playgrounds did not close. With the aid of Lanham Act funds supervisors were provided at eighteen parks and playgrounds during the summer of 1943. A year later there were 33 in operation, and the city was putting up three times as much money for them as it had in 1943. The *Virginian-Pilot* commented in a mild understatement: "This alone is a major achievement in a community which has not been notably forward in its solicitude for recreational needs."[18] Even more remarkable was the fact that the council voted funds to pay for a survey of the city's recreational needs. An expert from Ohio State University, W. C. Batchelor, was called in for a study. His report laid shockingly bare how far Norfolk was falling short of its responsibility for providing recreation for its citizens.[19]

All of these activities together came nowhere near achieving the goal avowed by President Bibb of the Norfolk Citizens' Committee when he said: "We are determined to have here a regular paradise for both servicemen and civilians."[20] Norfolk was not yet a heaven on earth, although at least it had moved farther away from the opposite extreme. Norfolk's belated effort to overcome its Navy reputation was an uphill battle against established prejudices. Thousands of sailors who expected no good of Norfolk had little trouble in finding the bad. There were still many who sympathized with the one who wrote: "My postwar plan for Norfolk . . . is as follows: Bring all the ships of the Navy to Norfolk as soon as possible after peace has been declared and anchor them out in the bay. . . . After the ships have been provisioned and

[18] *V-P*, June 19, 1944, p. 4.
[19] *V-P*, June 23, 1945, p. 14; W. C. Batchelor, *Recreation Survey and Long-Range Plan, City of Norfolk, Virginia*, 1946.
[20] *V-P*, October 30, 1943, p. 14.

their magazines filled to capacity, I suggest these ships shell Norfolk and all its money-hungry citizens off the face of the earth."[21]

Nevertheless, that was no longer the dominant attitude among Navy men. Sailors now had an adequate opportunity for good, clean fun on their trips downtown. There were now seven full-time USO recreation centers in the downtown area, without counting the new auditorium, besides the centers operated independently by the Lutheran Church and the Masons. Nearly ten million visitors swarmed into the USO clubs in the city during 1944. Sailors tramped up the stairs to the Catholic center in such numbers that they wore out three sets of stone steps. Workhorse of them all was the Navy Y which somehow managed to care for almost five million visitors in a single year. Its 400 bedrooms held an average of 528 persons a night, and thousands more slept on chairs or the floor in the lobby.[22]

All these centers were in large part the contribution of the people of Norfolk. Local gifts to the War Fund furnished nearly one-third of the money spent by the USO in the city. The city furnished more than 18,000 volunteers to the USO centers alone, including 2,500 junior hostesses to serve as partners at skating rinks or dances. These were some of the formal statistics that indicated Norfolk's new attitude toward the Navy. The stony stare had given way to the welcoming smile. There was a satisfying reward in reading some of the letters from sailors that now began to appear in the papers, like one which declared:

Personally, I am a strong Norfolk booster and have nothing but favorable criticism to offer the city for the way it has accepted service men, particularly in view of the manner in which the average enlisted man conducts himself. I can't remember a day since arriving in Norfolk that I haven't been offered a lift both to and from work while waiting for a bus or a street car. . . I still contend that the citizens of Norfolk have gone "all out" to extend every courtesy to the sailors stationed here.[23]

[21] V-P, August 15, 1944, p. 6.
[22] V-P, February 4, 1945, Part II, p. 4.
[23] V-P, September 18, 1943, p. 4.

26

SIN AND A SHAME

ADMIRAL Leary stayed only five months in Norfolk before he moved on to a new post in New York City, but few commandants had ever created so much disturbance among the civilians in the Fifth Naval District. Scarcely had the smoke settled from the barrage laid down over Norfolk County than the doughty admiral swung his guns on the Negro population of the city. The very day before he turned over his command to Rear Admiral David McD. Le Breton, Admiral Leary threw another out-of-bounds order around most of the Negro section of the city in the area between Princess Anne Road and Main Street.

The reasons for this arbitrary action were buried in Naval documents and were never revealed to the public. All an outsider could do was to try to reason from a few paltry facts. Within a period of six days during October, 1943, there had been a robbery and two stabbing affrays, in which four servicemen were cut, one, a soldier, fatally, in the area near Charlotte and Church Streets. In the same section a few days later a Navy officer and his girl were attacked by a group of Negroes; both were robbed and beaten, and the girl was raped. These crimes by Negro thugs were certainly regrettable, but similar crimes were being committed in other sections of the city by both colored and white civilians and sailors.

The only conceivable reason for issuing the out-of-bounds order was that the admiral feared that the continued presence of white sailors in the Negro section might lead to racial friction and riots. This was indicated by the odd terms of the order which applied only to white servicemen between the hours of sunset and sunrise. The boundaries of the forbidden district had been drawn in a confusing manner, if that was the case. One relatively innocent block of East Main Street with white residents was included, while the rest of Main Street was unrestricted. The prohibited zone completely encircled the Masonic Service Center. What made the order seem somewhat more ridiculous was that the scene of most of these crimes had already been out-of-bounds since April 10, 1942.

The Navy itself seemed highly embarrassed by the admiral's order. The news was not revealed until November 3, three days after Admiral Le Breton had taken over. The only explanation came from Police Chief Woods, who sounded as if the shore patrol had not done a very good job of convincing him when he said, "While these restrictions are drastic, and they may appear to be even more drastic than they are, we feel that if citizens understood why they were imposed they would agree with us that they are necessary." The best that could be got out of the Navy was an anonymous statement that the action was taken for the mutual protection of all concerned.[1]

The *Journal and Guide* indignantly termed this "most amazing order" "harsh, hasty, inept, and uncalled for." It declared:

By making out-of-bounds the entire Negro business district and the adjacent residential sections. . .the official edict puts all of Negro Norfolk outside the pale of decency, makes it suspect, and by inference labels it as unfit for contact by decent service men; that is, white wearers of uniforms.

. . .the Navy has given the Negroes of Norfolk, as such a black eye. It has damned the good Negroes with the bad without distinction. It is making the innocent suffer along with the guilty. This is against the civilized conception of justice and equity. And it certainly does nothing to enhance good relations between the military services and the Negro citizens.[2]

If there were any plotted race riots, the order prevented them. It did little else, for, as the shore patrol admitted, it was almost impossible to enforce. If the shore patrol could not keep men out of the smaller area which had been restricted for a year and a half, it could have little hopes of policing the enlarged territory. All it could do was to patrol the area and pick up any white sailors found inside. Of course, very few white servicemen had ever gone into the area anyhow, and perhaps the out-of-bounds order discouraged that small minority that would have ventured

---

[1] *V-P*, November 4, 1943, p. 20.
[2] *Journal and Guide*, November 13, 1943, p. 8.

into the colored section. At any rate, nothing more was ever heard of the order.

Meanwhile the echoes of Admiral Leary's first broadside against Norfolk County were to go on reverberating through Virginia politics long after the admiral had departed the scene. The grand jury which had been investigating the charges when the Navy put the county back in bounds reported what was common knowledge—that gambling, the illegal sale of alcoholic liquor, and the operation of houses of prostitution had been carried on openly in the prohibited zones and that the county police must certainly have known about them. The grand jury made the sweeping recommendation that nine of the county's nineteen officers be dismissed and that four more be reprimanded. Against Officer Benjamin T. Cullen it returned an indictment for operating a house of ill fame known as "The Pines."[3]

The county now went through the motions of reform. Officer Cullen was suspended and brought to trial. No one, however, seemed able to produce any evidence to indicate that the cabins at "The Pines" had been used for any illegitimate purpose. Judge Carney therefore ordered Officer Cullen restored to duty with back pay for the period of his suspension. After hearing the other officers criticized by the grand jury, the judge found that these charges were equally baseless. Nevertheless, Judge Carney decided to reorganize his police force. One officer, who had gone on a drinking spree in the county jail which had been joined by at least one of the woman prisoners, "was sort of prompted to resign," as he expressed it. Deputy Sheriff Wilson told him that, if he resigned quietly, Judge Carney would try to reappoint him later after this thing blew over.[4] Two other officers were quietly eased out, and Deputy Wilson was named chief of police to give the organization a badly-needed head.

This last appointment was somewhat ill-timed since Deputy Wilson was responsible for the operation of the county jail, which the State had just ordered closed because of its unsanitary conditions. Major Rice M. Youell, State Commissioner of Corrections, declared that the jail was next to the worst in the state.[5]

[3] *V-P*, September 24, 1943, p. 22.
[4] Statement of W. F. Butwell, *V-P*, March 2, 1944, p. 14.
[5] *V-P*, December 30, 1943, p. 16.

To redeem the honor of the county, Delegate James N. Garrett pushed a resolution through the Virginia House of Delegates calling for an investigation. The committee, headed by E. O. McCue of Charlottesville, held hearings in the county court room and turned up the same conditions that had been found by the Governor's private investigation and by the grand jury. It heard about the open gambling and prostitution, about the casual tolerance of the officers or their direct financial profit from these transactions, about several questionable practices in which Judge Carney himself had been involved. It also heard several of his ex-friends regret the decline in the judge's health. As an incidental sidelight, it discovered that the A. B. C. agents did not know what had happened to the more than 700 pints of whiskey seized in the raid on Shack's Place shortly after Pearl Harbor. When Deputy Wilson announced indignantly that it was still safe in the county jail, Shack promptly brought suit to recover his whiskey. The A. B. C. agents got ahead of him by claiming the confiscated liquor, but they discovered that 253 of the 760 pints deposited seemed to have evaporated, bottle and all.[6]

While the House of Delegates adopted a resolution asking the Supreme Court of Appeals to retire Judge Carney for disability, the judge demonstrated the vigor of his health by working out a new reform. County Sheriff A. A. Wendel, criticized by the McCue committee, found that his own health had fallen off and resigned. The judge then named Officer J. A. Hodges, one of the seven who had been exonerated by the committee, as county sheriff and head of the police. As part of the arrangement, Sheriff Hodges retained Deputy Wilson, who had resigned his chief of police job the day after the McCue committee was named. Deputy Wilson, it was announced, would no longer be in charge of the jail after its filth had been cleaned up, but would be confined to acting as a court officer.[7]

Even had Sheriff Hodges been given full authority to purge the

[6] V-P, March 5, 1944, Part II, pp. 1, 2; March 7, 1944, p. 12; March 10, 1944, p. 18.

[7] V-P, April 4, 1944, p. 14. The county's new purity still did not satisfy Judge Carney's critics. After the Supreme Court refused to retire him, the House of Delegates at the special session in 1945 voted to remove him from office, but the resolution was defeated in the Senate by one vote. Some months later the judge voluntarily asked for retirement, which was granted.

police, he would still have been unable to whitewash the county's Augean stables. There was no appropriation to pay for an adequate police force and there were no available candidates if there had been. The city itself was able to find only ten men suitable for police work in more than three years to replace the sixty men it lost. Although police salaries were raised, they were still too low to compete with war jobs. There were suggestions that women and Negroes could handle certain police duties, but, though Portsmouth did appoint a woman, Norfolk clung cautiously to its old standards. The auxiliary police were willing to help on a part-time basis, but Norfolk was reluctant to cope with the problem of controlling volunteers. All that saved the situation was the shore patrol, which continued to assign its men to fill the city's vacancies until there were 35 Navy men riding the city's scout cars.

The city police thus were too busy controlling traffic and handling major crimes to devote much time to the suppression of vice. The problem was a difficult one, in any case. A policeman had to be careful in picking up prostitutes, now that the familiar faces in the trade had become lost in a sea of newcomers. Even the vagrancy charge might backfire, as one policeman found out at the cost of $1,000. In July, 1942, he had questioned two Pennsylvania girls in the company of two Coast Guardsmen at the Arab Night Club. When the girls told him they were staying at the Monticello, he checked, found they were not registered there, and hauled them off to the police station as vagrants. Next morning, when they proved that they had stayed at the Monticello the night before and had then moved to the Atlantic Hotel, the charges were dismissed. The indignant girls, however, sued for false arrest and won $1,000 in damages, even though the unfortunate police officer appealed to the Supreme Court.[8] After that, police officers were even more cautious about picking up girls.

Another difficult question was the hotels, which were the city's counterpart of the county's cabins. The best hotels kept the house detective busy making sure that only married couples occupied the same rooms; less careful managers failed to notice when bellboys smuggled girls into the rooms; in the cheapest hotels the clerks asked no questions at all when a sailor and a girl came in and rented a room for an hour. The police knew the

[8] *V-P*, May 2, 1944, p. 14.

hotels; if not by common reputation, their names were learned from the Navy's reports of venereal disease contacts. Chief Woods had no hesitation in stating that a chain hotel was the worst offender in the city.[9] Getting evidence for a conviction, however, was another matter. Individual couples could be caught only by keeping a policeman on constant watch at the hotel; general raids were likely to round up legally-married couples and bring on a suit for false arrest. Convicting the management itself was so difficult the police never tried it.[10]

The sailors' liquor created another problem for the police. The State law which made it illegal to buy whiskey except by the bottle at the A. B. C. stores had always been a complaint of the Navy, but now that a sailor had to acquire a ration coupon before he could buy, get downtown early before the stores closed, and then stand in line indefinitely, he was more willing than ever to acquire his whiskey in the black market. The resulting demand drove the price of bootleg whiskey up to fantastic levels. A fifth which cost $2.20 at the A. B. C. stores was worth $14 after dark. Large and small smugglers rushed to get into the business, buying up liquor in the privately owned stores of Washington, Baltimore, or New York, and hauling it to Norfolk. Crew members of the boat from Baltimore packed every available hiding place with whiskey bottles before the steamer left Maryland. Truckers going into New York brought back as many cases as they could hide. The A. B. C. agents struck out in all directions trying to stem the flood of bootleg liquor. They raided the Baltimore boat so often that the discouraged crew abandoned the business for a time; they stopped trucks on the highway, catching one luckless driver literally napping. With the help of the shore patrol in plain sailor clothes they trapped unwary pint peddlers. Raiding the carefully acquired hordes, they took 240 pints from a Lamberts Point Negro and hauled away 1,162 fifths from a cache in Ocean View while the ex-owner groaned.[11] Down in the Dismal

---

[9] *Hampton Roads Investigation*, p. 167.

[10] Some managers did cooperate. A sign on the door of the Arcade Hotel said: "Positively no girls. Do not disturb the management by asking for them." One rooming house had a placard in the window: "This is a stag house and WE MEAN STAG." *V-P*, June 28, 1944, p. 16.

[11] *V-P*, May 29, 1943, p. 16; May 31, 1943, p. 20; August 27, 1943, p. 22; January 29, 1944, p. 10.

Swamp the moonshiners brought out their stills and went back to work. Bootleg sugar went to $15 a hundred-pound bag with whiskey worth $75 a keg. Several distillers set up shop in the Seashore State Park. Half the Federal Court docket was taken up with moonshiners.[12] There was even some hijacking; three Norfolk policemen yielded to temptation and took part in one such enterprise. The good old prohibition days seemed back again with all their erstwhile excitement.

The danger lay in the threat that the forgotten evils of prohibition might also return. Smuggling in liquor was an illegal competition with the State monopoly, but few people in Norfolk wasted enough love on the A. B. C. Board to worry if it was cheated out of a few dollars, especially since it seemed to have made such a failure of supplying legal liquor. The bootleg liquor trade was dangerous, however, because, being illegal, it could not be regulated. The persons who carried it on were encouraged to further violations of the law for profit; pint-peddling led to robbery and even to murder.[13] The sailors who bought were outside the law and had no protection against being defrauded except their fists.

Hand in hand with whiskey and women went the pandering pirates who operated for-hire cars. Whiskey had to be peddled from a ground base, since it was too easy to be caught with it in the cab, but women could be carried in the car. With a girl in the front seat beside him, the driver set out looking for a sailor or even a car load. Then he parked in a quiet spot and went for a walk. The girls got as much as eight dollars apiece from the sailors, half of which went to the drivers. The city managed to restrain this practice by revoking the license of any driver caught riding girls in the front seat, but the police could not stop it entirely, and there was no check at all beyond the city limits.

The city had trouble enough keeping the drivers within their legal fees. Ineffective as the requirement for posting rates in the cabs was, some drivers failed to do even that until the police began fining all offenders. When the meters finally arrived early

---

[12] *V-P*, May 12, 1944, p. 20.
[13] The soldier who was killed on Charlotte Street in October, 1943, was enticed into an alley by two Negroes who pretended they were going to sell him a pint.

in 1944 and the police began ordering all cars without working meters off the street, all but fifteen of the for-hire operators went on strike. When anyone called up to ask for service, they refused and told the inquirer to ask city hall for an explanation. They could not get the meters repaired, they asserted, since there was only one mechanic in Norfolk who could work on them.[14]

Although City Manager Borland granted the cabs another month to get their meters into shape, when June 1 came around, the operators protested that the devices were beyond repair and obtained another four-month extension. When the meters were still not operating by October 1, the police began to suspect that there might be some connection between the drivers' dislike of the meters and the consistent failure of the devices to function, since the taxi company never seemed to have any trouble with its meters. The cabs were therefore at last required to get their meters working, and by a miraculous transformation the mechanical breakdowns ceased.[15] Of course, many drivers were still absent-minded about knocking down the flag when no policeman was around, and then they were forced to estimate the charges.

Meanwhile, the county trade was suffering from too much competition. The county's free-enterprise system had by the fall of 1944 attracted 250 cars into the business, which fought for a gradually declining trade as soldiers and sailors shipped out of the area. The newcomers resented the special privileges of the 150 county cars which had been licensed to pick up passengers in the city a year earlier. When they tried to assert the same right, the police clamped down. Stiff fines of $50, with $100 for repeaters, took most of the profit out of the practice.[16]

Some of the drivers turned from lesser illegalities to major crimes; robbery was common, and several passengers were even murdered. An indignant city grand jury demanded an investigation of every cab driver in Norfolk, declaring that at least eleven for-hire operators had been sent to the penitentiary in the last five months. Chief Woods protested that the offenders were mostly county drivers as the county had no authority to regulate them. The city, he said, cleared every application with the FBI and

---

[14] *V-P*, January 5, 1944; April 28, 1944, p. 18.
[15] *V-P*, June 1, 1944, p. 16; October 7, 1944, p. 4.
[16] *V-P*, October 6, 1944, p. 20.

denied a license to any man who had a police record. The police
kept as close a check as possible on those who were granted licenses, the chief pointed out; in the last eleven months 75 city
drivers had lost their permits for overcharging, speeding, or hauling "cab-girls."[17]

The city council tried to meet the situation by an even stiffer
ordinance. Each driver was required to have his photograph
posted on the back of the front seat so that passengers might
identify him if necessary. He was required to post a "vacant" or
"on-call" sign so that he could be detected if he refused to give
service. So that the police could check him, he was required to
keep a record of all trips.[18] At the same time the police were
aided in their crusade against cab criminals by the confessions of
three young "cab-girls" whom they picked up. Their stories in-
criminated nearly fifty of the for-hire operators. Since virtually
all of these were county drivers, the county men let out a howl of
outrage that the charges were a plot cooked up by the city operators to drive them out of business.[19] The city drivers decided
that they needed an organization to protect themselves and joined
the Teamsters Union.[20]

The story of the three "cab-girls" was significant of a problem
which had been growing in Norfolk. The oldest was seventeen, a
Texas girl who had come to the city with a sailor in April, 1944,
and drifted into the cab business. Another was sixteen, from
Muncie, Indiana, who had come to Norfolk in August, 1944, to
marry a sailor but had changed her mind. Not yet hardened to
the trade, she was ready after five months to go back home.
Toughest of all was a fifteen-year-old child, who had run away
from her home in Durham, North Carolina, at the age of thirteen.
She had first arrived in Norfolk on September 7, 1942, and had
been twice picked up and sent home. Each time, however, she
had again run into difficulties with her stepmother and returned
to Norfolk.[21]

The calmness with which this North Carolina youngster de-

[17] *V-P*, December 5, 1944, p. 14; December 7, 1944, p. 20.
[18] *V-P*, January 31, 1945, p. 14.
[19] *V-P*, January 18–20, 1945, January 28, 1945, Part II, p. 1; February 6,
1945, p. 12.
[20] *V-P*, February 21, 1945, p. 14.
[21] *V-P*, January 18, 1945, p. 16; February 21, 1945, p. 14.

scribed how she had gone out in a cab with five sailors at one time was a shocking indication of a wartime infection of American youth. The steady growth of juvenile delinquency was a problem not peculiarly Norfolk's; every war town in the country had its uniform-crazy "V-girls", who became "VD-girls" through their contribution to the morale of the armed forces, its youths who were tempted by the easy money to be gained by dabbling in crime. Like other cities, Norfolk had its quota of "latchkey" children, given the run of the town while both parents were working.

The city, however, turned up more than its share of juvenile delinquents because the advertising it had received made it a mecca for discontented children from hundreds of miles around, like the girl from North Carolina. Every week a few runaways drifted in, looking for some sailor, seeking the independence that comes with a job, or merely hunting excitement. Jobs were fairly easy to find for the boys, with employers not too insistent on a birth certificate, but girls had a tougher time and the work they did get was at low pay. One girl looked in vain for a week while she slept in the rest room at the bus station until she was picked up by the police.[22]

Many of those who did get jobs found independence too much for them and drifted into irresponsibility. One fourteen-year-old boy, who had made his way through the fourth grade, was walking past the cotton mill in Danville, where both his parents were working, when he decided to come to Norfolk. Hitching a ride on a truck, he had a $35-a-week job before nightfall. Soon he met a sixteen-year-old New Jersey lad, paroled from a reform school, and the two gave up working, making their home in an old truck-trailer. Out with another sixteen-year-old boy, who had a mother in Norfolk and a father in West Virginia, the Danville youth wondered if he could drive a car. Stealing an auto out of a parking lot, he discovered that he could. The couple then picked up the New Jersey boy and started off to visit the father in West Virginia. On the way they wrecked the car and were hitch-hiking back to Norfolk when the State police picked them up in Farmville.[23]

[22] *V-P*, December 31, 1943, p. 18.
[23] *V-P*, February 6, 1944, Part II, pp. 1, 9.

Other youngsters overdid their working. One boy of sixteen worked six days and three nights a week to pay off a loan and buy a car and a diamond ring until his stepfather was called in by the juvenile court and told to see that the boy took better care of his health. One boy of fifteen, whose father was remarried and living somewhere in the West, was brought to Norfolk from a North Carolina farm. Then his mother followed the ship to another port, leaving him with the apartment and no money. He worked some and stole some until the police caught him. Another sixteen-year-old youth was picked up peddling bootleg liquor.[24]

The girls generally got into trouble with sailors. Lonely runaways or discontented local residents, they sought escape in companionship with friendly servicemen. Dates led to drinking parties and reckless abandon, sometimes to a trip to South Mills for a hasty marriage. This Gretna Green had been set up in North Carolina by a retired farmer named J. G. Etheridge. Being both register of deeds and justice of the peace, he could issue the marriage license and perform the ceremony immediately afterwards under North Carolina law. His willingness to open up his office at any hour of the day or night had built his business up to forty or fifty couples a week.[25]

Some girls seemed to be almost making a profession out of marrying servicemen. One girl at fourteen married a soldier in South Carolina in 1942. When she did not hear from him after he had been shipped overseas, she decided to marry a sailor in Oklahoma a year later. Then the sailor found out about her first marriage and told her he was getting an annulment. She thereupon slipped down to South Mills and married another sailor. She had had a baby before the Federal authorities finally caught up with her a year later.[26] She was topped by an Ohio girl who picked up two sailors and a soldier in six months at a Norfolk skating rink and married all three of them at South Mills. Mr. and Mrs. Etheridge explained that they could not remember faces since they had so many couples coming. They also had a poor memory for names as the girl had given the same name and address each time.[27]

[24] *V-P*, February 6, 1944, Part II, pp. 1, 9.
[25] *V-P*, August 18, 1944, p. 6.
[26] *V-P*, November 10, 1944, p. 20.
[27] *V-P*, August 8, 1944, p. 14; August 18, 1944, p. 6. North Carolina in 1945 enacted a law padlocking this marriage mill.

One West Virginia girl married a sailor at South Mills, found he already had a wife and family in Ohio, and went off to a hotel with another sailor to spite him. Another girl, sixteen, was picked up with a sailor of seventeen in a squalid hotel. The couple had signed the register, presided over by a sixteen-year-old night clerk, as man and wife. She admitted that she was married to another sailor, away at sea. Her husband would tell her that he wanted a divorce and then that he did not; she didn't know what was the matter with him. Her mother was dead, her father was married again. She had never had a home of her own, living with one family after another.[28]

There was little that could be done to mend these broken lives. For the drift girls the police adopted the simple expedient of sending them home when they were picked up. The Travelers Aid cooperated by furnishing funds when necessary; one day the Travelers Aid picked up a girl itself, an eleven-year-old child who was turned back at the bus station.[29] Some of them, however, had no home to go to, and some refused to be sent. When the police picked up two sixteen-year-olds one night and asked them who their parents were, they merely giggled, "A kiddledeedivy doo, wooden chew?"[30]

These were a problem, for the city had no place to put them. Some were crowded into the women's quarters of the city jail as the only available spot, but that was a violation of State law as well as being inhumane. In desperation the city had taken over a room in the building designed for Negro women prisoners on the city farm. The girls under eighteen were confined in this barren, bleak room, day and night, without the slightest provision for anything for them to do. There was no privacy anywhere, even in the bathroom; there were no curtains on the shower, no booths around the toilets. The only health measure was a rule that girls with venereal disease were supposed to use one toilet, those free of infection the other.[31]

The girls attacked the matrons with the chairs, and the chairs were taken away from the room. Then there was nothing left but the cots. The girls set fire to the bed clothes and threw them out

[28] *V-P*, February 6, 1944, Part II, pp. 1, 9; March 21, 1944, p. 14.
[29] *V-P*, January 3, 1944, p. 12.
[30] *V-P*, February 6, 1944, pp. 1, 9.
[31] *V-P*, June 27, 1945, pp. 18, 2.

the window, horrifying the matrons by starting a blaze in the grass below. When the girls finally went on a riot and broke every window in the room, they were transferred back to the city jail for a time. The city applied to the FWA for funds to build adequate detention quarters.[32]

Since reports of youthful delinquencies were protected by the privacy of the Juvenile and Domestic Relations Court, they attracted little public attention until early in 1944. Then Judge Herbert G. Cochran, disturbed by the increasing number of violations coming up before him, embarked on a determined publicity campaign to obtain action to curb them. After telling his story repeatedly to the newspapers and before civic organizations, he asked the city council to bar persons under eighteen from dance halls in which liquor was permitted, but nothing happened.

Two months later he tried again with another request, for an 11:00 P.M. curfew for everyone under eighteen. After six more weeks the council decided to hold hearings on the curfew, and in three more weeks finally adopted it. As enacted, the ordinance provided that the police should send home every child under sixteen found on the streets after eleven or take him home, if necessary. A summons was then to be served on the parents for allowing the child to be out. For good measure the council also approved Judge Cochran's other request, banning persons under eighteen from dance halls where alcoholic beverages were permitted.[33]

Although the city police had been reluctant to accept one more law enforcement task, they found that the new ordinance helped them to enforce others. Two young Negro boys, picked up after eleven, turned out to have been working in a restaurant, and the operator was fined for violating the child labor law; a girl who was questioned proved that she was old enough to be out on the streets but too young to hold the job she had. The police dusted off an old ordinance which prohibited minors from being admitted to poolrooms and swept the youngsters out of the billiard parlors, incidentally sweeping many truants back into the schoolroom. The police remembered another ordinance, adopted back in 1920,

[32] *V-P*, December 31, 1943, p. 18; November 21, 1944, p. 16.
[33] *V-P*, June 4, 1944, Part II, p. 1; July 26, 1944; August 16, 1944, p. 16. Portsmouth adopted a curfew ordinance a week earlier, on August 8, Norfolk County on November 14.

which required the operator of any hotel or rooming house to report within twelve hours the name of any person apparently
under twenty who registered without parent or guardian. This
law was revived and enforced against several rooming-house operators. Judge Cochran handed out stiff punishments to all who
came before him. When parents were brought up for allowing
their children to roam the streets, he gave them the choice of
serving time or moving away; four families left town in two
weeks. He ordered a $100 fine for the operator of a rooming house
who had rented a room to a seventeen-year-old girl without reporting it.[34]

Meanwhile the Navy was cooperating with an equally tough
clean-up campaign. A Joint Army-Navy Disciplinary Control
Board met with civic officials on October 18 to discuss the problem of keeping the servicemen under control. A special liberty
card for sailors under 21 to keep them out of barrooms, where as
civilians they would have been legally barred, was suggested, or
a curfew for all servicemen. Just a week later Admiral Le Breton
took stern action. He ordered that all enlisted men be off the
streets and out of public places from 1:00 A.M. to 5:00 A.M. from
November 1 on. The curfew was in effect at midnight in the
night spots for all practical purposes, since sailors would have to
leave by then to get back to the Base by the deadline.[35]

The indignant complaints of the sailors at this abbreviation of
their liberty echoed to the heavens. Young men yelled the loudest, but one older sailor commented, "They ought to chase those
kids off the street at ten o'clock." One sailor mourned that he
had been meeting his girl every night at one when she quit her
work at the telephone company. "She'll either have to get a day
shift," he complained, "or our romance is ended." The chief criticism came from the order's exemption of commissioned officers.
Enlisted men insisted that this was just one more instance of unfair privileges granted to the officers.

However much the order interfered with the sailor's pursuit of
happiness, it protected their life and property better. The Navy
men were off the streets shortly after midnight, and those who

[34] *V-P*, September 21, 1944, p. 18; September 24, 1944, Part II, p. 1; October 1, 1944, Part II, p. 1.
[35] *V-P*, October 19, 1944, p. 18; October 26, 1944, p. 18.

made a legitimate or illegitimate living off them were forced to close up shop. Profits vanished from the for-hire business since sailors went home while the street cars were still running. The number of robberies declined; the shore patrol arrested fewer sailors. Norfolk after midnight had a sedate look that *Collier's* would never have recognized. The most pungent comment came from the manager of the all-night restaurant in the Greyhound bus station, who pointed out that the curfew had been much more needed a year earlier. Like all of Norfolk's reforms, it had come a little late.[36]

[36] *V-P*, November 26, 1944, Part II, p. 1.

27

THROUGH THE CEILING

THE truce that followed the battle with Richmond over the ration board in February, 1943, turned out to be a permanent peace treaty. The new board under the chairmanship of Raymond C. Mackay operated so smoothly that it was held up by the OPA as a paragon of perfection instead of a horrible example. Representatives of other boards came to Norfolk to study its methods in order to improve their own.[1] The Richmond feud did rear its head again in August when the independent district office was put to death after a brief and fitful life of six months. Suspecting the Machiavellian touch of J. Fulmer Bright, Congressman Harris angrily cried out that the city had been betrayed into the hands of the enemy. General Bright, however, explained that the move was made necessary by Congress's cut of the OPA appropriation and was not inspired by a desire to recapture Norfolk. The district office gave way to a field office under the control of Richmond, and in another three months the field office was reduced to an enforcement department.[2]

To make up for this enforced curtailment of service to Norfolk, the OPA gave the Hampton Roads area the benefit of its first big drive to enforce price ceilings. The OPA had tried to place a lid on prices in the spring of 1942 by ordering prices frozen at the levels of March of that year. This was in effect a request for voluntary compliance since the order was unenforceable; not even the storekeeper himself could be sure of what his March prices had been on every item, and it was virtually impossible to prove any violation. In the first flush of patriotism obedience had been good, but, as shortages increased through 1942, producers got an

[1] *V-P*, February 20, 1944, Part II, p. 2.
[2] *V-P*, August 18, 1943, p. 20; August 19, 1943, p. 20; November 6, 1943, p. 14.

extra fee for favoring wholesalers in shipments, wholesalers collected from the retailers, and retailers passed the charge on to the public. Most businessmen clung to the spirit of the price ceilings in that they felt they should not seek an extortionate profit, but they believed they were justified in raising their own prices whenever they had to pay more to get a product.

The OPA then decided to sit on the lid by introducing a new type of ceiling. For the old system, under which each dealer had his own ceiling for each item, it substituted a new set of standards. A ceiling price was fixed on many brands of foods and grades of meat with some variations permitted according to the class of store. These new price lists were then published in the papers and sent to the stores, which were ordered to post them. It was expected that this would make the customers an enforcement agency, since the public would now know what the ceiling prices were and could report any violations to the local ration board.

This system went into effect throughout the country during 1943 but without the hoped-for results. The customer who knew he was being overcharged paid without protest to make sure he got the meat, and many dealers kept him from seeing the new ceilings. In Norfolk, for example, by July, 1943, it was noticed that many dealers did not have their meat-price charts up.[3] The OPA district office therefore launched a campaign in August to obtain compliance through persuasion. A meeting of 200 grocerymen was held in Blair Junior High School to hear Maurice Bennett, who in the meantime had moved through the alphabet from OCD to OPA, appeal for their patriotic cooperation in fighting the black market. All of them signed the pledge to obey the rationing rules and the price ceilings. A campaign was also launched to have every housewife take a similar pledge.[4]

Unfortunately, no matter how willing a grocer was to obey the regulations, he could not comply and stay in business. In June when the grocers were paying ceiling prices for onions and cabbages, they could buy none. To get these vegetables, they often had to pay as much as, or more than, the retail ceiling, a practice covered up by faked bills. The situation was even worse for meat, which was complicated by ceilings for four different grades. Dis-

[3] *V-P*, July 11, 1943, Part II, p. 1.
[4] *V-P*, August 26, 1943, p. 20.

tributors charged grade A prices and shipped grade C, and retailers who complained got no meat at all. Wholesalers in turn passed the blame back to the farmers, and the farmers blamed the high prices they had to pay for everything.

Difficult as the task was, the OPA decided to try to roll prices back all the way to the producer by starting with the retailer and began the drive by concentrating agents from all over the Southeastern region in Hampton Roads. On October 1 a force of sixty investigators began checking compliance in hundreds of stores and restaurants all over the area. Since this was the first effort at enforcement, they found most stores totally unprepared. OPA regulations were often confusing and unintelligible, and short-handed operators had not bothered to comply with many technicalities. Many meat department managers apparently had not taken the time to study the price charts. They freely quoted the prices they were charging to the investigators and signed their names to the statement.

The general opinion seemed to be that this new move by the OPA was another bid for friendly cooperation, to be followed by conferences to correct the difficulties. This mood was fairly well maintained in the hearings of restaurant operators and dealers in women's apparel. These businessmen were tried by a jury of their peers, the price panel of the local rationing board, fellow merchants, although in different lines of business. Since the price panel could exact no penalty except a voluntary contribution to the Red Cross or the U. S. Treasury, there was no danger that their action would be arbitrary.

The price panel proved moderate and understanding. When two beer dealers were charged with selling for more than their posted ceilings, panel members pointed out that every beer dealer in town was violating the ceilings and that it would be unfair to single out these men.[5] The panel heard the charges brought by the investigators, listened to the merchants' defense, and then reached an agreement with the offender on the penalty, assessing some $600 in voluntary fines, to cover the extra profit made from unintentional violations. Only in one instance did the panel decide that there was wilful violation. It ruled that the overcharges of

[5] *V-P*, October 9, 1943, p. 14.

the Norfolk Undersellers were too serious for it to handle and turned the firm over to the OPA for action.[6]

Norfolk businessmen accepted this method amicably, and only one or two objected to paying the fines. The OPA, however, in order to speed up procedure, brought in a hearing commissioner to sit on some of the charges before they had been heard by the price panel. Most of the grocery stores were called up before the hearing commissioner, who had the power to suspend dealing in all rationed commodities. The merchants trembled at the prospect of being brought up before a judge who had the power virtually to put them out of business for what they considered minor violations. Moreover, they had no faith in the fairness of the judge. It was bad enough to have one set of OPA men bring the charges while another OPA employee decided their justice, but in this case the hearing commissioner was T. Nelson Parker, the Richmond lawyer who had served as General Bright's ambassador in the February battle. Few local people were persuaded that he had wiped himself clean of that association by resigning from the OPA and accepting the present post only as a temporary assignment, entirely independent of Richmond.

Echoes of the old fight were roused again when the OPA called 25 of the Colonial Stores units up for hearings before Parker. Hunter C. Phelan, president of the company and one of Norfolk's leading citizens, at once suspected the justice of the charges, since he had always been insistent that every store obey the rules faithfully. In violent anger he stormed into the hearings in person. Company Counsel W. C. Pender began a careful lawyer's argument in defense of the firm, but President Phelan could not control himself. Jumping to his feet, he broke into Pender's plea to denounce the OPA's "confusions and complications." He complained that the company had had to make more than two million changes in prices and point values to comply with regulations and invited the investigators to examine the company's records for proof that every effort had been made to meet the law. "Our first job is to feed this war critical area," he stormed. "We are feeding this community, and I will not be displaced in the eyes of the people I serve. The question of this company's reputation is at stake. I will not see it smeared and will fight to the end for it."

[6] *V-P*, October 9, 1943, pp. 14, 7; October 16, 1943, p. 14.

When a Government lawyer stood up as if to interrupt, Phelan waved an indignant finger at him and shouted, "I'm going to finish this and there's no use for you to object. I represent something in this community and, by God, you're not going to refute it." Calming down, a little later he agreed that his managers might have been at fault, since it was impossible to find competent help. Commissioner Parker courteously agreed to allow the company the maximum extension of time to prepare a legal defense, even though the hearings were supposed to dispense with all legal technicalities. Feeling better satisfied, President Phelan left the room, which was fortunate for his blood pressure, as a few minutes later another Government lawyer said that "the public had been defrauded" by the Colonial Stores.[7]

The question of the company's honor threatened to protract the proceedings indefinitely. The hearing of the charges against the first store dragged out all day as the company tried to demonstrate its efforts to enforce price ceilings. Processes were speeded up eventually by an agreement to consolidate the charges against the other stores and present them in writing. The manager of the first store explained with disarming frankness why he had not checked the ceilings before he quoted prices to the investigator. "I did not realize the seriousness of the thing," he said. "I was trying to hurry things up. If I had realized the importance, I would have been more careful."[8]

Other managers had more time to think up excuses. They had been mixed up when they recited the prices and had not read the statement they signed. Some were confused about the grade of meats, and some thought the price tags must have fallen into the wrong trays. The one manager who admitted that he had to mark the meat above ceiling prices to show a profit was promptly fired as an evidence of the company's good faith.[9]

The hearings of the charges against scores of other meat dealers presented the same general picture. A few frankly confessed their guilt; one man who had a stall at the city market said that he had been so scared by the OPA investigation that he had sold his stand and quit the business.[10] Most of them presented more

[7] *V-P*, October 8, 1943, pp. 24, 13.
[8] *V-P*, October 12, 1943, pp. 20, 9.
[9] *V-P*, October 17, 1943, Part II, p. 1.
[10] *V-P*, October 10, 1943, Part II, p. 1.

or less ingenious explanations, which were of little help. Virtually all of those brought up were found guilty and suspended from selling meat for thirty or sixty days, depending on the seriousness of the offense. The penalty was much lighter than it appeared, however, since suspension was actually enforced for only one or two weeks, with the rest of the period probationary.

Since it was hard to get enough meat anyhow, the punishment imposed a relatively light penalty on the storekeepers. What hurt much worse was the feeling that they were being punished for doing what everyone else was doing. Even the stores which had escaped the OPA net seemed not to have been less guilty but more careful. One manager, for example, who had no prices marked in his meat trays, went to the OPA price charts to consult them before he quoted prices to the investigators. In the meantime, his clerks, who seemed to have much better memories, went on selling meat without looking up the prices.[11] How widespread violations were was revealed when charges were brought against one of the stores owned by a member of the local price panel, who promptly handed in his resignation.[12]

Grocers felt that the OPA's "crack-down" policy was branding them as profiteers in the eyes of the nation, whereas most of the violations had been minor ones, forced on them by the overcharges of the wholesalers. It seemed decidedly unfair to punish them while the distributors went unmolested. As indignation smouldered, another member of the local price panel, Harvey W. Barker, Jr., resigned to organize the Norfolk Independent Food Dealers Association to protect the merchants against the OPA. "The dealers have not been given a fair chance," declared Barker, as he announced plans for making a test case of the OPA's right to hand out suspensions.[13]

The man in charge of price control in the OPA's field office in Norfolk, Louis J. Smithwick, ignored his administrative loyalty to denounce "the present hysterical enforcement methods." General Bright in Richmond read his statement in the afternoon papers and wired a request for his resignation. Smithwick quit next day

[11] *V-P*, October 10, 1943, Part II, p. 1.
[12] *V-P*, October 13, 1943, p. 18.
[13] *V-P*, October 14, 1943, p. 22; October 15, 1943, p. 26.

and went back to his old job as secretary of the Tidewater Whole-sale Grocery and Feed Association.[14]

In reply a voice spoke up for the consumers. John C. Russell, chairman of the OPA's Hampton Roads Labor Advisory Committee, declared that for months his group had insisted that the local OPA office was stacked with individuals who were trying to hamper the execution of the price programs and now the charge was proven. Russell also blasted Barker's new organization, accusing it of attempting to weaken the war effort. The association indignantly denied any attempt to fight the OPA. Its principal object, reported the new board of directors, "is to crush the black market in Norfolk. Members of the association will have nothing to do with such a market. On the contrary, they will walk hand in hand with the OPA and make a profit if they can."[15]

One reason for this sudden change of front was the hope that the OPA's enforcement drive would succeed in forcing wholesale prices back to their legitimate levels. Already cabbage had tumbled down from its peak of $2.75 a basket, above the retail ceiling, to the legal $1.60. With evidence furnished by the accused merchants, the OPA was able to get at the black market wholesalers. A $6,000 damage suit against one local produce dealer was launched and a meat distributor in Newport News agreed to make a voluntary settlement.[16] Unfortunately, however, the OPA agents could not stay. The staff of investigators who remained in Norfolk had a hopeless task, and prices again soared upward. By the spring of 1944 onions were selling in local stores at twice the OPA ceilings. Retailers explained that the lowest price on the wholesale market was $9.00 a bag, while the ceiling was $3.89.[17]

Beer was as scarce as onions at ceiling prices. Distributors were respecting the OPA rules, but there was not enough beer to slake all the thirsty throats in Norfolk. One naive dealer called up his distributor to find out why he was getting no beer. "Hasn't the truck been around this week?" the distributor asked. "I haven't

---

[14] *V-P*, October 19, 1943, p. 18; October 20, 1943, p. 20.

[15] *V-P*, October 19, 1943, p. 18; October 21, 1943, p. 20. It was also announced that members would appeal their punishments to Washington and that proceedings thereafter would be secret.

[16] *V-P*, October 17, 1943, Part II, p. 1.

[17] *V-P*, April 20, 1944, p. 16.

seen one of your trucks for four months," the retailer replied. A few questions disclosed the answer. His competitors had discovered that a "tip" to the truck driver insured supplies. "We are not supposed to talk about that system," one dealer explained. "All we do is tip the driver a few dollars on each delivery of beer, depending on how much he brings in to us. If we forget to tip, he forgets to stop in on his next round. We can't discuss it. We might not get any more beer."[18]

The tipping dealers naturally passed this charge on to their customers and provoked complaint from them. This had been one of the sailors' criticisms taken up by the Norfolk Citizens' Committee, which had asked the OPA to proclaim an area ceiling for beer retailers. The harried OPA, realizing the problem of setting price levels fair for all concerned, as well as the difficulty of enforcing the regulation, worked on the question for months before it found a workable answer. Finally on July 1, 1944, it announced its solution. Dealers would be put into three classifications according to their price levels of April, 1943. Those in 1-B would be permitted to charge 20 cents for ordinary beer and 25 cents for premium brands; 2-B ceilings were 15 and 25 cents, and 3-B levels were 11 and 16 cents, the normal pre-war prices with an extra cent for increased taxes.

President Bibb of the Norfolk Citizens' Committee promptly denounced the new regulation because it permitted a 25-cent maximum and seemed to approve the current high prices. The OPA thereupon tried to satisfy him by "explaining" that all dealers would be classified as 3-B unless they could prove they were charging more in October, 1941. Since only a few swank night clubs had been getting more than fifteen cents then, the order promised a roll-back for most taverns.[19] At this point it was the retailers' turn to blow up. The 3-B ceilings provided a fair, if not fat profit on beer bought at the wholesale ceilings. Little of the beverage was being obtained at the legal prices, however; dealers were paying as much as $3.08 to $3.25 a case for unlisted brands, which they were supposed to sell for $2.64 at 3-B prices. When they discovered, therefore, that most of them were going to be classified 3-B, they decided on stern measures.

[18] *V-P*, April 20, 1944, p. 18.
[19] *V-P*, July 2, 1944, Part II, p. 1; July 4, 1944, p. 12.

On Friday afternoon, July 7, the beer dealers announced that they would be unable to operate under the new ceilings and would therefore be forced to stop selling bottled beer on Monday when the new rule went into effect. Just to make sure that no one was crazy enough to suppose he could make money at these prices, the dealers planned to have a special committee to check on "chiselers." Monday was a very dry day. Sailors threatened to empty the barrels of draft dealers, who met their ceiling problem by selling more foam, until the tavern keepers had to ration one glass to a customer. Other thirsty sailors made the best of a bad situation by trying to drink wine. In one block two drugstores, which were not on strike because they had been classified in 2-B, were startled when servicemen suddenly swarmed over their counters instead of going to the customary sailors' hangout at the nearby taproom.[20]

The thirsting public condemned the tavern keepers. The Kiwanians talked about organizing a buyers' strike against the dealers. The Department of Justice was said to be investigating the beer blockade. The A. B. C. Board stared steadily in the other direction. An organization with the tongue-tangling name of the "Association of Civic and Union Cost of Living Committee sponsored by the Hampton Roads OPA Labor Advisory Committee" called upon the retailers to join them in a drive to roll back wholesale prices. An OPA price executive from Richmond told the dealers they could expect no relief until the brewers had their prices rolled back. He also told them there was only one brewer that the Richmond office could control.[21]

In the meantime, however, the local ration board had let it be known that they might have made some mistakes in their original classifications, which had placed all but 25 of Norfolk's 700 beer dealers in 3-B. The taproom men rushed to file appeals for reclassification, and all but 21 of those who applied were raised into the 2-B, or 15 and 20 cents, class. After a long, dry week the beer began to flow again.[22]

Fortunately there was plenty of water to drink, for the city's second line to Lake Prince had been in operation for more than a

[20] *V-P*, July 8, 1944, p. 12; July 10, 1944, p. 14; July 12, 1944, p. 16.
[21] *V-P*, July 9, 1944, Part II, p. 1; July 14, 1944, p. 18.
[22] *V-P*, July 9, 1944, Part II, p. 1; July 19, 1944, p. 14.

year. The new line needed to supply Virginia Beach, however, was not finished in time for the summer trade. As the flood of tourists threatened to empty the pipes over the long Fourth of July week-end, Admiral Le Breton saved the day by calling the Navy out. Both the Army and the Navy placed the Beach out-of-bounds for servicemen until the crisis was past, keeping them at Ocean View over the holiday.[23]

Milk was not so plentiful for those who insisted on using that for a beverage. That problem had reared its head in the summer of 1943 when City Health Commissioner J. C. Sleet had discovered that much of the milk being shipped into the area from hundreds of miles away would not test above grade C, while a city ordinance prohibited the sale of any but grade A milk. Since enforcing the law would mean cutting the city's milk supply in half, Doctor Sleet conferred with City Manager Borland, who agreed that it was better to change the ordinance. The proposal to label the imported milk as grades B and C brought opposition from the distributors, who feared that the public would not buy the lower grades, especially since they would be sold for the same price as grade A. The city council tried to appease the milk dealers by an exercise in semantics, calling the lower grades only "Norfolk Approved Pasteurized Milk," but that brought on so much protest that the council finally accepted the model ordinance recommended by the U. S. Public Health Service, which it had rejected two years before, calling for specific grade labels.[24] Norfolkians went on paying grade A prices for B and C milk as before, but they at least knew what they were getting.

By the summer of 1944, as American soldiers fought their way out of the Normandy beach heads and General Patton's Third Army began its race for the Rhine, the war seemed almost over in Norfolk. Everything the city had been demanding for years to take care of its excess population was being delivered at last, now that the excess population had already started home. Except for Leigh Memorial, which was not to be finished until the end of the year, the work on the hospitals was done. The new de Paul Hospital on Granby Street was occupied in May, and old St. Vincent's

[23] V-P, June 29, 1944, p. 18; July 6, 1944, p. 16.
[24] V-P, December 26, 1943, Part II, p. 1; January 12, 1944, p. 14.

was immediately abandoned.[25] Extensions were being completed to Granby High and the Titustown School, and the FWA had approved a grant to enlarge the Bay View School.[26] Even the long-delayed sewage-disposal system got under way as the Hampton Roads Sanitation District Commission reached an agreement with the FWA to share expenses.[27]

Life was easier for the average Norfolkian than it had been for four years, in spite of the polio epidemic that alarmed parents, in spite of the smell of garbage rotting because the city could not hire anyone to collect it. The crowds were thinner downtown, the bus service better, except for the luckless souls living on the end of the shortened lines. Food was easier to find. The OPA cut point values in March and April. In September the OPA optimistically took most meat cuts off the ration list and left nothing on the blue point list but canned fruits and tomatoes.

As Patton's army ran out of gas at the German border and the war settled down to another winter, however, it turned out this action had been too hasty. By fall a new shortage had appeared, and people were standing in line for cigarets. Butter got so scarce that a customer in a Main Street cafe was smacked over the head with a plate when he asked for a second piece.[28] Then came the OPA's "Christmas present to the nation" when outstanding ration stamps were cancelled, followed by the return of most foods to the ration list. Coal was scarce and went under informal rationing. To save coal supplies, the brownout was introduced early in 1945, and Granby Street returned to the appearance of its dimout days.

One shortage which had never disappeared, at least on paper, was the labor shortage. The Navy Yard clamored the loudest for more men but suffered a net loss of 4,000 during 1944, as war workers started their exodus back home to look for jobs with peacetime security. Appeals to their patriotism would have been more successful if it had not been for the policy practiced by the Yard, in common with most war plants, of holding labor to care

[25] *V-P*, May 13, 1944, p. 10. One reason the civilian hospitals never reached the overflowing point was that the Naval Base Hospital began admitting servicemen's families in February, 1943, taking a substantial load off the city's hospitals.

[26] *V-P*, December 31, 1944, Part II, pp. 1, 3.

[27] *V-P*, April 14, 1944, p. 18.

[28] *V-P*, October 14, 1944, p. 12.

for peak loads, which meant that men stood idle during slack periods and earned the Yard a reputation for encouraging loafing.

The War Manpower Commission exercised its ingenuity to devise new regulations to herd workers into the war plants. In the spring of 1944 it introduced a system of manpower priorities. All essential employers were to file requests for priorities, and all available workers would be referred to the plant with the highest priority until its needs were satisfied. Ceilings were placed on all employers at their January level, and no firm was permitted to have more workers than it had in that month unless it obtained special permission. These two devices together were intended to make sure that all workers moved into the most urgent jobs without being attracted into the less essential industries.[29]

The establishment of a camp for German prisoners of war in the spring of 1944 at Camp Ashby on Beach Bordward furnished a little relief to the labor situation, but nothing could satisfy the enormous demands listed by the war plants. These demands, the WMC was beginning to realize, were intended more for bargaining purposes than to portray actual need; although the industries kept clamoring for more men, they refused to take as many women as they had asked for. The WMC office therefore thawed women out of the job freeze in the summer of 1944, permitting employers to hire them without restrictions. Gate-hiring of men was also simplified by permitting workers in less essential industries to go into war plants by submitting a certificate of prior employment instead of requiring them to obtain a release first.[30]

The priority referral plan met with much complaint from the workers. When a man applied at the USES office, he was assigned to the job for which he was most needed, not to the one which he best liked. Once he accepted a position he was frozen in it; releases could be pried out of the Navy Yard only with a crow-bar. If he quit without a release, he could not legally hold another job for sixty days. The result was a thriving black market in labor, as the WMC did not have the staff to police the hundreds of little employers all over the city, who were too busy to keep up with the complicated regulations anyway. Moreover, private enter-

---

[29] *V-P*, March 24, 1944, p. 18; April 9, 1944, Part II, p. 1; Area Office, War Manpower Commission, "History," p. 27.

[30] *V-P*, June 3, 1944, p. 12; Area Office, War Manpower Commission, "History," p. 31.

prise, over which the WMC had no control, was often more lucrative than an overtime job at the Navy Yard. The employment agency reported indignantly that one expert electrician was running a bar, another operating a taxi.[31]

The WMC fought the situation as valiantly as it could. It enforced its employment ceilings by cutting off from the services of USES all firms which failed to declare their ceilings. This at least somewhat reduced the demand for the available labor.[32] It appointed a steering committee of citizens to discuss ways of getting men into war jobs. The committee suggested a drive on persons engaged in illegal activities, threatening them with arrest under the vagrancy laws unless they took a war job. Nothing came of this proposal, but the work-or-fight threat of James F. Byrnes of the Office of War Mobilization frightened several hundred 4-F's into the Navy Yard.[33] The local WMC office at last began a compliance drive in the spring of 1945, which revealed that 63 of 294 firms inspected had obeyed all the regulations. Of a total of 8,055 workers covered by the inspections 958 had been hired illegally. Almost all of this bootleg labor was voluntarily turned loose by the employers.[34]

While the homeward-bound war workers were intensifying the labor shortage, they were relieving the housing shortage. By the fall of 1943 the last nail had been driven, the last grass seed planted on virtually all of the vast housing projects, which had added 14,166 new homes on the Norfolk side of the river, just about one new house for every three that had been there in 1940.[35] The problem of finding places for war workers to live had,

[31] V-P, August 18, 1944, p. 18.

[32] Area Office, War Manpower Commission, "History," p. 28. This action was taken in September, 1944.

[33] V-P, September 4, 1944, p. 14; January 11, 1945, p. 16.

[34] Area Office, War Manpower Commission, "History," p. 25.

[35] V-P, January 2, 1944, Part II, p. 1. These homes included: 7,132 units, privately-owned, but FHA-financed; 2,442 permanent units owned by the Navy or the Norfolk Housing Authority; 4,592 temporary units owned by FPHA. In addition there were 250 trailers and 540 dormitory beds. Similar figures for the Portsmouth side were: 3,258 FHA units; 1,673 permanent, publicly-owned; 6,472 temporary FPHA units. Portsmouth also had 2,450 trailers and 2,222 dormitory units. There was in addition a substantial amount of private building during 1940 and 1941, which was not under the war housing program. Privately-owned trailers, perhaps 3,000 in number, are not included in the above figures.

in fact, been so thoroughly solved that the War Housing Center closed its doors on April 1, 1944. The public housing projects alone had room for all who might come.

The over-all housing problem, however, had not been solved but merely transformed. Under the rules established early in 1942 the families of servicemen were ineligible for residence in any of the newer projects unless they happened to number a war worker among their members. These service families had been squeezing in wherever they could, but in 1944 they were coming in ever-increasing numbers. The USO information center in the old city hall reported that it had received 616 applications for rooms in October, 1943, but by June, 1944, the monthly total had reached 7,676, practically all of them servicemen and their families. Not all of them could be placed, especially those with children; only 4,433 of those who applied in June found quarters. One Navy warrant officer who arrived with his wife and five children went bedless for three nights, parking the older children with friends, while the parents slept in the car with the youngest child.[36]

The hotels worked out a scheme for rationing their rooms which was recommended to the rest of the nation by the WPB. Each hotel agreed to reserve some rooms every night until six to take care of essential war travelers, and guests were limited to a five-day stay. The hotels promised to work together to hunt for rooms for guests who had to be turned away. The Tidewater Hotel Association advertised in out-of-town newspapers to warn off summer visitors, asking them to stay away until victory.[37]

The hotels and the USO information center provided only for temporary quarters while the families looked for more permanent homes. On Sewells Point Road 200 apartments for service families were going up, the first such housing to be built since the completion of Benmoreell back in 1941, but that was a mere drop in the bucket. To keep all available homes mobilized, the city's USO council rushed to fill the gap as soon as the news of the closing of the War Housing Center was announced. A grant from the War Fund's surplus enabled the Norfolk Housing Authority to keep the same service going as the Housing Information Cen-

[36] *V-P*, July 28, 1944, p. 6; September 24, 1944, Part II, p. 1.
[37] *V-P*, March 7, 1944, p. 12; July 28, 1944, p. 12.

ter. In spite of generous response to its appeals for furnished quarters, the Housing Information Center found its burden constantly increasing. In its first month of operation, April, 1944, it received 495 applications and was able to place 356 of these families. In January, 1945, 1,641 applications came in and homes could be found for only 531.[38]

Every project had its waiting lists. One reporter counted 4,500 names on the waiting lists of the public housing projects with thousands more waiting to get on.[39] When the Navy decided to put 150 more names on the waiting list for Oakdale Farms, Navy officers stood in line for 24 hours to get their names down.[40] So urgent was the shortage that the National Housing Agency began to plan for more public housing for the area. There was also talk of more FHA loans to encourage private builders. It seemed almost like old times again when Otto Hollowell announced that local agencies would not look with favor on any more permanent construction in the area.[41]

[38] *L-D*, March 8, 1945, p. 4.
[39] *L-D*, May 7, 1945, p. 12.
[40] *V-P*, November 15, 1944, p. 18.
[41] *V-P*, February 10, 1945, p. 12.

28

VICTORY

EVEN before the Civilian Defense organization had been perfected, it had started to fall apart. As early as October, 1942, South Norfolk had discovered that it could no longer get volunteers to man its control center at night and had asked the Norfolk warning center to transfer calls at off-hours to the police station, and Norfolk County had taken a similar step the following May. By the fall of 1943 the confidence inspired by victories in the Mediterranean spurred on a more rapid demobilization. The Army antiaircraft command dropped its direct telephone line from the Norfolk warning center in September, and South Norfolk dropped its control center altogether. Public morale was increased when the Army relieved the airplane spotters of the Aircraft Warning Service from active duty on October 4, even though this move was as much the result of improved radar equipment as it was of growing confidence. In November the Red Cross stopped manning its direct phone at night, and the Naval Base gave up its control center.[1]

All of this led to confusion for the volunteers at the Norfolk warning center. Instead of making practically all of their calls over direct lines, they had to place them over the regular telephone system through the operator. The array of alternate numbers was a source of delay and confusion. When the volunteers passed on the test white flashes which they received over the CARW equipment, the person on the other end of the line often did not know what it was all about. When one of the Navy officers who had been listed to receive the calls from the warning center was aroused after midnight by a test flash, he asked whether this disturbance would go on all night. On the morning of the

[1] Memorandum in Civilian Defense: Norfolk Warning Districts, 1943, file, NWHC records.

November 17 daylight drill no one in Norfolk County could be located at all.[2]

At the end of the year the Army decided to cut down on some of the expense of operating the CARW equipment and closed several of the warning centers, adding Suffolk and Franklin to the calls to be made by the Norfolk volunteers. This move was kept secret to keep it from being interpreted as one more excuse for breaking up the Civilian Defense system. The organization was put on the alert by a blackout on January 11, 1944, the first test called by the Army since the daylight confusion of November 17. This time the signals came in their proper order, and no one got mixed up. There were few complaints of lights being left on in spite of the continued difficulty in hearing the siren. There were some protests over the timing of the blackout which blanketed a radio address by President Roosevelt. In several hotels and apartment houses managers threw the main switches to cut off the lights and incidentally shut off the radios. Democrats jestingly said the Republicans had arranged the blackout to keep listeners from hearing the President's talk, while Republicans replied that the Democrats had planned the test to keep the people by their radios.[3]

Next day the Army announced that drills would be held thereafter only once every three months. Coordinator Marshall took advantage of this relaxation to reorganize the warning center, which was having its troubles in finding volunteers. He worked out a system to let his own office force handle the calls during working hours, while the operator at the VEPCO switchboard, which maintained a 24-hour schedule, took over the calls at other times. Since a single operator could not put through all the calls very rapidly, the VEPCO girl was asked to notify only five persons of surprise tests or actual air raids. These five Civilian Defense heads would then fan the calls out to the other persons to be warned.[4]

[2] Memorandum, Civilian Defense: Norfolk Warning Districts, 1943, file, NWHC records. The operator's call sheet for the November 17 drill, however, shows that Norfolk County was reached as usual.

[3] V-P, January 12, 1944, p. 14; Civilian Defense: Blackouts, Incidents, file, NWHC records.

[4] Civilian Defense: Norfolk Warning District, 1944, file, NWHC records. Volunteers went off duty at the warning center January 22.

The new system got its first chance to go into operation three months later. At 9:30 P.M. on April 13 the warning yellow signal announced an impending blackout. The VEPCO operator passed the flash along to Coordinator Marshall and his aides, who relayed the message to the other centers. Then twenty minutes later, instead of the scheduled blue, there came a white, or all clear. The test, it appeared, had been scheduled for Pennsylvania, but someone in Third Service Command headquarters had accidentally included Virginia. The white went out to all the Civilian Defense centers, and the sirens sounded the all clear. Someone heard the sirens and switched off the street lights. The public, waiting for the promised drill, automatically began turning off its lights. Fortunately, most people missed the alarm entirely, and the lights gradually came on again.[5]

Virginia's scheduled test came the following week on April 18. Norfolkians who had turned off their lights on the all clear the week before now forgot to turn them off on the blue or even the red. Some people did not hear the sirens, and those who did hear them could not tell what signal was being given. All over town lights glared on through the blackout in stores and homes, forgotten by a public grown careless. In Norfolk, as elsewhere, no one seemed to take a blackout seriously anymore.[6]

Coordinator Marshall decided it was about time to call the whole thing off. The remaining military warning lines had meanwhile been disconnected, and the direct phone to Portsmouth was the only one of the original ten still in use. Calls over the regular telephone system took so long the blackout was likely to be delayed. Many wardens were not taking their jobs seriously, and those who were found that the public did not care. Marshall told Governor Darden that he thought there should be no more blackouts, but Third Service Command neither called blackouts nor called them off.[7]

While the Army in Baltimore deliberated over holding further drills, its Norfolk branch dismantled the equipment for calling them. On May 29, 1944, the Norfolk Wing of the First Fighter

[5] Civilian Defense: Blackouts, Incidents, file, NWHC records.
[6] Civilian Defense: Blackouts, Incidents, file, NWHC records.
[7] Marshall to Darden, April 19, 1944, Civilian Defense: Correspondence, Richmond, file, NWHC records.

Command closed up the information center, doing it gracefully at last. The volunteers there had been thrown into confusion the previous October when a brusque announcement from the War Department in Washington had demobilized the Aircraft Warning Service without prior notice, and it was not until later that the women had learned that they would still be needed. This time the local commander was able to give all the volunteers advance warning, and they knew that their job was ended before they read it in the papers. The CARW wires were ripped out, and J. Branham Cooke's force of volunteers also received an honorable discharge on June 9.[8]

The soldiers too left town. By July the Norfolk Wing was inactivated. The information center equipment was moved across Hampton Roads to Langley Field where Air Force trainees could practice with it. The men who had manned the antiaircraft guns on "No Man's Land" and the Sarah Constant Shrine in Ocean View since the week after Pearl Harbor moved out. The Army took down the observation tower on the grounds at Lincoln School and vacated Lafayette Park. It prepared to dismantle the barracks erected in Lee Park only the year before to house the soldiers of the Norfolk Wing, but asked permission to turn the WAC building over to the USO as quarters for servicemen's families.[9]

Coordinator Marshall also began dismantling. He had done some economizing in February by moving the Civilian Defense Volunteer Office in with his own, eliminating one secretary, and dropping the special salvage telephone. When the public relations secretary resigned at the end of July, he closed up the public relations office. Some of the emergency medical stations had begun folding up the previous fall, and now all the supplies were moved into a central storage place.

What was left of the Civilian Defense organization was called out to stand by in September when a hurricane roared up the Atlantic Coast and threatened to send a tidal wave swirling through Norfolk. Zone Warden M. G. Duffy of Ocean View mobilized his men to prepare for evacuating his district. The antici-

---

[8] *V-P*, May 29, 1944, p. 12; Civilian Defense: Cooke, J. B., file, NWHC records.

[9] *V-P*, August 6, 1944, Part II, p. 1; November 9, 1944, p. 18.

pated disaster was averted, however, when the storm swerved out to sea and struck the city only a glancing blow at low tide. The wardens helped to repair the damage in Ocean View, but there was no need for any of the other Civilian Defense groups to function.[10]

Not one member of the Civilian Defense volunteers was summoned a month later when the first bomb finally landed in Norfolk; in fact, it was not until the day after that anyone knew it had fallen. The cook in the home of James M. Wolcott noticed a loud thud on the afternoon of October 12, but paid no further attention. Next day the gardener came in to announce that there was a big hole in the back yard with something sticking out of it. The Navy came and dug up a 235-pound bomb which had accidentally fallen off one of its planes.[11]

Finally in November the Army announced officially what everyone had long taken for granted: there would be no more blackouts. Coordinator Marshall had 28 telephones removed from his control center, and the wardens packed away their tin hats and armbands. Six weeks later, just as the Battle of the Bulge was breaking, State Coordinator Wyse issued a warning that the Army was considering the possibility of a "buzz-bomb" attack and that Civilian Defense groups should be kept on the alert. Coordinator Marshall dutifully sent notices to all his department heads, asking them to keep their staff alerted for such occasion as might arise.[12]

Not even a buzz-bomb, however, could frighten Norfolk in 1945. The Civilian Defense organization had fallen apart, and not all the king's horses and all the king's men could put it together again. All that survived were the auxiliary police, still waiting to be called to active duty to aid the regular force, and the volunteer firemen, who were keeping their engines proudly polished. The only other protective force that was left was the Virginia Protective Force, by now the Virginia State Guard, with its little brother, the Virginia Reserve Militia.

The First Battalion had come a long way since it had been relieved from the grind of sentry duty on the Elizabeth River

[10] V-P, September 15, 1944; Civilian Defense: Histories file, NWHC records.
[11] V-P, October 13, 1944, p. 22.
[12] Civilian Defense: Norfolk Warning District, 1944, file, NWHC records.

bridge early in 1942. Under its new commander, Lieutenant Colonel James W. Roberts, who had taken over when Colonel J. Addison Hagan had joined the Marines in 1942, the last bit of raggedness had been ironed out by weekly drills. The battalion had carried on even when it had had to surrender its rifles for unmilitary-looking shotguns during the summer of 1942. The State had made summer drills more comfortable by supplying cotton khaki uniforms to supplement the heavy wool outfits, which the city had been forced to pay for back in 1941. The War Department had also issued them the spruce green uniforms turned in by the youths of the Civilian Conservation Corps, although they were a tight fit on the middle-aged members of the V. P. F.

By September, 1942, the entire battalion was ready to spend a week end at Camp Pendleton on maneuvers, marching proudly in review before Governor Darden. Interest was added to the drills by a cup donated by the V. M. I. Club as a prize for the most efficient company. As a result, the battalion showed marked improvement in its reviews at the summer encampments at Camp Pendleton in 1943. Target practice at the Lakewood rifle range in August increased the accuracy of the volunteers' marksmanship. When the OPA issued Ration Book Number 4 in October, the V. P. F. was called upon to guard the books until they had been given out.

In tribute to the battalion's record Colonel Roberts was named Norfolk's First Citizen of 1943, and the companies responded by even better performance. The War Department cooperated by returning their rifles and issuing them standard Army uniforms. When the battalion held a public review on May 21, 1944, under its new name of the State Guard, its soldiers could hardly be distinguished from the old National Guard in spite of their expanded waistlines. The waistlines shrank slightly during vigorous week-end maneuvers held at Camp Pendleton each month of the summer. By August General E. E. Goodwyn, state commander of the Guard, pronounced the First Battalion the most efficient in the State.[13] All this had been accomplished in the face of heavy casualties caused by the draft and war jobs. As the battalion

[13] *V-P*, June 13, 1943, Part II, p. 1; December 12, 1943, Part II, p. 1; August 28, 1944, p. 12; *Report of the Adjutant General of the State of Virginia*, 1942–1944.

celebrated its fourth birthday in 1945, it called for fifty recruits to bring it up to its authorized strength of 353 men and officers. In four years it had lost more than 700 members.[14]

Still in action, too, were the Virginia Reserve Militia, who demonstrated their vigor by turning out in a state-wide mobilization on April 22, 1945. The three companies from the city joined five others in a muster in South Norfolk, reviewed in person by the state commander, Brigadier General S. Gardner Waller. The V. R. M., better known as the "Minute Men," had been formed in June, 1942, as an organization of sportsmen to back up the V. P. F. in emergencies. Under no requirement to drill, they furnished their own weapons; all that the State provided was the V. R. M. insigne worn on the right breast of the hunting jacket, or on the authorized green uniform, if the member chose to buy one. The three Norfolk companies had never had any occasion to be called to active duty, except to stand by during the September hurricane.[15]

No further emergencies were to be expected, now that Norfolk was preparing for the end of the war. For months a stream of discharged soldiers and sailors had been trickling into the city and soon the returning veterans would become a flood. W. T. Wright, vice-president of the Royster Guano Company, gathered a number of public-spirited citizens to make plans to receive them. When the plans had reached a definite stage, the city council on November 14, 1944, formally appointed a Veterans Assistance Committee of a hundred members. The committee, with Wright as chairman, promptly approved the idea of establishing a Veterans Information and Service Center. Raymond C. Mackay, who had organized the Civilian Defense control center and put the ration board back on its feet, was named as director. The city agreed to provide quarters and equipment in the old city hall, and the United War Fund allotted $25,000 for operating expenses.

As a full-time assistant director, Lieutenant Sidney Ussher, who had been doing rehabilitation work at the Naval Base, was borrowed from the Navy. Mrs. Ussher, who had had some experience in social service work, was named special consultant. Space

[14] V-P, February 20, 1945, p. 14.
[15] V-P, April 23, 1945, p. 12; Report of the Adjutant General of the State of Virginia, 1942–1945.

was provided for representatives from the Red Cross, the Veterans Administration, and the U. S. Employment Service so that the veteran might find the answers to all his questions in one spot. Fully organized and ready for business, the center opened its doors on March 14, 1945.[16]

Day by day Norfolkians waited for the imminent announcement of the German surrender when suddenly they were shocked by unexpected news. On April 12, while newsboys were delivering the afternoon papers with headlines revealing that the Americans were only 57 miles from Berlin, A. J. Hollingsworth, director of the Goodwill Industries, was driving past the Norfolk Newspapers Building when a news bulletin interrupted the program on his car radio. Stopping his car, he called out to the *Pilot*'s city editor on his way to work. "There's a flash coming over the radio," he said, "that the President is dead. What have you heard?" Without waiting to reply, the city editor bounded up the stairs and rushed into the wire room to see the news coming over the teletype.

In the newsroom telephones jangled as hundreds of others called up, hoping they had not heard correctly. "Tell me it isn't so," voices pleaded. "There's nothing to that report, is there?" In the Y. W. C. A. diners in pleasant conversation pushed their trays along the rack until they reached the cashier. As she announced to each one, "The President is dead," talk suddenly lost its importance, and customers walked away in stunned silence. All over the city flags dropped to half-mast. Sailors who had come to the Moran Avenue USO for a dance instead sat quietly through a memorial service.[17]

To Norfolkians, as much as to any Americans, Franklin D. Roosevelt had been a personal friend. They remembered his cheery smile on that scorching July day when they had last seen him five years before. They recalled how he had taken office when the country seemed trembling on the brink of dictatorship and had inspired the nation with a new conception of democracy, the idea that men must care for their brothers, even if they are poor and lowly. They could not forget how they had followed him

[16] *V-P*, November 18, 1944, p. 12; "Veterans Information Center," *Know*, July, 1945, pp. 127, 144, 145.
[17] *V-P*, April 13, 1945, pp. 22, 19.

in his fight to contain the dangerous infection of Nazism when much of the nation had been afraid. No one could replace Franklin D. Roosevelt, but Death had made a new president, a humble man named Harry S. Truman.

No matter how President Truman—how strange the phrase sounded—might turn out, it was too late for the change to make much difference in Europe. As German defenses crumbled, the end could be only a matter of days. On Saturday night, April 28, when a broadcast from San Francisco announced that news of the German surrender might be expected momentarily, Norfolk started to celebrate. The sky to the north was full of light and sound as Navy ships turned on their searchlights and blew their whistles. Restaurants and taverns closed up to get out of the way of the celebration. Auxiliary police called headquarters to ask for their instructions on handling the crowds. The staff in the *Virginian-Pilot* newsroom stood by, waiting for confirmation to get out an extra. Instead a half hour later came official word from President Truman that the report was without foundation.[18]

When the news came at last, there was no moment to celebrate. On Monday morning, May 7, the Associated Press announced that the Germans had surrendered. The story was precise enough to show that it was true, but no one else announced it. All day long Norfolkians, certain that the war was over, waited for official confirmation but had to go to bed without it. Next morning at nine o'clock President Truman gave the official word in a radio broadcast. At the end of the speech sirens, bells, and horns let loose, but the edge had been taken off the excitement. A steady rain dampened whatever high spirits might have been left in the celebrants. Although the larger stores closed according to prearranged plans, the rest stayed open without incident. That night special services in the city's churches rendered thanks for victory in Europe and prayed that triumph in the Pacific might not be too long delayed.[19]

The war against Japan, however, was not to be Norfolk's war, and peace seemed almost here. Governor Darden revoked the State's blackout rules and announced that the State OCD would close on June 30, along with the national OCD. Colonel Borland

[18] *V-P*, April 29, 1945, Part II, p. 1.
[19] *L-D*, May 8, 1945.

talked the matter over in Richmond before he announced that the city's Civilian Defense office would close the same day. For months there had been little to do in the VEPCO office. Mrs. May Potter, Coordinator Marshall's capable secretary, closed up files and shut up shop. The auxiliary firemen and policemen waited hopefully for an extension of their life, but their organizations too came to an end on June 30. Only the salvage volunteers lingered on, gathering a record half-million pounds of waste paper on July 29.

By the end of June shiploads of soldiers returning from Europe were coming into Hampton Roads on their way to redeployment, but spreading the atmosphere of victory. On July 22, a Portuguese freighter looking for coal came into Hampton Roads, the first neutral vessel to enter the port since early in 1942. The Navy announced that it would close up its Landing Force Equipment Depot in the fall and sell the plant back to the Ford Motor Company, and the Army promised to return the grain elevator pier to private hands. The Navy turned the Nansemond and Cavalier hotels back to their owners on July 1, but visitors too eager to wait for their reopening swarmed over Virginia Beach on the July 4 week end to give it its biggest crowd in history, or slept on the beach at Ocean View.

The first postwar problems reared their head as the city was reminded that in peacetime it would have to stand on its own financial feet. The State ended five years of debate over who should pay the cost of new quarters for women prisoners by ordering the city to start to work on the project. Realizing that there was no longer any chance of getting anyone else to share the expense, Colonel Borland proposed to move the women still crowded in the jail to temporary quarters in the old police station on 44th Street, but city council turned down the idea when local residents protested. Reluctantly the council ordered a new building to be completed at the city farm by April 1, 1946.[20]

The Navy abruptly dropped the share of the city's police burden it was carrying when it ordered its 35 shore patrolmen out of the city's scout cars. Left with only 171 policemen of its own, the council adopted desperate measures. It dug deep in the city's

[20] *V-P*, June 21, 1945, p. 20; July 4, 1945, p. 16; July 11, 1945, p. 18.

pockets to vote immediate raises to policemen and firemen to attract new recruits to the jobs. Chief Woods took some of the attractiveness out of the job by putting his force on a seven-day week to make up for the shortage. The late auxiliary firemen and police, remembering the rejected offer of their services, rumbled ominously and organized themselves into a Greater Norfolk Citizens Forum.[21]

Suddenly the background noises of the war in the Pacific roared into a loud thunder. The city was brought sharply to attention by the news that the world's first atom bomb had been dropped on Hiroshima on August 6. Three days later the second atom bomb fell and Russia entered the war against Japan. As the Japanese government began negotiations for surrender, people impatiently for the news that the war was over. On Sunday night, August 12, Norfolkians listening to the American Album of Familiar Music heard the program interrupted by a flash that the President had announced the Japanese surrender. In a few moments Granby Street was flooded with sailors, shouting, "The war's over!" Horns honked, and a crap game started in the middle of Plume Street. Then the news came that it was all a mistake; no one knew how the message had got on the United Press wires. The premature celebration died out in disappointment.[22]

The false flash did not take the edge off the big celebration two days later. At 7:00 P. M. on August 14 President Truman's announcement that the Japanese had surrendered came over the radio in a car in front of the Post Office, and the driver pressed hard on his horn button. Another echoed him, and in moments Granby Street was jammed with honking autos. Two sailors stared in open-mouthed astonishment at the forming procession. Then one realized what was occurring and swore indignantly: "Of all the damned places to be when this thing happened, we had to be here." Four others joined hands exuberantly, swept a girl in a green dress into their circle, and danced around her, singing "Roll Out the Barrel." Sailors came out on the balcony of the Catholic USO, tearing telephone books into shreds and tossing the confetti on the crowds below.

[21] *V-P*, June 20, 1945, p. 18; June 22, 1945; July 19, 1945, p. 18; July 20, 1945, p. 20.
[22] *V-P*, August 13, 1945, p. 12.

East Main Street was closed tight, but forehanded Navy men took swigs out of anonymous bottles in brown paper bags. Two sailors sat on the curb with a case of beer between them, solemnly downing one bottle after another without a word, in spite of the crowd's wisecracks. Two others, impatient to get out of uniform, discarded their bell-bottom trousers immediately. One sailor picked up a garbage can, and a friend jumped to his shoulders to ride piggy-back and clang the lid against the can.

Excited girls kissed Navy men in gratitude for the victory. Discovering that they were heroes for the occasion, sailors took advantage of the opportunity to kiss every girl they met, with or without protest. Joining hands, they snake-danced in and out among the stalled cars on Granby Street. They put their heads inside car windows to ask, "May I kiss your wife, mister?" and did not wait for an answer. A clanging motorman tried futilely to pilot his trolley through the din, a washtub tied to its rear. An inquiring reporter yelled at a sailor, "What are your postwar plans?" Back came the grinning reply: "I'm going to report in in about three more days—after I sober up."[23]

[23] *V-P*, August 15, 1945, p. 22.

GOLD STAR HONOR ROLL OF THE CITY OF NORFOLK

THIS honor roll is based on a list of the Norfolk war dead compiled by the Norfolk War History Commission from information supplied by friends and relatives. To it have been added the names of those on the official Army and Navy casualty releases whose next of kin had a Norfolk address. Since this next of kin was frequently a wife only temporarily in the city while her husband was on duty in the area, a number of persons are included who had only a slight connection with Norfolk. In a few instances where the Commission was able to learn that the man should not have been credited to the city, the name has been omitted; when there was any doubt, the name has been included. Although repeated appeals have been made to the public to supply the names of all Norfolk men who died in World War II, there are undoubtedly some cases where friends and relatives have failed to provide this information. The Commission deeply regrets that the names of these men cannot be included on this list.

Whenever available, the following data have been given for each person: rank, branch of service, place and date of birth.

ADAMS, CHARLES LEROY, JR., Pfc., Army, b. Norfolk, Dec. 6, 1919.

ADKINS, FRANCIS EDWARD, Lt. Col., Army; b. Clarksville, Tenn., Nov. 20, 1914.

ALBRIGHT, EDWARD MATTHEW, JR., 1st Lt., Army; b. Norfolk, Aug. 26, 1916.

ALLEN, EDWARD LEON, Pfc., Army; b. Norfolk.

ALLEN, ROBERT BRANNER, Sgt., Army; b. Baltimore, Md., Nov. 10, 1924.

ANDERSON, IRWIN CORINTHIAS, Mess Attendant 1/c, Navy; b. Norfolk, April 24, 1916.

ANDERSON, WALTER T., Pvt., Army.

ANDREWS, CHARLES JAMES, JR., American Field Service; b. Norfolk, March 10, 1916.

ANDREWS, HAROLD T., Seaman, Navy.

ANDREWS, JOHN H., Commander, Navy.

ANDREWS, JOHN HENRY, Pvt., Army; b. Robersonville, N. C., 1914.

ANDREWS, RALPH F., Capt., Army.

APPLEWHITE, WILLIAM WRAY, Pvt., Army; b. Portsmouth, March 5, 1921.

ARCANJO, ANTONE, Fireman 1/c, Navy; b. Cambridge, Mass., Jan. 25, 1925.

ARMSTRONG, WILLIAM HENRY, JR., S/Sgt., Army.

ASHE, ANDREW LEE, JR., Pvt., Army; b. Portsmouth, Sept. 2, 1922.

ATWELL, MELVIN KENNETH, Lt., Navy; b. Pontiac, Mich., July 17, 1909.

AUGUST, PAUL A., Pvt., Army; b. Wilmington, Del., Jan. 25, 1916.

AULT, WILLIAM BOWEN, Commander, Navy; b. Enterprise, Ore., Oct. 6, 1898.

AUSTIN, ORION WILMER, Seaman 1/c, Navy.

AVANT, CHARLES T., T/5, Army.

BAILEY, ELMER D., Pfc., Army.

BAILEY, FLOYD WILLIAM, Cook 3/c, Navy.

BAILEY, JOHN EVERETT, Cpl., Army; b. Norfolk, Sept. 12, 1923.

BAIN, BENNIE, Water Tender 1/c, Navy.

BAIR, CLYDE THEODORE, Lt., Navy.

BAKER, CLARENCE PEED, Lt., Navy.

BAKER, RAYMOND DOUGLAS, 2nd Lt., Marines.

BAKER, WILLARD READ, Seaman 2/c, Navy; b. Norfolk, Jan. 22, 1925.

BALDWIN, FRANK D., 2nd Lt., Army.

BALDWIN, HARRY CONNOR, 2nd Lt., Marines; b. New Orleans, La., Oct. 11, 1916.

BARAS, EMANUEL, Pfc., Army; b. Portsmouth, April 6, 1925.

BARBER, BILLY LEE, 1st Lt., Army; b. Norfolk, Dec. 11, 1919.

BARKER, LEE JACKSON, JR., Fireman 1/c, Navy.

BARNES, CLYDE BERNEST, JR., Seaman 1/c, Navy; b. Norfolk, June 3, 1924.

BARNES, JOHN GOODE, S/Sgt., Army; b. Suffolk, June 18, 1906.

BARNHILL, JOSEPH WAVERLY, Pfc., Army; b. Halifax Co., N. C., Feb. 27, 1922.

BARRETT, LEON E., 1st Lt., Army.

BASDEN, ROLEN GALLOWAY, JR., 2nd Lt., Army; b. Bellhaven, N. C., June 6, 1916.

BASS, JOSEPH FRANK, Cpl., Army; b. Knoxville, Tenn., April 1, 1924.

BATEMAN, WILLIAM W., 2nd Lt., Army.

BATES, CLAYTON ELMER, Ens., Navy.

BATTRAM, GEORGE LEE, JR., Airship Rigger 1/c, Navy.

BAUGHMAN, RICHARD KIDDER MEADE, Pvt., Army; b. Baltimore, Md., Nov. 22, 1924.

BAYLOR, ROBERT PAYNE WARING, JR., Pfc., Marines; b. Norfolk, Feb. 27, 1923.

BEARD, WILLIAM F., Aviation Machinist's Mate 3/c, Navy.

BEISINGER, WALTER BROWN, JR., 1st Lt., Army; b. Danville, Ill., Oct. 15, 1916.

BELL, JOSIAH SCOTT, Pfc., Marines.

BELL, ROBERT GOURLEY, 1st Lt., Army; b. Norfolk, Dec. 30, 1919.

BELOTE, JAMES ROBERT, JR., Pvt., Army; b. Onancock, June 18, 1919.

BENDER, FREDERICK GEORGE, 1st Lt., Army.

BENNETT, CHARLIE RICHARD, Chief Electrician's Mate, Navy.

BENTROD, WILLIAM JARVES, Chief Aviation Pilot, Navy.

BERGER, LESLIE LEO, Water Tender 2/c, Navy.

BERNSTEIN, JOSEPH, S/Sgt., Army; b. Detroit, Mich., Feb. 4, 1924.

BERRYMAN, RAYMOND HAMPTON, Pfc., Army; b. Lewiston, N. C., July 16, 1918.

BESHORE, EDWARD ARTHUR, Aviation Metalsmith 2/c, Navy; b. St. Louis, Mo., Jan. 22, 1910.

BEW, FLOYD L., S/Sgt., Army.

BIGGERS, THOMAS ADOLPHUS, Lt. (jg.), Navy.

BILLUPS, CHARLES OGLETREE, Third Assistant Engineer, Maritime Service; b. Portsmouth, March 19, 1912.

BINDER, WILLIAM HICKEY, Pvt., Marines; b. Newport News, Oct. 17, 1924.

BISHOP, LEROY, Sgt., Army; b. Bath, N. C., April 25, 1922.

BLACKSTOCK, FRANK ALLEN, Chief Boatswain's Mate, Navy.

BLALOCK, GEORGE THOMAS, Chief Radioman, Navy.

BOENI, ALBERT ALOUSIS, Boatswain's Mate 1/c, Navy.

BOGART, PERRY SMITH, T/5, Army; b. Smithville, N. Y., Aug. 9, 1921.

BOND, RICHARD WADE, Lt. Comdr., Navy; b. Portland, Me., Oct. 30, 1917.

BONTECOU, PIERRE R., 1st Lt., Army; b. Beacon, N. Y., Aug. 9, 1921.

BOOTHE, JAMES HENRY, JR., Army; b. Suffolk, April 4, 1915.

BORUM, JOHN RANDOLPH, Lt. (jg), Navy; b. Norfolk, Dec. 8, 1907.

BOTTOMS, CHARLIE LEE, S/Sgt., Army; b. Rocky Mount, N. C., Oct. 16, 1923.

BOWERS, HAROLD EUGENE, Aviation Pilot 1/c, Navy.

BOYCE, CHARLES LOUIS, Seaman 2/c, Navy.

BOYD, JOSEPH TODD, T/Sgt., Army; b. Cleveland, O., July 4, 1918.

BOYD, SHERMAN TAFT, Water Tender 1/c, Navy; b. Kemp, Tex., 1909.

BRACE, JAMES DOUGLAS, T/5, Army; b. Roanoke, Jan. 15, 1915.

BRACKETT, FRED A., Flight Officer, Army.

BRADLEY, JAMES VINCENT, JR., Major, Marines.

BRAITHWAITE, JAMES FRANKLIN, Aviation Chief Metalsmith, Navy.

BREEDEN, ALBERT PRESTON, JR., Ens., Navy; b. Norfolk, March 18, 1921.

BREEDEN, HERBERT FITTS, 1st Lt., Marines; b. Hardiman Co., Tenn., Dec. 22, 1918.

BRESS, PHILIP, Major, Army; b. New York, N. Y., Jan. 1, 1908.

BREWER, WALTER DOUGLAS, S/Sgt., Army, b. Dendron, Feb. 16, 1917.

BRINKLEY, GEORGE WILLIE, Pvt., Army; b. Corapeake, N. C., Nov. 22, 1915.

BRINKLEY, LONNIE WILLIAM, Pfc., Army, b. Norfolk, April 19, 1920.

BRISTOW, HOWARD EARL, Chief Quartermaster, Navy.

BROWN, HOWARD, Steward's Mate 1/c, Navy.

BROWN, James Meredith, Fireman 1/c, Navy.

BROWN, Lloyd L., Pvt., Army.

BRYANT, JOSEPH FRANK, JR., Army; b. South Norfolk, Oct. 28, 1921.

BUCHANAN, THOMAS JENNINGS, JR., Lt., Navy.

BUCK, CLYDE LEONARD, Pvt., Army; b. Disputanta, March 2, 1923.

BUCKINGHAM, NORMAN DAVIS, Sgt., Army; b. Norfolk, May 4, 1920.

BULLS, MELVIN RAY, 1st Lt., Army; b. Surry Co., Va., July 6, 1922.

BUNCH, KENNETH CECIL, Aviation Radioman 1/c, Navy.

BUNTON, EDWARD WILBUR, Officers Steward 2/c, Navy.

BURCH, MELVIN JEROME, Pfc., Army; b. Portsmouth, Aug. 2, 1918.

BURTON, EDGAR WHITE, Aviation Radioman 2/c, Navy.

BUTLER, SANDY ALLEN, Army.

BYERS, NORMAN URSUS, Chief Yeoman, Navy.

BYRD, HAROLD THOMAS, JR., 1st Lt., Army; b. Norfolk, March 29, 1915.

CAKE, HENRY EPES, Ens., Navy; b. Norfolk, March 15, 1916.

CAMPBELL, GLENN HAROLD, Pfc., Army; b. Beggs, Okla., Sept. 8, 1924.

CAMPBELL, RAEFORD LENORD, Pfc., Army; b. Pittsboro, N. C., Nov. 29, 1918.

CANNON, FREDERICK BERTRAND, Cpl., Army; b. Chesapeake City, Md., April 15, 1917.

CAPETANAKIS, TONY ANTHONY, Pvt., Army; b. Merona, Crete, July 20, 1925.

CARAWAN, BERT BRANDON, Lt., Coast Guard; b. Lowland, N. C., March 25, 1904.

CAREY, HAROLD CLEMENT, Lt. (jg), Navy.

CARNLEY, DOUGLAS MYRON, 5TH, Aviation Pilot 1/c, Navy.

CARROLL, RAY CLIFFORD, Chief Motor Machinist's Mate, Navy.

CARROLL, THOMAS MARVIN, Pvt., Army.

CARTER, CHARLES JOHN, 1st Lt., Army; b. Long Beach, Cal., May 13, 1923.

CARTER, JOSEPH FOUNTAINE, Chief Machinist's Mate, Navy; b. Stoutsburg, N. Y., Oct. 16, 1905.

CARTIER, JACQUES JENNINGS, Water Tender 2/c, Navy; b. Manchester, N. H., Jan. 9, 1917.

CASEY, WILLIAM FRANKLIN, Sgt., Army; b. Norfolk, April 30, 1924.

CAUDILL, GILBERT H., Ens., Navy.

CECIL, HENRY EDWARD, Chief Machinist's Mate, Navy.

CECIL, PAUL FRANKLIN, 2nd Lt., Army;
b. Richmond, Aug. 8, 1917.

CHADWICK, LOUIS GUION, Capt., Army;
b. Portsmouth, Nov. 5, 1908.

CHANDLER, J. W., Chief Gunner's Mate,
Navy.

CHAPMAN, EDWARD L., Aviation Chief
Radioman, Navy.

CHOUINARD, LLOYD JOSEPH, Aviation
Machinist's Mate 3/c, Navy.

CHRISTIAN, JAMES EDWARD, JR., Pvt.,
Army; b. Portsmouth, Feb. 11, 1922.

CHURCH, HERMAN LLOYD, JR., 1st Lt.,
Army; b. Norfolk, March 16, 1918.

CLARK, ELBERT IRVIN, Pvt., Army; b.
Jonesboro, N. C., Jan. 7, 1926.

CLARK, LOUIS CRAWFORD, Ens., Navy.

CLOONAN, PHILIP PATRICK, Chief Boilermaker, Navy.

CLOUGH, RICHARD KENNETH, Machin-
ist's Mate 2/c, Navy; b. Vt., Nov. 4, 1917.

COHEN, BERNARD, 1st Lt., Army; b.
Norfolk, June 13, 1913.

COHEN, HARRY, 2nd Lt., Army; b.
Norfolk, Jan. 22, 1924.

COHN, LAWRENCE WILLIAM, JR., Lt.
(jg), Navy; b. Norfolk, July 4, 1918.

COLEMAN, GEORGE CARTER, JR., Cpl.,
Army; b. Norfolk, April 13, 1925.

COLLINS, DAVID HARRISON, Lt. (jg),
Navy; b. Newport News, Jan. 28, 1921.

COLONNA, FRANK CARLTON, JR., Pfc.,
Army; b. Exmore, Sept. 18, 1921.

COMER, JOSEPH GUY, Chief Electrician's
Mate, Navy.

CONDON, ROBERT FRANCIS, T/Sgt.,
Army; b. Norfolk, Oct. 11, 1920.

CONNER, EARL VINCENT, Cpl., Army;
b. Norfolk, Aug. 9, 1924.

CONSOLVO, FREDERIC EGNER, JR., Capt.,
Army; b. South Norfolk, Dec. 20, 1915.

CONWELL, WILLIAM YEATES, Ens.,
Navy; b. Milton, Del., Nov. 23, 1912.

COOK, ERNEST MELVIN, Aviation Chief
Ordnanceman, Navy.

COOK, WILLIAM RAYMOND, Lt., Navy.

COON, DEMPSEY WORTH, Aviation
Machinist's Mate, Navy.

COOPER, EPHRAIM COLON, Pvt., Army;
b. Columbia, N. C., Feb. 17, 1925.

CORBEILLE, MAXSUM E., Pvt., Army.

CORBETT, ODIS LEES, Aviation Chief
Ordnanceman, Navy; b. Troy, N. C., July
3, 1914.

COREY, RAYMOND, Sgt., Marines; b.
North Edgecomb, Me., May 22, 1924.

CORRELL, CARL EUGENE, JR., 1st Lt.,
Army; b. Salisbury, N. C., July 16, 1921.

CORYELL, RUPERT VANCE, Pvt., Army.

COVINGTON, WILLIAM ROBERT, T/Sgt.,
Army; b. Pocomoke City, Md., Jan. 24,
1925.

COX, CLAUDE, Pfc., Army.

CRAIG, TYLER MARSHALL, JR., T/Sgt.,
Army.

CREDLE, GEORGE AUGUSTUS, Radioman
3/c, Navy.

CREEKMUR, THOMAS CLIFTON, 1st Lt.,
Army; b. Portsmouth, June 24, 1921.

CREIGHTON, DONALD SEBASTIAN, Seaman 1/c, Navy; b. Port Norris, N. J., Aug.
8, 1925.

CROMMELIN, RICHARD GUNTER, Lt.
Comdr., Navy.

CRONIN, ROBERT CHARLES, Lt. (jg),
Navy.

CUBBERLY, GEORGE ELLIS, Capt.,
Army; b. Richmond, May 30, 1909.

CULLEN, STEWART BREWER, Seaman
1/c, Navy.

CULPEPPER, ALSTON, JR., Pvt., Army;
b. Northwest, July 20, 1924.

CUMMING, JAMES DICKSON, 2nd Lt.,
Army; b. Parkersburg, W. Va., Sept. 8,
1920.

CUMMINGS, POLLARD WRIGHT, Seaman,
Merchant Marine; b. Richmond, July 11,
1918.

CURLING, HEYWOOD WARREN, JR., 1st
Lt., Army; b. Portsmouth, Oct. 20, 1919.

CURTIN, JOHN FRANCIS, JR., 1st Lt.,
Army; b. Laurel, Md., Jan. 12, 1921.

CURTIN, LEO A., JR., S/Sgt., Army.

CUSHMAN, JOHN HERBERT, Lt. (jg), Navy; b. Cleveland, O., Sept. 15, 1917.

CUTHRELL, HARRY HAMILTON, Cpl., Army; b. Norfolk Co., April 23, 1922.

CUTHRIELL, NORMAN FARQUHAR, JR., Electrician's Mate 1/c, Navy; b. Portsmouth, Aug. 10, 1920.

CUTRELL, MITCHELL RAY, SR., Pfc., Army; b. Tyrell Co., N. C., Dec. 22, 1917.

DALE, RAYMOND.

DALTON, CLAUDE LAFAYETTE, JR., T/5, Army; b. Byllesby, March 30, 1924.

DANCE, ROBERT CHRISTIAN, Ens., Navy; b. Norfolk, Jan. 13, 1922.

DANIEL, JOHN CALHOUN, JR., 2nd Lt., Army; b. Lynchburg, Oct. 8, 1918.

DAVIS, EDWARD WALLACE, Lt., Navy; b. Carteret Co., April 1, 1891.

DAVIS, EUGENE RUSSELL, JR., 1st Lt., Army; b. Norfolk, Feb. 26, 1922.

DAVIS, FRANK COX, JR., 2nd Lt., Army; b. Eaton, Ind., March 11, 1920.

DAVIS, KENNETH SEARLE, Lt., Navy.

DAVIS, SAMUEL LEONARD, JR., 2nd Lt., Marines; b. Norfolk, May 16, 1923.

DAY, SHIRLEY OTIS, Water Tender 2/c, Navy.

DEAFENBAUGH, RAYMOND DALE, Pvt., Army.

DECKER, GEORGE SAM, Painter 3/c, Navy; b. Norfolk, Oct. 17, 1915.

DEDCOVICH, NEWELL SMITH, JR., Machinist's Mate 2/c, Navy.

DEITRICK, WILLIAM ALEXANDER, Lt. Comdr., Navy.

DENERY, HAROLD HARRIS, Lt., Navy.

DENTON, HAROLD VINCENT, T/Sgt., Army; b. Norfolk, Aug. 28, 1925.

DEPEW, GARLAND LEE, Boatswain 1/c, Navy.

DEVINE, JACK WARREN, Ens., Navy.

DICKERSON, MELVILLE LUCIUS, Aviation Radio Technician 2/c, Navy.

DICKSON, RICHARD, Major, Marines.

DIEMER, LESTER EMREY, Chief Fire Controlman, Navy.

DILDINE, ARTHUR LEWIS, Chief Commissary Steward, Navy; b. Elmira, N. Y., Nov. 16, 1884.

DILSBURG, WILLIAM CARROLL, JR., Sgt., Army; b. Norfolk, Nov. 23, 1923.

DIXON, OZZIE DEMERRITT, Sgt., Army; b. Roxboro, N. C., April 13, 1913.

DONATO, MAURY, Navy.

DOOLEY, VINCENT DUTTON, Pfc., Army; b. Norfolk, Jan. 7, 1912.

DORITY, ROBERT WILLIAM, Sgt., Army; b. Malden, Mass., July 20, 1923.

DOUGHERTY, JAMES VINCENT, Pvt., Army; b. Norfolk, Jan. 1, 1921.

DOUGHTIE, RUFUS, JR., Pfc., Marines; b. Cypress Chapel, June 7, 1923.

DOWDEN, JAMES ABRAHAM, Chief Water Tender, Navy.

DOWDY, DOUGLAS MUSKE, Storekeeper 3/c, Navy.

DOWNING, FREDERICK PAUL, 1st Lt., Army; b. Norfolk, March 28, 1917.

DOWNING, WILLIAM EMMETT, Lt. (jg), Navy; b. Norfolk, Jan. 22, 1920.

DOWNS, VERNE KENNETH, Chief Motor Machinist's Mate, Navy.

DOZIER, DAVID APOLLOS, 2nd Lt., Army; b. Norfolk, Feb. 26, 1918.

DOZIER, ROY OCIE, JR., 2nd Lt., Marines; b. Norfolk, April 25, 1920.

DOZIER, WILSON LLOYD, JR., Lt., Navy; b. Norfolk, Jan. 22, 1916.

DUKE, CLIFTON M., Pvt., Army.

DUNN, JOHN EDWARD, Lt. Comdr., Navy.

DUNNAVANT, JESSE HUGH, Motor Machinist's Mate 1/c, Navy.

DURANT, DOLIVE, JR., Lt., Navy.

DUVAL, HARRY WILSON, S/Sgt., Army; b. Norfolk, Jan. 17, 1922.

DYSON, ALONZO FRANKLIN, Boatswain's Mate 2/c, Navy.

DZURENKA, LOUIS, Shipfitter 2/c, Navy.

EASTWOOD, WILBURN FRANCIS, JR., Cpl., Army; b. Norfolk, Oct. 23, 1922.

EATON, WILLIAM GUY, SR., Commander, Navy.

EDGERTON, WILLIAM MANIN, T/5, Army.

EDISS, AL, Pharmacist's Mate 1/c, Navy.

EDMUNDS, MILTON BAILEY, Lt. Comdr., Coast Guard.

EDWARDS, CHARLES LUTHER, Boatswain's Mate 1/c, Navy; b. Baltimore, Md., March 15, 1919.

EDWARDS, HEYWOOD L., Lt. Comdr., Navy.

EDWARDS, JOHN MANNING, Ens., Navy; b. Norfolk, June 29, 1922.

EGAS, ROBERT HENRY, Pvt., Army; b. Norfolk, Dec. 10, 1919.

EGGLESTON, JOHN MARSHALL, Lt. Comdr., Navy; b. Norfolk, May 30, 1900.

ELDRIDGE, JOHN, JR., Lt. Comdr., Navy.

ELLERTON, GEORGE CLIFTON, JR., Lt. Comdr., Navy.

ELLETT, CLARENCE HENSON, JR., Boatswain's Mate 2/c, Navy.

ELLIOTT, HARRY MAXWELL, 1st Lt., Marines, b. Monroe, La., Nov. 28, 1912.

ELLIOTT, HUBERT LATHAN, Sgt., Army; b. Norfolk, Dec. 25, 1912.

ELLIOTT, ROSS TOMKINS, JR., Ens., Navy; b. Riverton, N. J., Sept. 17, 1920.

ELLIS, JOHN ALVIN, Second Assistant Engineer, Merchant Marine; b. Norfolk, March 17, 1906.

ELY, RICHARD JOHN, Royal Canadian Army.

EPPERSON, EWELL, Seaman 1/c, Navy.

EUBANK, PHILIP STEELE, Pfc., Army; b. Norfolk, May 26, 1926.

EVANS, THOMAS EISFELTER, Chief Pay Clerk, Navy.

EVANS, WILLIAM LEE, Seaman 2/c, Navy.

EWELL, ROBERT STANLEY, JR., Fireman 1/c, Navy; b. Norfolk, Dec. 5, 1913.

EWING, ALEX ALEXANDER, Chief Metalsmith, Navy.

FANTONE, JOHN SHEPPARD, Capt., Marines; b. Norfolk, Nov. 6, 1916.

FARTHING, HAL BUCKNER, Ens., Navy; b. Sugar Grove, N. C., Oct. 3, 1917.

FIDLER, CHARLES WILLIAM, Chief Machinist's Mate, Navy.

FISHER, LINWOOD JAMES, Second Cook and Baker, Maritime Service; b. Norfolk, Oct. 14, 1911.

FISHER, PAUL HAYWOOD, JR., Sgt., Army; b. Norfolk, Oct. 30, 1924.

FITZGERALD, LORENZA NATHANIEL, Seaman 1/c, Navy; b. Norfolk.

FLECK, HARRY LLOYD, Chief Machinist's Mate, Navy.

FONTANILLA, SERAFIO, Chief Steward, Navy.

FORBES, MARVIN JAMES, 1st Lt., Army; b. Portlock, Aug. 20, 1918.

FOREMAN, ISAIAH, T/5, Army; b. Princess Anne, Dec. 17, 1921.

FORSTER, EDWARD WILLIAM, Chief Machinist's Mate, Navy; b. Jersey City, N. J., Oct. 8, 1888.

FOUDRAY, DEMOSTHENES, Carpenter, Navy.

FOWLER, JAMES FRANKLIN, Boilermaker 1/c, Navy.

FOWLKES, CALVIN OSCAR LEWIS, T/Sgt., Army; b. Petersburg, Dec. 16, 1921.

FOX, EDWARD JOSEPH, 2nd Lt., Army; b. Norfolk, June 6, 1916.

FRADY, JUNIOR RICHARD, Pvt., Army.

FRANK, JOHN DISMAS, Lt. (jg), Navy.

FREEMAN, MARVIN SMITH, Shipfitter 2/c, Navy.

FRENCH, ALBERT SYDNEY, Chief Petty Officer, Navy; b. Bayborough, N. C., April 2, 1905.

FRENCH, HAROLD DOLPHIN, Chief Petty Officer, Navy; b. Narrows, June 29, 1902.

FRIAS, ALVIN ODIS, Sgt., Army; b. Norfolk, July 29, 1922.

GALLUP, BILLY LOCKWOOD, Sgt., Army; b. Norfolk, Aug. 9, 1921.

GAMSEY, ARNOLD MELVIN, 1st Lt., Army; b. Norfolk, Aug. 31, 1920.

GARDNER, HOWARD NATHANIEL, Electrician's Mate 1/c, Navy; b. Geneva, N. Y., 1903.

GARRELFS, VICTOR R., Pfc., Army; b. Norfolk, July 21, 1924.

GAULT, DAVID DUKE, Chief Machinist's Mate, Navy; b. Dallas, Tex., Jan. 25, 1901.

GERHARDT, CHARLES WALTER, Lt. (jg), Navy.

GIBSON, GEORGE DAVIS, Lt. Comdr., Navy.

GILBERT, HILARY, JR., Sgt., Army.

GIVAN, JAMES ALEXANDER, Lt. Comdr., Navy.

GLASSER, STANLEY F., Sgt., Army; b. Norfolk, Nov. 2, 1914.

GLENNAN, MICHAEL, III, Sgt., Army; b. Norfolk, Sept. 1, 1912.

GOGGIN, JAMES ROBERT, S/Sgt., Army; b. Ashland, Ky., 1923.

GORDON, EUGENE, T/4, Army.

GORDON, JAMES SHELTON, Pvt., Army.

GOWEN, FLOYD HOMER, JR., S/Sgt., Army; b. Drakes Branch, Feb. 21, 1915.

GRACIE, ROBERT PENTER, 1st Lt., Army; b. Jersey City, N. J., Oct. 28, 1919.

GRANT, SAMUEL HARVEY, S/Sgt., Army; b. Norfolk, May 6, 1919.

GRAVES, ELMER PRESTON, Aviation Chief Metalsmith, Navy.

GRAVES, ESTLE JENNINGS, Chief Electrician's Mate, Navy; b. Sharps Chapel, Tenn., Sept. 12, 1898.

GRAY, HAROLD WILLIAM, Ens., Navy.

GRAY, JOHN EDWARD, S/Sgt., Army; b. Scotland Neck, N. C., Oct. 20, 1915.

GRAY, WALTER STEPHEN, Lt. Col., Army; b. Norfolk.

GREEN, ROBERT LEE, 2nd Lt., Army; b. Camden, N. J., Jan. 5, 1925.

GREENE, FRANCIS WHITTLE, Ens., Navy; b. Norfolk, Aug. 21, 1921.

GREENE, ROBERT NIXON, 2nd Lt., Army; b. Norfolk, Sept. 21, 1923.

GREGG, ROBERT ALTON, Storekeeper 1/c, Navy.

GRIFFITH, PERRY IVAN, JR., Ship's Cook 2/c, Navy; b. Norfolk, Dec. 24, 1921.

GRIGGS, GEORGE RAYMOND, Boatswain's Mate 2/c, Navy.

GRILLO, EUGENE, JR., Pfc., Army; b. Norfolk, June 18, 1921.

GROBOSKI, FRANK, Pvt., Army.

GUTHRIE, JOHNNY DELMAR, Gunner's Mate 1/c, Navy; b. Ransomville, N. C., Sept. 8, 1918.

HAENEL, OTTO WILLE, Lt. (jg), Navy.

HAFNER, WILLIAM MEADE, 1st Lt., Army; b. Little Rock, Ark., Nov. 4, 1918.

HAGERMAN, SAMUEL NASH, Capt., Army; b. Bedford, June 6, 1912.

HALL, CLARENCE SAMUEL, Pfc., Army; b. Hickory, July 8, 1924.

HALL, GARLAND LOUIS, Cpl., Army; b. Portsmouth, July 27, 1922.

HALL, RAYMOND ELNOR, Chief Shipfitter, Navy.

HALSTEAD, BERNARD JAMES, Cpl., Army; b. Norfolk, Jan. 26, 1923.

HANK, WILLIAM EDWIN, Commander, Navy; b. Norfolk, Sept. 25, 1902.

HANLON, LOUIS JOHN, Aviation Machinist's Mate, Navy.

HARDY, HUGH PARROTT, JR., Capt., Army; b. Littleton, N.C., Jan. 10, 1916.

HARDY, JAMES EDDIE, Chief Warrant Carpenter, Navy; b. Dothan, Ala., July 16, 1918.

HARP, CALVIN NELMS, JR., 2nd Lt., Army; b. Norfolk, June 25, 1922.

HARRELL, CALVIN GIBSON, Pfc., Army; b. South Norfolk, Oct. 14, 1924.

HARRIS, JOHN WINSTON, Pfc., Army; b. Norfolk, March 16, 1925.

HARRIS, LECIL E., Pfc., Marines; b. Parrish, Ala., Dec. 24, 1922.

HARRIS, WILLIAM JESSE, 1st Lt., Army; b. Bath Co., May 23, 1919.

HARRIS, WOODWARD, Pvt., Army.

HASKETT JAMES WARREN, Sgt., Army; b. South Norfolk, April 24, 1914.

HAYCOCK, EUGENE RUSSELL, JR., Pfc., Army; b. Portsmouth, Nov. 4, 1924.

HEGE, RAYMOND WEBSTER, Capt., Navy.

HELMS, JOHN ALLEN, Ens., Navy.

HELSLEY, HENRY HERBERT, Seaman, Merchant Marine; b. Norfolk, Dec. 27, 1912.

HEMPHILL, KERMIT, Machinist's Mate 1/c, Navy.

HENDERSON, CLAUDE THOMAS, JR., Cpl., Marines; b. Norfolk, June 11, 1920.

HENDERSON, GEORGE EVERETT, Pvt., Marines; b. Kincaid, Kans., Jan. 1, 1926.

HENDERSON, NERO, Pvt., Army; b. Lynnhaven, Feb. 29, 1924.

HIBBITTS, JAMES O., JR., Pvt., Army.

HICKEY, WILLIAM JOHN, Chief Store-keeper, Navy; b. Norfolk, March 18, 1885.

HILL, ROBERT AMBLER, Chief Warrant Officer, Navy.

HINES, OCEOLIA, Pfc., Army; b. South Norfolk, August 12, 1916.

HOCKADAY, WENDELL WALLACE, 2nd Lt., Army; b. Norfolk, March 9, 1923.

HODGES, BURRELL DAN, JR., Pfc., Marines; b. Norfolk, Jan. 11, 1925.

HODGES, EARL LINWOOD, JR., Pfc., Army; b. Norfolk, Jan. 6, 1925.

HODGES, JOHN MASON, JR., Sgt., Army; b. Norfolk, Nov. 22, 1924.

HOEDING, EUGENE LAWRENCE, Sgt., Army; b. Wilmington, N. C., April 4, 1919.

HOEY, GRANVILLE BENJAMIN, Capt., Navy.

HOLLENBECK, CHARLES ERNEST, JR., S/Sgt., Army; b. Danville, Dec. 7, 1914.

HOLLENGER, EDGAR ALLAN, T/5, Army; b. Norfolk, Aug. 4, 1925.

HOLLIDAY, DANIEL DAVIS, Aviation Machinist's Mate 2/c, Navy; b. Jamesville, N. C., Sept. 8, 1913.

HOLLOWAY, THERMAN NATHANIEL, Steward 3/c, Navy.

HOLLOWELL, JOHN AMBROSE, Commander, Navy.

HOLT, GRANVILLE SANFORD, Aviation Machinist's Mate 2/c, Navy.

HONEYBELL, JAMES H., Pfc., Army.

HOPKINS, SAMUEL, Chief Electrician's Mate, Navy.

HORNSBY, STANLEY MONTGOMERY, JR., Pvt., Army; b. Seaford, June 6, 1925.

HUDGINS, JEFFERSON ABSOLOM, JR., Aviation Machinist's Mate 3/c, Navy; b. Portsmouth, March 7, 1926.

HULL, DELMAR DELBERT, Boatswain's Mate 1/c, Navy.

HUNT, EARL RODNEY, JR., Cpl., Army; b. Norfolk, Sept. 10, 1923.

HUNTER, RALPH LEO, Pvt., Army; b. Loogootee, Ind., Aug. 5, 1917.

HUNTER, VICTOR IRVIN, Pfc., Army; b. Loogootee, Ind., April 14, 1922.

HUTCHINSON, RONALD BAXTER, Lt., Navy.

INGERSOLL, ROYAL RODNEY, Lt., Navy.

IRBY, EDWARD LEE, Pfc., Army; b. Danville.

IRVIN, SAMUEL LEWIS, Pfc., Army; b. Bellefonte, Pa., Sept. 18, 1920.

IRWIN, RAYMOND RICHARD, Aviation Radioman 2/c, Navy.

JACKSON, EDMOND PEEL, Seaman 1/c, Navy; b. Everetts, N. C., Feb. 20, 1924.

JACKSON, EDWIN FILMORE, Capt., Army.

JACKSON, ERNEST LINWOOD, JR., Pfc., Army; b. Norfolk, Nov. 24, 1923.

JOHNSON, ARCHIE JAMES, Motor Machinist's Mate, Navy.

JOHNSON, BENJAMIN FRANKLIN, JR., Pvt., Army; b. Norfolk, Jan. 25, 1924.

JOHNSON, DAVID ANDREW, JR., Officer's Cook 2/c, Navy.

JOHNSON, HOWARD LEWIS, JR., Pfc., Army.

JOHNSON, JAMES ALOYSIUS, Machinist's Mate 2/c, Navy.

JONES, ANTHONY, Steward's Mate 3/c, Navy.

JONES, COVELY, S/Sgt., Army; b. Tenn., Sept. 19, 1922.

JONES, JAMES EVERETT, Seaman 2/c, Navy.

JONES, JESSE, Seaman 1/c, Navy.

JONES, JESSIE FREEMAN, Boatswain's Mate, Navy.

JONES, NORMAN MEREDITH, 1st Lt., Army; b. Norfolk, March 4, 1922.

JONES, RAYMOND THOMAS, Pvt., Army; b. South Norfolk, April 21, 1925.

JONES, ROBERT PAUL, Chief Pattern-maker, Navy; b. Coakley, N. C., 1892.

JONES, ROBERT WAYNE, 2nd Lt., Army; b. Worthington, Minn., June 22, 1919.

JONES, WILLIAM LEON, Pvt., Army; b. Norfolk, July 14, 1924.

JORDAN, JAMES PARHAM, S/Sgt., Army; b. Norfolk, Aug. 19, 1923.

JORDAN, PAUL IRWIN, Aviation Machinist's Mate 2/c, Navy.

JOYNES, CHARLES RANDOLPH, Water Tender 2/c, Navy; b. Norfolk, April 23, 1920.

KATZOFF, SIDNEY M., Pvt., Army.

KAUFMAN, ALBERT EDWARD, 2nd Lt., Army; b. Norfolk, March 6, 1920.

KEELING, ROBERT MAURICE, Pvt., Army; b. Norfolk, Jan. 6, 1916.

KELLY, WILLIE FRANCIS, Officer's Cook 3/c, Navy.

KEMP, MARY LEE, Machinist's Mate 3/c, Navy; b. Columbia, N. C., May 5, 1922.

KEPNES, HAROLD ARTHUR, Lt., Navy.

KERNS, CORNELIUS REID, 2nd Lt., Army.

KIJEWSKI, HENRY JOSEPH, Aviation Machinist's Mate 2/c, Navy; b. Buffalo, N. Y.

KING, ARCHER EMMET, Commander, Navy; b. Roanoke, Sept. 14, 1893.

KING, CALVIN E., 2nd Lt., Army.

KING, ELMER GORDON, Chief Shipfitter, Navy.

KING, WILLIAM BENJAMIN, Aviation Radioman 1/c, Navy.

KINNE, JOHN HENRY, Seaman 1/c, Navy; b. Brooklyn, N. Y., July 13, 1921.

KLOEPPEL, PETER KOTSCH, Chief Water Tender, Navy.

KOONTZ, ROBERT WARREN, Ens., Navy.

KOPCHOK, PAUL, Pharmacist's Mate 2/c, Navy.

KUNER, ROBERT RUSSELL, Gunner's Mate, Navy.

LACKIE, WESLIE KAIL, Aviation Radioman 1/c, Navy.

LAMPERT, SADRON CLYDE, JR., Pfc., Army; b. Powellton, W. Va., Aug. 9, 1918.

LAND, GEORGE RHEA, JR., 2nd Lt., Army; b. Norfolk, July 3, 1917.

LANE, ELMER VERNON, Ship's Cook 2/c, Navy; b. New Haven, Conn., Oct. 22, 1909.

LANGSTON, ROBERT LEE, Steward's Mate 1/c, Navy.

LANNING, RONALD ROSS, Pharmacist's Mate 2/c, Navy.

LAPE, WILLIAM ALVIN, Seaman 1/c, Navy.

LARGE, JULIUS DEWEY, JR., S/Sgt., Army; b. Buffalo, N. Y., May 20, 1919.

LASSITER, GRAYSON BLACKWELL, Pharmacist's Mate 3/c, Navy; b. Portsmouth, Aug. 13, 1925.

LAUGHRAN, DONALD, Aviation Ordnanceman 1/c, Navy; b. Waterford, N. Y., June 14, 1923.

LAWLESS, VALENTINE BROWNE, T/Sgt., Army; b. Norfolk, April 19, 1908.

LAWRENCE, CHESTER WADE, 1st Lt., Army; b. Brownsville, Tex., Feb. 28, 1921.

LAWRENCE, HUGH AUGUSTUS, Aviation Chief Metalsmith, Navy.

LAWRENCE, JOSEPH G., Pfc., Army.

LEA, JAMES LOWRY, Commander, Navy; b. Charleston, S. C., July 31, 1898.

LEACH, OLIVER D., Pvt.

LENTSCH, WILLIAM JOSEPH, Boatswain's Mate 2/c, Navy.

LESLIE, CLAUDIUS WILLIAM, Seaman 2/c, Navy.

LETTERMAN, CHARLIE ALFORD, Chief Water Tender, Navy.

LEWIS, MARS, JR., Lt. Col., Army; b. Norfolk, April 7, 1920.

LIEBRA, OTTO, Chief Machinist's Mate, Coast Guard.

LINDBLAD, AXEL THED., Comdr., Navy.

LITTLE, JAMES NORMAN, Painter 1/c, Navy.

LOFTIS, REX HENRY, Machinist's Mate 1/c, Navy.

LONDEREE, SIDNEY HERBERT, JR., Seaman 1/c, Navy.

LOREN, NATHAN, Pvt., Army; b. New York, N. Y., Aug. 1, 1914.

LUCAS, FRED R., Pfc., Army.

LUTHER, WILLIAM TYSON, Chief Signalman, Navy.

LYNES, FRANK MOURFIELD, Chief Gunner's Mate, Navy.

McCALLUM, DANIEL, Lt., Navy; b. Newark, N. J., Oct. 11, 1885.

McCLANAN, OSCAR LEE, Cpl., Army.

McCLOUD, THOMAS JEFFERSON, T/Sgt., Army; b. South Norfolk, Oct. 25, 1913.

McCORD, LANGFORD SCOTT, Seaman 1/c, Navy.

McCOY, HENRY ELTON, Pfc., Army; b. Hickory, July 31, 1923.

McCOY, JAMES PETER, Boilermaker, Navy; b. South Mills, N. C., March 16, 1895.

McELHENIE, WENDELL DALE, Chief Motor Machinist's Mate, Navy.

McGINNIS, NOAH EDWARD, JR., Pharmacist's Mate 3/c, Navy.

McGOVERN, FRANCIS JOSEPH, Chief Water Tender, Navy.

McLEOD, DUKE ANGUS, 1st Lt., Army; b. Jonesboro, N. C., Oct. 12, 1924.

McRAE, JOHN MELVIN, Gunner's Mate 2/c, Navy.

McROBERTS, JAMES JOHNSTON, Lt. Comdr., Navy; b. St. Louis, Mo., Sept. 12, 1905.

McVAY, EDGAR C., Flight Officer, Army.

MACHEN, THOMAS SIDNEY, JR., 1st Lt., Army; b. Norfolk, Nov. 26, 1919.

MADDOX, CECIL HAGEN, Sgt., Army; b. Roanoke, May 29, 1925.

MADDOX, JAMES LOWERY, Aviation Machinist's Mate 1/c, Navy.

MAIN, FRED ROBERT, Aviation Machinist's Mate, Navy.

MANN, JOSEPH PATRICK, Utility Man, Merchant Marine; b. Rochelles, N. J., Feb. 4, 1895.

MANTEL, JULIUS ARTHUR, Painter 1/c, Navy.

MARKS, GEORGE ANDREW, Boatswain's Mate 1/c, Navy; b. Norfolk, July 21, 1909.

MAROULIS, GEORGE G., Sgt., Army.

MARRIOTT, OSCAR FERDINAND, Chief Electrician's Mate, Navy.

MARRON, JOHN MARTIN, Aviation Machinist's Mate 2/c, Navy.

MASON, STEDMAN KEITH, Motor Machinist's Mate 3/c, Navy; b. Morehead City, N. C., Sept. 17, 1922.

MASON, WALTER NORRIS, JR., Capt., Army; b. Parksley, Dec. 30, 1910.

MASTHAY, JOHN WILLIAM, Seaman 2/c Navy.

MASSEY, DAVID NATHANIEL, T/5 Army; b. Mount Airy, N. C., March 26, 1924.

MATHEWS, RICHARD HUDSON, Fireman, Navy; b. Norfolk, Oct. 30, 1919.

MATTHEWS, CLARENCE McCOY, Fireman 3/c, Navy; b. Suffolk, April 11, 1924.

MATTHEWS, LUTHER PRESTON, JR., 2nd Lt., Army; b. Norfolk, Jan. 5, 1917.

MAUCK, JAMES MILTON, 1st Lt., Army; b. Norfolk, Jan. 3, 1920.

MAYER, CHARLES, Chief Radioman, Navy.

MEADS, ERNEST McMULLAN, T/5, Army; b. Weeksville, N. C., July 13, 1916.

MECLEWSKI, ROMUALD PETER PAUL, Commander, Navy.

MEEKS, SAMUEL H., Pfc., Army.

MERRILL, WILLIAM JOSEPH, Hospital Apprentice 2/c, Navy; b. Pungo, Dec. 25, 1925.

MESSICK, CHARLES THOMAS, Sgt., Army; b. Norfolk, March, 1912.

MIDDLETON, BENJAMIN HOWARD, Seaman 1/c, Navy; b. Norfolk, Dec. 30, 1925.

MILES, LION TYLER, Lt., Navy; b. Williamsburg, March 4, 1910.

MILLER, JOSEPH CORNWELL, Seaman, Merchant Marine; b. Petersburg, Sept. 3, 1916.

MILLER, MASON, Aviation Machinist's Mate 2/c, Navy; b. Norfolk, April 1, 1924.

MILLER, MORTON MARCHANT, JR., Lt. (jg), Navy.

MILLER, WILLIAM DECATUR, T/Sgt., Army; b. Norfolk, Dec. 6, 1917.

MILLS, WALTER JUNIOR, Pfc., Army; b. Norfolk, Nov. 22, 1923.

MOLLER, HENRY, Aviation Chief Ordnanceman, Navy; b. Krupp, Wash., Jan. 6, 1896.

MONTGOMERY, HOWARD, Chief Carpenter's Mate, Navy.

MOORE, CHARLES WILLIAM, Pfc., Army; b. Mt. Vernon, Ill., Aug. 28, 1923.

MOORE, ORVILLE ROBERT, Lt. (jg), Navy; b. Rose Hill, Iowa, June 28, 1919.

MOORE, PAUL WILLIAM, Metalsmith 1/c, Navy.

MOORE, WILLIAM CORNELIUS, Pfc., Army; b. Norfolk, April 13, 1914.

MOREHEAD, CLIFFORD W., JR., Pvt., Army.

MORGAN, THOMAS GALE, Chief Water Tender, Navy.

MORGAN, WILSON, Sgt., Marines.

MOSELEY, SIDNEY JAMES, JR., Lt., Army; b. Norfolk, April 8, 1918.

MOSIER, MANLEY D., JR., 2nd Lt., Army; b. Norfolk, April 25, 1923.

MOSS, CLARENCE ELMORE, Gunner's Mate 1/c, Navy; b. Newport News.

MUENCH, ALBERT, Chief Machinist's Mate, Navy.

MULLIKIN, MAXWELL NESBIT, Motor Machinist's Mate, Navy.

MUNDEN, HORACE G., JR., T/5, Army; b. Norfolk, Jan. 22, 1924.

MURDOCH, JAMES FREDERICK, Pvt., Army; b. Norfolk, Feb. 18, 1925.

MURPHY, GEORGE GENTRY, Pvt., Army; b. Back Bay, Dec. 6, 1922.

MURPHY, ODELL O., S/Sgt., Army.

MURRAY, FRANKLIN MURLIN, Lt., Navy.

MURRAY, HOWARD LEROY, Lt. (jg), Navy; b. Greensboro, N. C., Sept. 8, 1918.

NEAR, RAY WILLIAM, Major, Marines; b. Struthers, O., Jan. 29, 1896.

NEEDHAM, WILLIAM OSCAR, Lt., Navy.

NEWTON, RAYMOND BARNARD, JR., Chief Water Tender, Navy.

NICHOLS, HEWLETT ALVIN, 1st Lt., Army; b. Portsmouth, May 13, 1913.

NICHOLS, JOHN THOMAS, JR., Lt., Navy; b. Portsmouth, Feb. 19, 1918.

NIVEN, WILLIAM G., Pvt., Army; b. Norfolk Co.

NOBLE, WILLIAM P., JR., 2nd Lt., Army.

NORTHINGTON, JOHN ANDREWS, 2nd Lt., Marines; b. South Hill, Aug. 11, 1923.

NORTON, CHARLES EDWARD, Pvt., Army; b. Neon, Ky., March, 1922.

NOTTINGHAM, CLAUDE DANIEL, JR., Pvt., Army.

O'BRIEN, WILLIAM GILBERT, Aviation Machinist's Mate, Navy.

ODELL, CHAUNCEY NEWTON, Pfc., Army; b. Norfolk, July 19, 1925.

ODELL, IRVIN SCOTT, 2nd Lt., Army; b. Norfolk, Sept. 29, 1914.

O'HEARN, JOHN JOSEPH, JR., Capt., Army; b. Williamson, W. Va., Oct. 1, 1914.

OLD, EDWARD HENRY HERBERT, Capt., Navy; b. Norfolk, Sept. 28, 1876.

OLD, ROGER A., S/Sgt., Army.

OLIVER, EUGENE LEROY, 1st Lt., Army; b. Norfolk, Aug. 7, 1913.

O'NEAL, WILLIAM THOMAS, Third Engineer, Merchant Marine; b. Bluff Springs, Fla., Aug. 31, 1908.

OVERTON, ANDREW LEE, Seaman 2/c, Navy; b. Suffolk, June 13, 1923.

OVERTON, JAY EDWARD, Pvt., Army; b. New York, N. Y., July 22, 1922.

OWEN, WILLIAM LEA, Ens., Navy.

PALUMBO, PATRICK NICK, JR., Seaman 2/c, Navy; b. Philadelphia, Pa., July 24, 1923.

PARKER, DONALD HARVEY, Seaman 2/c, Navy.

PARKER, EVERETTE H., Lt., Army.

PARKINSON, WILLIAM RIDDICK, 2nd Lt., Army; b. Norfolk, June 12, 1921.

PARSONS, JAMES RAYMOND, JR., 1st Lt., Army; b. Norfolk, March 10, 1919.

PATE, McCALL, Lt., Navy.

PATRICK, WILLIAM McCLEESE, JR., Pfc., Army; b. New Bern, N. C., Jan. 8, 1914.

PATTERSON, HOWARD RUSSELL, Aviation Radioman 2/c, Navy; b. South Norwalk, Conn., Nov. 4, 1915.

PAUL, STANLEY CORPREW, 2nd Lt., Army.

PAYNE, GEORGE HARRISON, JR., Cpl., Army; b. Monterey, Oct. 10, 1923.

PEACE, ALONZO FRANKLIN, Boatswain's Mate 2/c, Navy.

PEELE, EDWARD ROBIE, JR., Pfc., Army; b. Norfolk, Oct. 8, 1925.

PENDERS, ROBERT JOSEPH, Chief Machinist's Mate, Navy.

PETERSEN, ROBERT LEWIS, Pfc., Marines; b. Newport News.

PETERSON, BERNARD MILLER, Lt., Navy.

PETERSON, HARVEY, Aviation Machinist's Mate 1/c, Navy.

PETTITT, RALPH J., Pfc., Marines.

PFAEHLER, FRED OTTO STROBLE, JR., Sgt., Army; b. Norfolk, June 23, 1923.

PHELPS, FRANK EUGENE, Seaman 1/c, Navy.

PHILLIPS, CHARLES MORRIS, Seaman, Merchant Marine; b. Little Rock, Ark., Sept. 5, 1918.

PHILLIPS, PAUL LANGE, Commander, Navy; b. Norfolk, Dec. 16, 1904.

PICKRAL, ALBERT HERBERT, Gunner's Mate 1/c, Navy; b. Washington, D. C., Oct. 24, 1916.

PICKRELL, JOHN ALLEN, Ship's Cook 3/c, Navy.

PITT, GUYLER STORM, Ship's Cook 2/c, Navy.

PLESANT, LEE EDAGAR, Aviation Chief Radioman, Navy.

POFF, CHARLES WILLIAM, Cpl., Army.

POINTER, LESTER LaVERN, Aviation Ordnanceman, Navy.

POOLE, WALKER PHILLIPS, Water Tender 1/c, Navy; b. Surry Co., Feb. 9, 1923.

POPE, CARL NORTON, JR., Pvt., Army; b. Norfolk, Sept. 3, 1919.

PORTER, LYTLE RIDGWELL, Cpl., Army; b. Norfolk, March 14, 1922.

POWELL, OTIS GORDON, Pvt., Army; b. Suffolk, Sept. 19, 1921.

POWER, JOSEPH, Chief Water Tender, Navy.

PRATT, GEORGE A., JR., Pfc., Army; b. New York, N. Y., May 6, 1918.

PRAUSE, ROBERT HENRY, JR., Lt., Coast Guard; b. Charleston, S. C., June 22, 1915.

PRICE, CLAY CLARENCE, JR., Pvt., Army; b. Norfolk, Sept. 26, 1925.

PRICE, GORDON GRATIOT, 1st Lt., Army; b. Norfolk, Nov. 21, 1919.

PRITCHARD, EDGAR HARRIS, Ens., Navy; b. Norfolk, Oct. 25, 1913.

PRITCHARD, HERBERT A., S/Sgt., Army.

PRUDEN, JAMES NORFLEET, Steward's Mate 2/c, Navy.

PUTNAM, PAUL, Chief Metalsmith, Navy.

RABER, WARREN HOWARD, Lt. (jg), Navy; b. Portsmouth, March 11, 1921.

RADFORD, CYRUS S., JR., Commander, Navy.

RAGUET, CONDE LEROY, Lt. Comdr., Navy.

RAINES, HORACE FRANKLIN, Signalman 1/c, Navy.

RAINEY, IRVIN B., Pvt., Army.

RASH, OSCAR SILAS, Chief Water Tender, Navy.

RAWLINGS, HOWARD FREDERICK, Seaman 1/c, Navy; b. Portsmouth, Oct. 1, 1920.

REID, CHARLES L., T/5, Army.

RENGER, LAWRENCE HAROLD, Fire Controlman 3/c, Navy.

REYNOLDS, GEORGE W., Chief Machinist's Mate, Coast Guard.

RHODES, WILLIAM JOSEPH, Pvt., Army; b. Windsor, April 17, 1925.

RICHARDS, HURLEY JAMES, Pfc., Army; b. Everetts, Sept. 22, 1912.

RICHARDS, JOHN ANTHONY, Seaman 1/c, Navy.

RICHARDSON, BURBLE, JR., Pfc., Army; b. South Norfolk, Dec. 12, 1922.

RICKARDS, GARRETT VAN SCHAICK, Capt., Army; b. Norfolk, April 17, 1917.

RICKETTS, MILTON ERNEST, Lt., Navy; b. Baltimore, Md., Aug. 5, 1913.

RIDDICK, NARRIO, Machinist's Mate 1/c, Navy.

RINICK, DANIEL Lee, Aviation Ordnanceman 2/c, Navy.

RITTER, RAYMOND W., Pvt., Army.

ROACH, MELVIN CLEVELAND, Lt., Navy.

ROACH, ROBERT BEIRNE, Aviation Chief Electrician's Mate, Navy.

ROBERSON, WILLIAM GORDON, Pfc., Army; b. Norfolk, July 24, 1920.

ROBERTS, CLARENCE THORNTON, Coxswain, Navy.

ROBERTS, MAXWELL HOWARD, Yeoman 1/c, Navy.

ROBERTS, ROBERT EWING, Chief Commissary Steward, Navy.

ROBERTS, STUART WELLER, Lt., Navy.

ROBERTS, WALKER DANIEL, Sgt., Army; b. Newport News, Sept. 19, 1916.

ROBERTSON, CECIL MINOR, Lt. Comdr., Navy.

ROLFE, CHARLES WILBER, Water Tender 1/c, Navy.

ROMANO, SIMON, Officer's Cook 1/c, Navy.

ROMM, EDWARD DUNSTON, Lt. (jg), Navy; b. Norfolk, Sept. 7, 1909.

ROOSEVELT, ROBERT BARNWELL, Ens., Navy.

ROWLAND, FLOYD WALLACE, Pvt., Army; b. South Norfolk, Nov. 5, 1912.

RUBIN, CARL MORRIS, 1st Lt., Army; b. Norfolk, June 23, 1919.

RUDIGER, WARREN LEROY, Sgt., Army; b. Norfolk, Jan. 21, 1924.

RUDOLPH, HENRY FRANCIS, Fireman 1/c, Navy.

RUPERT, WALTER DAVID, JR., Lt., Navy.

RUSSELL, ERNEST RAYMOND, Cpl., Marines; b. Gold Hill, N. C., Feb. 26, 1922.

RYAN, CLAUDE HOYT, Chief Boatswain's Mate, Navy.

SAARI, ANTON ANDREWS, Sgt., Army; b. Norfolk, Oct. 26, 1921.

SANDERLIN, MILLARD THOMAS, Pvt., Army; b. Norfolk, Aug. 29, 1922.

SARGEANT, FRANCIS SHELDON, JR., Capt., Army; b. Norfolk, Sept. 21, 1913.

SAUNDERS, HARDY ALFRED, 1st Lt., Army; b. Norfolk, Feb. 20, 1920.

SAWYER, FOSTER LOWRIE, Gunner, Navy.

SAWYER, WILLIAM CARL, Sgt., Army.

SCARBOROUGH, ERNEST WARREN, Pfc., Army; b. Norfolk, March 21, 1922.

SCHAFFER, EARL JUNIOR, Aviation Machinist's Mate 1/c, Navy.

SCHILLING, WALTER O., Capt., Army; b. Roanoke, Feb. 27, 1908.

SCHRAM, LOUIS JOSEPH, Ens., Navy.

SCHULER, CARL FEHRENBACH, JR., Seaman 1/c, Navy; b. Norfolk, July 20, 1925.

SCOTT, FREDERICK POWER, Chief Metalsmith, Navy.

SCOTT, ROLAND EARL, Pfc., Army; b. Robersonville, N. C., Sept. 15, 1922.

SEABORN, ELMER LEWIS, Lt. Comdr., Navy.

SETTLE, ROBERT LUNSFORD, Lt., Navy; b. Fincastle, Feb. 6, 1919.

SHAFFSTALL, LEVERNE EUGENE, Aviation Machinist's Mate, Navy.

SHARPS, JUNIOUS PERCEL, Seaman 1/c, Navy.

SHELL, JOHN PERRY, Aviation Chief Machinist's Mate, Navy.

SHEPARD, ISHLER VINSON, Fireman 1/c, Navy.

SHIPP, JOHN LEWIS, JR., Seaman 1/c, Navy; b. London Bridge, Nov. 9, 1925.

SHRADER, ARCHEL PERSHING, Ship's Cook 2/c, Navy; b. Cass, W. Va., April 18, 1918.

SHROYER, KEITH FRANCIS, Chief Ship's Service Man B, Navy; b. Eckley, Col., March 10, 1910.

SHUMWAY, DeWITT WOOD, Commander, Navy.

SIBERT, JAMES BEVERLY, 1st Lt., Army; b. Norfolk, June 2, 1919.

SIECK, LUDWIG V. T., Chief Machinist, Coast Guard.

SIEGRIST, FREDRICK W., S/Sgt., Army.

SILADIO, FRANCISCO, Officer's Steward 1/c, Coast Guard.

SIMMONS, RALPH LEROY, 2nd Lt., Army; b. Norfolk, July 15, 1918.

SIMMONS, WILLIAM RUSSELL, 1st Lt., Army; b. Washington, D. C., June 21, 1920.

SIMPSON, RANDOLPH FOSTER, Seaman, Merchant Marine; b. Norfolk, Aug. 9, 1919.

SIMS, WILLIAM TRABUS, Chief Carpenter's Mate, Navy.

SINGLETON, WOODROW WILSON, Seaman 1/c, Navy.

SIZEMORE, STANLEY LOUVORN, Ens., Navy.

SKIDMORE, CHESTER HUGH, II, Lt. (jg), Navy.

SMALLWOOD, JOHN EDWARD, Painter 1/c, Navy.

SMITH, ALTON B., Pvt., Marines.

SMITH, BERNARD LEROY, Cpl., Army; b. Fentress, March 13, 1920.

SMITH, CLAY STUART, Cpl., Army; b. Norfolk, July 27, 1923.

SMITH, CLYDE ADELBERT, Aviation Chief Machinist's Mate, Navy; b. Lewiston, Ida., May 29, 1918.

SMITH, DONALD BLAKE, Radioman 1/c, Navy.

SMITH, DONALD EMANUEL, Lt. Comdr., Navy.

SMITH, GEORGE BLANE, Gunner's Mate 1/c, Navy.

SMITH, GEORGE LEONARD, JR., Pvt., Army; b. South Norfolk, Aug. 19, 1920.

SMITH, GEORGE MASON, JR., 2nd Lt., Army; b. Norfolk.

SMITH, JAMES EDWARD, Lt. (jg), Navy.

SMITH, JOHN CALVIN, JR., Seaman 1/c, Navy; b. Schuyler, Dec. 7, 1925.

SMITH, JOHN HAROLD, Electrician's Mate 1/c, Navy.

SMITH, PAUL FRANKLIN, Specialist 2/c, Navy.

SOUTHWORTH, VARNUM COCHRAN, Lt. Comdr., Navy.

SPANNUTH, ROBERT DONALD, Lt., Navy.

SPARE, LOUIS JAMES, Chief Pay Clerk, Navy.

SPEAR, GEORGE LORNE, Aviation Chief Radioman, Navy.

SPENCE, JOHN LEE, S/Sgt., Army; b. Conway, N. C., June 8, 1922.

SPENCER, AUGUSTUS RUDD, 1st Lt., Army; b. Newport News, Dec. 22, 1918.

SPIVEY, HERMAN C., T/3, Army; b. Norfolk, Jan. 8, 1922.

STALKER, HOWARD WAYNE, Yeoman 2/c, Navy; b. Farmer City, Ill., Nov. 17, 1915.

STARR, BERT, 1st Lt., Army.

STATON, JOHN A., JR., Pfc., Army.

STEINER, HENRY, Chief Aviation Pilot, Navy.

STELL, VIRGINIUS RAWLS, JR., 2nd Lt., Army; b. Norfolk, Feb. 16, 1921.

STERLING, JAMES WENDELL, Water Tender 2/c, Navy.

STEVENS, CLAXTON, Pfc., Army; b. Norfolk, July 22, 1922.

STEWART, HENRY, T/5, Army; b. Martinsville, May 29, 1924.

STIDHAM, EARL ZEATON, Storekeeper 1/c, Navy.

378   CONSCRIPTED CITY

STIM, CONSTANTIN, Chief Machinist's Mate, Navy.

STINNETTE, MURRELL FLEMING, JR., Sgt., Army; b. Norfolk, May 25, 1922.

STONE, LEONARD W., Pfc., Army.

STROUD, AUBREY LEWIS, Pfc., Army.

STURTEVANT, JOHN FRANCIS, Aviation Machinist's Mate 3/c, Navy.

STYRON, WILLIAM GLENWOOD, Pvt., Army; b. Norfolk, Dec. 19, 1922.

SUMMERS, RAYMOND WARREN, Pfc., Army; b. Norfolk, Aug. 25, 1924.

SUNDQUIST, CHESTER ROYAL, JR., Seaman 2/c, Navy; b. Cincinnati, O., March 4, 1926.

SUTHERLIN, HARRY MELTON, Torpedoman's Mate 3/c, Navy.

SUTPHIN, JOHN ROBERT, Chief Machinist's Mate, Navy.

SUTTON, LEON C., Jr., 2nd Lt., Army.

SWANEY, RALPH LOREN, Pfc., Army; b. Norfolk, Dec. 26, 1921.

SZEBELEDY, LOUIS, Chief Pharmacist's Mate, Navy.

TANN, RAYMOND M., T/4, Army.

TATEM, CECIL V., Chief Engineer, Merchant Marine; b. Norfolk, May 2, 1911.

TATEM, LESTER HORACE, Pfc., Army; b. Dozier's Corner, Nov. 14, 1910.

TAYLOR, JAMES UNDERHILL, Coxswain, Navy; b. Cartersville, April 13, 1919.

TAYLOR, WILLIAM HORACE, Cpl., Army.

TENNANT, JOHN GARDNER, Commander, Navy.

THURMOND, RICHARD HARRISON, Chief Yeoman, Navy.

TILLMAN, BILLY LEE, Pfc., Army; b. Scottsville, Dec. 18, 1919.

TOFFTON, RICHARD CHARLES, Sgt., Army; b. Norfolk, Jan. 28, 1920.

TOLSON, RUMAN CROMWELL, JR., Able Seaman, Merchant Marine; b. Portsmouth, Sept. 20, 1915.

TREAS, CARLOS, Chief Steward, Navy.

TRUSS, JERRY CLEVELAND, Lt., Navy.

TUCKER, ALFRED BLAND, III, Lt. Comdr., Navy; b. Berryville, Dec. 26, 1909.

TURNER, LOREN ELLSWORTH, Water Tender 2/c, Navy.

TURNER, ROBERT THORNTON, Pvt., Army; b. Norfolk, Sept. 21, 1922.

TWIDDY, CLARENCE AUGUSTUS, JR., Lt. (jg), Navy; b. Norfolk, July 5, 1917.

TWIFORD, ANDREW BROWN, JR., Pfc., Army; b. Elizabeth City, N. C., Sept. 27, 1923.

TWILLIE, CLARENCE ALTON, Fire Controlman 3/c, Navy; b. Columbus, Ga.

UNDERDOWN, RAYMOND STUART, T/Sgt., Army; b. Norfolk, April 29, 1924.

VAN HOUZEN, WILLIAM MARTIN, Aviation Machinist's Mate 2/c, Navy.

VANTURE, GEORGE DEWEY, Lt. Col., Army; b. Staunton, Aug. 25, 1898.

VENETIDY, THEODORE, Pfc., Army; b. Norfolk, July 19, 1923.

VERHAAGEN, RICHARD WOODROW, Sgt. Army.

VINSON, LINWOOD, JR., Capt., Army; b. Norfolk, Aug. 31, 1918.

VOTSIS, SAM A., S/Sgt., Army.

WADE, GEORGE RALEIGH, JR., Ship's Cook 3/c, Navy; b. Norfolk.

WADE, RONALD PEAKE, Pvt., Army; b. Gladys, Sept. 19, 1919.

WADSWORTH, ALEXANDER SCAMMEL, III, Lt. Comdr., Navy.

WAGECK, JOHN, Chief Warrant Machinist, Navy; b. Freeport, N. Y., April 26, 1895.

WALKER, RICHARD IVES, Lt. (jg), Navy.

WALKER, THOMAS CLIFTON, Chief Carpenter, Navy.

WALTON, WILLIE JACKSON, JR., Mess Attendant 1/c, Navy.

WARD, MILTON TAYLOR, JR., Fireman 1/c, Navy; b. Marionville, May 8, 1918.

WARE, CHARLES H., JR., 2nd Lt., Army; b. Norfolk, Aug. 13, 1922.

WARE, ROBERT EDWARD, Pfc., Army; b. Newport News, Oct. 13, 1918.

WATTS, LEWIS ALFRED, JR., Pvt., Army; b. Norfolk, May 14, 1924.

WEATHERFORD, FRED GARY, Lt., Navy.

WEEKS, ROBERT MAYO, Chief Machinist's Mate, Navy.

WEBB, MAURICE GODWIN, Warrant Machinist, Coast Guard; b. Norfolk, Oct. 21, 1902.

WEBSTER, WILLIAM B., JR., 2nd Lt., Army.

WELLS, CLEO, Aviation Machinist's Mate 1/c, Navy; b. Miller, Mo., Feb. 4, 1910.

WELLS, EUGENE BERNARD, JR., Seaman, Merchant Marine; b. Greensboro, N. C., March 7, 1907.

WEST, CLYDE GRAY, Capt., Navy.

WHITE, ALBERT LOTZE, JR., Seaman 2/c, Navy; b. Norfolk, Dec. 1, 1920.

WHITE, JOSEPH ANTHONY, Pfc., Army; b. Norfolk, July 23, 1919.

WHITE, WILLIAM NELSON, JR., Pfc., Army; b. Florence, S. C., Aug. 22, 1925.

WHITEHURST, ALAN EDWARD, Sgt., Army; b. Va., Nov. 21, 1924.

WHITEHURST, CALVERT STANHOPE, JR., S/Sgt., Army; b. Norfolk, Jan. 16, 1923.

WIGGINS, THEODORE BURR, Chief Pharmacist, Navy.

WILBERN, DONALD ELMORE, Pfc., Army; b. Norfolk, March 19, 1919.

WILBERN, PAUL H., Sgt., Army.

WILDER, ROLAND JETHOR, Pvt., Army; b. South Norfolk, Aug. 7, 1914.

WILKINS, JOHN LLOYD, Water Tender 1/c; b. Jacksonville, N. C., May 3, 1915.

WILKINSON, JOHN MILLARD, JR., Seaman 1/c, Navy; b. Norfolk, Nov. 23, 1924.

WILLCOX, WESTMORE, III, 1st Lt., Army; b. Norfolk, April 13, 1919.

WILLIAMS, FORREST BLAN, Motor Machinist's Mate 3/c, Navy; b. Mundens, July 8, 1926.

WILLIAMS, GEORGE, JR., Capt., Army; b. Norfolk, March 23, 1919.

WILLIAMS, JAMES LIONEL, Pvt., Army; b. Norfolk, Feb. 28, 1913.

WILLIAMS, JUNIUS, Steward's Mate 1/c, Navy.

WILLIAMS, WALLACE PERRY, Aviation Ordnanceman 3/c, Navy.

WILLOUGHBY, JOHN CLIFTON, Pfc., Army; b. Norfolk, Jan. 7, 1920.

WILLOUGHBY, RICHARD E., Pvt., Army.

WILSON, ALBERT LYTLE, Aviation Machinist's Mate 3/c, Navy.

WILSON, ALFRED GENERAL, Cpl., Army; b. Norfolk, July 16, 1916.

WILSON, JAMES HARVEY, JR., Pvt., Army; b. Norfolk, April 8, 1914.

WILSON, WILLIE, Steward's Mate 1/c, Navy.

WINGFIELD, KENNETH RAY, Pvt., Army; b. Norfolk, May 7, 1926.

WINSLOW, JOSHUA EDWARD, Pvt., Army; b. Belvedere, N. C., Dec. 9, 1908.

WINSLOW, WILBUR P., Pfc., Army; b. Norfolk, June 23, 1908.

WISE, CHESLEY GERALD, SR., Pfc., Army; b. Stumpy Point, N. C., Sept. 12, 1918.

WOOD, EUGENE WESTMORELAND, 2nd Lt., Army; b. Norfolk, Jan. 26, 1920.

WOOD, GLEN DOUGLAS, Lt. (jg), Navy.

WOOD, LEROY DWIGHT, Fireman 1/c, Navy; b. Great Bridge, May 25, 1925.

WOOD, THOMAS CARL, T/Sgt., Army; b. Norfolk, May 30, 1910.

WOODHOUSE, HORATIO CORNICK, JR., Lt., Col., Marines; b. Norfolk, Aug. 27, 1913.

WOODHOUSE, WILLIAM THOMAS, Fireman 1/c, Navy; b. Norfolk, Aug. 6, 1922.

WOOLDRIDGE, KENNETH LEE, Pfc., Army.

WOOLFORD, THOMAS RALPH, Pfc., Army; b. Portsmouth, Dec. 10, 1917.

WORLEY, HARRY WILTSIE, Lt., Navy; b. Futsing, China, April 5, 1920.

WREN, BEVERLEY KENNON, Sgt., Army; b. Gilmerton, Oct. 14, 1919.

WRENSINSKI, ROBERT L., Pvt., Army.

WRIGHT, ROLAND ANDERSON, JR., Aviation Cadet, Navy; b. Lynchburg, Dec. 14, 1921.

WRIGHT, WILLIAM JOSEPH, Pfc., Army; b. South Norfolk, April 12, 1917.

YACKEE, RAYMOND FRANCIS, Carpenter's Mate 2/c, Navy.

YEATES, ARTHUR BERNARD, JR., Lt. Comdr., Navy; b. Bath, N. C., March 20, 1915.

YOHO, JOHN RICHARD, Lt. Comdr, Navy.

YOUNG, LEE ALLEN, S/Sgt., Army; b. Norfolk, Jan. 18, 1920.

ZIRNHELD, GEORGE RAYMOND, S/Sgt., Army; b. Portsmouth, March 17, 1918.

ZOCK, THOMAS JOHN, Aviation Machinist's Mate 3/c, Navy; b. Altoona, Pa., June 17, 1919.

INDEX

Forty-First Street, 231
Franklin, 353
Freemason Street, 4, 130, 272, 314, 317-318
Frontakowski, Leonard, 114
Frontakowski, Mrs. Elsie Mae, 114
Fuel oil rationing, 236-237, 241

Gaiety Theater, 6, 124
Garden Clubs, 298
Gardner, H. L., 278
Garrett, James N., 277, 325
Gasoline rationing, 178-179, 237-238
Gasoline shortage, 108-111, 152-153, 241-243, 265-268, 270
German surrender, 360
Germany, 1-2, 4, 113-115
Ghent, 102, 105
Ghent Methodist Church, 170
Gill, Corrington, 256
Girl Scouts, 105-106
Glenwood Park, 32
Goldberg, Dr. J. A., 29
Goochland, 182
Goodwill Industries, 141, 359
Goodwyn, Brig. Gen. E. E., 45-46, 357
Graham, Aubrey G., 41
Granby High School, 5, 64, 92, 169-170, 347
Granby Street, 3-6, 8, 12-13, 32, 36-39, 64, 68, 100, 119, 124, 130, 154, 158, 199, 205, 240, 254, 292, 296, 315, 347, 362-363
Granby Street hospital, 88, 94, 158, 231, 252-253, 300, 346
Granby Street school (proposed), 64, 93, 176
Granby Theater, 124
Grand Ole Opry, 313
Grandy, C. Wiley, 15 n., 73
Gray Ladies, 240, 308
Great Neck road, 66
Greater Norfolk Citizens Forum, 362
Green, Thomas S., 55-56
Green Bay, 251
Greer, 113-114
Greyhound bus station, 266, 336
Greyhound Lines, 68
Grunert, Gen. George, 293

Guadalcanal, 228
Gurkin, John A., 5, 13
Gutheim, Frederick, 257
Guy, Louis Lee, 27
Gygax, Admiral Felix X., 87, 108

Hagan, Lt. Col. J. Addison, 357
Hague Club, 316
Halperin, John, 87
Hamilton Avenue, 114
Hamlet, Lynette, 11, 49-50, 138-140, 283
Hampton Boulevard, 5, 12-13, 32, 37, 152-153, 157, 179, 210, 231, 254, 296; resurfacing of, 38; underpass on, 5, 13
Hampton Roads, 1-3, 10, 24-26, 31, 34-36, 42-43, 60, 63, 70-71, 75, 80-81, 106, 115, 125, 131, 146-147, 166-168, 190, 192-193, 205, 211, 213-214, 240, 255, 257-258, 261-262, 296, 337, 339, 355, 361
Hampton Roads Area, Temporary Committee for the, 25-26, 33
Hampton Roads Defense Rental Area, 175
Hampton Roads OPA Labor Advisory Committee, 343, 345
Hampton Roads Rapid Treatment Venereal Disease Hospital, 300
Hampton Roads Regional Defense Council, 26-27, 33-34, 37, 41, 48-49, 52, 55-56, 59, 63-64, 66, 70, 76, 82, 84-86, 89, 94, 96, 107, 111, 115-123, 125-126, 129, 131-132, 135, 142, 144-145, 147
Hampton Roads Sanitation District, 35-36, 88, 177, 253, 347
Hanes, Tom, 160, 224, 232, 315
Hardiman, Larry H., Jr., 227, 259, 297-299
Harney, W. S., 81-82
Harper, Charles E., 37
Harris, Rev. B. W., 64
Harris, Winder R., 26, 44, 73, 80, 89-90, 93, 98, 132, 178, 220, 235, 237, 248, 251-252, 255, 337
Health and hospitals, 63-64, 93-97, 157-158, 252-253, 256, 299, 346-347
Health for Victory Club, 298
Hemphill, W. Edwin, viii
Henderson, Leon, 110, 221

ABOUT THE AUTHOR

Dr. Marvin W. Schlegel, a former professor of history at Longwood College and Norfolk State University, is among the country's outstanding historians of the home front during World War II. Schlegel has written or contributed to eight books, including many on what happened stateside during the war. Schlegel also wrote the first guidebook for local war historians, *Writing Your Community's War History*.

During World War II, Schlegel was in charge of Pennsylvania's war history program. In 1947, he came to Norfolk to teach in the St. Helena Extension of the College of William and Mary. The following year, he joined the faculty at Longwood College in Farmville, Va. In 1966 he went to Norfolk State, where he was a professor of history until he retired in 1976/ Since coming to Virginia, he has contributed to The Pursuits of War, the Albemarle County war history, and has written Virginia On Guard, the story of the state's civilian defense program. In 1962, he edited and wrote chapters for Norfolk: Historic Southern Port, a history of the city.

Born in Thompsontown, Pa., in 1910, Dr. Schlegel graduated from Susquehanna University in 1928. he later received his M. A. and Ph. D. from Columbia University, where he worked with Columbia's famed historian Allan Nevins, twice winner of the Pulitzer Prize. His first full-length publication was Ruler of the Reading in 1947, a study of coal mines and railroads in eastern Pennsylvania.

In addition to his writing, Schlegel has traveled extensively through Europe. Among other places, he has visited England, Scotland, France, Italy, Germany, Portugal, Tangiers, Yugoslavia, Greece, Russia, Israel, Syria and Switzerland.